D1324546

THE LIE

BOOKS BY KATHRYN CROFT

The Girl With No Past

The Girl You Lost

While You Were Sleeping

Silent Lies

The Warning

The Suspect

The Lying Wife

The Neighbour Upstairs

The Other Husband

The Mother's Secret

THE LIE

Kathryn Croft

Lms
19.4.24
A really enjoyable book

bookouture

Published by Bookouture in 2023

An imprint of Storyfire Ltd.
Carmelite House
50 Victoria Embankment
London EC4Y 0DZ

www.bookouture.com

ISBN: 978-1-83790-111-1
eBook ISBN: 978-1-83790-110-4

For Gosia and Joanna
Dwie wspaniałe kobiety

PART ONE

"Hope" is the thing with feathers -
That perches in the soul -
And sings the tune without the words -
And never stops - at all -

Emily Dickinson, '"Hope" is the thing with feathers'

ONE

LUCY

We all have secrets, don't we? Things we want kept hidden, even from ourselves. Never run away, they say. It might work for a while, but sooner or later whatever it is we've escaped will catch up with us. And then things can only get worse.

'What are you thinking about?'

Tom's voice catches me off guard, causing me to jolt round so that coffee from my mug sloshes onto the floor. It's barely five in the morning, and, other than me, nobody in the house stirs before seven. Especially on a Sunday. This quiet stretch of time is sacred, a brief respite before I'm plunged into the day.

I grab a cloth and wipe away the dark brown puddle. 'I was just about to clear up outside,' I say, standing up and nodding towards the garden, where litter from yesterday evening's barbeque remains strewn across the lawn. Despite the mess unnerving me, my lips form a smile. It was a successful evening; everyone seemed to enjoy themselves. It was a step towards becoming part of this community.

Tom stands beside me and nods. 'I'm surprised you didn't want us to deal with it last night.'

'Hmm. I'm regretting that this morning.' How different the

garden looks in the aftermath: wretched and neglected. The newly blossomed peonies in the raised beds do nothing to detract from the mess.

'Leave it for now, Lucy, I'll help you later. Go back to bed for a bit. It's Sunday.' Tom chuckles. 'How's your head? You were putting them away last night. I didn't even hear you come to bed.'

'I'm fine,' I say, too defensively. Although I don't tell him I can't face the thought of breakfast. And I'll probably avoid lunch later too.

'It's just not like you to drink like that,' Tom continues.

'You mean you can't remember the last time I enjoyed myself?' I deliver a light punch to his arm. 'Are you saying I've become dull and middle-aged?'

He drapes his arm across my shoulders. 'No, not at all. You've been so focused on the move. Setting up the business. And the kids, of course. It was nice to see you relaxing for a change. And I would have joined you if I hadn't been on those.' He points to the bottle of antibiotics on the worktop.

But I hadn't been relaxed, even with alcohol loosening me up. I was watching Ava like a hawk, scrutinising everything she did. Or didn't do. Tom thinks now that we've moved, we can all rid ourselves of the past, as easily as pushing a switch. That along with a new life for all of us, this is a new me.

'Are you happy being here?' I ask, turning to face him, so he knows this conversation is serious. 'Do you miss London?'

He pulls me closer. 'No. I still work there so it hasn't been too much of a change. Except that it's far more peaceful here. And greener, of course. Brighter. We actually know our neighbours here.'

Despite his assurances, a sliver of guilt rushes through me. 'I know I've thrown myself into the business. You've hardly seen me lately. But it's Easter.'

Tom seems to understand that there are peaks and

troughs in the floristry business, and that I have to capitalise on the moments when business floods in. He never complains when I'm shut in the greenhouse or my workshop for days on end, or in the cutting garden, visible yet out of reach. We uprooted our lives for me to do this, so I'm determined to make it work. Of course, this isn't the only reason we've moved from London to Surrey, but the other one I force from my mind.

Tom opens a cupboard and pulls out a mug. He's not going back to bed, then, despite his suggestion that I should. 'It's fine, Lucy,' he says. 'You're not the only one who's been busy with work. There's no reason for you to feel guilty. The kids do their own thing most of the time anyway. It's not like they're little and want to be with us all the time. It can't stay that way forever, can it?' He squeezes my shoulder. 'Moving here was the right thing for all of us.'

'Especially Ava.'

He nods.

'She barely spoke to anyone at the barbeque,' I say. 'Even though I invited several parents from her year. She just didn't join in with those kids.'

Tom shrugs. 'She's just shy. We know that. It doesn't mean anything.'

His words cause me to shiver, because my instinct as a mother tells me there's something more than just shyness.

'You need to relax,' Tom continues. 'She'll be fine. She was talking to Rose a lot. Did you notice?'

'Yes, but Rose isn't in her year. She needs to make friends with year eight kids.'

Tom pours his coffee and sets it aside while he begins unloading the dishwasher. 'She's nearly thirteen, Lucy – it's an awkward age, isn't it? Don't you remember what it was like? I know it was a long time ago...'

I ignore his tease. 'Jacob's so different. At that age he just seemed to have more confidence in himself. To know who he was. Ava seems to be afraid of... *everything*.'

'Honestly, Lucy, there's nothing wrong with Ava. Nothing other than the fact that she's becoming a teenager. I know she's finding it hard to make friends, but the other day she told me it's better than her old school.' He abandons the dishwasher and stands before me, placing his hands on my shoulders. 'We got her away from that place for a reason, didn't we? At least now she has a chance to reinvent herself. To start again. You've got to stop this worrying. This...'

Paranoia? I'm about to respond, but think better of it. We've had this discussion too many times now and never end up agreeing. There is no middle ground. Tom thinks Ava will be fine now that we've moved to Surrey. I have my doubts. As with every other time this comes up, he will just point out that my concerns come from fear. For now, I file it all away; it is something I will deal with myself.

'Speaking of our children,' Tom says, reaching for his coffee. 'Is everything okay with Jacob and Rose? They didn't seem to talk much at the barbeque.'

I force my mind to recall, but my memory is a black fog. 'I think Ava was hogging all her time.' Now that I'm thinking of it, I don't remember seeing much of Jacob. 'I hope Rose didn't mind.'

'Well, Jacob seemed to,' Tom says. 'He didn't look happy. A bit like how he was when Isla moved away.'

I freeze at the mention of her name. In London, Jacob hadn't shown much interest in girls until he'd met Isla. Then everything changed. *He* changed. He thought about nothing else, and his whole world revolved around her. He seemed to lose focus. We'll never confess this to Jacob, but we were both relieved when her family moved away. We'd assumed that Jacob would revert to the boy he'd been before he became involved with her, but that didn't happen. Jacob insisted they were still together, that they were having a long-distance relationship until they finished school and went to university. But then he met Rose.

Since Jacob turned sixteen, I've tried to stay out of his personal life, but his relationship with Isla was baffling. It still is. He's a handsome boy, and before Isla, despite his indifference, he'd never lacked female attention. Perhaps his lack of interest somehow made him more appealing. A complexity of human nature.

The hardest thing for me has been to accept that Jacob has gradually stopped sharing everything that's going on in his life. He's no longer the small child I knew everything about. And now, at almost six feet, he towers above me, changing the dynamics of our relationship.

'How long have they been together now?' Tom enquires.

'About six months, I think.'

Tom ponders this. 'How quickly he forgot about Isla. Well, that was for the best. We don't even know what was going on there.'

I nod. 'I just wish—'

On the kitchen counter, my phone rings.

Tom raises his eyebrows. 'Bit early, isn't it?'

I reach for it and stare at the screen. 'It's Carrie. That's odd. She never calls me. She must have left something behind yesterday.' I take a deep breath and prepare myself. I might not have known her for long, but unlike her daughter, Rose's mother is a difficult woman to read. 'Hi Carrie, everything okay?'

She doesn't bother with pleasantries. 'No, it's not. Is Rose there?' Her voice is husky; something I've never noticed before.

Frowning, I glance at Tom. 'No, she isn't. And Jacob's still asleep. Why, what's going on?'

Carrie takes a deep breath. 'I'm... not sure she came home last night. After your barbeque, I met up with my friend from work at the pub. Rose had already gone home. So when I got here and found her bedroom door shut, I thought she was asleep. She never shuts it unless she's asleep.' She pauses to blow her nose. 'I fell asleep on the sofa. I just woke up and went to check on her and she's not here. Doesn't look like she slept in her bed. It's too tidy. She never makes the damn thing, even at her age I still have to do it. Oh God, where is she? Her phone's switched off!'

'Carrie, please try not to worry. We'll sort out what's happened. Maybe she's just gone for a walk?'

It might have only been a few months ago we met Rose, but already I know that she, like me, loves being surrounded by nature. She's even spent time with me in my cutting garden, sitting on the grass, listening intently while I've taught her about the different flowers I grow. I can picture her face now, staring with wonder at the wreaths I create. 'There's nothing more beautiful than a flower,' she'd said once. 'Nothing purer or more innocent. Simple and complex at the same time.' I'd been surprised by her mature and philosophical interpretation.

'Let me go and wake Jacob,' I tell Carrie. 'Hang on, I'll hand my phone to Tom for a minute.'

Tom tries to protest, but I force it into his hand. 'Talk to her,' I mouth.

Upstairs, I push open Jacob's bedroom door and step into the darkness. The previous owners left the blackout blinds they'd installed for their young children, and even though Jacob doesn't need it – his dark blue curtains already shut out the light – he pulls it down every night. I head across to his bed, the scent of Lynx mingling with the stale odour of sweat.

He doesn't stir as I approach. He's always been a deep sleeper, even as a baby. While other new mums would struggle with their newborn babies' sleep patterns, Jacob was calm and docile, sleeping through the night after only a few weeks. He lulled me into such a false sense of security that when Ava was born, I struggled to adjust to a baby who wouldn't sleep for longer than twenty minutes at a time. A lifetime ago.

'Jacob,' I whisper, gently nudging him. 'Wake up.'

He mumbles something incoherent, but doesn't move.

'Jacob.' Louder this time. 'It's important. Carrie's on the phone and she's looking for Rose.'

His eyes snap open. 'What?'

I perch on the side of his bed. 'Carrie thinks Rose might not have come home last night. Do you know where she could be?'

Jacob stares at me and seconds tick by before he pulls himself up. 'But... but she went home. I walked her home from the barbeque. I saw her go inside.'

'Are you sure?' I wonder if he's aware that I'm questioning his recall because there's every possibility that he and Rose could have sneaked some alcohol into their drinks. Didn't I used to do things like that when I was a teenager?

Without a reply, Jacob snatches his phone from the bedside table and begins tapping, holding the phone to his ear and turning from me. 'Voicemail,' he says, ending the call. Even in this darkness I can tell his face has paled. With his fingers moving frantically, he begins typing a message.

'Are you sure you don't know where she could be?'

He shrugs. 'No.' He throws his duvet aside and jumps up, scanning the room.

'So, you definitely walked her home after the barbeque? Are you sure she went inside her house? Was she planning to go anywhere else?'

'Yes, I'm sure and, no, Mum, I don't know where she is!' He grabs some jeans which have been abandoned on the floor and pulls them on. 'She's probably doing...'

'What?'

'Nothing. Can you let me get dressed, Mum?'

I glance at the door. Jacob's raised voice is bound to wake

Ava. 'I need to go and tell Carrie. She's still on the phone talking to Dad.' I head towards the door.

And then I remember. Last night, I'd started watching a film on TV and had fallen asleep on the sofa. But I'd woken up when I heard Jacob come in. I'd checked my phone and it was past one a.m. I was going to confront him but I was too tired, my head feeling like it was being crushed. I'd decided to wait until the morning to lecture him about coming home by his curfew.

I turn back to him. 'What time did you walk Rose back to her house?'

He shrugs. 'I don't know. About nine thirty, I think.' He pauses. 'Yeah, it was definitely around then. She said she was tired and wanted to sleep. I remember thinking how early it was.'

'So, where did you go after that?'

'Mum, what's with all the questions? I came straight home. Everyone was asleep. Can you please stop asking me all this stuff!' He rushes out into the hall. 'I need to look for her,' he shouts, already halfway down the stairs.

I follow him down, staring at his back. He's mistaken, that's all it is. He won't have thought about the time, and just assumed it was earlier. Because I'm right about how late it was. I know it.

In the kitchen, Tom still clutches my phone to his ear, his calming voice issuing reassurances to Carrie. 'Of course she'll be all right. An early morning walk, that's what it will be. I'm sure she'll be home any minute now.' He glances at Jacob standing in the doorway. 'Oh, here he is now. I'll put him on.'

'Tell her I'm coming over now,' Jacob says, pulling on his coat.

He's gone before I have a chance to tell him to take something to eat with him.

I hear Tom relaying that Jacob's on his way, and then he is handing back my phone.

'Carrie, Jacob says he walked her home and saw her go into the house. Then he came home. It was around nine thirty.'

'Oh. I don't understand where she could be.'

'Jacob will help you look for her,' I assure her.

'I've got a bad feeling about this,' she replies. 'This isn't like Rose. She wouldn't let me worry like this. You hear about it all the time on the news, don't you? Young girls being—'

'Don't think like that,' I interject. 'Rose will come home. I'll just jump in the shower and then I'll come over too. In the meantime, you need to call the police.'

Carrie falls silent. 'I was about to. I wanted to call around first before bothering them. I just thought she'd be with you. Where else would she be? Nina hasn't seen her either.'

We end the call, and I place my phone on the worktop. It's only now I notice that my hand is shaking.

Tom walks over to me and wraps his arms around me. 'She'll be fine, Lucy. It's not like—'

'Yeah, of course she will.'

And this is what I have to believe.

On my way upstairs I don't notice Ava is sitting at the top until I'm almost tripping over her. 'You scared me! Are you okay?'

She nods. 'What's going on? Where's Jacob gone?'

I sit beside her, push back a dark strand of her hair that's fallen across her eye. 'He's gone to help Carrie look for Rose.'

Ava stares at me. 'What d'you mean? Where is she?'

Long ago I decided I would never keep things from Ava, even if staying silent might protect her. There is nothing more destructive than lies. I should know. 'Carrie thinks Rose didn't come home last night,' I explain.

Ava frowns. 'You mean after the barbeque?'

I nod.

'But she must have. Why wouldn't she go home? She never said anything.'

'I'm sure it's just a misunderstanding,' I say.

'Rose said we could go for a walk this morning to the nature reserve. She said it would... help me feel better if I get out and just take in my surroundings.'

This doesn't surprise me – Rose is always looking out for Ava. 'That's kind of her. Did you arrange this at the barbeque? Did she say what time she'd be here?'

Ava nods. 'Straight after breakfast. So, there's nothing to worry about. Rose will be here soon.' She smiles. 'Rose never breaks promises.'

'I'm sure you're right.' I pat her arm. 'Jacob didn't mention she was coming here.'

Ava shrugs. 'He probably didn't know. They didn't really talk that much at the barbeque. I think Rose was... angry with him.'

'What makes you think that?'

'I don't know. But it's okay, Mum. People argue all the time, don't they? You always say that if you and Dad ever argue. You always tell us it's normal to have disagreements. That's what people do.'

'Yes, Ava, it's true. I'm sure everything's okay. Why don't you go and get dressed, and once I've had a shower I'll make some French toast?'

While she goes back to her room to get dressed, I head to the bathroom and turn on the shower. By the time I've finished and have got dressed in jeans and a loose V-neck jumper, concealing the dark circles under my eyes with make-up, I still have no appetite.

And there is no sign of Rose.

TWO

CARRIE

She stands in the living room, staring out of the window. The street is quiet – it's still too early for most people to be up on a Sunday – and heavy grey clouds loom ominously in the sky. She pictures Rose walking up the short path to their door, as if there's nothing out of the ordinary. Carrie will let rip when she sees her – and make her daughter see how selfish she's been by disappearing like this. And then she'll wrap Rose in her arms and never let her go.

'Where are you?' Carrie says aloud. She tries to recall the last conversation she had with Rose, but her memory is hazy. She doesn't even remember Rose leaving the barbeque. Had she left before Carrie? Or after? Carrie hadn't even had a chance to talk to her daughter that evening, and can't remember seeing her much. Or Jacob. Rose will have been too busy to talk to her mum. That's what Carrie tries to convince herself of, but the truth is that it was the other way around: Carrie was the one who'd been preoccupied.

Had something been worrying Rose? Her daughter is headstrong, never allowing herself to dwell on things. Carrie would definitely have noticed if things had changed. They've always been close, able to talk about everything. At least until Joe crashed into their lives like a wrecking ball. If Carrie's honest with herself, their whole family dynamic has changed since she got involved with him. Not for the first time, she questions her own judgement. But hasn't she vowed to give her relationships a chance, rather than fleeing at the first sign of disharmony like too many people do?

Across the street, the Nelsons' door opens and the twins run out, dragging their scooters behind them. Their identical bright blond hair flops around their foreheads and looks unbrushed, as if they've just this second got out of their beds. There's no sign of Lia. Carrie tuts and shakes her head. She's far from perfect, but she'd never have let Rose play outside unsupervised at that age. She doesn't know for sure, but those boys don't look more than four. They might live in a cul-de-sac, but plenty of cars still make their way in and out. And those twins are unruly.

Carrie turns away and scans the room, trying to see the place through someone else's eyes. The police will be here any moment, and she knows they'll have judgements to make about her. Her house might be small, but at least it's clean. There'll be no dust to find on any surface. Perhaps it's a bit cluttered, but Carrie always keeps it tidy. Her mother instilled in her that it doesn't matter how much, or how little, money people have, having pride in yourself and your home is more important. Elizabeth always had pearls of wisdom to impart, most of which Carrie didn't listen to. Rose is different; she seems to listen when Carrie tells her things. An old soul in a young body – that's what Rose is, what she's been for as long as Carrie can remember.

Outside a car pulls up, and she watches as a uniformed police officer steps out. She wonders if there will be two of them, like they always show on television, but the passenger door remains closed. He's a tall man, and walks with an assertive stride. This should fill her with confidence, but instead she's nervous. As if she's done something wrong. He's wearing body armour and she wonders if he's sweating underneath it. It might only be April but the heat this morning is almost unbearable. A mini heatwave, it said on the news. And we'd better expect more of them in the future.

The doorbell rings and she shuffles towards it, delaying the moment she has to confront this reality. Rose really is missing, the officer at her door is proof of that, and there's nothing she can do to change it. Carrie was hoping Jacob would be here by the time the police came. He was the last person to see Rose so he should be telling them everything he can think of.

She still isn't grounded in reality when she answers the door. Perhaps it's shock, or something worse, because she feels in her bones that this is the beginning of something.

The officer introduces himself. PC Morgan. A name she must make an effort to remember, even though her mind is already expelling it. He's younger than she'd first thought, probably straight out of police training. Still, at least he is here. And don't younger people have more to prove?

'Can I get you tea or coffee?' she asks, because it feels like that's what she should do. Another thing her mum insisted she know. Treat everyone who comes into your home like a cherished guest. Tea. Coffee. Something to eat.

PC Morgan's lips form into a smile. 'Nothing for me, thanks. Shall we have a seat?' He gestures to the kitchen table, where the mug of tea Carrie finished over an hour ago still sits.

She does as he asks, and he pulls out an electronic device. It reminds her of a Blackberry, but she's sure it can't be. People don't use those any longer, do they?

'For taking notes,' he explains when he notices her staring at it. 'And if it's okay with you, I'd like to switch on my bodycam so I have a record of this conversation. It's just to save you having to go over everything again. Is that okay?'

Carrie nods, even though she's not sure she likes the sound

of this. It feels too formal. But refusing would make it seem that she has something to hide.

'I understand your daughter, Rose, hasn't come home,' PC Morgan begins. 'Can you tell me what's happened?'

But Carrie has already done this on the phone. Answered so many questions she didn't think they would ever stop. Isn't it a waste of time to keep going over everything? The police need to be looking for Rose, not just questioning her. Why does she need to repeat it like a broken record when it's simple? 'She's only just sixteen. And she didn't come home last night.'

'And when was the last time you saw her?'

'There was a barbeque yesterday afternoon. At her boyfriend's house. His name's Jacob Adams. It wasn't supposed to be a barbeque – more of a house-warming party really. But the weather forecast was so good that Lucy – that's Jacob's mum – changed it to a barbeque. Rose was there and she was fine. And then... I left. I went to meet my friend at the pub. My partner, Joe, was on a late shift at work so I thought I'd take the chance to see a friend.' Carrie should have stayed at the barbeque. Despite what had happened there, she shouldn't have left. Then maybe she would have seen what had been going on with Rose.

'And what time was it you left?' PC Morgan asks.

Carrie bites her lip. 'I'm not sure exactly. Maybe around nine?' Then I came home from the pub and Rose's bedroom door was shut so I didn't want to disturb her by opening it.' She stares at the floor. 'I know, it's terrible. I should have done. But she's such a light sleeper, so I didn't want to risk it.' She sighs. 'And then I watched TV and fell asleep on the sofa.' She points to the living room, as if she needs to show him. *I was drunk. Too intoxicated to notice that my daughter wasn't home.* Silently acknowledging this stops her breath. 'I thought Rose was upstairs asleep. I mean, why wouldn't she be? She's never stayed away from home before.'

Carrie feels the weight of the police officer's gaze on her. Swallowing her, then spitting her out. 'And what time would you have got home?'

'When the pub closed, just after eleven. It's only a short walk from here.' Her eyes flick to the front door. *What's taking Jacob so long?*

'So, you don't know if she came back last night? Could she have gone out this morning.'

'That's not likely,' Carrie says, firmly. 'I'm a light sleeper too. And you can't shut the front door quietly. I would have woken up.'

He regards her closely, and Carrie fights the urge to look away and avoid his scrutiny. 'Okay,' he says. 'Can you remember what Rose was wearing the last time you saw her?'

There is no hesitation in her answer. 'Light blue loose jeans and a green crop top.' It was new and Rose had asked her if she liked it. Carrie didn't want to tell her that she hates anything that shows stomach flesh so she said it was lovely.

PC Morgan nods. 'Did she have a bag or anything with her?'

'She's never liked bags. She prefers not to be encumbered. She just sticks her phone in her pocket and off she goes.'

'And have you noticed anything missing from her room? Clothes, footwear, anything like that?'

The first thing Carrie had done was to check, and as far as she could tell there was nothing out of the ordinary in Rose's bedroom. Apart from the bed being neatly made. She tells the police officer this, growing frustrated that she's repeating herself.

'Okay,' PC Morgan says. 'What about her mobile phone?'

'I told them this already. It's not in the house.'

'Can you think of any reason why Rose might have wanted to leave home? Anything at all. Could she have been upset about something? Bullying at school, anything like that?'

Carrie's stomach tightens. 'No, she was happy. Rose isn't the type to let anyone bully her. She's too... fierce. And she'd never do this on purpose. She would have told me if something was going on at school.'

'Being bullied isn't a sign of weakness,' PC Morgan states.

Carrie wonders if he's supposed to make personal comments like that. 'I know, I didn't mean it like that. I just meant that Rose doesn't let people mess with her, she isn't the type.'

'Sometimes teenagers might bottle things up. If there's anything at all you can think of, then please tell us. We just want to find Rose and get her home safely.'

She shakes her head. 'There's nothing. Nothing that I know about at least.' *Clearly there's something, though, because Rose isn't here, sitting eating her breakfast like she should be.*

'Could she have had an argument at the barbeque? Fallen out with anyone?'

'No, she was just with her boyfriend. They've been together for months. They're always together.' *Except they weren't together at the barbeque. What does that mean?*

'And how would you describe their relationship?' PC Morgan continues.

Carrie smiles. 'They love each other. Everyone can see that.' She pushes away the nagging feeling that something has changed.

The police officer asks if Carrie has a recent photo of Rose.

'On my phone.' She grabs it from the table and begins to scroll, handing her phone to PC Morgan.

'If you could email that to us, it would be really helpful.' He pulls a business card from his pocket and places it on the table.

'We'll also need a list of all her friends' names and numbers. And family members. Anyone you can think of who's in Rose's life.'

Carrie nods. 'I've called them all. Nobody's seen her.'

'It's good that you've done that but we do need to do our own questioning.'

She finds some paper and begins writing.

'While you're doing that, do you mind if I have a quick look around the house? I'll need to check Rose's room, just to make sure nothing is missed.'

'Okay,' Carrie agrees. She turns back to her list, surprised by how short it is when she's run out of names. While she's waiting for PC Morgan to finish his search, she texts Jacob, asking how long he'll be.

The police are here now. You need to come quickly.

It's less than five minutes before the officer returns.

'Rose doesn't surround herself with too many people,' she explains as she hands PC Morgan the sheet.

'Any particular reason for that?'

'She's comfortable in her own company. She's not like a lot of other girls. You know, dancing around on TikTok and only caring about what they look like. Rose is different. She's never followed the crowd.'

'And has she ever done anything like this before?'

'Never. I always know where she is.' *Or at least where she says she'll be.*

'We'll need Rose's mobile number and any social media handles. She may have posted something that might give us an insight into where she is.'

Carrie shakes her head. 'Rose isn't on any social media. None of them. Like I told you, she hates all that stuff.'

PC Morgan raises his eyebrows. 'We'll check anyway. Just to make sure. Sometimes kids like to keep things private from their parents. She could have been using a different name.'

Carrie finds it hard to believe that Rose could have a secret life on social media, not when she's always telling Carrie to get off Facebook. Carrie can hear Rose's words. *It's for sheep. Who wants to be like everyone else?*

'Does she have a computer?' PC Morgan asks. 'Or access to one?'

'I saved up and bought her a laptop for her birthday in the summer. It wasn't an expensive one, but she needed one for her homework. I just use the computers at work if I need to.'

'Okay. We'll need to take a look at it. And her boyfriend – you say he was with her at the barbeque?'

'Yes. His mum Lucy told me he walked her home. You can talk to him – he'll be here in a minute. He said he was on his way.' *Over an hour ago. Where is he?*

'We'll definitely need to talk to him. Does your partner live here with you and Rose?' PC Morgan asks.

'No. It's just me and Rose. Her dad left us years ago, when Rose was only five. He lives in Dubai.'

'I'll need his details.'

'He won't know anything. They barely even speak.'

'That might be the case but we need to check everything carefully. And your partner didn't come back here last night?'

'No. He was at home as he had an early shift at work this morning. He had to be in at five. He's left work early and is out looking for her now. I'm staying here in case she's lost her key and can't get in. I need to be here for her...' Carrie can't finish her sentence. She knows what this man must be thinking.

PC Morgan stands. 'For now, I need to get back and get this information logged so we can start looking for Rose. We'll be treating this as high risk, so I can assure you we'll be doing everything to find her as quickly as possible.' He glances around. 'We'll need to organise a full search of your house. It's standard procedure. And we'll also be searching the home where the barbeque took place, and the route your daughter and her boyfriend took home. That will be our starting point.' He pulls out a pen and writes a number on the back of the business card. 'This is your incident log number. Use it if you need to speak to us at any time.'

Carrie thanks him in a timid voice she doesn't recognise. Normally she confronts problems head on, deals with them with fierce strength and determination. She'd fallen apart when Hugh had left, and she refuses to let that happen again. But if Rose doesn't come home soon, that might just break her.

As soon as PC Morgan leaves, the door closing behind him, a shiver runs down her spine. Someone walking over her grave.

Almost an hour passes before the doorbell chimes, and for a flicker of a second Carrie allows herself to believe it's Rose, and that once again her daughter has left behind her key.

Even when she opens the door and takes in Jacob's pallid complexion and unruly black hair falling across his face, she looks behind him for Rose. The disappointment at her daughter's absence smashes into her chest, almost knocking her off balance.

Composing herself, Carrie steps forward and hugs Jacob, something she's never done until now. His body stiffens, but then he tentatively taps her back in return.

'The police will need to talk to you, Jacob. And to your parents. They want to see everyone who was at the barbeque. Your mum will remember who came, won't she?'

He nods. 'Yeah, I'm sure. I'm sorry I took so long to come. I... I was out looking for her. I went to the nature reserve. We go there sometimes to just... chill out. Embracing nature, Rose says. It's her happy place.' He stares past Carrie. 'I thought by the time I got here... you know...'

She glances across the street where the Nelson twins still play outside, firing at each other with bright orange water guns. Their mother has joined them now, and stands with her hands on her hips, watching Carrie and Jacob. Carrie pulls him inside and closes the door.

'Where could she be?' she says, going through to the living room. 'I've called Nina and she has no idea. She's Rose's best friend – she should know where she is! She said she'd message everyone they know from school. But what good will that do?'

Sweat pools on the small of her back and beneath her breasts, and she silently curses this unnatural weather. Surely nature should ease them into summer, and not confuse their bodies like this? Only a few days ago she'd been wearing her winter coat. Rose would tell her that humans are to blame for the weather becoming so erratic.

'I keep going over and over our last conversation,' Carrie tells Jacob. 'Wondering if I missed something. Was she trying to tell me anything? Is she in trouble?'

'Maybe someone's seen her?' Jacob suggests, avoiding her questions, avoiding her stare. He puts his backpack on the floor by the sofa.

Carrie wishes she could infiltrate his mind, rummage around to find out what's going on in there. He's been too quiet lately, nothing like the boy he was when Rose first brought him home months ago.

'D'you want something to drink? You probably haven't even had breakfast, have you?' She doesn't wait for an answer. 'I'll make you some toast. And then you can sit and tell me everything. You were the last person to see her, and I need to know every word she said.'

Jacob nods. 'Can I... see Rose's room first?'

Carrie's eyes narrow. 'Why?'

'I need to feel close to her. I'm worried, Carrie. She wouldn't run away. And she never turns her phone off, does she?'

'I know. But we can't assume the worst. I won't do that.' She picks up Jacob's backpack and takes it into the hall, placing it under the coat hooks, where he knows it should go.

While he's upstairs, she places the last two slices of bread in the toaster and hunts for the jam. It's Rose's favourite breakfast, and she'll need to get more bread because any minute now her daughter will charge through that door announcing that she's starving. But how can Carrie traipse around a supermarket, browsing through the aisles, when her daughter is missing? She pours orange juice for Jacob and boils the kettle for coffee. At least that's one thing that isn't running low in this house.

By the time the toast pops up, Jacob is still upstairs. She swipes butter across it and carefully spreads the jam, making sure she covers every millimetre of toast, just how Rose likes it, and then she leaves it on the table and heads upstairs, silence washing over her as if she's only imagined Jacob is here.

He sits on Rose's bed, tapping on his phone. He's so lost in whatever he's doing that he doesn't notice Carrie come in until she deliberately coughs.

'I was sending her a message,' he explains. 'I know her phone's off but...'

Carrie sits beside him. 'Jacob, did Rose say anything at all that might make you worry? Was she upset? Did anything happen at the barbeque?' She's firing questions at him just like PC Morgan did to her earlier – and it borders on an interrogation. But she needs some answers.

Jacob doesn't respond for a moment. 'No. She was fine. I mean, I didn't spend much time with her actually. You must have noticed.'

Carrie's body freezes. 'No.' *Because I've been too busy, haven't I?* 'Why was that?'

'I don't know. She just spent most of the barbeque with Ava.' He shrugs. 'I didn't mind, course I didn't. Ava's my sister and she loves Rose. But we just didn't have a chance to talk.'

'I have to ask you this Jacob, did the two of you have an

argument? You can tell me. You're not in any trouble. But it might explain why she didn't want to come home.'

'But I don't live here!' Jacob protests. 'Even if we'd had a fight she could have come home. But we *didn't*. And she was fine when I walked her home. Maybe a bit tired.'

Grabbing his shoulders, Carrie leans in to him, urging him to look at her. 'Jacob, you're going to have to do better than that. Was she tired, or was something wrong?'

'I don't know!'

'Did she say anything was bothering her? Anything at all?' A crushing weight descends on Carrie's shoulders. There are things unspoken that she doesn't know, that perhaps she never will, and she can't bear it.

Jacob buries his head in his hands. 'No, she didn't. She was fine,' he says. 'I would have known if something was wrong.' And when he turns to look up at Carrie, she feels as though he is invading her thoughts, seeing into her soul. A cold shiver runs through her.

Carrie stands and smooths out her skirt. 'You'd better come down. Toast'll be getting cold. Rose hates cold toast, doesn't she?'

With a nod, Jacob follows her out, and Carrie closes the door behind them. She's not sure why she does this, especially when soon enough the police search team will be here rooting around. But it's something Rose always does, even if she's only going to the bathroom.

'Where's Joe?' Jacob asks, once they're downstairs.

Carrie's eyes shift to the floor. 'He didn't stay last night. He had to be up for an early shift. He left work, though. Said he needs to help find Rose.'

Jacob doesn't reply, but sits at the table and picks up a slice of toast. It's easy to guess what he's thinking: why is Joe offering to help when everyone knows he and Rose can't stand each other?

'I just wondered if... maybe they'd had an argument?'

Carrie stares at him. 'No,' she says firmly. 'Joe wasn't even here.'

Leaving Jacob to eat his toast, she wanders to the living room window. Outside, the twins have swapped their water guns for bikes and are now pedalling up and down the road, their shouts of joy incongruous among her suffocating pain.

Back in the kitchen, Jacob stares at her. 'Rose will be back soon,' he says. 'She's just taking some time out. That's all it is.' He stands up. 'That's all it is.'

Something stirs in Carrie. A maternal instinct to protect. After all, Jacob is just a child too. No matter how grown up he and Rose might think they both are. 'Yeah, she'll come waltzing in any minute now, wondering what all the fuss is about.' She heads towards Jacob, noticing that he flinches as she approaches. 'Does Rose ever say anything about—'

She's cut off by the sound of the doorbell. It sounds shrill this morning, too loud and menacing. Carrie rushes to answer, and right behind her she senses Jacob following.

'Any news?' Lucy asks, before Carrie's fully opened the door. And then the woman is striding in as if it's perfectly natural that she should come inside without being invited. It seems this is an open house now, where anyone can come and view the show.

'She's not back, Mum.' Jacob says.

'I'm sure this will all get sorted out,' Lucy says, turning to Carrie. 'Have you checked her room?'

Carrie frowns. 'I'm sure I'd know if she was hiding in there.'

'I know, sorry. I meant have you checked through her things. Maybe there's something that might show us where she could be?'

Carrie silently berates herself for misunderstanding what Lucy meant. Maybe the woman should have made it clearer, though. 'I've checked and nothing seems unusual. The police officer also had a quick look. A search team will come too, to go through the whole house.' She turns to Jacob. 'Did you see anything unusual up there? Maybe I missed something.'

He stares at the floor. 'I wasn't looking through her stuff. I just... wanted to sit in there for a minute.'

Carrie notices the questioning look on Lucy's face. The flicker of confusion, which quickly transforms into something else.

Without warning, Jacob stands and rushes to the front door.

'Where are you going?' Lucy calls. 'Wait.'

'I can't just stand around here. I need to be out looking for her.'

He slams the front door behind him and Carrie rushes to the living room window, watching him sprint down the road.

Jacob is hiding something, she's sure of it.

THREE

ROSE

My life has been severed into two parts, leaving nothing but a jagged edge. A protective fence around two distinct Roses. You didn't know the Rose before, and I doubt you would have liked her. I might be barely sixteen, but I'm far more than that. Especially now.

Because of you.

It was Nina who noticed there was a new boy joining the school. Someone from London, who she decided we had to get to know before anyone else did. 'Why?' I'd questioned. But she couldn't come up with a convincing answer. London, although it's not far, is an exotic place to her. Full of possibilities. She's convinced her future lies there. That the streets are paved with gold, or some other bullshit. More like the streets are paved with dog crap. But it's somewhere she plans to run off to the second she's released from education. I've told her a thousand times that education shouldn't stop the second you walk out of the school gates. Learning should be lifelong.

'It's all right for you,' she always moans. 'You have your music. Talent. You'll make it in life whatever happens.'

She misses the point, though. Nothing is guaranteed. And

then a curveball comes your way and knocks you off course. Neither of us knew that was about to happen to me.

Anyway, that's why she wanted to know the new boy. 'Before Rowena Hill and her group of bitches get their claws into him,' she'd laughed. Nina and I always tried to rise above the bullshit popularity contest that is a constant thing at school. Every person walking those corridors lives in fear of judgement, but not us. It tries to sneak up on us, touches us once in a while, even clutches us in a vice grip, where it would be too easy to give in, but we fight back. Take us how we are, or stay the hell away.

Often, I could see Nina cracking, though. Fighting the urge to be accepted. I'd see her giving too much thought to what she was wearing, or asking me if her make-up looks okay. And I'd also catch her watching Rowena closely, almost admiringly. Mum says it's ingrained in us: that need to feel part of something, that we are just like everyone else. To belong. Unique, but no different. My mum talks a lot of sense sometimes, despite how her life's turned out. Despite the fact that she's desperately searching for something and isn't even aware of what that is.

'His name's Jacob Adams,' she reported to me that lunch time. Detective Nina on the case. 'And he's hot. Come on, let's go and look for him. Then you can see for yourself.'

I flicked hair from my eyes. 'Can't. I'm not interested. I'll see him whenever.'

'But he's *different*, Rose. You can tell he's from London. There's something about him. Something cool. He's nothing like the idiots in our year.'

I laughed. 'And you can tell this without even speaking to him. Okay, Nina.'

'He just looks... I don't know. Confident,' she insisted. 'But not in an arrogant way like Jamie and that lot. He seems... comfortable in his own skin. Like us. Or you, at least.' She grabbed my hand. 'Come on, *pleeeease!*'

And Nina was right, wasn't she? No one could say there wasn't something different about Jacob Adams, the mysterious boy from London.

It was on the school field that we found the new boy. 'Look at him sitting with his headphones on, eyeing everyone around him as if he's appraising them, not the other way around.' Nina couldn't stop staring. 'That's confidence, isn't it?'

But I very quickly learnt otherwise, didn't I?

FOUR

LUCY

The garden is tidy when I get home. Everything as it should be. All remnants from the barbeque removed, as if it never took place. Tom is still out there, rummaging around in the shed. From this distance, I can't see what he's doing, but can only assume he's sorting it out; something he's been meaning to do since we moved in.

I step outside in my bare feet and walk across the lawn. Something in the grass pierces my skin and I stop and lift my foot, watching as a tiny circle of blood oozes from my sole. Close by, a shard of glass shimmers in between blades of grass.

Tom looks up as I approach. 'You okay?'

'I stepped on some glass,' I say. 'I'll survive. I don't think we have any plasters.'

'Let me check it,' he says, moving towards me.

'No, I'm fine, honestly. It's nothing.'

'Okay,' Tom says. 'I knew the mess in the garden would be bothering you so I've been cleaning up. Also made a start on the shed.'

I smile. Tom knows this is my peaceful place, and that when it's in disarray then so, too, is my mind.

'Any news?' he asks, wiping sweat from his brow.

'No. The police had just been when I got there. Carrie says they'll need to talk to us all. Even Ava. And they'll be sending a specialist team to search our house.'

'Tom frowns. 'I didn't think about that. I've just cleared up. I shouldn't have, should I? They might need it to be exactly how it was. It was Jacob who put the idea in my head. He came home to get his phone charger and was staring out of the window. He said you'd hate the garden being like this, and said that he'd do it but he needed to look for Rose. I know I'm hard on him sometimes, but he's got a good heart.'

'Well, it's done now, and it's not like it's a crime scene.' But perhaps Tom is right and we shouldn't have disturbed anything. 'It was just some bottles and rubbish. You've still got the black bin bags, haven't you?'

'Yeah, they're by the bins if the police need to search them.'

'I don't like this,' I say. 'She'll come back, won't she? She's just gone off somewhere; nothing's happened to her.' I'm aware of the panic in my voice.

He takes my hand. 'She'll be fine. We'd better warn Ava, though. Seeing the police rooting through the garden might be a bit distressing for her. 'How was Carrie?'

'Not good. I don't think she wanted me there, but I couldn't leave her alone. I waited until Joe came and then I left. Carrie just seemed a bit... numb. Like she didn't know what to say or do.' I don't explain that Jacob hadn't gone straight there. Looking for Rose, Carrie had explained once he'd left. And I'd caught the flicker of doubt in her eyes.

'Rose will turn up,' Tom says. He's usually able to stay positive, even at the most challenging of times. Right now that's exactly what I need. What we all need. 'Don't worry.'

'If she doesn't... Jacob will be a mess. And Ava. Where is she?' I look up at the house and see our daughter in the window, watching us.

Tom gives her a wave. 'She shut herself in her room with your iPad,' he says. 'I didn't have the heart to demand she put it away. What's a bit of screen time with all this going on?' He sighs.

'Maybe you should go and check in on Carrie as well,' I suggest. 'I just feel like we're a part of this too. Rose has become like family, hasn't she?'

'You're right,' Tom agrees. 'I'll head over there in a minute.'

I'm not surprised that Tom hasn't objected to my suggestion; above all else his kindness is what drew me to him when we first met. 'I would come with you, but there's no way Ava will cope with it,' I explain. At least our daughter is here, though, where we know she's safe. *But where is Rose?* 'I should make some lunch for her,' I continue. 'She didn't have breakfast.'

Tom kisses my head and begins locking up the shed. 'Did you know Rose was supposed to be meeting Ava here this morning?'

'Not until she told me earlier. Jacob didn't know either.'

He frowns. 'Is that odd?'

I fight back the suffocating feeling that we're being kept in the dark about something. 'They're close, aren't they?' I respond.

'But it's strange that Jacob didn't know.'

'Who understands kids?' I say, and neither of us smiles at my joke. 'I should make a list of everyone who came yesterday. For the police.' Being practical is what I do best. It's the only way I'll cope if we can't find Rose.

Tom reaches for my hand. 'Don't worry, Luce,' he says again. 'Soon enough we'll be wondering what all the fuss was about.'

I force a nod, and head back to the house.

There's no answer when I knock on Ava's door. But I wait; as much as it makes me nervous that I can't see if they're okay, I will never go in without being invited. The kids need some privacy – it's a basic human right. I try again, and still silence is the only response. 'Ava, can I come in? I need to know you're okay.' No answer. 'Okay, I'm coming in.' I slowly push the door, half expecting the room to be empty. But Ava is there, lying curled up on the bed with her knees drawn to her chin, facing the wall.

I walk over and kneel by her bed. 'Ava, can you talk to me?'

She shakes her head. 'I don't want to, Mum.'

'I know you're worried about Rose – we all are – but—'

'Please don't tell me it will be okay and they'll find her. Just stop, Mum. Dad's been saying it all morning. Sometimes the police *don't* find people. It happens. They won't find her.'

'Ava, please look at me. Why do you think they won't find Rose?'

Slowly, she rolls over to face me, her eyes red and glistening. 'Because it's *Rose*. And she didn't turn up this morning. Before that, I thought she must be okay. But now... She would never run away. No way. It's not like she's a troubled teen who hates her home life. Well, maybe she can't stand Joe, but he doesn't even live with them. So, there's no reason for her to leave her mum. She loves Carrie. Which means...'

I can't let her finish that thought. 'We don't ever truly know what's going on in people's heads, do we? How can we? People show us what they want us to see. Maybe Rose has been upset about something and she just hasn't felt able to talk about it to anyone. Even Jacob.'

'Yeah, she *has* been upset! And you're all too blind to see it!'

My body tenses. 'Ava, what do you mean?'

She sits up and pulls her knees up to her chest, rocking slowly. She used to do that as a toddler, and even carried on when she first started school, but it shocks me to see her doing it now.

'She hasn't been happy, and it's all Jacob's fault!' Tears

erupt from her eyes and her body shakes with the force of her sobs.

My mind struggles to compute what Ava's saying. 'Did they have an argument at the barbeque?'

Ava remains silent, staring at her door as if she's considering bolting through it any second. 'No', she says eventually. 'I didn't mean anything. I'm just upset. I want Rose to come back.'

I lean in and wrap my arms around her. She may be almost thirteen, but she's still my little girl. 'I know Rose means a lot to you—'

'She's the only person who's kind to me. I mean, outside of our family. And she said she'd be here today. Nothing would make her break her promise.'

Unless it's something outside of her control. I would never say this to Ava, though, even though I think she's already reaching this conclusion by herself. 'The police are looking for her,' I assure Ava. 'Wherever she is, they'll find her.' I move a strand of hair from her eyes. 'They'll be coming to talk to us. And have a look around the house and garden. Will you be okay?'

Ava's eyes widen. 'No! I don't want to talk to them. I... I can't.'

'Ava, it's fine. I'll be right there with you, okay? All you have to do is answer any questions they have. They'll just want to know about the barbeque. And you did spend a lot of the evening with her. They'll want to know how Rose was acting, that kind of thing.' Something I was too distracted to notice, wrapped up as I have been in worry for my daughter. It never occurred to me that it might be my son who needed watching.

Ava falls silent. 'Will I get in trouble if I don't speak to them?'

'I don't know, but they'd want to know why. Look, we need to find Rose, and telling the police everything we know will help us do that, won't it?' Even as I say this my stomach wrenches. *Do I tell them that Jacob was confused about the time he got home?* I need to speak to him first, just to make sure, and I can't do that while he's out searching for Rose. 'We'll deal with it together,' I tell Ava. 'I just need to call your brother. He should be here when the police come.'

'But he needs to be out there, looking for her!' Ava protests.

'It's okay, your dad is going over to help. Right now, though, you need to have lunch.'

Reluctantly she agrees, and I relish the intense relief I feel at being able to do something normal, when nothing else is.

It's another two hours before Jacob makes his way home. There is nothing I can say that will comfort him, so instead I reach out and hug him. His body is rigid but he doesn't immediately pull away; he knows this is something I need to do for both our sakes.

He refuses to eat, and sits silently on the sofa, his head buried in his phone. When Ava says she'll take Cooper for a walk, I grab the chance to confront my son.

'Jacob, we need to talk.'

He looks up, scrunching his face.

'This morning you told me you came straight home from dropping Rose off at nine thirty. So, you would have been home by ten. But... I heard you come in. I woke up when you came in and it was nearly two a.m.'

Jacob stares at me. 'No. It wasn't. It wasn't that late. And wouldn't you have had a go at me for coming in so late?'

'Yes, normally. But I was tired, and I didn't feel well.'

'You mean you were drunk? In that case, how can you even be so sure of the time? I'm telling you, I walked Rose home at about nine thirty. And then I came back. End of. Can you stop interrogating me now?'

'Jacob, if you or Rose are in any kind of trouble, you know you can talk to me. We've always been able to talk, haven't we?'

He sniffs, still avoiding eye contact. 'I s'pose.'

'Well, that hasn't changed just because you're sixteen. I'm still here. Will you look at me, please?'

His head jolts up. 'Bloody hell, Mum, what is all this? I just want to find my girlfriend.'

If I don't drop this, it will damage our relationship. But there are so many questions burning through my mind, none of which I can ask him right now.

By evening I can no longer stand the heavy tension filling the house, so I head out to my workshop after dinner. Ava and Jacob were silent as they pushed spaghetti around their plates, barely lifting their forks to their mouths, and even Tom couldn't draw them out, as much as he tried to ignite a spark of conversation.

With a wedding in only six days, I need to write my flower recipes, and wash all my buckets and candlesticks so that they're ready. As much as it feels wrong to be carrying on with work while Rose is missing, I can't let my client down now. Besides, the police being here has unsettled me. I watched Jacob answer their questions, searching his face for any hint of dishonesty, but all I felt emanating from him was fear.

I look up at the house; Ava's bedroom light is on, and next to it so, too, is Tom's office light. I have no idea where Jacob is, so when I've finished washing the vases, I head back to the house to find out.

It's quiet as I step inside and walk through the conservatory. But then I hear voices as I reach the kitchen. Ava and Jacob's. Loud. Angry.

'I hate you,' Ava hisses. 'You must know where she is! This is all your fault!'

A menacing silence before Jacob speaks. 'Shut up, Ava. D'you hear me? Shut the fuck up!'

I stand open-mouthed, too shocked to move. Jacob's never

spoken to Ava this way. He bolts out of the living room and runs upstairs, unaware that I'm standing right there.

In less than a second I'm in the living room, sitting beside Ava, asking her what just happened.

'Nothing, Mum,' she insists, avoiding my stare. 'Just leave it. Jacob's... upset about Rose. He was... blaming me for arranging to meet up with her. For putting pressure on her to be my friend.'

'Ava, that doesn't make sense.'

'I can't explain why he's saying that stuff. Mum, can I just go and do my homework?'

With only one more day before school starts back, I'm certain that Ava will already have finished every task she needed to complete in the holiday. Yet confronting her now, trying to force her to talk, will only cause her harm. Ava is fragile right now, and I must do everything I can to protect her, even if it means it will be harder for me to uncover what's going on. Because with every passing hour it's becoming clearer that something awful has taken place.

And even though I don't want to believe this, my instinct is whispering that Jacob isn't telling us the truth.

FIVE

ROSE

That first kiss. Laced with excitement and fear.

We were at your house when it happened. I'd been going there for months, thanks to Nina. 'Jacob's not interested in *me*,' she'd announced a few weeks after that stalking incident at school. 'He's got some girl in London. Apparently, she moved away, but they're still in a relationship. Some long-distance thing. And we all know those never work. He definitely likes *you*, though.'

'How do you know all this stuff about him?'

'It's on Instagram. His life laid bare.'

'Oh,' I said. And I think I was disappointed to hear this. 'Anyway, I'm sure he doesn't like me.' But I must have been a bit intrigued because I questioned Nina further. 'What makes you think he does? You just said he has a girlfriend in London.'

Nina rolled her eyes. She has an infuriating habit of doing it, even when it's not warranted. I wonder if it's an unconscious action. 'Oh, come on, Rose, are you blind? He stares at you all the time. *All* the time. Like he's in a trance. It's actually a bit creepy. But anyway, he asked me for your number and I gave it to him. You don't mind, do you?'

I *did* mind. If there was a girlfriend in the picture, then there was no way I wanted to get involved. I didn't want to be a person who could do something like that. But I was too shocked to be annoyed with Nina. She was pushing us together when I wasn't even sure how I felt. I didn't want a boyfriend, especially one who already had someone. I just wanted to focus on studying and getting into uni. And on my music. Nina didn't let it go, though – it was like she needed to hear about Rose Nyler and Jacob Adams being together, like some twisted version of a celebrity couple, so she could live vicariously through us. She invented us. And that's where the problem began.

Your family were out that day when I first kissed you. I felt comfortable at your house, and with your family; Ava and I had clicked immediately and she'd started opening up to me, telling me things I'm sure none of you even knew were in her head. And then there was Lucy. She'd been good to me from the second she met me. I could tell she thought I'd be a suitable girl-friend for her son, even though we'd told everyone it wasn't like that. We were just friends. Jacob and Isla were still the great young love story, like Romeo and Juliet, although without the tragic ending hopefully.

I could tell right away that Lucy was overprotective, though, and I could also see it was something she tried to fight. As if her mind was in a constant battle between letting her kids go and wrapping them up in a bubble. But underneath that, she was cool. Down to earth. Always there if you needed her. She was wrong about me, though, wasn't she? I was far from a suitable girlfriend, when that's what I was forced to become.

We'd talked a lot, you and I, hadn't we? Got the measure of each other. And that intense urge for you took me by surprise. Absent one day and then setting me alight the next. It was new to me. Intoxicating. I'd had a couple of boyfriends before, but had never felt like this. *Alive.* The intensity of my feelings was overwhelming; I could barely see anything else. I got lost in you way before I was sure that you felt the same way. And even though guilt sat heavily within me, weighing me down, I pushed it aside because the pull of you was powerful.

That's why I kissed you that afternoon in the kitchen. It was a big risk – I didn't know what you'd do, but I didn't care. It was raining outside, and the spatter of raindrops against the window was comforting. Like we were in a bubble, protected from the outside world. It was wrong, wasn't it? Given what we both knew about each other... but I was powerless to stop myself.

You gave in to me for a moment. Seconds where I tasted the salt on your tongue, and felt how soft your lips were. And then you pulled away and I could see you were shocked. Scared. Vulnerable. I'll never forget that look because I never saw it again. And then the panic set in. 'No, I can't.' You nudged me away. 'I don't do things without thinking them through,' you'd said. 'I'm sorry. I shouldn't have—'

'*I* did it. It was me.' I looked past you to the garden and my eyes fixed on Lucy's workshop. It was a sacred space to her, and a beautiful place. I cherished the time I'd spend listening to her talk about the flowers she grew. Her passion was infectious, seeping into me. And I longed to feel that strongly about something. Anything. Perhaps it was my desperation to feel alive that drew me to you, despite knowing I should stay away.

It was in that awkward moment of silence that your family came home, and Ava appeared in the kitchen first. 'Rose!' she said. 'Jacob never said you were coming.'

'Well, Jacob never says much at all, does he?' I laughed, turning to you. Your cheeks were flushed, and I wondered if anyone would notice.

'It's lovely to see you, Rose,' Lucy said. 'Are you staying for dinner? I think we'll get fish and chips for a treat.' She smiled. 'It is Friday, after all.'

'Oh, I don't—'

'Please stay,' Ava pleaded, in her shy way.

I love that girl. My relationship with her brother might not be right, but I would never change the friendship I've come to have with her.

'I'd love to. Thanks, Lucy.'

'Will you come with me to take Cooper for a walk?' Ava asked.

'That's a lovely idea,' Lucy said, before I could answer. 'Jacob won't mind you going.'

It was a relief to get outside, to take in a lungful of frozen air. Inside, it had felt as though I'd stopped breathing.

Christmas was fast approaching and I didn't want to think about those long weeks being stuck at home because I knew that Joe would be there for so much of the holiday. He was spending far too much time at our house. I'd begged for extra shifts at the pet store so that at least most of the two weeks off school would be filled, but they weren't open on Christmas Day. So, my fate was inevitable. I tried to push this from my mind and focus on Ava. Sweet, young Ava. I worried about her, even then. I could see what none of you could. She was sinking fast and needed help.

'Are you and Jacob, like, *together?*' Ava asked, as we made our way to the nature reserve. 'I've tried asking him and he never tells me anything. It's so annoying.'

'We're just friends,' I explained.

She frowned, pulling Cooper's lead tighter. 'It doesn't look like it,' she said. 'You're always at the house. You're always *together.*'

'That's because we've become close. In a *friend* way.' I couldn't explain this to Ava but we understood each other. The darkness that was inside both of us drew us together. I thought of you and the kiss that had gone terribly wrong, and my cheeks began to burn from a mixture of guilt and fear. I hoped Ava didn't notice.

'But you're so pretty,' she said, oblivious to my distress. 'I know he likes you.'

'He has a girlfriend,' I said. *And lots of baggage, but I will never be the one to tell you about that.*

'Isla? How can that work when she lives miles away? Anyway, I don't think Jacob loves Isla. She's weird. But you fit so well together. You're just... *right*. Mum thinks so too.'

'Lucy said that?'

'Yeah. I don't think Mum likes Isla.'

But whatever the reason for this, I'd thought, I am worse than Isla, worse than anyone else could be, for her son. Guilt coursed through my body then. Briefly. Gone almost as soon as I'd registered it.

'Maybe Isla's crazy,' Ava said.

'She'd have to be to put up with your brother,' I'd joked, and Ava and I both laughed. It was one of the only times I saw Ava laugh with abandon.

We'd reached the nature reserve, and we walked along in silence, taking in our surroundings. There's so much beauty in this world – in nature – and we're all too busy to stop and take it in. I wanted Ava to see that. To know that whatever was troubling her, stopping to notice what's around us once in a while would be sure to help.

'It's beautiful, isn't it?' I said. 'Even in winter. Especially in winter. Being right in the middle of nature. It's like nothing else matters. Only the connection to what's around us.'

Ava briefly looked up and nodded, but I don't think she was convinced. She preferred being in her room with a book over going outside, even on the warmest of days.

'You know, I'm a pretty good listener,' I said. 'If there's anything you need to talk about.'

'Okay.'

'So, is there?'

'No.'

'But if there ever is, I'm here for you.'

She nodded again, falling silent and staring at her chunky boots. Perhaps I should have pushed her, but I didn't. I should have seen that she needed help to open up. And now it's far too late for me to do anything.

'Look at that swan over there,' I said instead, pointing to the lake.

Ava barely glanced at it. 'Even my dad likes you,' she said, as if this was a natural continuation of our conversation. 'And he's never shown much interest in Jacob's love life – I think it embarrasses him.'

'Well, it's nice to be appreciated,' I said.

We carried on walking in silence, and every so often I glanced at Ava, pleased to see that she seemed more at peace the longer we spent out there.

Then I thought of the kiss you and I had shared moments before in your kitchen, and how it will have changed everything.

And a suffocating dread surfaced within me, almost crippling me.

SIX

CARRIE

Waiting. That's all it feels like she's doing. Helpless. Futile. While Rose is... where? Carrie wants to be out searching with everyone else, but – as strange as it must seem – she's terrified to leave the house. She needs to be here to lay eyes on her daughter the second she comes back. Because Rose *will* come back. And with her reappearance, Carrie knows there will be a heap of devastation thrust upon them. Rose has disappeared for a reason. Something has made her do this. What is she running from?

The sound of a car engine forces Carrie to rush to the window. People gather in the street, all of them having been rallied together within minutes by Lia Nelson, the twins' mother. Carrie shouldn't have judged her all this time. It's hard being a parent, no matter what age the kids are. She's probably trying her best, just like Carrie has always done, and it can't be easy having twins. And Carrie knows everything is twice as hard when you're doing it alone. When Rose is back, Carrie will buy Lia some flowers to say thank you. Red roses to match her fiery red hair.

It's Joe's Volvo she heard, and she watches him clamber out

and scurry towards the door. She's tempted to ignore him. To stay right where she is until he gives up and leaves. Joe doesn't give a damn about Rose – he never has – so why should he be here now, feigning concern? Putting on an appearance for others, that's why he's shown up. Regardless, she needs all eyes out looking. Even Joe, who she imagines will stop off at every pub along the way.

'Thanks for coming,' she says, standing at the door, her arms folded.

'She's doing this on purpose, Carrie,' Joes mumbles, striding into the house. 'To make you worry. I hope you can see that?'

'Rose would never—'

'Damn it, Carrie – she's not the perfect little angel you think she is. Rose could do anything and you'd make an excuse for her.' He pulls off his jacket and hangs it on the coat hook. He looks scruffy this morning. Carrie wishes he'd shave more often; his stubble feels like sandpaper against her skin. And he needs a haircut – his dark hair flops across his face and it irritates her that he's always running his hands through it.

Resisting the urge to pound her fist into his face, Carrie closes the door. Yes, she would make an excuse for Rose any time because she knows that her daughter is a decent person. Kind. Carrie has never understood why Joe is unwilling to see that. *It's jealousy, that's what it is. He hates that I had a life with someone else.* He's never been able to deal with the fact that Rose's dad is more successful, more together, than Joe will ever be. Even if Hugh did move to another country and barely has time to speak to his daughter. *What does that say about Joe?* Still, she has to focus on the positives – Joe does look out for Carrie in his own way.

'She hasn't done this on purpose,' she says. She's drained; there's no space in her head for one of their arguments. Right now, she couldn't care less if Joe thinks he's got the upper hand;

she will let this one go. 'Not for this long. She wouldn't deliberately let me worry like this.'

She raises her eyebrows and stares at Joe, defying him to contradict her. And then she thinks about Jacob, how with every inch of her being it felt that he was hiding something. Still, that's none of Joe's business.

'I've been out searching since you told me,' he says. 'And I'll get no thanks when she finally rocks up.'

Shut the fuck up! Carrie screams in her head. 'The police will want to talk to you.'

'Well, I don't know anything, do I? I wasn't even at that barbeque. And I wasn't here after either. I didn't see her, did I?'

'No, but you're my... partner.' The words cling to the roof of her mouth, reluctant to leave. Partner makes it sound as though they're a team – which couldn't be further from the truth. And she will never call him her boyfriend. At forty she feels far past that.

'Course I'll talk to them but they're wasting their time,' Joe says, snapping her back to the present. 'I've got nothing to tell 'em.' He rolls his eyes. 'Least you can do is get the kettle on.'

'Do it yourself,' she snaps, leaving him in the hall and heading back to the front window. She ignores Joe's cursing and smiles to herself when the kettle begins its familiar rumble. A small victory. But the feeling quickly evaporates; what does getting one up on Joe matter when Rose is missing?

After a few minutes of clattering around in the kitchen, Joe joins her in the living room and hands her a mug of tea. 'It's strong, how you like it,' he says.

She takes it silently and turns back to the window. There are still several people wandering around, and it strikes Carrie that they don't seem to be doing much searching. Rubberneckers, more likely. Here only to have something to gossip to their friends about. Carrie sighs. She doesn't want to think so negatively – when did she become so cynical?

'D'you think something happened at the barbeque?' Joe asks. He is softer now, offering her a glimpse of the man she fell in love with. It had been three years ago. A lifetime in so many ways. Joe could make her laugh – that's what got her. No matter how she was feeling, he helped her laugh her way through it. 'She was fine yesterday morning,' he continues. 'I was here, wasn't I? Didn't seem there was anything wrong.'

Carrie feels that tightness in her chest again, and wonders for a moment if she's having a small heart attack. A silent one. Can that happen? She goes over yesterday morning: the three of them had sat down to breakfast together. None of them had spoken much, but that doesn't mean anything was bothering Rose – she and Joe never have much to say to each other. And Carrie couldn't even look at him that morning. Rose had gone to her room to revise after that, and then Carrie had left for work. The next time she saw Rose was at the barbeque.

'I've been going over and over it,' she tells Joe. 'Wondering if I've missed something. But Rose seemed fine. Normal. I would have noticed, wouldn't I, if anything was wrong? I'm her mum. It's my job...'

She lets her words evaporate, become part of the ether. Because Carrie knows she could have easily missed something. She and Joe had argued a couple of nights ago when she'd caught his eyes falling too appraisingly on that new barmaid at The Tavern. Carrie had seen the lascivious glint in his eyes. She could have dismissed it, put it down to the alcohol and the novelty of a new young woman behind the bar, but he sought her out too many times. And after a few pints, his attempts to be discreet crumbled. But still, Carrie had sat there quietly, biding her time. She knows too many people around here and she didn't want to cause a scene. So, she'd waited until they got home – stumbled home, in Joe's case – and then she'd ripped into him.

'Do you think I'm a fool?' she'd demanded.

'What are you on about?' he'd slurred, his eyes unable to focus on her. He even tried to reach for her – in that way that meant he wanted something. There was no way Carrie would let him touch her that night, though, not after what he'd done.

'You're pathetic,' she'd told him, shoving him away.

When she'd left him in the living room, she found Rose sitting at the top of the stairs, her arms folded across her chest. 'What are you doing with him, Mum?' her daughter had asked. Carrie had felt her chest constrict, because it was messed up that her daughter should have to talk to her like this. Their roles had reversed, and she was now the child.

'I'm making it work,' she'd replied, turning away from the disappointment scrawled on Rose's face. 'We can't just throw relationships away without fighting for them.'

Rose shook her head. 'Mum, you're not a failure for ending a relationship that's not working.'

Sometimes her daughter shocked her with the things she came out with. 'You see, that's just the problem. People are too quick to walk away from things, to throw away relationships. They take hard work, Rose. Commitment. It's important to see things through.'

'Yeah, I know all that, Mum, but do you love him? I don't know how you can, but I think you *must* to put up with him.'

Carrie took her time to consider this. 'I love the person Joe is when he isn't drinking,' she'd said eventually. 'Or hungover. Yes. I'm going to get *that* person back. Alcohol changes people, Rose. Masks their true nature.'

'I don't believe that. Maybe alcohol actually shows you exactly who the real person is. And maybe you've never even known who Joe really is.' She stood then, heading back to her bedroom and closing the door behind her.

Now, looking at Joe, Carrie thinks maybe Rose was right.

'This is what I reckon,' he says, his hands forming a steeple. 'She got mad about something. Did a runner. Wants a big fuss made of her. End of. She'll come back when she's hungry.' He reaches for her hand and squeezes it.

As much as she appreciates that Joe is making an effort, all he's doing is proving how little he knows her daughter. Rose would never seek attention in this way. If anything, the opposite is true; the only time she ever wants any eyes on her is when she's playing her guitar and singing the songs she writes herself. And even then, it's about the music, not Rose. She makes it that way.

'Listen,' Joe says. 'Let me grab a sandwich and then I'll get back out there, okay?'

Carrie nods, unable to thank him with words. She'll make him that sandwich, though. She supposes it's the least she can do.

The next time she answers the door, she's surprised to see Jacob's dad, Tom, standing on her doorstep. She stares at him, her brain recognising him yet unable to understand that he's there. She'd been in Rose's room, folding her washing and hanging up her school uniform, making sure it's tidy for when she comes home, so Carrie didn't see or hear his car pull up outside. Otherwise she would have been prepared.

Tom's never been to her house before, and for a fleeting moment she doesn't want to let him in. He's always dressed so smartly – even today when he's not working. Expensive-looking jeans and a designer short-sleeved polo shirt. He's a handsome man, his dark eyes and tanned skin a striking contrast to his dark blonde hair. If she's honest with herself, she finds him intimidating in the cold light of day, away from the informal atmosphere of the barbeque. When she's stone-cold sober.

Carrie finds her hand reaching to smooth down her hair. She can't even remember if she's brushed it this morning, so she must look a mess. She doesn't really care. She just wants her daughter home.

'I hope you don't mind me coming,' Tom says. 'I'd like to help with the search. Rose is family to us.' He hovers on the doorstep.

'That's very kind,' she says, still not letting him in.

'Lucy wants to help too – she's just getting Ava sorted with some lunch.' He rolls his eyes. 'Sorry, that must seem insensitive when Rose is missing.'

'Everyone's got to eat,' Carrie says. 'Do you want to come in?' She regrets the offer as soon as it's spoken, but she can't take it back now. 'How's Jacob doing?' she asks, as Tom steps inside and she closes the door behind him.

'Um, he's out there searching. I think he just needs to be doing something to find her. He can't think of anywhere she could be. Or any reason she wouldn't come home. This is really hard on him.'

Carrie's eyes narrow. 'I'm sure it is.' She gestures to the living room. 'Come and sit down, I need to ask you something.'

Tom Adams sits on her sofa. Her faded chintzy sofa that needed replacing years ago. There's even an indent in the seat Joe always plonks himself on. Carrie almost laughs out loud. This man is incongruous in her house, and she wonders if he feels it too. Despite yesterday, he doesn't fit into her world. 'You've never been here before, have you? She asks. 'Not even to drop Jacob off or pick him up.'

His face flushes. 'Er, no. Lucy usually—'

'Funny, that. When Rose and Jacob have been together for... what is it now... six months?'

'I'm always at work. In London. The commute means my working day is long. Painfully long, actually.'

'I'm sorry, you don't have to explain yourself to me. I'm... this is just...'

He holds up his hand. 'I can't begin to imagine what you're

going through, Carrie. If it was Ava, I'd be going out of my mind. Don't apologise for anything.'

She stares at him. 'There *is* something I need to apologise for.' Now it's her turn to look flustered. 'I... drank too much at the barbeque yesterday. And probably talked way too much.' She remembers pulling on Tom's arm, trying to force him to dance with her. Giggling like a child. He'd looked embarrassed but she didn't care; all her inhibitions were lost. And he was kind enough to humour her a bit. Heat floods to her cheeks as she recalls this. Why is it that alcohol always makes her feel like she's twenty again? Reckless.

Tom holds up his hand. 'No need to apologise. Lucy had a bit too much as well, and she rarely drinks.'

'Too focused on her business?' Carrie suggests. 'I was supposed to do a shift this afternoon. Overtime. But how can I?'

'Course you can't. You work at the hospital, don't you?'

She nods. 'I'm a healthcare assistant. I've been planning to do my nurse's training. I know it's quite late in life but...' She stops short, unsure why she's telling him this. Why should he care what her life plans are?

'That's great,' Tom responds, smiling.

'You're a lawyer, aren't you?'

'Solicitor. Corporate law. All very dull.' He offers a thin smile.

Carrie tries to respond, to show some interest, but her brain is foggy. She can't think of anything other than Rose. 'Where is she?' she asks.

Tom reaches for her hand. 'The police are looking. Everyone's out looking. Your neighbour across the road said she's calling everyone she knows. She's posted on the local Facebook group too – that will help. Someone will have seen her. We'll find her, Carrie.'

She tries to take comfort in his words. He speaks with such

confidence, but she knows that's only because his children are safe at home.

'What did you want to ask me?' Tom continues.

'What?'

'Just now. You said you needed to ask me something.'

'Oh, yeah.' She pauses, wondering how to proceed. There's no way to know how he'll react to what she's about to say. 'Have you noticed Jacob's been a bit quiet lately?'

Tom scrunches his face. It ages him, yet he still looks distinguished. Kind. His face isn't harsh like Joe's. 'I don't think so. Why do you ask?'

'He's just always so chatty when he comes here. Polite. You know. Asks how I am. That kind of thing. We often have a long chat in the kitchen before he even goes up to Rose's room. But that all stopped a couple of weeks ago. And he's been a bit... withdrawn.'

Tom frowns. 'I think he's a bit worried about the exams. That's all it will be.' When he studies her face, for an irrational moment Carrie wonders if he can read her mind.

'Yeah. That must be it, then,' she says.

He rises slowly. 'I'll get going. Drive around. Is there anywhere you can think of that Rose likes to go?'

Carrie shakes her head. 'Rose likes being at home. When she's not at school or working, she's usually in her room writing new stuff. Playing her guitar. If she's not with Nina or Jacob, then there's nowhere else.'

'Except the place she is right at this moment. And we'll find her, Carrie.'

'Jacob knows something.' Carrie hasn't planned to say this, but the words flood from her mouth, a tsunami she's powerless to stop.

Tom stares at her, blinking. 'What? Why do you say that?'

That's the problem; it's nothing concrete, she has no evidence to support this accusation. 'He's the closest person to

Rose. He's been acting out of character. I think... maybe they were having problems and... and she left because he's upset her. I don't know, Tom. It would have to be something really awful to upset Rose, though. She's so strong, she never lets things get to her. So going off like this...'

Tom frowns and folds his arms. 'I... can't imagine that's the case. I hope it's not. Those two are so close. Jacob would never—'

'What? Hurt her? That's what I thought about my ex-husband until the day he told me he was moving to Dubai for work, and that he didn't want me or Rose to come with him.' It feels strange mentioning Hugh to Tom, but then this whole day so far has been anything but ordinary.

Tom stares at her. 'I'm sorry. I didn't know that's what had happened. That's awful.'

'So, you can see why I don't just believe what appears to be true on the surface? I have to question everything, Tom.'

He nods. 'Listen, Carrie. I understand. And I promise you that if Jacob knows anything, then I'll find it out. Okay?' He takes her hand, and she feels a surge of something. Excitement? How can it be that when she's so worried about Rose?

'Thank you,' she says, standing up. 'You'll let me know if you find her?'

'Of course.'

At the door, she watches him climb into his slate grey BMW. And then she remembers his supportive words about her dream of training to become a nurse. And his promise to speak to Jacob. He seems like a kind man; she shouldn't have accused Jacob like that. Not to his own father. She needs evidence first. Otherwise, she's just a distraught mother who no one will listen to.

Back in the living room, Carrie stands by the window once more and pulls her mobile phone from her pocket. She taps Rose's name, clasping the phone to her ear while she waits for the inevitable voicemail message. She's lost count of how many times she's called this phone today.

'Rose. Please call me. I'm worried sick. Whatever's happened, you can come home and we'll get through it together. Isn't that what we always do? We're a team, aren't we? Just you and me. Please call.'

Carrie ends the message and sinks to the floor, covering her ears tightly with both hands to drown out the sound of the Nelson twins shrieking as they chase each other down the road.

SEVEN

LUCY

It's past dinner time before Tom comes home. I rush over to him and hold him tightly, feeling guilty that I'm grateful it's not Ava or Jacob who are missing. 'Anything?' I ask, even though I already know. He would have called immediately if there was any news.

Tom shakes his head. 'We need to stay positive, though. Is Jacob back?'

'No. He called and said he was with Nina and they're both still out looking. I told him to be back before dark. He was planning to grab some food at Nina's.' I don't add that I'd nearly demanded that he come home and explain the argument I overheard him having with his sister. I'd tried to talk to Ava but she'd shut down, and I know better than to push her when she clams up like that. I'm sure I won't have much more luck with Jacob.

I watch Tom as he fills a glass with water, and I open my mouth to tell him what I'd overheard, and also that Jacob was back later than he'd claimed. But I don't. The words won't come, because I know that Tom will assume the worst. He'll never say it to me, but I believe he's found bonding with Jacob difficult. Jacob was already three years old when I met Tom, and before we had Ava, Tom often joked that he feels like a usurper, taking over the role of father from someone else. He did his best, though, yet there is a silent tension between them, underlying every encounter, which isn't there with Tom and Ava. So I stay silent. I will deal with whatever is going on myself.

'Have you eaten?' I ask Tom. 'There's plenty of lasagne left.'

'Maybe later. I need to go through some files for a client before our meeting tomorrow.'

This doesn't surprise me; Tom and I are often up until the early hours of the morning working. We tell ourselves that it won't always be like this; but we do nothing to change it.

'How was Carrie?' I ask.

He takes a long drink of water before answering. 'Worried, of course. There wasn't much I could say to comfort her. Strange thing, though.' He frowns. 'She asked me if I'd noticed whether Jacob's been acting differently lately. Withdrawn, she said. Quiet. She wondered if he and Rose were having problems. I told her he's just worried about his exams.'

My stomach clenches. 'He's been fine,' I say. 'Maybe a little stressed about exams, but he's dealing with it well. I think Carrie's just desperate for answers.'

'Yep,' Tom agrees. 'That's understandable.' He walks over to me and kisses my forehead. 'I'll be up in my office. Are you working tonight as well?'

'Later. I need to take Cooper for a walk. Maybe I'll ask Ava to come – she needs to get out of the house for a bit.' Dog walks are one of the ways I can spend quality time with the kids, and they're usually happy to speak about most things as we walk.

Upstairs, I knock on Ava's door, expecting to be greeted with silence.

'Come in,' she says, surprising me. She's lying on the floor this time, on her front, reading a book she's laid open on the floor. She doesn't look up as I come in. Ava is painfully thin, even though she eats plenty. It used to worry me, but it's just her genetic make-up; she's tall like Tom, too, and that makes her appear even skinnier.

'Is it good?' I ask, sitting beside her on the floor.

'Yep. Rose gave it to me. To keep. She said it was her favourite book when she was my age.' She closes it and pulls herself up so she's sitting cross-legged. 'I can't imagine Rose ever being thirteen. She seems so... mature.'

'She does, doesn't she? As if she went straight to sixteen and skipped the early years.' I smile. 'She's a special girl.' I reach across and turn over the book. 'That's nice of her to give you it.' My breath catches in my throat as I read the title. *Girl, Missing*.

'Oh,' I manage to say. 'That's...'

'It's not what you think,' she says, flicking a strand of dark wavy hair from her face. 'It's about a girl who finds out she's adopted. She runs away to find her biological parents. And to find out why everyone's lied to her.' Ava rolls her eyes. 'It's just a coincidence, Mum. Rose gave me this book months ago. I've just had so many other books to read, so I only started it the other day. Besides, Rose isn't adopted, is she? Her mum would never lie to her.'

I haven't known Carrie that long but it seems that what you see is what you get with her. 'No, I don't imagine she would.'

'Did you need me for something?' Ava asks, taking back the book.

'I wondered if you wanted to take Cooper for a walk with me? He's desperate to get out.' *And you need to as well, even if you don't realise it.*

She shakes her head and folds her arms. 'No thanks. I just want to read.'

'Okay.' I pause. 'Ava, are you and Jacob all right?'

'I told you, Mum, everything's fine.'

'It didn't sound fine earlier.'

'We fight sometimes. It doesn't mean anything.'

But this was about Rose. It has to mean something.

I stand up and walk to the door, glancing back at Ava. 'If you change your mind about coming for a walk, then call me and I'll come back for you. Okay? Or Dad can drop you to wherever we are. We can walk back together.'

She holds up her book. 'I'm fine, Mum.'

It's a relief to step outside. The atmosphere in the house is off, tainted by something I can't identify. It's cooler now – there's no trace of the unseasonably warm weather we've been having. Cooper pulls on his lead, excited to be out, frustrated that I'm not keeping up. I quicken my pace. 'You'll have to wait,' I say. 'Just a bit longer. When we reach the Downs, I'll let you off.'

I head along quiet roads, and all the time Rose is in my thoughts. I try to focus on the dog's heavy panting to ground myself, but it's futile. She is all I can think of. Did I talk to her at the barbeque? I don't recall anything other than a greeting and offering her food, the compliment she gave me on my dress. It was royal blue and Rose said the colour suited me. I was too busy rushing around, too consumed with worrying whether everyone was having a good time. But most of all whether Ava was okay. Nothing struck me as out of the ordinary. Rose had been talking to Ava a lot. It didn't occur to me at the time, but now I wonder if she was avoiding Jacob. I don't remember seeing them together.

Cooper tugs harder on his lead and it almost slips from my hand. 'What is it?' I ask. Then I see Jacob on the other side of the street, walking towards us. Even though his hood is up and I can barely make out his features, I know it's my son. And evidently our dog does too.

I cross the road and call to him. He doesn't respond – he's too busy staring at his phone, but then he gets closer and finally looks up, shoving his phone in his back pocket.

'Hey, boy,' he says, leaning down to ruffle Cooper's fur.

'Nothing?' I ask.

Jacob shakes his head. 'Nina's with her dad now, driving around. We've just been at the school, but she wouldn't be there, would she? It's the Easter holidays – it's the last place she'd go.'

'Well, it's worth trying everywhere,' I reply, reaching for his arm. It's barely a second before he awkwardly pulls away. 'Will you walk with us? We can retrace the route you took yesterday when you walked her home.'

'I already have. And the police have too. I've seen them out, knocking on doors.' He stares at the ground, shoves his hands in his pockets.

'Come on,' I urge, sliding one of his arms out and placing the lead in his hand. 'You can take this. He's been dragging me along this evening, and I'm sure you've got more energy than I have.'

Jacob looks as if he's about to object but he does as I ask. He's silent as we head along London Road, staring at the ground. It strikes me that he should be looking around, keeping an eye out for Rose rather than focusing on his trainers.

That's when I notice. 'Jacob, are those new trainers?'

'No. Why?'

'They're bright white. I haven't seen them that colour since the day you got them.'

'I washed them. The other day. What's the big deal?'

'Nothing. I'm just surprised.' I have never known Jacob to wash his trainers. In fact, hasn't he told me before that they look better when they look worn?

I turn to him. 'Jacob, I need to ask you something.'

'What?'

'Why were you and Ava arguing?'

'When?'

'At home earlier. I overheard you. She was angry with you about something.'

He turns and stares at me. 'That was nothing, Mum. Just Ava being... annoying.'

I try to read his expression but there's nothing to give me any insight into his thoughts. 'She said you know where Rose is. That it's your fault she's gone.'

'Jeez, Mum, and you believe her?'

'I'm not saying that. I'd just like to know what's going on, that's all. Do you—'

'Don't even ask me that! Course I don't know where she is!'

As I stare at my son, every part of me wants to believe him. I can't lose my faith in him, not when I'm the only person in this family he has a strong bond with. He might have had issues in the past, but that doesn't mean he's lying to us now. *Except about the time he got home last night. What does that mean?* I force this thought from my mind. I have to trust him.

'Okay, Jacob, I believe you. But if you do know where she's gone, or if you're keeping any kind of secret for her then you need to talk to me. And we'll deal with it together.'

Slowly he nods. 'I know, Mum. But there's nothing. I don't know where she is. If I did, then I'd be there now convincing her to come back. Ava's just upset because she thinks me and Rose must have argued. She... thinks that's why Rose left.'

'Jacob, you did tell the police everything you could think of, didn't you?'

'Course. I'm not a liar, Mum! I told you, I don't know where she is or why she's gone!'

'Okay, let's just concentrate on trying to find Rose,' I say. 'Maybe we could ask Carrie if she wants us to print some posters? I know it's out there on Facebook but there are plenty of people around here who don't use it. Seeing a poster of Rose might spark a memory?'

Jacob nods. 'Yeah, thanks. That's a good idea.'

We reach the intersection and I stop and turn to him. 'Which way did you go last night?'

He points to New Inn Lane. 'There. We went the back way.'

Away from the main road, there will be less chance anyone saw them. 'Okay, let's go.'

'What's the point of this?' he asks. 'It's not like she'll be walking the same way right now, is it?'

'No, but... I don't know. Maybe you missed something?'

'Like what?'

'I don't know, Jacob! I'm just trying to help. And we need to walk Cooper anyway, so what harm will it do?'

When he stares at me, he feels like a stranger. 'All right,' he mumbles. 'But we won't find her here.'

The silence between us is painful as we head towards Rose's house. I long to push him for more information, but he's shutting me out, and I have no idea how to reach him. The streets are quieter now, and I'm surprised that no one is out. No police knocking on doors. Nobody looking for Rose. It's as if with the approaching night, she's been forgotten about.

When we turn onto the road that leads to Rose's house, Jacob stops. 'Mum, can we go home now? Please.'

'But we're nearly there. I think we should check in on Carrie. See if we can do anything.'

He shakes his head. 'No, I don't want to.'

I frown, scanning his face. 'Why? What's going on?'

'I... I'm scared, Mum.'

'I know. We're all worried about Rose. We just—'

'You don't even know her. She's... Nobody knows her. There's stuff people have no idea about.'

'Jacob, what are you talking about?'

He stares at me, his eyes wide. Wild. And then he runs.

EIGHT

CARRIE

Joe's cooking her dinner, even though she insisted she can't eat. The thought of food makes her nauseous. And she'd never be able to swallow anything; it would feel like knives cutting into her throat. It's been twenty-two hours since Rose was last seen, and with each passing minute Carrie's insides rip further apart. It's easy to dismiss a few hours, to put that down to a misunderstanding, or lack of communication on Rose's part. But twenty-two? And Rose has always been conscious of keeping in contact when she's out. A message here and there. A silly emoji. Something to let Carrie know she's okay.

She sits on the sofa in the dark with the curtains open, staring through the window while Joe busies himself in the kitchen, the smell of beef mince drifting through the house. Outside, the street is silent now, the crowds having dispersed long ago. The police warned her about this. Searches become difficult once darkness sets in.

Still, she wasn't prepared to feel so bereft knowing that in a couple of hours nobody at all will be looking for Rose. Those who, only this morning, were eager to join the hunt will be going back to their lives, eating dinner, while her life is... what?

There is no word to describe this. Limbo? A slow, torturous state that Carrie doesn't know she'll survive.

But she must stay positive for Rose. She must find her daughter.

Her mobile phone rings and she grabs it from the coffee table, answering before she's fully registered that it's Hugh, her ex-husband, calling.

'She's still not home,' Carrie blurts out, before he's had a chance to ask. She'd texted him this morning to let him know their daughter hadn't come home, and it's only now he's bothering to call.

'What's going on? Where is she?'

'If I knew that, then I'd be with her,' Carrie hisses. 'And don't start trying to act the concerned parent now. You don't give a damn about Rose. When was the last time you even called her?'

'Actually, we spoke yesterday afternoon. Well, morning for you.'

This is news to Carrie. Strange. Rose usually tells her when she's spoken to her father. 'She would have told me. She tells me everything,' Carrie insists, fully aware she sounds like a petulant child.

'Clearly that's not true, otherwise you'd know where she is right now.'

Carrie ignores his retort. 'Did she say anything to you? How did she seem? Do you know where she is?'

'No, of course I don't,' Hugh says. 'And she seemed fine. Apart from having a run-in with your charming boyfriend the night before. She wasn't upset about it, though. Good old Joe. She can't stand him, can she? Which makes me wonder what you're doing with him.'

Again, Carrie ignores his comment. She's used to Hugh's snide remarks. Funny that he's so quick to deliver them when he's the one who left. And now he's shacked up with that woman. *Silvana.* Carrie can't bear to even think her name, let alone say it.

'What run-in? When?'

'I don't know when it was, Carrie. But if this has got anything to do with why she's run away, then you need to get that man out of Rose's life. Anyway, I told the police when they called me. They were very interested to hear about it. I don't think they knew.'

That's because Carrie didn't know herself. Still, this is none of Hugh's business. 'It was nothing,' she says. 'They just... disagreed about something. They always bicker. It doesn't mean anything.' She cranes her neck to catch sight of Joe in the kitchen. He's whistling while he's stirring the mince, her favourite teal blue tea towel thrown carelessly over his shoulder.

'The police will be the judge of that,' Hugh says. 'They asked me if she might try to come and see me, but her passport's still there, isn't it?'

It was the first thing Carrie had checked. 'I've got it with mine. And there's no way she'd miss school. Not for...' Carrie stops herself from saying *you*. She's too exhausted to fight with Hugh. They need to be united in this. Whatever's happened between them, they are in this together, whether they like it or not.

'I have to go,' Hugh says. In the background, that woman's voice calls to him. 'Message me the second she gets home. Please.'

'Aren't you worried?'

'No,' he says, the word delivered with authority. 'She'll be okay. This is Rose we're talking about. She's always okay. I don't know anyone tougher than her.'

As if you know her. There was a time when Carrie would have been reassured by anything Hugh said. But Hugh is right. She hangs up. Still holding her phone, she walks to the kitchen. Joe's put on the radio, nodding his head to an eighties tune she can't remember the name of. Something about building a bridge to someone's heart. Anger swells in the pit of her stomach.

'What did you and Rose argue about?'

Joe stares at her, wiping his hands on her dish cloth.

'On Friday night. You had an argument with Rose.' Carrie had been out with some of her work colleagues, and Joe had been here when she'd come home. He'd been drunk. Pawing at her when all she'd wanted to do was sleep. Rose hadn't been awake, but she hadn't mentioned any kind of argument the next morning. And then there was the barbeque.

Joe frowns. 'Oh, that. That was nothing. Rose being Rose. I told her she had to clean up the kitchen – it was a bloody state after she'd made herself dinner. She kicked off about it. The usual stuff about me not being able to tell her what to do. I'm not her *dad*. It was nothing. Hardly the reason she's gone off.'

Carrie glares at him, at the flecks of grey in his stubble, wishing her stare could burn his skin, cause him some pain. 'Why didn't you tell the police?'

He rolls his eyes. 'Because it's not important.'

'Of course it is!' she shouts, unable to keep control. 'My daughter is missing and you had a fight with her. What planet are you living on if you think that's not important?'

Joe picks up the wooden spoon he's been cooking with and turns back to the food. 'I'll let this go, Carrie, because you're so... upset. And I get it, course I do. But the little tiff I had with Rose has got nothing to do with anything. We've had worse before – you know we have – and she's never done a runner. So can you just drop it? If you want to tell the police and make me look like a liar, then do it. You'll just be wasting their time and making them focus on me instead of on finding Rose. Well, that's your choice, ain't it?' He tastes some of the sauce on the spoon and puts it back in the pan to stir again.

Carrie watches him for a moment. 'The police already know. Hugh told them.'

She sets the table for one. She imagines the anger swirling inside him, how any minute now he will erupt and launch them into another slanging match. For the first time, Carrie doesn't care. *Bring it on.*

'It's okay,' Joe says quietly, turning off the hob. 'I'll just explain it to them. Hugh's mistaken. It was just me telling Rose to clean up the kitchen. Simple as. They'll know what teenagers are like. We argue all the time and she's never run off before, so it's nothing to do with me. They'll see that.' He starts whistling again as he dishes up the food.

'I'm going for a bath,' Carrie says, walking out of the kitchen. 'Don't bother serving up any food for me.'

It's eleven p.m. now and Joe is slumped on the sofa, intoxicated as usual. Carrie's been upstairs in Rose's room, rooting through everything again, poring through her notebooks and schoolwork, just in case there is something there. The television is on and she prises the remote control from his hand, turning it off before throwing it at Joe's lap. He doesn't flinch. He's off work tomorrow, yet even if he wasn't, he'd still have consumed all the Heineken she has left in the house. She wants one herself but she needs to have a clear mind. There must be something she's missing.

Glancing at Joe again, Carrie shuts the living room door and grabs her denim jacket. She writes a note for Rose, telling her she's out looking for her and will be back soon, and sellotapes it to the front door. She doesn't have to worry about Joe; Carrie's quite sure he won't surface until the morning.

In the car, she turns on the engine and prepares herself to be out all night if she has to. There's no way she'll be able to sleep, so she needs to use this time constructively.

She drives for over an hour, making a circuit of the houses where Rose's classmates live. To begin with, this small and futile act goes a tiny way towards comforting her, but witnessing the desolate streets begins to eat away at her. Why is nobody out looking?

She stops outside Jacob's house and all is still and dark there too, no sign of anyone being awake. Briefly, she considers messaging Jacob, asking him if he'll join her, but she's realised that she no longer trusts him.

Resting her head against the steering wheel, she sets free the tears she's been holding back all day. Strong, practical Carrie. Carrie who can deal with anything, who just gets on with things. That's what she's had to be all day, but now that's slipped away.

A tap on the window forces her to look up. Through tear-streaked eyes, it takes her a moment to register that it's Tom Adams peering through her window.

'Carrie? Are you okay?'

She tries to compose herself and rolls down the window. 'Sorry, I'm okay. I was just driving around. Looking for Rose. I thought you were all asleep.'

'I wasn't,' Tom explains. 'I was working but I heard a car engine. I thought I recognised yours. Are you sure you're okay? Do you want to come in? Lucy's asleep but I can wake her.'

She shakes her head. 'No, no. It's late.'

'Okay. Tomorrow they'll start searching again. I know it must feel awful with everything going quiet.'

'Would you... sit with me for a minute?' Carrie doesn't know why she's asked this – what's given her the courage, especially with no alcohol inside her.

Tom's eyes widen, and he glances back at the house. 'I... um... yeah, okay.'

He doesn't want to; he's doing it out of pity. Still, Carrie can accept this. She just wants to talk to someone about Rose.

'I thought about asking Jacob if he wanted to drive around with me,' she begins, once Tom's in the passenger seat and the door clicks shut. 'But I know it's late. And he's been out all day looking. He must be tired.'

'I could come with you instead,' Tom offers.

She shakes her head. 'No. Thanks. I've been out for hours so I think I'll head home in case she comes back. She could do any minute.' Saying this, she feels a sliver of hope. 'Maybe she's back there now? Joe's there.' She doesn't mention the state he's in, that he wouldn't even notice if Rose came strolling in. Turning to Tom, she wonders if he knows about the toxic relationship he has with Rose. Does her daughter tell Jacob things which he in turn passes on to his parents?

Tom offers a thin smile. 'It's good that he's there, just in case.'

'I left a note on the door. For Rose.' Her hope dwindles and it hits her that she's been kidding herself. 'Stupid, isn't it? She's not coming back. Not in the middle of the night.'

Tom frowns. 'Maybe... do you think she just needed to clear her head? Perhaps the pressure of exams has been getting to her and she just needed an escape. They're so young, aren't they? Even at sixteen, their brains aren't fully developed. Perhaps running was the only way she could deal with it?'

Carrie wishes this were true. But surely Tom knows that Rose has been predicted all eights and nines for her GCSEs? Jacob must talk about this. He's proud of her, and he himself isn't too far behind Rose. She loves studying, makes it seem effortless, unlike Carrie when she was at school. Nothing came easily to her, but she got there with sheer determination. 'I don't think it's that,' Carrie explains. 'Rose has always dealt with exam pressure well. She's organised and meticulous, she was way ahead with her revision.'

Tom nods. 'She's actually been a really good influence on Jacob. Lucy and I are always saying that. We've been thrilled that the two of them found each other.'

Carrie's nose begins to run, but she's too embarrassed to

reach into the glove compartment for a tissue. It would mean leaning over Tom, being too close to him. 'That's what everyone says. They're the perfect young couple.'

He turns his head to the side, appraising her. 'Don't you think so? I know you think Jacob's changed lately. Lucy and I haven't noticed that ourselves. We were wondering what makes you—'

'I don't know. I did think they were good together. Love's young dream, if that's even a *thing*, but...'

He leans forward. 'What? Is there something we should know about Jacob? Has he done something? Carrie, you can talk to us. To me. I know he's my son, but if he's—'

'I'm probably just being paranoid. Questioning everyone and everything.' She searches his face. 'And please don't tell me that's understandable. I can't bear your sympathy. I'd rather you tell me to get a grip.'

'Okay, then get a grip, Carrie.' Tom smiles, and despite the situation, Carrie again feels that shred of hope. 'Rose will turn up with a whole story about where she's been and why she's gone off the grid.'

'Can I ask you something?' Carrie says.

'Ask away.'

'Do you feel differently about Jacob and Ava? Because you're Jacob's stepdad, I mean.' She's being forward and intrusive, but Carrie has nothing to lose.

'I have to correct you there,' Tom says. 'I adopted him when he was six. I'm his dad, Carrie.' He looks at her. 'But if I'm being honest, of course it's a little different. I try to treat them both equally, but when I look at Jacob, I only see Lucy's first husband. He and I are very different. I try not to see it, but... I'm only human.'

'Did you know him, then?' Carrie is curious. She's never heard any of this from Rose.

'Alistair? No. He died just before Lucy found out she was

pregnant. A brain tumour. And I didn't meet her until Jacob was three.' He smiles. 'She was doing an amazing job raising him on her own, and then I came along. Sometimes I feel like...'

'What?'

'No, nothing.'

Carrie won't pry, not when it's clear he doesn't want to tell her. 'But then you had Ava. Things must have felt better then?'

Tom smiles. 'The day she was born was the best day of my life.'

'Yes,' Carrie says. 'I know what you mean.'

'Listen to me – Rose will be found. Okay? You can't stop believing that.'

'Thanks.' She stares through the window, where small drops of drizzle patter against the windscreen. 'Tom, about what happened—'

'You don't need to explain anything. I won't say anything, I promise.'

'Thank you,' she says, her voice a whisper even though they're alone. 'I know you and Lucy are happy. I'd never—'

'Honestly, it's fine.' Tom's cheeks flush, and he looks away, watching the rain. It's a few moments before he faces her again. 'I'd better go. If you're sure you're okay?'

Guilt wraps itself around her, squeezing slowly. She's crossed a line, but she's sure Tom feels something too. She doesn't normally imagine these things. She nods while he tells her they'll check in on her tomorrow, and she watches as Tom walks back to the house, briefly waving before he closes the door.

Carrie switches on the ignition and drives away. To inebriated Joe. Back to the house that her daughter isn't sleeping in.

At home, she watches Joe for a moment as he lies asleep on the sofa. He looks peaceful, even with his heavy drunken breaths. *We all have secrets.*

NINE

ROSE

'Have you ever been in love?'

You asked me this question, not long after that first kiss. Even though we'd avoided talking about it, pretended it hadn't happened, something drew us back together, and here we were. You didn't seem worried this time, as if the days had given you the space to work out what you really wanted. Me. I know you did. Just as I wanted you.

Everyone was out, and we were alone in your house. I was always there, at your home more than my own. It got me away from Joe, but that's not why I wanted to be at yours whenever I wasn't at school. I was lying on your sofa while you were busy upstairs, but you came down to get me a drink.

I could tell you were nervous – your hand shook as you handed me a glass of coke. I put it on the table and told you to sit with me for a minute. 'That's a strange thing to ask me. Nosy.' I'd laughed.

But you looked so serious, so I answered you. 'No, I haven't. I've been waiting to fall.'

'I don't need to ask you the same question,' I said. There was an unspoken rule between us not to mention her, and it suited us both. Pretend the problem doesn't exist and then it will go away.

'Love can't be defined,' you explained. 'It's fluid. Ever changing.'

I'm not sure I understood what you were trying to say, but I didn't care. I was drawn to you with such intensity that I didn't care about anything else. About what we knew about each other.

And then your mouth found mine, your hands rough and gentle at the same time. 'You've done this before, haven't you?' you asked.

I laughed. 'No. Not yet.'

You froze. 'Really?' you said, resting your head on my chest. 'I can't be your first.'

'Stop then,' I said, calling your bluff. This dance between us had been going on for months and I wanted to finish what you'd started. But despite my words, I didn't expect you to pull yourself off me and rush back upstairs.

Humiliated, I left and went home, leaving you to explain to your family why I wasn't there to have dinner with them.

For days I was angry with you. It was the Christmas holidays and I avoided your house. It wasn't difficult. Everyone was too busy worrying about presents and parties to wonder why I was absent. I made excuses: I had to revise and do extra shifts at the shop to pay for Christmas presents. Too easy.

And then I was distracted by what was happening with Mum and Joe. I couldn't think about you because I was forced to think about *him*. Yes, you might wonder why I'm talking about him now, when this is *our* story, mine and yours, but you'll see that it's all related. Everyone has a role to play in what happened.

On the last day of school, I'd been at Nina's and it was late when I got home. It had started snowing, only light flurries which barely touched the ground before dissolving, but everyone was going on about how we might get a white Christmas for a change. I would never have stayed out that late but I knew Mum was working a night shift. Walking home, I'd planned to run a bath, light some candles and read my book while I soaked in the bubbles, but I quickly realised that wasn't going to happen.

I could hear Joe talking on the phone the second I stepped inside, even though the living room door was shut. I hated it when Mum let him stay there when she wasn't home. He had his own place – why did he have to keep turning up at ours when he knew she'd be at work? Especially when it was clear that he despised me. It was as if he did it on purpose to annoy me.

'Are you gonna do that thing you do to me?' he was saying, panting down the phone. It made my stomach heave. I could barely understand what Mum saw in him, let alone another woman. I should have run upstairs, pretended I didn't hear anything until I could tell Mum in the morning, but I was intrigued. I stood frozen in the hall, soaking up every word, every hideous sound.

'No, not here. Her daughter's always buzzin' around, like an annoying fly. Shame I can't swat her.' He laughed, not as if he'd just made an innocent joke. No, it was a deep, menacing sound that turned me cold. 'I'll come to you. I've only had a couple so I'll be fine driving. Gimme ten minutes. Oh, and be naked when I get there.' He was slurring. Clearly he'd had more than a just a couple of beers.

I made a show of slamming the front door, so he wouldn't know I'd heard his sleazy conversation. I pulled off my coat, hung it up and slowly walked into the kitchen. To Joe, I would have looked perfectly normal, but inside I was seething. And sickened.

He glanced up. 'Oh, you're back. Thought you'd be with Jacob as usual.'

I couldn't look at him. 'Nope, not tonight.'

'I'm just popping out,' he said, filling a glass with water. He probably thought that would sober him up enough for the drive to his other woman's house.

'Oh, going anywhere nice?' I tried my best to sound casual; I needed to catch him out in his lie, even though everything I'd heard confirmed what kind of man he was.

'My mate Niko's having a poker night at his place,' he said, the lie slipping easily from his mouth.

I nodded. It was showtime.

I walked towards the door and turned back to him. 'Have a nice time. I hope Niko does that thing you like him to do to you.' I didn't look at him as I made my way to the stairs, but I knew the fallout would come.

'What did you just say?' He slammed his glass down and followed me, just as I expected he would. Joe never misses a chance to verbally attack me. I wasn't scared, though, not then. Joe was all bark – he'd never hit either of us.

Standing on the bottom stair, I leaned on the banister. 'Does Mum know about your other woman?'

He went for me then. With no warning, and even though I'd expected a reaction, the force of his hand around my neck shocked me. 'Think you're clever, do ya? You've been waiting for an excuse to get me out of Carrie's life, haven't you, you little bitch?'

I squirmed, trying to free myself. 'Get off!'

'You say one word to her and I'll make sure you never talk again. D'you understand?'

Now, looking back, I'm mad at myself that I gave in. All I could do was nod. Shock rendered me inactive. Before that moment, Joe had just been annoying and sleazy. Now he'd become something else. And I was afraid. It wasn't just the words he'd spoken – threats are idle most of the time – but it was the rage in his eyes. The loss of control. On reflection, I think he was in shock himself.

His hand loosened then, and I raced upstairs, locking myself in the bathroom.

It was a long few moments before he left, slamming the door. Off to see his other woman.

And both of us knew that I couldn't tell Mum.

Straight after that, I found myself walking to your house, messaging you to meet me. It was more like begging, wasn't it? At first, you said you couldn't, that it was too late to go out, but then you were there with the dog, meeting me by the woods.

You took one look at me and knew exactly what to do. Taking me in your arms, you held me tightly and let me cry into your chest, while beside us Cooper sniffed at the grass. You tied his lead around a tree trunk and pulled me to the ground, right there in the woods, and we did what you'd told me, and yourself, could never happen.

Afterwards, when we finally came up for air, we lay there holding each other. It felt right, didn't it? My blood soaked into the ground beneath us but neither of us cared. In that moment it was just you and me.

So, you see, ultimately it was Joe who brought us together. If we'd never met in the woods that night, nothing would have happened. I'd have still been coming to your house all the time, but everything would have stayed the same.

'Everything's different now,' I said. 'What does this mean?'

You took a while to answer, but when you did your words were laced with resignation. And something else. Terror. 'It means a whole lot of trouble, Rose.'

TEN

LUCY

Monday morning brings rain with it, fierce pellets hammering against our bedroom window. I turn and glance at the clock. Seventeen minutes past seven, and I can hear Tom showering in the en suite. I pull myself up and reach for my phone. There are no messages from Carrie, so I can only assume that Rose still hasn't come home.

It's an inset day at school today but the kids are due back tomorrow, and I know from Jacob that Rose hasn't missed a single day in the last couple of years, something she's proud of. I need to see Carrie today, to assure her that I'm there for her, and that I understand.

Tom steps out of the bathroom, rubbing his hair with a towel, another one wrapped around his waist. I haven't told him about Jacob running off yesterday, and his claim that there are things we don't know about Rose. More secrets I'm keeping from my husband.

'I'm sorry I can't be here when the police do their search,' he says. 'I hope Jacob and Ava will be okay.'

I have my doubts. Ava seems to have shut down, and Jacob's behaviour is so out of character I don't even know what to think. He wouldn't talk to me after running off yesterday evening, and he shut himself in his room for the rest of the night.

'Alicia said we can pop next door if they need us to be out. She's got the day off work.'

Tom nods. 'That's kind of her.'

'I got the impression she just wanted to gossip about it, find out what's going on.'

'Jacob didn't seem right yesterday,' Tom says, changing the subject so suddenly that it catches me off guard.

'His girlfriend is missing.'

'Do you think he knows—'

'No, I don't. I keep asking him and he insists he doesn't know where Rose is. We have to believe him, Tom. If he doesn't have us to support him, then who has he got?'

'I know. I just... Never mind. The police will find her and then we can put this all behind us. It's not just Jacob it's affecting, is it? Ava's in a state.' He pulls on his suit jacket and stands in front of the mirror to straighten his tie. 'If it wasn't for this client meeting, I'd work from home,' he says, kissing my cheek. 'Keep me updated, though.'

Once Tom's left for work, I wake Ava and make the kids scrambled eggs for breakfast, all the while trying to maintain a semblance of normality. But Rose's disappearance hangs over us all – how could it not? Jacob and Ava are silent as they eat, their eyes focused on their plates, but the occasional glances between them don't escape my notice.

'Alicia said you could hang out next door this morning,' I tell Ava. 'Just while the police search team is here. She said she's baking cupcakes with the kids, so that should be fun.'

Ava frowns. 'Yeah, if I was five.' She turns to her brother then, her forehead creased. 'What about him?'

'I'll be out looking for Rose,' Jacob says. 'So I won't be here.'

Ava scrapes scrambled eggs from her toast and picks up the

empty slice. 'It's not good to lie to the police, is it, Mum? About anything. Even small things.'

'No, it's not,' I say, swallowing my guilt, because this is exactly what I'm doing. I know Jacob came home later than he claims.

The triumphant smile Ava throws Jacob's way speaks volumes.

Jacob pushes his plate aside. 'Cereal would have been fine, Mum.'

'I know. I just wanted to do something different. There's no time on school mornings, is there?'

Neither of them mentions that I haven't done this for the whole Easter break until now.

'Jacob's just being ungrateful,' Ava says, her eyes narrowing as she stares at him.

Ignoring her, Jacob takes his plate to the bin, scraping most of his breakfast into it before putting his plate in the dishwasher. 'I need to get going,' he says. 'I printed out posters last night and need to get them up.'

'Because you really want to help find Rose,' Ava mumbles.

'And what's that supposed to mean?' Jacob stares at her. 'Forget it, I'm outta here.'

And once again I'm left wondering what's happened between them.

A few hours later I sit in Carrie's living room, awkward silence floating between us, even though I try my best to fill it. She looks broken, like a glass full of cracks, and I want to reach out and hug her, to tell her that I understand her pain. Without make-up she is a ghost of herself, and her thick brown hair is tied back in a messy ponytail, loose strands hanging down each side of her face.

'Did it feel strange?' she asks. 'The police raking through your home and garden.'

'Yes, it did. Unsettling.'

She nods, her eyes narrowing. 'Funny. I didn't feel that way at all when they were searching here. I felt... comforted. Was Jacob okay when he spoke to the police? I got the feeling he wasn't comfortable doing it.' Her mouth twists, as if she's moulding it into a smile.

'He was happy to talk to them,' I assure her. 'He told them everything he could think of – I hope you know that, Carrie. He's printed hundreds of posters and is out there now hanging them up.'

'Someone knows where Rose is,' Carrie says. 'People don't just disappear. Someone's hiding something.'

I lean forward. 'Carrie, Jacob loves Rose. If he knew where she was, then he'd tell us. Please believe that.'

'But I can't, can I? I can't just believe everything I'm told. I have to work things out for myself. Get to the truth of things.'

'Of course you do. But you can trust Jacob. Trust in their love for each other at least.'

'They're sixteen! What *is* love, anyway?' Carrie replies. 'I'm not even sure it exists.'

'You love Rose, don't you?'

'I'm not talking about that kind of love.' She pauses. 'Our love for our children is permanent and unconditional. But romantic love? That's ephemeral. And fragile, too, like a spider's web. Full of conditions.'

'But it all comes down to the same thing,' I counter. 'Loving someone means you want the best for them, that you want to protect them. It's no different between couples. It's harder, yes, but that doesn't mean it can't be just as permanent.'

Carrie shakes her head. 'We don't walk away from our children, though. Yet it's all too easy to leave a relationship behind. Someone we're supposed to *love*.'

I don't know much about Rose's dad, but I do know that he left them both when Rose was five. It's no wonder this has shaped Carrie's view of relationships. I myself am a perfect example of how past trauma clouds our judgement. I also know how difficult it is to change that, even when you're aware that you need to.

'You love Joe, don't you?' The second I say it I regret asking such a personal question, and I'm shocked to see Carrie's expression soften.

'I try to. He doesn't make it easy.' Her mouth forms into a thin smile. 'How about you, then? Tom seems like a good man. A good father.'

'He is. I feel blessed. That's not to say it's perfect – nothing ever is – but it feels like we're a team. Like we're in it together. Whatever life throws at us.'

Carrie hangs her head. 'That must be nice.' When she looks up again, her eyes are glassy. 'Thankfully life hasn't thrown *this* at you. A missing child.'

'No, not that, but I—'

'Please don't tell me you understand. How could you? You have *no* idea.'

She turns from me but not before I see the tears trickle down her cheeks. I reach for her hand but she pulls away.

'My sister died when I was eight,' I say. 'She was four years old.'

Carrie looks up, her eyes wide. 'Oh... that's awful. I'm sorry. What happened?'

Even though I've shared this much with her, I'm not sure I'm ready to tell her the details. Still, if it helps Carrie to see that I understand pain, then it's what I need to do.

I take a deep breath and tell her the story that's haunted me since I was eight. How I'd been playing in the garden after school with a friend. We'd been so engrossed in our game that we'd paid no attention to what my little sister Sabine was doing.

And my parents... they had been busy in the garden. I explain to Carrie that they had a landscape gardening business; when they weren't with clients they were always out in our garden – summer or winter, it didn't matter. They just left us to our own devices out there. And it was a big garden; they couldn't see what we were doing most of the time. None of us were watching Sabine. And then I'd heard the thud. She'd somehow climbed up onto the shed roof using a ladder dad had left out. And she fell.

'There was nothing anyone could do to save her,' I tell Carrie. I rarely talk about this, and the pain of recalling it now overwhelms me.

'I'm so sorry, Lucy. That must have been—'

'There are no words to describe it. The pain of losing her. The guilt because I hadn't been paying any attention to her. I was her older sister. I was supposed to look after her. And as for my parents... they fell apart after that. Neither of them could carry on the business. They just gave up on life, and got divorced a couple of years after. They blamed themselves, and if I'm honest, I blamed them too. They should have watched her more carefully. Both of us. We were allowed free rein in that garden and there were so many hazards in it. It's why I might seem—'

'Overprotective?'

I nod, even though it's difficult to admit this to Carrie.

'I admit I made judgements about you,' Carrie says. 'First seek to understand, isn't that right? I'm sorry I didn't do that.'

Before I can reply, Carrie's mobile rings. She wastes no time answering it and walks to the window as she talks, turning her back to me.

'Yes, hi. Any news?'

Silence follows, and I wish she would turn around so I can get a sense of what she's being told. When the call ends, she turns to me, and even before she speaks, I know this isn't good.

'Carrie, what is it? What's happened?'

She stares at me. 'That was the police. A witness saw Rose having an argument with someone the night she went missing. They identified him from a picture. It was Jacob.' She shakes her head. 'What did your son do to her when he walked her home?'

'Nothing, Carrie. Jacob wouldn't—'

'And they've found house keys they think are Rose's. In a bush near your house.' She stares at me. 'They're hers, Carrie. It's her keyring with her initial on it. Are you still going to tell me Jacob doesn't know where she is?'

ELEVEN

CARRIE

'What?'

Carrie watches how Lucy's mouth gapes open, distorting her face and stripping it of warmth. Carrie's never seen her lose her composure.

She tells Lucy what the police have just informed her. 'A witness on Burnet Avenue saw Rose and Jacob arguing. It was just after nine. He was shouting in her face, grabbing hold of her when she tried to get away. I knew Jacob was lying! And why would Rose's house keys be in a bush near your home?'

'I don't understand,' Lucy says, rummaging in her bag. She pulls out her phone. 'Okay, maybe they had a disagreement, but it doesn't mean she ran off because of Jacob. And it proves Jacob was telling the truth about walking Rose home.' Even as she says this, flames of doubt flicker across her face – Lucy doesn't believe her own words. 'And Rose could have dropped her keys on her way home from the barbeque.'

'Then they would have been on the road, not hidden in a bush! And Jacob said he saw her go in the house. He waited until she was safely inside, that's what he said.'

Lucy's face drains of colour. 'Someone could have found

them somewhere else and thrown them in that bush. Kids maybe?'

Carrie wishes she could believe this, but the evidence is mounting that something has happened to Rose. Her daughter has no house keys. No way to get in her own home. Rose has never before lost her keys. 'Don't you see,' she tells Lucy, 'Jacob lied to the police. He didn't mention any argument. He specifically said they hadn't argued, didn't he? He told them everything was fine between him and Rose. And that's what he told me too.'

'Maybe he—'

'Forgot? Got confused? Come on, Lucy, I know he's your son but surely you can't defend lying to the police. And if he lied about that, then what else is he hiding? Does he know where Rose is? Do *you* know anything?' Carrie's voice is shrill, ear-shattering, and she steps towards Lucy. The woman is at least three inches taller than her, but Carrie doesn't feel intimidated.

Lucy backs away. 'Of course I don't. It must be a misunderstanding. Jacob wants to find Rose as much as you do. As much as we all do.'

'But he lied for a reason. I *knew* he was. I could feel it.' She wants Lucy out of her house now, she needs to organise her thoughts and she can't do that with this woman pecking away at her, trying to convince her not to trust her instinct.

'Carrie, I understand why you're upset. The police finding Rose's keys is... not good news.' Lucy reaches for her arm but Carrie pulls away.

'Don't patronise me. I want to talk to Jacob. Where is he?'

'I told you. He's out hanging posters. I don't know exactly where he'll be.'

Without a word, Carrie grabs her phone from the windowsill and starts scrolling through her contacts.

'Wait, no... let me speak to him first. Please. I'm sure we can clear this up. Jacob will explain everything. There'll be an explanation.'

Ignoring her, Carrie finds Jacob's number and presses call, blocking out Lucy's pleas to let her do it herself. When he doesn't answer, Carrie's fury kicks in. Why would he avoid her call when Rose is missing?

'Jacob,' she says to his voice message, 'I need to talk to you. The police know about your argument with Rose. You need to call me straight away.'

When she ends the call, Lucy is once again sitting on the sofa, shaking her head, tapping a message into her phone. 'This isn't fair on Jacob,' she says. 'You should have let me talk to him first. I'm his mum. Now he's going to think you're... accusing him of something.'

Carrie stares at her. 'I *am* accusing him of something. Lying.'

'But you haven't even given him a chance to explain,' Lucy protests. 'You already think he's guilty of something. He's just a child, Carrie.'

'And so is Rose. A child who's gone missing, while your son is lying about what happened between them. What am I supposed to think, Lucy? I just need to know where Rose is. I need to know my girl is okay.'

Lucy stands and shakes her head. 'I know my son. He's not lying. Maybe the witness was mistaken. Jacob would tell us if he knew where she was.'

In that moment, a flash of pity surfaces within her, but it's fleeting – gone as soon as she's acknowledged it. 'We're both fools if we think we know our children. They're on the cusp of adulthood. Who are we to walk around thinking we can second-guess their every feeling or action? Jacob can avoid me if he wants, but the police will talk to him, so he can't hide forever.'

'He's not—'

'I think you should leave now.'

'Carrie, please—'

'Just go. Just get out of my house.'

As evening approaches, a tsunami of fear rises inside Carrie, flooding her body and rendering her frozen. She's just spent hours at the police station, identifying Rose's house keys, begging for answers as to what it means. But nobody had any.

Tomorrow school starts back after the Easter break, and she knows, with the same certainty she knows summer follows spring, that Rose would never miss it. No matter what's happened, with her first exams only weeks away, she wouldn't let anything affect her studies.

Carrie has tried calling Jacob's mobile several times, but he never answers. His refusal to speak to her only reinforces her belief that he's hiding something. It's up to the police now. They will find out what's happened.

Joe is working this evening, and Carrie's relieved that she doesn't have to make excuses not to see him tonight. When Carrie had first met Joe, it bothered her that his job as a gas engineer meant he worked night shifts, and she wondered how they'd ever see each other. But she soon came to see it as a blessing. Joe also laps up any opportunity for overtime, and it makes her wonder, again, what the point of their relationship is. Still, she got into this, she felt love for him in the beginning, she can't just walk away.

Unless he is the reason Rose left. Carrie's had time to reflect on this, and she can't see Rose being upset about anything Joe says or does. She loathes him, yes, but it's more in a mocking way. Her sixteen-year-old daughter looks down on her mum's boyfriend. Carrie would laugh if it wasn't so tragic.

The evening stretches ahead of her, isolating and empty; all she can do is wait and wonder, alone with her thoughts and fears. The police have been slow to speak to Jacob; she's not even sure they've done it yet. It's beginning to feel like Carrie is the only person who wants to find Rose.

Almost on autopilot, she heads into the kitchen and searches the cupboards. It's funny with alcohol – she can take it or leave it, but right now she needs something to numb her senses. Of course Joe will have finished all the beers, and not bothered to replenish them. Carrie doesn't want to feel anything; it's too painful, because underlying it all is the question she hasn't wanted to answer: did Carrie herself do something to drive Rose away?

There's nothing in the cupboards – it's never her priority to stock up on wine or Prosecco – and she can't bear the thought of traipsing to the Costcutter down the road. Instead, she fills a glass with tap water and forces it down; perhaps that will stop her longing for a drink.

Outside, the dog next door begins to yelp, locked out of his home again. A gloomy soundtrack to her fear. Carrie picks up her phone and calls Jacob again. Still no answer. So now Carrie has no choice but to go to him.

Her heart pounds as she strides along Jacob's front path and reaches his front door. It's too cold for just her denim jacket, but that's the first thing Carrie grabbed from the coat rack. And she could have done with jeans instead of leggings, but she'll be back in the warmth of her car soon enough. Lights shine from the ground floor windows so it's clear someone's home, although there's only one car parked on the drive.

'Where is he?' she cries, before the door's fully opened and she can register that Tom Adams has answered.

'Carrie, what's going on?'

'Lucy didn't tell you?'

Tom takes her arm. 'No. Look, just come in. Then you can tell me what's going on.'

She doesn't move. 'Where's Jacob?'

'Lucy's taken the kids out for dinner. It's her brother's birthday so it was planned months ago. I've had to work late so couldn't go. They'd already left before I got home. Now can you please tell me what's happened?'

She steps forward then, and lets him shut the door behind her. She's still cold, and keeps her arms folded. 'The police have found Rose's house keys. In a bush near here. And a witness saw Jacob and Rose arguing when he walked her home after the barbeque. Your son's been lying to the police, Tom! And he must have had her keys and tried to hide them!'

Tom's face pales. 'What?'

'Lucy knows. Why hasn't she told you? Don't you two talk?'

'I've been in back-to-back meetings most of the day. She was probably waiting until they got back from this birthday dinner.' He turns and walks through to the kitchen, urging her to follow.

'Because this isn't important, is it?' Carrie asks.

'No, I didn't—'

'Why is Jacob lying to the police? What's he hiding?'

Tom falls silent for a moment, and Carrie stares past him to the garden outside. The last place she saw Rose. She can't recall any moment when Rose was with Jacob, no matter how much she tries to force it.

'I don't know why Jacob lied to the police, and I'm sorry they found Rose's keys. I know you must be thinking all kinds of things right now. But there could be a simple explanation. She might have lost them on the way home from the barbeque?' Tom says.

'That's impossible. I already told Lucy this. Jacob said he saw Rose go in the house.'

Tom considers what she's saying, and realisation seems to dawn on his face. 'I don't understand any of this, Carrie, but I can promise you I'll try my best to find out. I'm as confused about this as you are. I really don't know what Jacob's playing at. But if he's been lying, then I'm so sorry.'

Carrie sinks onto the L-shaped sofa in the corner of the room – so much more comfortable than her own – and buries her head in her hands. Tom's kindness is too much to bear. 'How come you're not defending him?' she asks. 'Like Lucy did.'

He comes to sit beside her and takes her hand. 'Because I know my son isn't perfect. And if he's lied, then there is no way I'll defend that. If he knows anything about Rose's keys, then—'

'I don't think Lucy feels the same way,' Carrie interjects. 'She insisted there must be some kind of misunderstanding. She refuses to believe that Jacob knows something.'

'Listen, Carrie. I'm not actually saying Jacob knows anything. We can't assume that. But clearly he's lied to the police and we need to know why. I have to say, though, it's too much of a leap to think he knows where Rose might be. I hope you can see that?'

When he smiles at her she wants to reach out and touch his face, feel the smoothness of his skin. Just like she did at the barbeque. *I'm not thinking straight. Tom is a married man and my daughter is missing. My mind is playing nasty tricks, and it needs to stop.*

'Can I wait for him? Please. And Ava. She spent a lot of time with Rose at the barbeque – maybe she can tell me something?'

'She's already spoken to the police. I really don't think Ava knows anything. She's been so upset about Rose, and—'

'Please, Tom. Let me stay. It's a school night – surely they won't be too much longer?'

His forehead creases and he lets out a deep sigh. Carrie knows he wants her to go. If it comes to it, Tom will have to forcibly remove her because she's not going anywhere until she's seen Jacob. That boy has avoided her for too long.

Eventually, Tom agrees. 'But I need to text Lucy to warn her. I'll tell her not to let Jacob know.'

Carrie nods. It's the least she can do when she's planning on tearing pieces out of the boy.

'Have you... got anything to drink?' she asks.

'Sure, tea or coffee?'

'I meant something stronger.'

Tom stares at her. She wants to smooth away the frown distorting his face. 'Is that a good idea? Didn't you drive here?'

'One small glass of wine or a beer won't hurt, will it? Please, Tom. I really need it. Look, I'm shaking.' She holds out her hand.

Tom stares at it. 'Just a small one, then,' he agrees, and she watches as he finds a glass and opens a bottle of red wine. 'Is this okay?'

She nods. 'Thank you.'

He doesn't pour himself one, but fills a glass with tap water instead.

They sit silently while Tom messages someone on his phone. Lucy, she assumes. Warning her that Carrie is here.

She finishes her drink too quickly, and almost asks for another one, until it hits her that she needs to keep it together for Rose's sake. Her daughter could come back any minute now, and she'll need Carrie more than she ever has before. And what will that mean for their two families? Will Rose and Jacob still be together?

'Lucy doesn't like me, does she?' Carrie blurts out, unable to keep track of her own train of thought.

Tom looks up from his phone. 'That's not true. Lucy likes everyone.'

'I'm very perceptive, though, Tom. I feel things. Sense things about people. What they think of me. I always just seem to... *know*.'

'She's never said a word against you, Carrie. I can assure you of that. And she loves Rose.'

'I'm not Rose, though, am I? Lucy doesn't have to like me. Even if Rose and Jacob end up married one day, our families don't have to get along, do they?'

Her head swirls; Carrie knows that this will never happen. There will never be a wedding day for Rose. *It's my mind playing tricks again. I need to stop. I need to believe.*

'You're right, we don't have to get along. But we like you, Carrie. *I* like you. I'm on your side here too. Whatever's happened, we'll find out.'

She reaches for his hand, ignoring the way he flinches at her touch. 'Thank you.' And then she is pushing herself into him, finding his mouth with hers. It only lasts a second before Tom pulls away. 'Carrie, stop—'

The sound of the front door forces them both to freeze. Carrie ignores the flood of shame she feels and rushes to the door, ignoring Tom's plea for her to wait. She grabs Jacob's arm before he's through the door. 'What were you arguing about, Jacob? Tell me. What do you know about Rose's door keys?'

Lucy appears behind him, and prises Carrie's arm from him. 'Carrie, please just calm down. Let's talk about this properly, okay? Come in the kitchen and sit down.' She turns to Ava. 'Please can you go and get ready for bed. I need you upstairs right now, okay?'

'No, Mum! I want to hear this.' Ava folds her arms across her chest, reminding Carrie of Rose when she was a toddler.

Carrie walks over to her. 'Listen, Ava. Rose thinks the world of you. But I know one thing for sure – she wouldn't want you hearing about all this. This is for the adults to sort out.'

Ava shakes her head. 'Jacob's not an adult. And I want to know what he's done to Rose!'

'What do you mean?' Carrie asks.

'Rose wasn't happy with him at the barbeque. She didn't

want to be anywhere near him. Because he must have done something to her!'

'Ava, that's enough,' Lucy says. 'Please just go upstairs and I'll be up in a moment.'

'I hate you all!' Ava screams, before rushing upstairs.

Nobody speaks until her bedroom door slams.

When Jacob heads into the kitchen, Carrie is right behind him. 'Answer me, Jacob. You lied to the police. Why? And you hid Rose's keys in that bush!'

He sinks into a chair and buries his head in his hands. 'I don't know anything about Rose's keys. Have they been found?'

'Yes, and you'd better start talking.'

'It wasn't an argument,' he begins. 'Not really. Not like they're making it seem.'

'Then what was it? The witness said there was no doubt you were having a huge fight. You were grabbing her, trying to stop her walking away. How did you end up with Rose's keys?'

'I didn't! Rose had her keys – she opened the door and went inside. I saw her.'

'What were you fighting about?'

Jacob doesn't respond.

Carrie feels the weight of Lucy's hand on her shoulder. 'I think you should let the police sort this out. It's not right for you to interrogate Jacob like this.'

'Interrogate him? My daughter is missing and all you care about is protecting your son. He's lying, Lucy!'

'Jacob has explained himself, Carrie. He told you it wasn't an argument, and he knows nothing about the keys. What good is this doing?'

'He hasn't explained anything!' Carrie turns to Jacob. 'Why are you lying? You're still lying. Just tell the truth!'

'I think you should go now,' Lucy says, pulling her away from Jacob. 'Just please go. The police can sort this out tomorrow.'

'Hang on,' Tom interjects. 'Carrie's upset, Luce. Wouldn't you be too if it was the other way around?'

Lucy glares at Tom, her mouth hanging open.

He ignores her and leans down to Jacob. 'Listen, son, can you just tell Carrie what exactly you and Rose were arguing about. Even if you think it's not important. Just tell her.' Slowly, Jacob raises his head and stares at his dad. 'I told you, there was no argument. Why don't you believe me? If this was Ava, you wouldn't question her, would you? Any excuse to have a go at me!' He stands up, flinging his chair back so hard it crashes to the floor.

'Jacob, wait!' Lucy tries to grab his arm but he pushes past her and rushes out of the house, slamming the door behind him.

Carrie heads after him, but when she gets outside there is no sign of him. She turns back to the house and Tom is standing there in the doorway, urging her to come back.

Carrie turns away and makes her way to the car. She doesn't have the space in her head to think about what she just did with Tom, and how ashamed she should feel. Not now that she's more convinced than ever that Jacob is guilty of something. She just needs to find out what that is.

TWELVE

ROSE

This thing between us wasn't love. But engulfed as I was in the intoxicating haze of you, I couldn't see that then.

You took me out to dinner just after Christmas; such a grown-up thing to do. It wasn't my birthday for another few months, but you said it could be an early birthday present. You were trying to impress me – I know that now. Showing me how different you were. A league above anyone else I could hope to be with.

I wore a dress that I'd shopped for that day, and it still had the label on, tucked in the back. I couldn't afford it and it would be going back to H&M the next day. It makes me cringe to think I did that, when it was something I detested. Don't buy things you have no intention of keeping, I'd rant at girls at school who were wannabe influencers, doing clothes hauls on YouTube, like the mindless fake celebrities they idolised, then returning everything they'd ordered. But there I was, knee-deep in the shit I loathe.

We were both trying to impress each other, weren't we? You told me I looked different that night, that I was taking your breath away, like a girl who'd become a woman. And I lapped up your compliments, allowed them to soak into my skin, to shape me. Because I didn't know any better.

We went up to London on the train, and it excited me that we were doing something different. 'Guess what?' I said. I'd been bursting to tell you my news. I'd planned to save it for the restaurant, but I couldn't wait.

'What?' you'd asked, and I'd expected to see happiness in your eyes, but all I detected was fear.

'I've got a gig! My first one.'

Your shoulders unhunched a little, and you smiled. 'That's great. Where?' You turned to look out of the window. We were approaching London now and the scenery was transforming from green fields and trees to grey stone and brick.

'A pub in Aldershot. Joe's friend runs it and Joe talked him into—'

'Hang on a second. The same Joe who you had a huge fight with not long ago? How come he's helping you?'

I shrugged. 'Maybe he felt bad. More likely he's trying to get back into Mum's good books. Anyway, he spoke to his friend and he agreed to let me do a few songs this Friday. Joe told him I was eighteen.' I reached for your hand. 'Will you come?'

You looked me up and down, smiling. 'You do look like you could pass for eighteen.'

You still hadn't answered my question. 'So you'll come, then?'

'Rose, I don't know. I can't... It just won't be—'

'Please.' I said the word but it felt alien to me. I don't beg people for anything; it goes against everything I believe in. But it was important to me that you were there; a sign that I meant something to you. Despite my fierce independence, I was starting to realise that maybe I did need some kind of validation after all. From you. 'Mum can't come as she's working. She tried to swap her shift but they're really short-staffed at the moment and couldn't do it. She's gutted she'll miss my first gig.'

'I'll try,' you said, after a long pause.

I told you it started at seven, but that I'd need to be there a couple of hours before to get ready and prepare myself.

'I can't come before, but seven, yeah.'

There was no enthusiasm on your part, though, despite me explaining how much it meant to me. You didn't say it, but I knew what you were thinking. Who would want to go and watch a teenager sing and play the guitar? But you'd even said yourself, there was a maturity about me that you'd never seen in other girls.

'Thanks,' I said. 'You'll love it, I promise.'

I think it's important here that I add how lovely our evening in that restaurant was. We let ourselves feel like a normal couple, ignoring each other's baggage, all the things that threatened to throw us overboard. To drown us. We were able to forget them all, and pretend we were just like anyone else on a date. We were laughing so hard that we got a few looks. What were we doing in that fancy restaurant? But we didn't care. They didn't know us.

Nerves hit me on the evening of the gig. Anxiety like I'd never felt before. I was out of my league there. How did I think I could get up and sing my own music to this group of strangers. They were mostly middle-aged men, and none of them looked like they gave a shit about any kind of music. Nobody even glanced in my direction when I walked out and took my seat in front of the mic. People talk about stage fright, and it sounds so harmless, but the truth is it cripples you. I scanned the room – it was past seven and I was already late starting – but there was no sign of you. I would have spotted you immediately in this crowd.

I glanced at Rick, the manager who'd given me this gig, and he was busy serving behind the bar – he didn't look my way either. If I'd run, nobody would have noticed, and believe me, I did consider it. All I thought I needed was to see your face there, to know that you had shown up for me. That you were my person. That would have made everything okay.

I began to stand, but something made me stop. This was an opportunity I'd dreamed of – why was I squandering it? I went back to the mic and started strumming, and as soon as I played that first note, something changed. The chatter died down and people turned to look at me.

You weren't there but I no longer cared. I could do this on my own. I didn't need anyone to lift me up. All I needed was my guitar and my voice.

That power I felt then – how I wish it had lasted.

THIRTEEN

LUCY

Jacob sits on the sofa, his eyes fixed on the carpet. I turn to DC Gillary, who's sitting across from him, and notice how deeply his brow furrows as he closely watches my son.

'I have to go to school,' Jacob says. 'I'll get in trouble if I'm late.' He glances at the living room door. Ava is sitting on the stairs, and I wonder if Jacob has noticed she's there.

'This won't take long,' the police officer says. 'And then you can be on your way.' He doesn't wait for a response. 'Now, can you tell me what you and Rose were arguing about?' He smiles. 'I know it might not seem like a big thing – maybe you couldn't agree on what film to watch or something like that – but the more information we have, the sooner we'll be able to find Rose. And we all want that, don't we, Jacob?'

His overfamiliar tone won't work with Jacob. He'd have a better chance of getting through to him if he was more authoritative. A bad cop. Police tactics, but Jacob will see straight through this.

'Do you have any idea how Rose's keys might have ended up in that bush two roads down from here? Do you know anything about that?'

'No. I keep saying this. I don't know how they got there. I watched her unlock the door and go into her house. It doesn't make sense.'

'And you still have no idea where she could be?'

'No. I don't know where she is. You should be out looking for her, not questioning me about nothing.'

'We have a search team out looking, Jacob, please don't worry about that. But I'm here to gather more information. Anything that will help the search. And that's what we all want, isn't it?' He narrows his eyes. 'Were you and Rose having trouble in your relationship, Jacob? Because if you were, I think you should tell us. Was Rose trying to leave you, perhaps?'

I wait for Jacob to object, but he says nothing, and doesn't look up. I long for him to glance at me, so I can at least nod to him, show him that everything will be okay.

'It was nothing,' Jacob said. 'That's why I didn't say anything. Rose just... she accused me of liking her friend, Nina. And I don't, not like that. But Rose wouldn't believe me. She went a bit... nuts. I'd never seen her like that before. She was being so... so weird. Psycho.'

The words are clear, but my brain can't digest them. Rose has never seemed like the possessive type. And she trusts Nina; the two of them have been friends since primary school. What Jacob is saying doesn't fit with anything I know about Rose. And now I just want DC Gillary to leave – I need to question Jacob myself.

It's another five minutes before he does go, leaving us with assurances that they'll need to speak to Jacob again.

Ava rushes in and pummels her fists into Jacob's stomach. 'Why are you lying to everyone? I hate you!'

I prise her off him and tell her it's time for school. 'We're running late now, so I'll drop both of you.'

'No,' Ava insists. 'I'm not getting in the car with him. I'll walk.'

There is no point protesting; Ava will walk quickly and make sure she isn't late, and I need this time to talk to Jacob.

'I'm dropping you at school,' I tell him. 'I'm afraid you don't have a choice.'

'Whatever,' he mumbles, heading off to grab his bag.

For over ten minutes we're stuck in traffic, and all hopes of getting Jacob to school on time are rapidly fading.

'It would have been quicker to walk,' Jacob points out. 'I'm getting out.' He reaches for the door handle.

'No, wait. We need to talk.'

He lets go of the door and turns to me. 'Mum, I'm late for school. I don't want a late mark.'

'I'll call and explain that it's my fault.'

'No, don't. You'll just make things worse.' Again, he reaches for the door handle, and this time tries to open it, forgetting that I always have the locks on when we're driving.

'Were you telling the truth about the argument with Rose? I need to know, Jacob.'

'Yeah, course.' He doesn't look at me. 'Why won't you believe me?'

'It's just that... it seems so out of character for Rose.'

He turns, his eyes piercing mine, and I barely recognise him. This isn't the first time my son has felt like a stranger since Rose disappeared. 'I told you before there's stuff you don't know about Rose. You don't know her. None of you do! Why can't you just believe me?'

'I do, Jacob, but you won't tell me what you're talking about, so I have no idea! I just—'

Without another word, he unlocks the doors and flings his open, jumping out before I can utter his name. And I am left to wonder what exactly I should believe.

.   .   .

Tom calls me later, when I'm de-thorning and conditioning some roses. He's outside somewhere – I can hear the drone of traffic in the background. 'I came out to grab lunch,' he explains. 'I didn't want anyone overhearing me. How did it go with the police? Did Jacob admit that they argued?'

I relay Jacob's claim that Rose had accused him of being interested in Nina.

'That's weird,' Tom says. 'What the hell is going on? Why did he lie? That witness saw him grabbing her. It doesn't make sense. I don't like this, Lucy. It doesn't sound like the truth.'

'What exactly are you accusing him of?' I try to keep my voice measured; I need to make sure Tom doesn't claim that I'm letting my emotions control my responses. 'We need to show him we're both on his side.'

'How can we be on his side, Lucy, if he's lying to the police? There's only one reason to lie, and that's to cover something up. I've been going over and over it – what would Jacob need to cover up?'

'Maybe Rose doesn't want to be found. Maybe he's protecting her?'

'From what? Her loving mum? The school she's doing so well at? It just doesn't make any sense.'

Tom is right, but I can't let myself believe an alternative. At least if Rose has chosen to disappear, then she should be safe. 'I messaged Carrie this morning to see if Rose has turned up at school but she didn't reply. I tried the school but they wouldn't tell me anything.'

'Carrie's upset,' Tom says. 'It's understandable she might be a bit off with us, after Jacob lying to the police like that.'

'If Jacob knew anything, he wouldn't let Carrie suffer. He's a good kid. I wish you could see that.'

The sigh down the phone drowns out the hum of traffic. 'I do, Lucy. But he's been lying. That speaks for itself. You need to take your rose-tinted glasses off when it comes to Jacob. He's not perfect, like you seem to think he is.'

'It's our job to protect him. To be there for him, no matter what.'

'And I am.'

Yet Tom's words tell a different story.

'Why are you so hard on him?'

There's a long pause. 'I'm not. You're just—'

'I have to go,' I interrupt. I don't want Tom telling me again how overprotective I am.

For the rest of the day, I distract myself with work. I take solace in browsing through *The British Flowers Book* and Pinterest to put together a proposal for a wedding in August. I don't move from my workshop until Ava bursts through the door, her cheeks red and tear-stained. She throws herself onto a chair and buries her head in her hands. I hear the words even before she's uttered them. 'Rose wasn't at school.'

I make my way over to her and fling my arms around her. Even though I've known this would be the case, the suffocating swell of anxiety renders me speechless. I hold on to Ava, taking comfort from the fact that she is here with me, safe. And eventually I find some words. 'We mustn't assume the worst. We've got to keep hopeful. I've researched it and people go missing all the time and then turn up soon enough. Rose will come home.'

Ava pulls away from me. 'No, she won't, Mum! Don't you see? She would never miss school. Never!'

I gently pull her towards me again, letting her cry onto my sleeve.

Through her sobs she manages to speak. 'The kids at school are being so nasty. They're saying she's doing it for attention and no one should waste their time talking about it.'

'Well, they don't know Rose, then, do they? But *we* do, and whatever's happened, she's only done it because she's felt she doesn't have a choice.' I smooth down the stray strands of hair that have come loose from Ava's ponytail.

She looks up at me and for a second she looks like a frightened infant. My stomach lurches. 'How about this?' I say. 'Why don't we go into town and pick out a little something for Rose to give her when she comes home? You can choose it.'

Ava's face brightens. 'That would be nice. Something from Smiggle?'

'Sure. Whatever you think she'd like.'

'Let me just get changed. I don't want to wear my school uniform in town.'

As she walks away, I call her back. 'Did you see Jacob at school today?'

'Only at lunchtime. He was huddled with Nina, whispering about something.'

'Probably talking about where Rose could be.'

'You weren't there to see them, Mum. It didn't look like that. They looked... weird. Worried.'

'Of course they're worried—'

'No, not that kind of worried, Mum. I wish you could just see what's going on.' Ava turns and disappears upstairs. And I'm left wondering how I will convince not only Tom, but Ava too, that we need to believe in Jacob.

In the evening, exhaustion takes hold of me and I fall asleep on the sofa. Jacob was silent all through dinner, skulking off to his room as soon as he'd finished, and Ava read her book while she ate. I noticed the glances she occasionally threw Jacob; I only wish I knew what they mean. I have no idea where Tom is. The solid foundation I thought my family was built on seems to be crumbling, slowly, menacingly. While I walk along blindfolded.

I reach for my phone and send Tom a message, checking if he's okay. It's not just the kids I worry about; the fear of Tom being in an accident often cripples me. Losing my sister and then Alistair has irrevocably altered me, and everything I do is shadowed by their deaths.

After five minutes, there's still no reply, so I go and check on Jacob. I don't expect to be invited into his room, so it's a surprise when he beckons me in.

He sits at his desk, his pen hovering over a page in his blue exercise book. It's his English one, his favourite subject, so I'm not surprised he's doing his homework this late at night. 'I know I've been... a bit off,' he begins, not looking up.

'You're upset,' I offer, walking over to his bed and smoothing out his duvet before I sit down. The smell emanating from his sheets is a mixture of sweat and Lynx.

He turns and fixes his stare on me. 'I need you to believe me, Mum. I don't know where Rose is. Everyone at school is saying she's run away because of me. But I haven't done anything. I swear. I didn't do anything to make Rose run away.'

'You have to ignore them all, Jacob. The second Rose comes back this will all blow over, I promise.'

He places his pen on his desk and swivels his chair around. 'What if she—'

'You mustn't think like that. Okay?'

Although he nods, there is a frown on his face.

'Jacob, what were you talking about when you said we don't really know Rose?'

He doesn't answer.

'Jacob, I need the truth now. I know you're scared and that might be why you've not said anything, but I also know you didn't get home until after one a.m. So please, no more lies.'

He doesn't answer for so long that I know I won't like what I hear. I hold my breath, vowing to myself that we can deal with whatever has happened. No matter how bad it is.

'I was... with Nina.'

He says it so softly I have to ask him to repeat himself.

'After walking Rose home, I messaged Nina and told her I needed to see her. To talk. She told me to come to hers and she'd sneak me in through the back.'

It takes me a moment to realise the significance of his words. 'Oh, Jacob. So Rose was right – there *is* something going on between you and Nina.'

'Please just listen. There's nothing going on. We're just friends. I needed someone to talk to about Rose.'

At least this explains why he got home so late. 'Why, though? What happened with you and Rose?'

'Nothing. It doesn't matter. Nina's my friend, too, okay? Can't I spend time with her without it meaning anything?'

Jacob has a point, but he said only moments ago that he needed to talk about Rose. *Don't push him. At least he is saying this much.* 'So what happened when you were there?' I ask. There are too many gaps – too much I'm unsure of. 'That's a lot of hours you spent with Nina.'

Jacob slams his fist on his desk. 'I'm not interested in Nina! We just talked, okay? It's not a crime.'

'Then why didn't you just tell the police?'

'I just panicked. I... I thought it would be better if I said I came straight home. And then when I said it, it was too late to take it back. They'd think I'm lying about everything. Please don't tell them, Mum.'

I can't. I am now as deeply entrenched in Jacob's lie as he is. His logic may be flawed but part of me understands. 'Okay. No more lies, though, Jacob. You need to promise me.'

He nods and looks away from me, tapping his pen on his exercise book, where I can see the beginning paragraphs of an essay. 'Mum, I need to finish this. It was due in today but I... I've had other things on my mind. Miss Wright said it was fine to have an extra week but I said I'd hand it in tomorrow.'

I stand up. I will get nothing more out of him tonight. 'I am proud of you, Jacob. For how you're handling all of this. And thank you for telling me the truth about being at Nina's. I hope you know that you always can. Whatever it is.'

'Yeah, I know, Mum.'

I lean down to hug him and am again haunted by this stranger's body I'm holding.

Sacha Owens is a tall woman, imposing and elegant as she stands framed in the doorway of their three-storey townhouse. It's clear that she spends time on her appearance – her precision-cut bob is immaculate and her make-up appears professionally applied. She looks confused, as if she can't place me. 'Jacob's mum,' she says, when recognition finally dawns. 'He isn't here, I'm afraid.'

I step forward, muster a smile. 'I know. I was just wondering if Nina was in?'

Her forehead creases and she rubs her chin. 'Is everything okay?'

'I'm not sure if you know, but it seems Jacob and Rose had an argument while he was walking her home.' I ignore the way Sacha's mouth gapes open. 'And according to Jacob, Rose might have been under the impression that he was... um... interested in Nina.' I've said it now; the words are out in the ether to cause what destruction they may.

'I see.' Sacha opens the door wider. 'You'd better come in.'

'Is Nina at home, then?' I ask, stepping inside the hallway. Everything is white, with clean lines and no clutter. Too clinical. And there's not a hint of a flower or plant anywhere.

'Yes.' She lowers her voice. 'Since Rose disappeared, I've been saying she can't be out late. It's just... Well, it's worrying, isn't it? They're so young still. I know they want their freedom and all that, but at what cost?'

I nod. 'You're right. But I'm sure Rose has a reason for not coming home. The other kids will be safe.' Even as I say this,

I'm aware that I can't relax until I know Jacob is home. But it was like that even before Rose went missing.

'People are talking,' Sacha says, her voice still barely above a whisper. 'And it's upsetting Nina. She doesn't want to hear people bad-mouthing her best friend.'

'What are they saying?' I ask.

'Mostly that Rose has done this on purpose. To upset people. That she'd planned it for ages. To get attention.'

'Mum!'

Nina's voice makes us both turn to the stairs. She's dressed in khaki joggers and a fitted white T-shirt, her curly blonde hair floating around her shoulders. She looks so much younger than sixteen. 'Nina, hi, how are you holding up?'

Slowly she walks downstairs, her arms folded across her chest. She reaches the bottom and glances from me to her mum. 'Has something happened? What's going on? Have they found Rose?'

'Not yet,' I say. I don't mention the police have found Rose's keys. 'I'm sorry. Can I talk to you quickly about Jacob? There's nothing's wrong – he's safe at home.'

She looks at her mother, who gives an almost undetectable nod, before agreeing.

'Why don't we go in the kitchen?' Sacha suggests. She offers me something to drink, but there's no way I can sit here sipping coffee, or even water.

I wait until we're all seated. 'Nina, I know this might be hard to talk about, but can you think of any reason Rose might suspect Jacob liked you as more than a friend?'

Her eyes widen. 'No! Not at all. We're just friends. I would never...'

I reach for her arm. 'I know that, and you're not in any kind of trouble. I just need to know the truth. You see, a witness saw Jacob and Rose arguing while he walked her home after the barbeque. And when I asked Jacob, he told me that Rose had accused him of liking you.'

Nina stares at me, while my words scatter around us, darkening the atmosphere.

'It's not true, is it?' Sacha asks. 'If it is, it's not your fault. Things happen, don't they? People can't help who they like.' Then she looks at me. 'I mean, Nina's a beautiful girl...'

I offer a nod. 'Yes,' I assure her. 'And whatever has made Rose leave, it's not your fault.'

There are tears in Nina's eyes, but she doesn't speak. Instead, she stares at her neatly polished nails. 'Jacob isn't interested in me – it's not true. And Rose would never think that. She just wouldn't. I don't know why Jacob said that.'

A flash of anxiety passes through me. 'Nina, Jacob also said that he came here to see you the night Rose went missing.'

Nina frowns. 'No, he didn't. Definitely not that Saturday. But he was here for a few minutes looking for Rose the day before the barbeque. She wasn't here so I invited him in. He was only here for about ten minutes.'

'Yes, I remember,' Sacha says. 'That was definitely Friday night because I was getting ready to go for a business dinner.'

'Are you sure? Because Jacob—'

Sacha's phone rings, and Nina and I both turn to watch as she answers.

'Hi, Joe.' She glances at me while she listens to Carrie's partner. After a moment her face drains of colour. 'Don't think like that,' she says. 'There's every chance it's not. Do you want me to come with you? Okay. Call me as soon as you can.' Sacha hangs up the phone and reaches for Nina's hand.

'I don't know how to say this, love. That was Carrie's partner, Joe. The police have... they've found a body.'

FOURTEEN

CARRIE

One second is all it takes for someone's world to fall apart. The words coming from DC Gillary's mouth shatter her existence, and now Carrie is freefalling into an abyss. 'They've found a body. Female. Similar height and build to Rose.'

'Where?' Joe asks. He's standing beside her, and Carrie's grateful that he is. He'd just turned up, minutes before DC Gillary rang the doorbell. A coincidence.

'DC Gillary looks at Carrie, even though she's not the one speaking. 'In Merrow Woods. Someone out walking their dog found her and called us.'

The sensation that she's falling continues relentlessly – there's no end – maybe she'll be hurtling downwards forever. It doesn't have to be Rose. Teenage girls run away all the time; Rose won't be the only one. It's not her. *Please don't let it be her.* Carrie doesn't know who she's praying to – she gave up believing in God long ago, but now... now she thinks she might have been too quick to dismiss the notion that there is something greater than all of them.

'Carrie! Say something!' Joe's voice pulls at her, stops her from withdrawing deeper. She can't disappear; she needs to see for herself that it's not Rose they've found.

She looks at DC Gillary. 'Is it my Rose?'

He tells her they can't be sure, but they'll keep her informed. 'We wanted to tell you in case you heard about someone being found. On social media. Sometimes people find out about things before we know ourselves.' His mouth is a flat line – neither a smile nor a sad expression – rather something that is desperate to be both. 'We'll be in touch as soon as we know anything more,' he says. He turns to Joe. 'Will you be here with Carrie?'

'Yeah, course. I'm not going anywhere.'

DC Gillary lets himself out, and Carrie watches from the window. As soon as his car disappears, she grabs her phone and heads for the front door.

Joe grabs her arm, too roughly. 'Wait, where are you going?'

'It's not Rose. I won't let it be Rose.'

'No, Carrie, the police said to wait. They'll be in touch as soon as they know more. We need to listen to them, Carrie.' His grip tightens. Perhaps Joe has her best interests at heart, but she's not convinced. And when did he start listening to authority? He's always been the type to have a problem with following orders.

Carrie yanks her arm from him. 'There's no way in hell I'm going to sit here and wait while...' She can't finish that thought. 'Move out of my way.' She pushes past him and throws herself into her car, slamming the door shut and locking it before Joe can stop her.

Moments later she's driving on autopilot, faster than is safe on these roads. She doesn't care about breaking the speed limit. None of that matters. She just needs to get there and see that it's not her daughter lying in the woods. Some other poor child, yes, but not her Rose.

Heavy rain spatters against the car, forcing her to slow

down. The weather report has warned of a thunderstorm tonight, but she'd hoped they were wrong because she can't bear to think of Rose out there in this, even though her daughter loves thunder and lightning. Even as a toddler Rose would stare out of the window, mesmerised by the power of nature.

Carrie leaves the car on the main road, half of it on the pavement. She doesn't waste time turning off the car headlights or taking the key with her. She's too busy running, following the lights she can see through the bushes. She knows she's running too fast; the tightness in her lungs tells her she's pushing her limit, but it also feels like she's moving in slow motion, her feet crunching on gravel, and then sliding through damp grass.

Whatever she finds when she gets to the police cordon, life is about to change, whoever's body has been found. She knows she will never be the same after seeing some poor girl lying dead in the woods. It will haunt Carrie until she takes her own last breath. But at least it won't be Rose.

Twigs snap under her feet – a soothing sound of destruction. And then up ahead she sees the white and blue crime-scene tape. The uniformed officer guarding the area holds up his hands, shouting out that she can't go in there, but Carrie ignores him and ducks under the tape.

And then she sees the girl, lying flat on the ground, her face down, buried in the mud. Her hair is wet, sodden from the rain that's fallen all night and day, a mass of tangled strands. Carrie's heart pumps faster; she can almost hear it beating in her chest. It's not Rose. This poor girl's hair is too straight. Rose's could never look like that, even when wet.

But she needs to be sure, so she continues running. Desperation blocks out all else, and she barely registers a familiar voice urgently calling her name. DC Gillary. But she can't tear her eyes from the girl. Someone's daughter. Possibly someone's sister. Whoever she is, there will be people in this world who love her.

'Please, Carrie. You can't be here.' DC Gillary reaches her now, gently tries to hold her back. He's frantically spouting something about forensic evidence and preserving the crime scene, which would all make sense to Carrie if she was able to register it. If she was able to care. All she wants to do is go to this girl and see the face of a stranger. From this distance nothing is certain; the claustrophobic darkness stands between her and peace of mind.

Doubts set in as she gets closer. The shape of the girl's body: the thin arms and legs, the long back – it's all too familiar. And then Carrie sees that the hair she'd thought from a distance was poker straight is actually a mass of damp chaotic waves.

Arms reach for her as she sinks to the floor. Too many arms to belong to one person. She doesn't know who's got hold of her, and doesn't care. 'Rose!' she cries, trying to squirm from the grip that's too strong, too constricting.

And then someone is holding up an evidence bag – a bright red jacket inside it. The one Rose saw in that charity shop and had worked extra shifts to buy, even though Carrie had offered to buy it for her. 'No, Mum,' Rose had insisted. 'I want to get it myself. It's the right thing to do.'

Carrie's tears mingle with the rain, blending together so that Carrie no longer feels she is a separate entity. Is this what Rose meant all those times she'd urged Carrie to be at one with nature? Now, she wishes she'd listened to her daughter. Now, when it's too late for Rose to know that, finally, Carrie understands.

The banshee scream that erupts from her mouth forces the two officers who have hold of her to loosen their grip, and then Carrie really is falling, smashing to the ground and pummelling her fists into the mud. Her daughter is dead, and she doesn't know how she'll go on living. But Carrie also sees with absolute clarity that she needs to get justice for Rose.

FIFTEEN

ROSE

We had a couple of months, didn't we? When the sea was calm and there were no waves in sight. Although it had hurt me that you didn't turn up to my gig that evening, I was too proud of myself for seeing it through to be angry with you for long. You explained your reasons, which I roughly translated as fear. Fear of us. Fear of the future.

I knew we couldn't sail along like this so smoothly, but I refused to give any headspace to all the voices screaming at me that this couldn't last, and that eventually it would implode.

I just didn't expect it to all come crashing down when it did.

The rest of your family were away for a few days over the February half-term, so we got to play house. I don't know how you got away with not going with them, but you'd convinced Lucy you needed to stay at home. I brought a bag of toiletries and spare clothes and had no intention of leaving until they came back.

'What's all this?' you said, laughing, when I turned up at your house. 'Are you moving in, then?' But your smile soon faded when I didn't reply.

'I'll just stay for a day or two. We never get the chance to do this. Come on, it'll be fun.'

'But your mum will wonder where you are. She'll know you're here and she'll come looking for you.'

'Let her,' I said, laughing.

Your eyes widened, a mixture of fear and horror. Ignoring it, I pulled you towards me and nuzzled your neck. 'She's working nights for the next couple of days. She won't even notice I'm gone.'

Despite what I was doing to you with my hands, the stubborn frown on your face remained, so I gave up and retreated to the sofa to read, putting my feet up and making myself at home, just to annoy you. It was childish and petty but I didn't care. It's only now I can see that this was the first bubble of resentment brewing inside me.

You ignored me, and went to sulk upstairs. A couple of hours later, when you finally came back downstairs, I was still there, this time sitting at the kitchen table.

'I thought you'd gone home,' you said.

And I probably should have, but even if we weren't in the same room, I didn't want to leave your house. I hated myself for the power I let you hold over me, but in your presence my reserve whittled away, leaving me with no self-protection.

'What have you been doing?'

'Homework.' This, and my music, were my only distractions from you; the only things that could keep me from losing myself. I loathed who I was becoming. The gig at the pub should have screamed out to me that I didn't need you, and that if anything, you were toxic for me. And sitting there in your house, after you'd left me to my own devices all morning, I almost told you I was leaving, that whatever was happening between us was over. I'm sure I even opened my mouth to utter the words, but they withered away when I thought of not seeing you again, of never again having your arms around me.

'I was watching you from the hall,' you said, sitting next to me. 'You look sexy when you're studying. It's... almost too much. Your mind. It makes me...' You didn't finish your thought, whatever it was. I like to think that I, too, held some power over you – that this wasn't just one-sided. 'Let's order some food,' you said, changing the subject so abruptly I felt like I'd been left behind on a motorway while you sped off.

'Okay.'

'The Thai place in town delivers now.'

'Can't we just have Domino's?' I asked, laughing.

You didn't seem to get the joke, and frowned at me, trying to work out if I was serious.

We had sex on the sofa while we waited for the food, and if I'd known then that it would be the final time, the last moment when you'd hold me, and want me, I would have savoured it more, devoured every second of you being mine, before you snatched it away. You stroked my hair afterwards, and I longed to be able to vanquish all our problems. Because there were so many, weren't there? And nothing we could do about them.

The food was nice, even though I silently longed for pizza. I didn't notice that you were distracted while we were eating. I was filling the house with excited chatter about summer, which wasn't too far away. 'Freedom from exams. Well, for a few months at least. Time just feels like it's rocketing away, doesn't it? I thought it was only old people who felt that.' I didn't wait for an answer. Perhaps I'd already sensed there was something heavy ploughing towards us, towards me, and I wanted to delay it for as long as I could. 'Maybe we could go somewhere together?' Even as I said it, I knew that would never happen.

'Mmm,' you mumbled, prodding your fork into your chicken, staring at it but not lifting it to your mouth.

'There's always a way if you look for it,' I continued.

'Rose, stop!' You hammered your fist on the table. It wasn't a violent action, not really. It was more to get my attention. And you certainly did that.

'We need to stop, Rose,' you said, softly now. 'We can't do this any more.'

But hadn't we been here before? Your fear forcing you to end things when that's not what you wanted.

'You always do this. Yet here we are.'

'No, not this time,' you said, placing your knife and fork together. 'I can't do it any more. I won't.'

You stared right at me, defiant, and that's when I knew this time it was different. There was no going back for you. 'I'm sorry, Rose, I really am. But we both knew this couldn't work, didn't we? There's too much... It's time now to move on. Focus on exams. Enjoy the summer.'

What happened next felt like the actions of someone else, not my own. I could almost witness it as I slammed my fists into your chest, pummelling until my knuckles were red and swollen. I lapped up the pain.

You tried to restrain me and gripped my wrists so hard they had puce-coloured rings around them for days afterwards.

Eventually I got up and walked out of your house, holding my head high. I wasn't going to beg you. But I walked home drowning in guilt and shame.

It was only much later I realised the extent of what you'd done.

PART TWO

And sweetest - in the Gale - is heard -
And sore must be the storm -
That could abash the little Bird
That kept so many warm -

Emily Dickinson, '"Hope" is the thing with feathers'

SIXTEEN

LUCY

How quickly things fall apart. Carrie's life lies shattered, and so too does Jacob's. Rose was found two weeks ago, and in that time he's barely eaten, or slept. And neither have I. There's an empty space in our house, one that only weeks ago was filled by Rose, and we all feel her absence.

Although I try my best to keep us anchored, slowly, piece by piece, we are becoming fragments of a family, untethering from each other.

I've been to too many funerals already, and now I sit here at Rose's, in the back row of the crematorium, with Ava cuddled against me and Tom on her other side. We watch as Carrie stands at the front in a black mid-length dress that's too loose on her, leaning on her friend's arm, sobbing onto her black trench coat. I want to go to her, to hold her in my arms and tell her I'm sorry this has happened, but it would only distress her. I'm the last person she wants comfort from.

It's drizzling outside, and the rain spatters against the windows, a melancholic musical score. On the other side of the crematorium, police detectives sit conspicuously, despite trying to blend in with the other mourners. DC Gillary is here, and

Michelle, the family liaison officer. And next to them is the new homicide detective who has taken over; her stern eyes dart around, taking in every detail of us all.

They will be wondering why Jacob isn't here, and I, too, am perplexed by his refusal to attend.

'I don't need to go to remember Rose,' he'd insisted that morning, when I'd attempted to rouse him from his bed. 'She would have understood. She was always talking about not conforming.' From underneath his duvet, he'd stared at my clothes. 'And why are you wearing black? Rose would have hated that.'

'Do it for Carrie, then,' I'd tried to convince him, but to no avail. We'd had no choice but to leave him in bed and head to the crematorium, where the weight of everyone's stare is upon us.

The service is short and poignant; Rose wouldn't have liked a big fuss, Carrie explains as she ends her eulogy, a broken woman.

Beside me, Ava blinks away tears and clutches my hand. We all rise and that's when I notice Jacob standing at the back of the building, watching from the open door, his hair damp and his arms folded.

I'm about to rush over to him but the new detective gets there first.

'You nearly missed it,' she's saying to Jacob when I reach them. 'Everything all right?'

Jacob nods and shoves his hands in his pocket, shifting from one foot to the other. 'I felt sick,' he says. Another lie.

'I'm DC Joanna Keller. Good of you to show,' she says. She gestures to his yellow T-shirt and blue jeans. 'Even if you didn't have time to dress for it.'

I take Jacob's arm and lead him outside. 'Thanks for coming.'

'I only came because... Look at this.' He reaches into the

back pocket of his jeans. 'I found this on the doormat.' He shoves a folded piece of paper into my hand. I unfold it and read the words.

You deserve to die too.

'What is this?'

'Someone put it through the door! I don't know who.' He snatches it back and starts to rip it.

'Stop, we need to show it to the police.' I snatch the note and turn to where the detectives are talking to Carrie.

I walk towards them, but Jacob grabs my arm. 'Not here, Mum. Not now. It's Rose's funeral.'

Jacob's right. I will wait until later to show it to the police. 'Shall we go home?' I say to Jacob. There are too many eyes on us. We move off towards Tom and Ava when I hear Carrie's voice.

'You shouldn't be here,' she says, staring at Jacob.

'He's paying his respects to Rose,' I say. 'He wanted to be here. I'm sorry if that upsets you, Carrie, but Jacob hasn't done anything wrong.'

She ignores me and keeps her eyes fixed on my son. 'Get out of here. It's your fault she's lying in there waiting to be incinerated. It's all because of you!' She jabs her finger towards him and Jacob flinches, staring at the ground. On the other side of the path, DC Keller is watching us closely.

'I'm sorry,' Jacob says. 'But I didn't do anything.'

'Just leave. Now.'

'We were just leaving anyway,' I say. 'I'm sorry, Carrie.'

She ignores me and turns away, heading back to her friend, who holds out her arms to Carrie.

And in that moment, I know things are going to get worse.

. . .

The following morning, I'm in the supermarket, grabbing some vegetables for dinner, when a hand lands heavily on my shoulder. I spin around and Joe Aldridge is standing there, his face so close to mine that I can smell a vile mix of coffee and cigarette smoke on his breath. 'How's Jacob?' he sneers.

I glance past him; there's no one else in our aisle. Joe's never been a pleasant man, but now his tone is menacing. And I know what everyone around here thinks of my son.

'He's not doing well, but that's to be expected. How's Carrie doing?' I step back from Joe and scan the shelves to avoid looking at him.

'Terrible,' he says. 'I suppose you heard that she left me? I don't know how that news got out but people have been plastering it all over social media. All that shit about couples not being able to last through tragedies like this. But it's all bollocks, ain't it? Cos Carrie and me, we were... we were solid.' His voice cracks, and I feel a twinge of sympathy. No matter how much Rose disliked Joe, through Carrie she was still a huge part of his life.

I don't admit that I already knew this, that Carrie had told Tom when he'd visited her a few days ago, checking up on her because I'm not able to. She has shut me out of her life, Jacob too, and Tom and Ava are the only ones she'll speak to.

'It's because she doesn't think you can be impartial,' Tom says when I bring it up. 'And she's convinced Jacob knows something.' This is why I have barely seen my husband over the last two weeks. He doesn't trust his son.

'I'm sorry about that,' I tell Joe, forcing myself to look at him. 'It's just so awful.'

He moves closer to me. 'What's your Jacob hiding, Carrie? Did he do it? Squeeze her neck so hard until she had no breath left in her? That's what happened to the poor kid. Was it him?'

The image of Rose being strangled from behind forces its way into my head. The brutal way her life was cut short has haunted me since we heard the details. I've got used to hearing these accusations over the last couple of weeks. Wicked words get hurled at us all like weapons, and the only way we can fend them off is to turn away from them, ignore the venomous shouts. The fury and hatred. But there is something worse about Joe's words, his devastating description of Rose's murder. Despite the claustrophobic warmth in this shop, a shiver runs down my spine.

'Jacob doesn't know anything,' I say. 'And if that's what you've been telling everyone, then please just stop.' I try to keep my voice calm; getting angry won't help. 'What good does spreading rumours do? He's a child, Joe. And he's grieving. People need to leave him alone.'

He edges closer to me, leaning into my ear. 'Not if he's a murderer,' he hisses. 'Child or not, he needs to pay for what he's done to Rose.'

'Was it you who put that note through our door? Because I've given it to the police.'

Joe's eyes become slits. 'I don't know what you're talking about. What note?'

'It was a threat. To Jacob. Someone put it through our door.'

'Did they, now?' He smirks. 'Can't say I'm surprised about that. He'd better watch his back, hadn't he?' Joe turns away from me and strolls off, as if we've just shared a pleasant chat about the weather.

I watch him disappear around the corner, and then I leave the supermarket, my hands shaking as I clutch my empty bags.

'Just ignore him, he's a piece of scum,' Tom says, when I call him from home later. He sighs, and I picture him checking his watch, turning his attention back to his computer screen, desperate to end this call.

I'm in my workshop, and I abandon the dried flower posy

I've started making. 'That's the thing, Tom – I would just ignore it, but the whole interaction with him felt... I don't know... sinister or something. And even though he denied it, I'm sure Joe is the one who sent that note.'

Again, a sigh. 'Well, he's not the nicest of people, is he? The best thing we can do is ignore his pathetic attempt to scare us. Carrie's well rid of him.'

The mention of Carrie's name constricts my chest. 'How's she doing?' I ask.

'As you'd expect,' Tom replies. 'But she did say I could bring Ava over to pick out something of Rose's to keep. That's decent of her, isn't it? Given that it's so soon. I'll take her over tonight.'

And now it's my turn to sigh. Tonight will be another evening Tom won't be around when there is so much we need to discuss. 'Okay.' The conversation is dwindling, but there's something else I need to know. 'Tom, does Carrie really believe Jacob knows something? Or worse, that he...' I can't bring myself to say it. 'I know she says all that stuff, but do you think it's just grief confusing her?' And I, of all people, can understand this.

'I don't know, Lucy. I'm trying to support her on behalf of all of us, but it's the lies she can't deal with. And the fact that Rose and Jacob argued. She doesn't know *what* to believe. And it doesn't help when the police have made him a person of interest.'

'He's not a suspect, though. Just a person of interest. They were clear about that. There's no evidence, Tom. That's what they said.'

'But they question him a lot. It doesn't look good, does it?' He pauses. 'Did he go to school this morning?'

'Yes.' I don't mention that he went only after a lot of coaxing and encouragement on my part.

'Well, good. How many days has he missed now? And his exams are only weeks away.'

I hold back from defending Jacob. It won't do any good;

Tom won't hear anything positive about our son at the moment. 'The staff at school understand.' It's all I can manage to say.

'I've got a late meeting this evening,' he says, and it's a relief that he's changed the subject. 'I'll swing by and pick up Ava then head straight to Carrie's.'

I give a pointless nod and we say goodbye. That word has never felt so loaded.

I've just finished eating a cheese bagel and salad for lunch when the call from school comes. At first, I assume something has happened to Ava – we only ever got calls about her when we were in London, so it's hardwired into me to assume it's my daughter they're calling about – but this time Vicki from the office is calling about Jacob. I listen and try to comprehend her words, all my fears squeezing my ribs, crushing me as my mind assumes the worst before she's even finished. There's been a fight. A serious one. And I have to come and get Jacob now.

Adrenalin floods through me and I'm already grabbing my car keys before Vicki's finished speaking. 'Is he okay? Is Jacob badly hurt?' I ask, my breaths short and heavy.

'Mrs Adams, I don't think you understand. Jacob's not the one who's hurt. It's the other boy who's been taken to hospital.'

We sit in the car outside school, and I wait for my son to speak. Outside, a patch of dark grey cloud threatens to erupt over us, making me think of how the rain had destroyed any DNA that might have been left on Rose's body. A fleeting thought comes to me – *was it Jacob's DNA that was washed away?* – and I banish it before it takes hold of me. His DNA was bound to be all over her – they were in a relationship.

'Are you going to tell me what happened?' I ask.

Jacob stares out of the side window, towards the school.

'Did you hurt that boy? Felix.'

He gives an almost imperceptible nod. 'Yeah. But only because he was threatening me. He said I need to pay for what I did to Rose.' Jacob turns to me, and for a second he looks like the toddler I used to hold closely whenever he needed me. 'I didn't mean to... to do *that* to him. I just... I just... snapped.'

His confession sits heavily between us for a moment. 'He could have a broken nose.' I wince when I say this; there has already been too much violence in our lives over the last few weeks.

'I know, Mum. I'm sorry.' He hangs his head.

'You've never had an anger problem. Where's this coming from?' *Maybe not anger, but look how quickly he got over Isla – a girl he professed to love.*

We both know the answer. His anger comes from losing his girlfriend in such a heinous way. From the devastating unfairness of it all. One life obliterated and many others destroyed. From the fact that everyone believes it was him.

'It's all my fault, Mum,' Jacob says, looking up at me with tears in his eyes.

I reach for his arm. 'I'm sure Felix will be okay. Luckily there were witnesses who said he went for you first. And that bruise on your face is evidence too. Everyone will see that it was self-defence.'

Jacob turns away. 'I don't mean Felix.'

I freeze.

'I mean Rose. It's all my fault she's dead.

SEVENTEEN

CARRIE

Two weeks have felt like two years to Carrie, and yet at the same time like it was only two seconds ago she was staring at her daughter's body, splayed on the muddy ground like an abandoned rag doll. Rose's death has distorted time, scrambled everything in Carrie's world. She is a lost soul, ambling through her days, the very definition of an automaton. Justice is the only thing that will get her through this. Knowing that whoever did this will be caught. Michelle, the family liaison officer, has cautioned her against jumping to conclusions about Jacob, and assured her that their questioning of him doesn't mean he's guilty of anything other than lying about the argument with Rose. Carrie sees things differently; his lie is a sure sign of guilt.

Carrie has always felt sadness watching tragic news stories, and now she is part of one herself. A story that strangers will talk about, detached and unaffected. She can't bring herself to read the news on her phone, or to watch it on TV.

It's nearly seven p.m. and she stands by the window waiting for Tom and Ava. Tom had warned her he'd be late – a work meeting that ran over for far too long. She admires his work ethic – it's much like her own. In fact, she called her boss a couple of hours ago to tell her she needed to come back to work. Without having that to focus on, Carrie might just wither away. Rose wouldn't want that; she would want her to carry on, to fight for them both.

'It's too soon,' her manager Abigail had warned. 'You need to take more time. We can manage here. I've juggled the rotas, and everything will be fine until you're ready to come back.'

'I'm ready *now*,' Carrie had insisted. Demanded, even. And although she didn't say it, she knows that Abigail will be struggling to fill her shifts, and that because of Carrie's absence, all her colleagues will be working overtime they can barely manage. She can't have that on her conscience.

Eventually Abigail had reluctantly agreed, but on the condition that she gave it a few more days. It's Wednesday today, and Carrie's emphatic response was that she'd be in on Monday for the early shift she would have been on anyway. If things had been different.

Tom's car pulls up outside, and she heads to the door. She likes Ava, and it will be nice to have their company. When she's around others it means she can turn the focus away from her grief, however temporary and half-formed the respite is.

Ava's not standing beside Tom when Carrie opens the door. She looks past him, but there's no sign of his daughter.

'I'm so sorry, Carrie – Ava's caught some sickness bug from school. She's in bed and she's really upset she couldn't come. Is it okay for me to still be here? If you don't want company, I understand. I know I'm not as interesting as my daughter.' He offers a small smile.

'Come in,' she says. 'I'll go mad if I have to just keep staring at the walls. Or out of that window' She points to the living room. 'I'm not used to being so inactive. It doesn't sit right with me.' *Nothing does any longer*. But she keeps this to herself.

'If you're sure?' Tom steps inside, and Carrie shuts the door, locks out the world that has become so unfamiliar. 'Let me make coffee,' he offers.

'I'm perfectly capable of boiling the kettle,' Carrie remarks. 'You're as bad as Michelle.' His lips tighten. 'Sorry, no offence. It's just... Well, it might sound daft but even doing the small things like making a hot drink is a distraction from grief.' *Take things one second at a time, don't think beyond that.* The counsellor had told her this in their first session, but Carrie's not sure she's doing it very well. It's difficult not to think of the day Jacob will be exposed for what he's done, no matter how far in the future that may be.

'Please,' Tom says, placing his hand on her upper arm. 'You don't have to apologise for anything.' He averts his eyes. 'Not after... you know. Jacob's lie. I feel dreadful that he did that.'

In that moment, Carrie knows exactly why Tom is here, why he keeps coming here to make sure she's okay. He knows his son is guilty, and he's trying to make some amends for that. This thought comes to her with such clarity that she can't see why it hasn't occurred to her before. And she may not be able to get the truth out of Jacob, but perhaps through Tom, there is a way.

'It's tearing me up,' he says, releasing his hand. 'I... I just can't get my head around it. The police don't trust him. And I hate to say it but... I'm not sure I can either.'

Carrie takes Tom's hand and leads him to the sofa. 'Sit down,' she says. 'I'll make that coffee.' More caffeine is the last things she needs; it's already impossible to sleep for longer than an hour or two.

'Lucy trusts him implicitly,' Tom continues. 'It's as if she can't even entertain the notion that he might be hiding something. I can't talk to her any more – it's like she won't hear anything I say.' He sighs. 'I wish it was that easy for me to be convinced about Jacob.'

Sitting beside him, Carrie places her hand on his knee.

'She's a mother. That's what we do. We fight for our kids, no matter what they've done. It has to be that way.'

He looks at her for a moment, taking in what she's said. 'I know, Carrie. It's just driving such a wedge between us.' He stares at his hands. 'I'm sorry, I shouldn't be talking about all this. Not when you're—'

'Try not to blame Lucy,' she forces herself to say. 'Losing her little sister like that when she was just a kid herself has scarred her. And then her husband.' Just like Rose's death has severed Carrie. She and Lucy should be united, yet there couldn't be more distance between them. She doesn't understand it, she only knows it to be true.

Tom's eyes widen.

'You're surprised I'm defending her when I won't even talk to her?'

'Something like that,' he agrees.

Carrie shrugs. 'I suppose, ultimately, Lucy's not the one who's hiding things. Sorry. You don't need me to keep going on about Jacob. It's awkward, isn't it? This... friendship of ours.'

Tom leans back, resting his head against the sofa. 'Yes, it is. But... I'm not going to stop coming. I need to be here for you. We... I can't explain it, but there's some sort of connection with us, isn't there?' He averts his eyes from her. 'Even before all this.'

Yes. And it started at the barbeque. Not an affair of any kind, far from that, but a silent acknowledgement that something existed between them.

She stands to go and make coffee, leaving his words to disperse around them.

She's smiling as she walks to the kitchen, feeling his eyes on her. *This will work.* This is her way to get justice for Rose. It will be Tom who helps her, even though he won't know that's what he's doing. It's fallen into place like a piece of a jigsaw.

While the kettle boils, Carrie watches him. It's strange not to see Joe there on the sofa, hunched over a beer, eyes glued to the television, a far cry from the man who sits there now. Tom is happy to sit and wait, alone with his own thoughts. Joe couldn't tolerate silence.

Carrie hands him his coffee. 'I know it would be nice for Ava to pick it herself, but why don't you come upstairs and pick something of Rose's to take back for her? I'm sure she won't mind her dad choosing for her. Like I said, I know Rose would want her to have something. Maybe a book? Ava loves to read, doesn't' she?'

Tom smiles and thanks her as he takes the mug. Carrie assumes he's used to proper coffee cups in his house, not huge chunky mugs like the ones filling her cupboard. It doesn't bother her; she is who she is and she won't put on airs and graces for anyone. Even Tom Adams. Although he's never given her the impression that he looks down on her, she's fully aware they live in different worlds. *But not now; now our worlds have collided and we're stuck with each other through this tragedy. He can walk away, but it won't change anything. Rose and Jacob. Forever linked.*

'Thanks, Carrie. It means a lot. To all of us.'

Parting with something of Rose's is not as difficult as she'd expected. It hurts, of course it does, to think that the book Tom has chosen will now be in Ava's possession, but she assures herself it doesn't matter. Rose didn't care about material things – all she wanted to do was write music and sing. That's it. *And love that boy who is likely the one who took her life.*

'Come here,' Tom says, holding out his hand.

This isn't how it's meant to be, not this soon. And not here in Rose's room. But she goes to him anyway, and he pulls her towards him, holding her tightly, his arms strong and secure. 'For as long as you need,' he says, and she buries her head in his chest. They stay like that, a frozen tableau, for too many minutes to count.

EIGHTEEN

LUCY

'It's all my fault she's dead.'

Jacob's words have circulated around my mind since he uttered them in the car yesterday, and even now, when I've had hours to digest them, to manipulate them like dough, trying to mould them into a form that makes sense, I still can't be sure of their meaning.

'You mean because of the argument?' I asked. 'I told you it's not—'

'No! Because... because we had that fight. And she was mad at me. She tried to walk off without me but I made sure I followed her home. I swear. I saw her go in the house.'

'Then it's not your fault, is it? You've got to stop thinking like that.'

'You don't understand! She only went in for a second, and then I saw her leave again. She left the house! And I... I didn't follow her. I just left her. I was so angry. I didn't even care where she was going. I thought she must be going to the petrol station for chocolate or something. She loved Lion Bars and that's the only place that does them.'

Hearing this confession, the weight of an ocean crushed my

chest. More lies. 'Another thing you didn't tell the police,' I'd said. 'You could have admitted it when you admitted to arguing.' He seemed to crumple before me, but then there was a flicker of something, too fleeting to grasp. Was it defiance?

'I've already told you I was scared. And then once I'd kept it from them, how could I tell them the truth? And now Rose is dead and if they find out I saw her leave the house, then they'll definitely think it's me. They'll say I followed her. And it *is* my fault because if I'd gone after her, then she wouldn't be dead.'

Sometimes we make decisions acting only on instinct, with no thought or reason involved, only that urge to protect at all costs. 'Jacob, look at me. Don't tell this to anyone else,' I said. 'And I mean *anyone*. Not your dad. Not Ava. No one.'

He stared for a moment, possibly trying to work out if that command had really come from my mouth. And then he gave a small nod, and neither of us has mentioned it since. Despite being wracked with guilt, I won't feed my son to the wolves.

Jacob refuses to go to school this morning, or get out of bed. The bruise on his face looks even worse today – a deep burgundy colour grotesquely plastered under his eye. Still, the other boy fared far worse.

'You need to get up, Jacob,' I say gently, pulling at his duvet. He ignores me and rolls over. 'Look at this,' he says, passing me his phone. 'Look what they're saying about me at school.'

I stare at the vitriolic words, feel the crushing weight of them; Jacob shouldn't have to endure this. 'We've always taught you and Ava to ignore the trolls, haven't we? They're cowards who hide behind their screens. Don't let it be your reality, Jacob. Remember?'

Jacob sits up, drawing his knees to his chest. 'That's just it, though, Mum. They're not just trolls. They're kids I go to school with and see every day. They don't just hide behind screens, they say this stuff to me in person. Or put threatening notes through our letterbox. I just... I don't know what to do.'

I sit on the edge of his bed. 'Apart from hitting that boy, you've done nothing wrong, have you? So, you need to hold your head up high, always. What would Rose tell you to do?'

At the mention of her name, Jacob stiffens. He's grieving, it's bound to be hard when anyone speaks of her.

'She'd tell me to push through,' he replies. 'Ignore those arseholes.' He glances at me. 'Sorry.'

'Bad language is the least of our worries,' I say. 'So, do you think you can do it, then? Ignore them and go back to school tomorrow, head held high?'

He shrugs. 'I'll try.'

'Good. And in the meantime, how about getting some fresh air? We can take Cooper for a walk.'

'I will,' he says, pulling the duvet aside. 'But would you mind if I went alone? My head feels fuzzy and I need time alone to put it straight.'

Despite my disappointment, I agree. Ava's still not well and I need to be here for her. I hope she understands why Jacob's been getting so much of my attention over the last few weeks, especially given that for at least a year before we moved, the majority of our focus had been on Ava.

Once Jacob's gone, I check on his sister and find her asleep, an open book folded across her chest. I tiptoe in and close the curtains, then head to my workshop. I still haven't finished a wedding proposal I promised to have done by tomorrow, and I can't let my clients down.

It's not long before Ava appears, standing in the doorway with her arms folded over her stomach.

'How are you feeling? Did sleep help?'

She nods. 'A bit. Where's Jacob?'

'He's taken Cooper for a walk.'

Ava heads over to me and sits cross-legged on the floor, her arms still folded protectively across her body. 'Is he going back to school tomorrow?'

'I don't know. I hope so. It won't do him any good hiding away at home.'

She spreads out her hands and studies them. 'The kids at school are being... awful.'

'I know. Have they said anything to you?'

Her eyes flick to me then back to her hands. 'Only that Rose is dead because of him. They're saying that if even if he didn't do it himself, she would never have run away from him and ended up dead if he hadn't argued with her.'

'You know that's not true, don't you Ava? What do you say to them?'

'I don't say anything. Because I don't know anything! I hate this, Mum. I wish I could defend him and tell those people to leave him alone, but how can I when I saw how Rose was acting at the barbeque? She was staying away from Jacob, avoiding him the whole evening. She didn't want to be anywhere near him. Why? And now he's broken Felix's nose it just doesn't look good. That's why I don't say anything. I can't.'

'I understand this, Ava, but we have to stick together as a family. We have to be there for Jacob. That's all that matters.'

'No, it's *not* all that matters,' she insists. 'Rose matters.'

'Of course she does, but your brother isn't responsible for what happened to her.'

She stands. 'You just can't see it can you, Mum? Even Dad can.'

I stare at her. 'What do you mean? What's your dad said?'

'He's scared, Mum – can't you see that? He doesn't want to believe his son could be mixed up in this, but there are too many lies and inconsistencies in Jacob's story. He says he was with Nina, but she said she didn't see him that night. How can you explain that?'

'How do you know she said that?' I ask. I haven't breathed a word of what Nina said to Ava or Tom.

'I saw her at school. She told me Jacob had been saying he

was with her. But it's not true, Mum! He's lied again. He just keeps on—'

'Jacob explained all that; he got confused. It was the night before that he'd gone to Nina's. Her mum even said that was true.' *And I still have no answer for where he was the night he walked Rose home.*

'Yeah, he went there looking for Rose and was there for about a second. How could he get that mixed up with being at Nina's for hours?'

I've trawled through my mind to come up with an answer for this, but I've failed. All Jacob says is that he must have been out walking and lost track of time. I understand why Ava, and everyone else, is sceptical, but I know my son. Whatever his faults, he didn't do anything to Rose. His lies are manifested through fear.

'This has made everything horrible,' Ava says. 'All you and Dad seem to do is argue. You barely even speak any more,' she says, pulling herself up.

'I'm sorry for that. I'm trying to put things right, but your Dad—'

'You can't blame him for believing what everyone else does!'

I'm about to explain to Ava that Tom and I will be fine, that we'll get through this, but how can I offer her that reassurance when I'm not sure I believe it myself.

'I'm going to make some toast,' she says, disappearing through the door and clicking it shut behind her.

Consuming myself with checking over my proposal for the wedding flowers, dinner doesn't even cross my mind until a text message appears on my phone. It's Tom, and a wave of sadness passes over me when I see his name. It used to fill me with warmth whenever I'd receive a message from him; now it's as though tension is fuelling every communication between us.

To my relief, he's only asking how Ava is doing. I let him

know that she's a little better, then lock up my workshop and head back to the house.

Inside, Ava's watching TV in the living room. I ask her if she's seen Jacob and I'm greeted with a shrug. 'Nope.'

I call his name, but silence is the only response. And there's no sign of Cooper either. The panic is instant, coursing through my body. The twist of nausea. I check my phone. It's nearly six now and Jacob left just after two.

Grabbing my phone, I call his mobile, forcing deep breaths while I wait for him to answer. But he doesn't, and when his voicemail kicks in I leave a frantic message. Even to my own ears I sound hysterical. 'Jacob, where are you and Cooper? I'm really worried – you've been out for hours. Please call me as soon as you get this.'

I head outside and check our road. There's no sign of them. I call Tom; there's nothing he can do from work, but we're in this together. Surely he won't tell me I'm being paranoid when it's been almost four hours and we've never taken Cooper out for this long?

'Lucy, I'm just about to have a client meeting – can it wait?'

'Jacob hasn't come home. He took Cooper out for a walk at two, and there's no sign of them. He's not answering his phone.' My words tumble from my mouth, and I only hope I'm making sense.

There's a heavy pause before Tom answers. 'He's sixteen and has dug himself into a huge hole – maybe he just wanted some space? I can't blame him for that. It's got to be hard for him.'

'I'm not just being paranoid this time, Tom. It doesn't feel right. If he hadn't taken Cooper, then maybe I wouldn't worry so much, but he knows the dog needs to eat. He'll be thirsty too.'

Tom's silence tells me I might have got through to him. 'Okay, it does seem a bit strange. I'll leave as soon as this meeting's over, okay? We can go out and look for him.'

As soon as we've ended the call, the doorbell rings. I hold my breath as I answer, praying I don't see police officers standing there, delivering a message I won't be able to hear.

It's Jacob, his face streaming with so much blood that I can't tell where it's coming from. His T-shirt, once blue, is bright red now, sticking to his chest. I stifle my cry, force myself to remain calm as I lead him inside. 'What happened?' I ask, desperately trying to crush the panic.

And then he crashes to the floor, and there's silence.

NINETEEN

ROSE

They tell us that anger isn't healthy. Release it. Let it go. Don't let it consume you. What they don't acknowledge is that sometimes it's a driving force for good. It pushes you to see things you might have overlooked.

After leaving your house that day, I walked for hours, a thick black cloud of fog filling my head, leaving me unable to take in my surroundings, to appreciate them like I normally would when I'm outside. And that made me hate you. It wasn't because you had ended what we had so abruptly, it was the fact that you'd changed me beyond recognition, stopped me seeing the beauty in life, and all for nothing. For your own selfish needs.

I knew Mum was working a night shift, but I didn't expect Joe to be home when I got back to the house. He was sprawled on the sofa, a can of beer in his hand. Perhaps it was my anger with you that made me confrontational, but instead of going upstairs and shutting myself in my bedroom, I plonked myself on Mum's armchair and stared at him, daring him to start an argument.

'What's up with you?' he asked, his eyes fixed on the TV.

'Nothing.'

He snorted or sniffed; I couldn't tell which. 'You don't normally sit anywhere near me.'

'That's 'cos you're a sleazebag, Joe.' I said, preparing myself for the inevitable fight. I didn't care; Joe could hit me with his best shot, it would only ricochet off me. I hugged my knees to my chest and watched him.

'You're probably right,' he said, flicking his head upwards. 'Ha, I've been called worse.'

I frowned. What game was he playing? It wasn't like Joe to be self-deprecating. And I couldn't name a time he'd spoken to me without contempt. Even the gig he'd got me at that pub was only done as a favour to his friend. Joe had owed him for something, and he'd repaid the favour by getting me to sing in the hopes of pulling more drinkers in.

'Are you feeling all right, Joe? Had a lobotomy or something?'

He really laughed then, and it lit up his face. I actually caught the tiniest glimpse of what Mum might see in him.

'Where's your woman, then?' I asked, because despite the apparent warmth he was emitting, I couldn't forget what I knew about him.

'How come you haven't told your mum?' he asked.

I met his stare. 'Because I don't want to hurt her. And because maybe, just maybe, I understand a tiny bit. But if you're still doing it, I won't hesitate.'

He took his time to respond, looking away from me and staring out of the window. 'I love your mum,' he said eventually. 'It's just... complicated.'

'No, it's not,' I countered. 'Mum's love is pretty straightforward. Till death do you part, or whatever.'

Joe rubbed his chin. He'd actually shaved for once. 'Okay, then *I'm* complicated.'

I crossed my legs and folded my arms. 'Stop making excuses,

Joe, you just like sleeping with different women. One just isn't enough for you.' As soon as I'd spoken, I was astonished by my boldness – yet still I continued. 'You're right that this is on *you*, though. It's got nothing to do with Mum. You won't be happy whoever you're with.'

He looked at me then, and it felt like I was seconds away from an attack. 'Well, well, well. Who'd have thought it? Rose Nyler might actually be right about me. I'm a mess and I need to clean up my act or I'll lose your mum forever. I don't want that.'

He stood up, and I imagined him striding over to me and pummelling his fists into my face. I don't think I cared. I would welcome the pain.

'D'you know what, Rose? You actually have a wise head on your shoulders. What do they say? An old soul in a young body.' He looked me up and down, then walked across to me, gently lifting my chin with his hand. 'But listen to me carefully. Don't forget that you're still a child. D'you hear me? Oh, you're not a woman yet, Rose.'

I didn't want to stay at home after that. Joe's words crashed around my head, because despite what I thought of myself, how mature I considered myself to be, he was right, wasn't he?

It was late but I sent Nina a message, telling her I needed to see her. She replied straight away – that's just the kind of friend she was – and I left the house without another word to Joe.

We sat in her bedroom and my tears fell like a waterfall, never-ending, blurring my vision so that not only was my brain distorted, but now everything in my physical world was indistinct.

Nina looked pretty, sitting in her spotted pyjamas with no make-up. Why are girls our age in such a hurry to grow up? To be considered women? This was better, wasn't it? Just being able to be comfortable in your pyjamas with your hair tied back. Not Instagram-worthy or any of that bullshit, but just stripped back to our essence. And then I realised that this is how I used to be, and you had destroyed that.

'Is this about you and Jacob?' Nina asked, cradling me in her arms, like I was a baby.

I could only nod. I couldn't even begin to tell Nina the whole truth. Never.

She took my hand and we sat in silence for a moment. Then when she spoke, her words shocked me. 'I think it's for the best, Rose, isn't it? I'm sorry to say this but... I could tell something was wrong between you. And then there's his girlfriend in London. I mean, what happened there? Everyone says how much they were in love, so it's weird that he suddenly cut her off when he met you. I mean, that says a lot about him, doesn't it? The poor girl.'

I shuddered at the mention of Isla, because I knew the whole truth. But my focus quickly turned to disbelief at what Nina was saying. I thought I had hidden things well, that to the outside world my relationship appeared solid. How could I have got everything so wrong?

'What do you mean, you could tell something was wrong with us?' I asked Nina.

The sheepish look on her face was one I'd never seen before. 'I can't explain it,' she replied. Maybe I just *felt* it, you know? Instinct. I'm good with that. Mum always says I seem to see things others can't.'

None of this was Nina's fault, but suddenly I felt this huge rage towards her. I hate myself for what I did next. For how I treated her. I can never take it back.

'You like him, don't you?' I said, firing my accusation at her.

Her cheeks reddened and she shrunk back. 'What? Who?'

I jumped up. 'Jacob, of course. You've always liked him. Is

that why your *instinct* knew it wasn't right with me and him? Is that what you were hoping?'

'No! Rose, stop it, you're scaring me!'

I'm not going to repeat all the hateful things I said to her then. The accusations I threw her way hurt her like physical bullets – I could see the pain on her face, and I did nothing to alleviate it. In fact, I was glad that her pain matched my own. That I wasn't the only one suffering. I had never been so cruel in my life, and I loathed myself for it, at the same time as I couldn't stop.

'What kind of friend are you?' I spat my words at her. It was awful, because she'd been the kindest friend I'd ever had. The only person other than Mum who'd been a constant part of my life. And now I was pushing her away, deflecting my pain at what you'd done.

'Why are you being like this?' she cried. 'I know you're hurt because you've split up with Jacob but I promise you there's nothing going on with us if that's what you think? You've known me long enough to know—'

I shouted at her to stop talking, and then I walked out.

'Do you know what, Rose?' Nina screamed, as I slammed the door. 'You don't deserve Jacob!'

I walked back to my house, but I was still shaken when I got inside. Joe was still lying on the sofa, a slow smile appearing on his face when I walked through the door.

'Oh, dear,' he said, taking in my tear-soaked face. 'I think you'd better come and tell me all about it.'

TWENTY

CARRIE

She has a purpose again – justice for Rose; this is what keeps her going. Each new day when she opens her eyes, she forgets for a fraction of a moment, and she can almost hear music drifting from Rose's bedroom. The strum of her guitar. Her soft throaty melodies. And then like a punch to her gut it hits Carrie that she will never again hear her daughter sing.

It's Thursday morning, not yet eight thirty, and she's just got off the phone with Tom. He called her from work, checking she's okay before his full-on day begins. Jacob got in a fight at school yesterday, he'd told Carrie. Almost broke a boy's nose. Carrie feels almost vindicated hearing this – it's proof that Jacob is capable of violence.

Carrie had let herself get lost in Tom's voice; despite her need for him being rooted in deception, she does like the man. Even if he is Jacob's father. 'Will you come over tonight?' she asks.

'I'll try,' he promises. 'It might be late, though.' There is so much unspoken between them, and Carrie prefers it this way. She's doing nothing wrong if no words are uttered.

She's not due in at work until ten, and she'd had to beg

Abigail for this shift. It's not good for Carrie to be at home, where all she can think about is Rose. At least today she has a couple of things to do to keep herself from drowning in an ocean of despair.

It's not easy to pull up outside Joe's flat. Too many memories swamp her mind, of when life was normal. When all she had to worry about was what they would watch on Netflix that night. *I'm forgetting the incessant flirting. The way Rose loathed him. It wasn't all picture-perfect.* She and Joe wouldn't have made it anyway; her leaving him has nothing to do with Rose's death, despite what he believes.

He answers the door in his pyjamas, his hair ruffled. His eyes grow wider as he registers that it's Carrie standing on his doorstep.

'How come you're here?' he says, looking behind her as if he expects to see someone with her.

Carrie places the large box of Joe's belongings on the doorstep and stands back. 'Just bringing the rest of your stuff. I've been having a clear-out.'

'Right,' he says, making no move to take the box. 'Are you... How are you?'

'I can't answer that question, and I wish people wouldn't ask it. What do you expect me to say? That I'm okay? Hunky-dory? I'll never be okay, Joe. Never.' She turns away.

'Carrie, wait! At least come in and have coffee. Or breakfast? I bet you haven't eaten. I'll do scrambled eggs. With tomatoes. How about it?'

Too little, way too late. 'I'm not going to have breakfast with you, Joe. Or coffee.'

'Please, Carrie.'

He's never begged her for anything before, and it convinces her to reconsider. What harm would a few minutes do? It's too early for Jacob to be up yet anyway. 'Okay, Joe. Coffee. Five minutes. Then I'm gone for good.'

The first thing she notices when she steps inside his flat is how musty it smells. Without a word she heads into the kitchen and throws open the small window. Dirty dishes lie stacked in the sink and her eyes fix on a scattering of breadcrumbs by the toaster. Joe was never the tidiest of men, but she's never before seen his flat in this state. It's as if he's given up on himself. On everything.

'I've been busy at work and the dishwasher's bust,' Joe mumbles, even though Carrie hasn't mentioned the state of his kitchen. 'And what's the point of clearing up? It's only me who has to see it – no one comes here.'

'I find that hard to believe,' Carrie says. 'I'm sure you wasted no time replacing me.'

He shakes his head. 'No, it's not like that. I don't want anyone else. I wanted *us* to work, Carrie.' He reaches for her hand. 'We still can.'

She pulls away. 'No. We're long past that being a possibility.'

Joe steps back and picks up two dirty mugs. 'Maybe when you've had more time... you know, to get—'

'Get what? Get over my daughter dying?'

'No, I didn't mean it like that, I—'

'Why don't you just get the kettle on?' she suggests.

Carrie takes the mugs from him and squeezes some wash-ing-up liquid onto a sponge. While she's here, she may as well clean up. It will keep her busy; standing still is the thing that crushes her. *Keep moving. Keep searching for a way to expose the truth.* And then she might just be able to find a way to live alongside her grief, for it to be merely a companion rather than an adversary.

'He'll bleeding well get away with it,' Joe says, when she's cleared up and they're seated at the table.

'Did you put that note through their door? Saying Jacob should be dead?' Tom had told her about it and Carrie had immediately thought of Joe. 'Because I don't need you to fight my battles for me. Do you hear me? Stay out of it.'

Joe picks up a slice of burnt toast he's made. The smell of it would normally awaken Carrie's hunger, but right now it turns her stomach. 'I don't know anything about that,' Joe says.

Carrie doesn't know what to believe. And she's not sure she cares either way whether it was Joe or some stranger. 'What makes you say Jacob will get away with it?' she asks.

'It's been weeks, and they still haven't got evidence to arrest him.' He shakes his head. 'I don't like how the police keep talking to me too. Like I'm guilty of something.'

'They're talking to everyone who was in Rose's life – not just you.'

'Still, that boy needs to be taken care of. Not only has he done that to Rose, but look what he's done to us too.'

'Stop, Joe. I keep telling you we're not over because of Rose. We're over because of *me*.'

But she agrees that Jacob needs to be dealt with – although not in Joe's way. Everyone deserves the right to a trial. To defend themselves. Carrie just needs to make sure the police find whatever they need to make that happen. 'The truth always comes out in the end,' Carrie says. 'Doesn't it?' She sips her coffee. Strong and yet too milky at the same time. It's as if her taste buds have died along with Rose.

Joe looks away. 'Yeah,' he says. 'I s'pose it does.'

'I've got to go,' Carrie says, standing and taking her cup to the sink. She won't bother washing it – she's already done enough for Joe.

He doesn't try to stop her, as she expected he might. But Carrie doesn't have time to dwell on what this means.

When she gets home after her shift, Michelle, the family liaison officer, is outside her house, waiting in her car. Carrie rushes up to the open window and leans in. 'Has something happened? Do you have news?'

Michelle shakes her head. 'Sorry. I'm just checking in. Can I come inside?'

Carrie wants to say no. She doesn't want company, and if Michelle can't offer any new information, then what's the point of talking to her? But she agrees, and once they're inside she boils the kettle.

'What exactly is happening?' Carrie asks. 'It's been weeks and Jacob hasn't even been arrested.'

'Remember, we've talked before about not accusing people without evidence. It's a dangerous game, Carrie. We can't arrest anyone until we've got all the evidence we need for a conviction. Otherwise it could damage our case.'

'Then what exactly is happening?'

Michelle places her hand on Carrie's shoulder. 'Please trust me when I say that we're doing all we possibly can. And without any DNA evidence, that's really challenging. There was no sexual attack which could lead us to someone. Nothing on Rose's body to give us any hint. But we're still following up on possible sightings, and we have a specialist team analysing the contents of her laptop. So far there's nothing. It can take weeks to trawl through all the CCTV as well.' She pauses. 'We'll find something, I promise. Whoever did this can't stay hidden forever.'

Carrie has heard enough. She knows the police are doing what they can but it's not enough. 'I have to go out now,' she says.

She sits in her car opposite Jacob's house. What she's doing could be considered criminal, but she doesn't care. This is nothing compared to taking someone's life. Besides, not one thing the police can do to her is worse than what she's already going through. Her daughter is gone, Rose's bright flame extinguished so easily.

Not for the first time, Carrie wonders if her daughter fought whoever did that to her. She can't imagine Rose making it easy for her attacker. But Michelle told her that it's likely she was attacked from behind, so perhaps Rose never even got to face her killer. To look Jacob in the eye and fix her last stare into his consciousness. Did Jacob have any marks or scratches on him when he came to the house the morning after? Carrie doesn't think so, yet how can she be sure when she wasn't looking out for that kind of thing?

It's just after six p.m. when she sees him walk up the drive. Something is wrong, though. He's not walking, he's staggering, clutching his stomach, doubling over as if he's in pain. She cranes her head but can't tell what's happened. Then she notices that it's not a red T-shirt he's wearing – what looks like blood has soaked his clothes. And then the door is opening and Jacob falls to the ground, while Lucy rushes forward, pulling out her phone.

It's time for Carrie to leave; later she can find out from Tom what's going on. Right now, despite her instinctive urge to protect and heal, she can't muster a single ounce of sympathy for Jacob Adams.

Poetic justice is what it is. Carrie is at home, surrounded by hollow silence. She makes herself a cup of tea, which will undoubtedly end up going cold, and messages Tom to see how his day has gone. She can't reveal that she knows Jacob's been hurt, but she hopes Tom will tell her what happened.

After an hour he still hasn't replied, and she begins to think that whatever kind of friendship she and Tom now share has been conjured by her mind. She's aware that grief can distort things, alter reality. She needs him, though. For Rose's sake. Carrie can't let this go; she'll do whatever she has to.

The doorbell interrupts her thoughts, and she freezes for a moment. It's probably Joe, interpreting her visit this morning as a sign that she'll take him back, even though Carrie insisted that was it. That's the trouble with Joe, he never sees beyond his own desires.

It rings again, an impatient chime, forcing her up. She'll tell him to leave her alone, she resolves, as she walks to the door. There's no space in her head for anything to do with Joe Aldridge.

But it's not Joe standing there; it's Tom, still dressed in his work clothes: a red silk tie and dark grey suit. His car is parked haphazardly outside. 'I'm sorry to just turn up like this. Can I come in?'

She opens the door wider and across the road sees Lia standing in her doorway yelling at the twins that their dinner's going cold. They're nowhere in view, and Carrie wonders how she can let them out of their sight, particularly after Rose. When Lia notices Carrie and Tom she stops and stares. *Let her think what she wants.* Carrie doesn't have time to worry about other people's judgement.

'Is everything okay?' She shuts the door and turns to Tom. Even though she knows what he's about to say, she forces her mind to become a blank canvas, ready to react appropriately. How should she react? She feels numb, as though she is an empty vessel.

'Jacob's been attacked, Carrie. He's in hospital.' He lifts the back of his hand to his head and rests it there for a moment.

Carrie reaches for his arm. 'I'm sorry. What happened?'

'He'd taken the dog for a walk and... There were three of them. They beat him and left him bleeding at the side of the road, not far from our home. He must have been on his way back. Somehow he managed to make it home and then... he just collapsed on the doorstep.'

'My God, that's awful. Was it kids? From school?' Even after everything, Carrie feels a wave of sadness that this has happened. This isn't what justice looks like.

'We don't know yet.' Tom takes her hand. 'I hate to ask this, but I need to get to the hospital and don't want to leave Ava on her own. You're the only person she wants. Would you... Do you think you could come to our house and just stay with her? She's been ill so she'll probably go to bed soon.'

There's no hesitation in her answer. 'I'm on my way.'

This is working out better than she could have hoped.

It's clear that Ava's been crying when she answers the door. She rushes into Carrie's arms, as a child ten years younger might do. For a second Carrie is too shocked to move, but then she wraps her arms around the child, glad that it feels so different to a hug from Rose.

'Everything's horrible,' Ava says.

Carrie smooths her hair. 'I know. I know. But we'll get through this, both of us, okay? Jacob will be all right.'

'That's just it,' Ava says. 'He probably deserves it, doesn't he? I feel horrible thinking that, but then I think of Rose and... I don't know what to think. Or feel. It was worse for her, wasn't it? At least Jacob's alive. She never made it.'

'Let's go in and we can talk about it. Shall I make us some hot chocolate?'

Ava nods. 'Yes, please.'

It doesn't take Carrie long to find everything; the kitchen is tidy and organised, much as she'd expect from Lucy.

'Are you having one too?' Ava asks, sitting at the table and pulling her feet up so she's cross-legged on the chair. Her hooded top is far too large for her, and Carrie wonders if it's Jacob's. Or even Tom's.

'I think I will,' Carrie says. 'Rose loved hot chocolate. If we ever ran out, there was trouble.' Carrie tries to smile but the gesture feels alien, as if the muscles in her mouth have unlearnt how to do it.

At the mention of Rose's name, Ava falls silent. It's a reminder to Carrie that she's not the only one grieving, even if hers is far deeper. She pours milk into a saucepan and lights the hob, before joining Ava at the table. 'Do you know what I do whenever I feel like I'm sinking?'

Ava looks up at her, her expectant eyes glistening. 'What?'

Carrie smiles. 'I imagine that Rose can see me, and I think... she wouldn't want me to be in this state. I'm still her mother. I have to keep being that role model she needed.' *If I ever was. Rose was disgusted by my relationship with Joe. But I've done it now, I've walked away from him.* 'She'd want me to soldier on, and try and find some comfort in the small things. Like having a cup of coffee.'

'Or hot chocolate?'

'Yep, definitely. And then that might help her be at peace. Wherever she is.'

Ava nods, her face brighter now. 'I'll try it. Can I ask you something, Carrie?'

'Anything at all.'

'What do you think she'd say to Jacob? And how would she want us to act around him? I can't even look at him. But then when he got attacked, I felt so sad and wanted to hug him. But I couldn't. Because Rose is always there in my head. It's like, part of me felt sorry for him and the other part feels like he deserves it.'

Carrie nods. 'I know how hard it is. He's your brother, after all. We just have to let the police find out what happened.' *But they're taking so long.* She hasn't been prepared for the long empty days and the feeling that nothing is moving forward. If there hadn't been a storm the day after the barbeque, they might have found something by now. 'They do say innocent until proven guilty, don't they?' she tells Ava, though Carrie can't apply this to her situation.

'We know we can't trust him, though. He keeps lying. About the argument, and about going to Nina's.'

'That's true, Ava. We all just have to wait for answers, I'm afraid.' But Carrie will make sure these come sooner than they might otherwise. 'I'd better check that milk before it boils,' she says.

They finish their drinks, and when Ava begins to yawn, Carrie suggests she goes to bed.

'I don't want to leave you on your own,' Ava insists. 'I can stay up a bit later, Mum and Dad won't care. Not with everything that's going on.'

'Don't worry about me. I need to check my emails and catch up on everything at work, so I can just sit and go through my phone. I'm sure either your mum or dad will come back soon.'

'I *am* a bit tired.' Ava stands and pushes in her chair.

'Yes, the yawning's being giving that away for the last half hour.'

Ava smiles and walks forward, wrapping her arms around Carrie. She says goodnight and heads upstairs, oblivious to the tears glimmering on Carrie's cheeks.

Jacob's room is a mess. His duvet lies in a heap on the floor, along with scattered piles of crumpled clothes. Textbooks and stationery cover the desk, and there's no order to anything. It makes things easier for Carrie; now she can carry out her search without worrying about putting things back as they were.

Even as she begins rummaging through Jacob's things, Carrie knows this is futile. The police have already searched his room, a forensic team carefully looking at every item, unlike her frenzied hunt. Still, he could have easily put something back in there that he'd kept elsewhere. The clothes he was wearing? Although he's bound to have washed those. Or thrown them away. She stops in her tracks when she finds a photo of Rose with Jacob, shoved underneath his wardrobe. Her head is nestled into the crook of his arm and he's looking down at her, smiling. The photo is bent out of shape, crumpled. In anger?

Carrie lets out a heavy sigh. It won't be evidence in the eyes of the police. She needs more than this. Pulling herself up, she's about to open the wardrobe when a sound disturbs her. She turns slowly, sensing that someone is there, though she didn't hear footsteps approaching, even in the still of this night.

'Is this what you're looking for?'

TWENTY-ONE

CARRIE

Ava stands in the doorway, watching her. She's dressed in a pink fleece onesie and holds a mobile phone in her hand, waving it at Carrie. Is she about to call the police? Quickly, Carrie searches her mind for a valid reason that she's in here rummaging through Jacob's possessions.

There isn't one. 'I... um—'

'Maybe this will help you,' Ava says. 'She holds out the phone, urging Carrie to take it.

'What is that?' she asks, but now she's closer to it, Carrie already knows. What Ava holds in her hand is Rose's mobile phone; she'd recognise it anywhere. The case is rose gold, and if she looks closer she'll see initials engraved on it. R.N. Carrie had advised her not to get it engraved, insisting that when Rose wanted to replace it nobody would buy it. *I don't care*, Rose had declared. *I'll just give it away, and whoever gets it will always have a reminder of Rose Nyler!* She'd laughed, and Carrie can almost hear it now. A piece of her daughter, here in this room with them.

She stares at Ava. 'Where did you get that, Ava? How have you got Rose's phone?'

Ava shuffles past her and sits on Jacob's unmade bed. 'Please don't be cross with me. I... I didn't know what to do. And then when we were talking downstairs before, you made me think about what Rose would do. I went to bed but I couldn't sleep; it was making me sick. I think Rose would want you to have this.' She places it in Carrie's hand.

Carrie examines it, turning it over to confirm what she already knows. 'Ava, I need to know exactly why and how you've got Rose's phone.'

A few seconds of heavy silence follow before Ava answers. 'I'm scared, Carrie. I don't know what to do.'

'Just tell me, then we can decide together, okay?' It's an effort to hold herself together. What is she about to hear? How can Ava be tied up in all this?

'I found it in here. In Jacob's room. A few days ago. He must have had it on him or something. It was in the pocket of his dressing gown. He never uses that thing. Mum bought it for Christmas years ago and it just hangs on the back of his door. Pointless.'

'What were you doing in his room?'

'Same as you. Looking for something. Anything. I think mostly I wanted to find something that would mean he couldn't have done anything to Rose. But instead I found that.' She points to the phone, tears falling onto Jacob's sheets. 'I couldn't tell anyone. I got scared. What if the police thought I was lying and that I had something to do with it?'

'No,' Carrie says. 'I know you didn't. But we need to put it back, Ava. Exactly where you found it. And then we need to tell the police it's there. All you have to do is be honest, and tell them the truth.' *This is it. The evidence that proves Jacob killed Rose.* Michelle had told her the phone was switched off before the barbeque, and there was no way to track it unless someone turned it on again, so it must have been off this whole time. Jacob is smart.

'Is this why you're so sure Jacob's guilty?' Carrie asks. 'Why you've been so angry with him?'

Ava nods.

'I'm sorry you've had to carry this burden. That must have been difficult.'

'But will it work?' Ava asks. 'When the police find it, Jacob could just say Rose left it here. Or... they might say it was me who put it there. Jacob could say anything – he's already lied!'

Carrie sees the fear in her eyes. 'That's not going to happen. You just have to trust me, okay?'

Ava doesn't respond.

'Leave it with me,' Carrie tells her. 'I'll sort this all out. Why don't you go to bed – you've got school in the morning.'

Slowly Ava stands. 'Okay.' At the door she turns back to Carrie. 'I'm sorry I didn't tell you straight away. I was scared.'

'I know. None of that matters because you've told me now. Hurry to bed – I don't know how much time we have before your mum or dad gets back.'

Ava leaves, and Carrie watches her every step until she's out of sight, her chest constricting with the effort of maintaining her composure. Now that she's alone she no longer has to hold back the pain that's exploding inside her, crippling her. She sinks to the carpet and tries to steady her breathing. She needs to focus her thoughts on an object – anything – so she fixes on a blue exercise book lying on the floor. Something normal, to ground her. It doesn't work, and her eyes drift to Jacob's shiny white trainer lying upside down next to it. And then all she can see is Jacob kicking Rose repeatedly until she has no more breath within her. It's not the way Rose died – she was strangled – but that doesn't matter. Now the image is in Carrie's head it's all she can see.

It's only when car lights illuminate the room that she stirs into action. She needs to get this phone hidden and rush downstairs before the front door opens.

TWENTY-TWO

LUCY

Hospitals are never silent, even this late at night. As much as I try, I can't drown out the whirring and beeping, or shoes squeaking along tiled floors. These noises are my companions as I sit by Jacob's side. He drifts in an out of consciousness, and it's hard to tell if he knows I'm here, despite the fact that I'm holding his hand.

His eyes are white pools in a ghastly sea of crimson and purple, and there's barely a trace of untouched skin on his face, only the bloodied bruising that looks as though it will never heal. And beneath the stiff hospital bed sheets, Jacob's ribs have been broken – every last one.

A nurse comes in to check his monitor and when she's gone, I once again take his hand. 'Jacob,' I say softly. 'Can you hear me?'

His eyes flicker like a butterfly's wings before he slowly manages to open them fully. He frowns and winces. 'Mum.'

He's already spoken to a police officer – no one we know from Rose's case, just an unfamiliar PC who doesn't seem to care about the damage that's been done to my son, and only wants to tick off questions. I listened while Jacob answered what he could: No, he didn't know them. There were three of them. Older, it seems. They came out of nowhere. He let go of the lead and Cooper ran off. Probably in fear. Our dog would never have abandoned Jacob otherwise.

I still have questions for Jacob, and he doesn't have the best track record of openness when it comes to being interviewed by officers.

'How are you feeling?' I ask.

'My throat's dry.' He tries to clear it, but it only causes him to wince again.

I use the remote control to lift the bed so he's upright, and fill a cup with water. 'Here, have some of this.' He lets me lift it to his mouth, even though he must hate every second of needing help. Of being vulnerable. Even as a small child he was fiercely independent, wanting to do everything for himself. Unlike Ava. He gulps the water without pausing, then with shaking hands attempts to put it back on the table.

'Let me.' I take the cup from him and place it on the tray beside his bed.

'Cooper,' he says.

'We don't know where he is. Your dad went out looking with Ava but no luck yet.'

'If anything happens to him, I'll... Those bastards.'

'We'll find him,' I assure Jacob. 'He's a big Labrador – someone's bound to notice him without an owner. Ava's already posted a picture of him on the local Facebook group.' I only silently acknowledge how he looks away when I mention his sister's name. 'Jacob, listen. Did you tell the police everything? You really don't know who did this to you? It wasn't anyone from school?'

'No. I've never seen them before. They were older than me. Maybe thirty. I've never seen them around. I thought I would die, Mum. I really thought... this is it.'

I squeeze his hand. 'You're here, and you're safe. Dad and I won't leave your side, okay?'

A tear forms in his eye. 'And then what? I still have to go to school and sit my exams. Live my life. And what will it be next? Everyone thinks I killed Rose, so I deserve to die.' He turns away from me. 'Even my own family think I'm guilty.'

'I don't,' I assure him.

'What about Dad? And Ava?' Thankfully, he doesn't wait for an answer. 'I want to go back to London. I hate it here. Life was good before, and now...'

'We can't go back there, Jacob. You know what happened to Ava. This whole move was for her.'

'She can still go to a different school. It doesn't have to be the place she was bullied.'

Hearing those words makes me cringe. That word doesn't even begin to describe what happened to Ava at her old school. And now a similar thing is happening to Jacob. Only this is far worse.

'Do you trust me?' I ask him.

The nod he attempts makes him wince again.

'Try not to move too much. I just need you to believe that I will sort this out, okay?'

He closes his eyes. 'There's nothing you can do, Mum. Not when the police think it's me. They're not even looking for anyone else, are they?'

'Listen,' I say, leaning forward. 'I'm sorting everything, okay? You just have to hang in there until you're well enough to leave here.'

'Okay.' He opens his eyes again and looks towards the door. 'Are Dad and Ava coming to see me?'

'Yes, they'll be here soon.'

'Will they? Dad hates me. And Ava can't stand being anywhere near me.'

'Your dad doesn't hate you, Jacob.' *He just needs to remember that he loves you.*

I stay with my son until he seems to fall asleep, and when I'm sure that he is, I step outside the room to call Tom. I'll be staying the whole night, and I need some clothes and my toothbrush. I'm just pulling my phone from my pocket when I see him walking towards me, scanning the rooms.

Despite the tension between us lately, I rush over to him and hug him, trying to ignore how his body stiffens.

'How's he doing? Is he okay?' Tom asks, pulling back.

I repeat what the doctor has told me: that he'll be okay, and that he's very lucky considering the scale of the attack. 'There were three of them, Tom. Three grown men!'

Tom shakes his head. 'I know. It's truly awful. Poor Jacob. I can't even imagine how terrified he must have been. What have the police said?'

'They're looking into it. Checking CCTV in the area.'

Tom lowers his voice. 'We got another note through the door. Luckily it was me who found it and not Ava.'

We haven't told her about the first note, wanting to protect her as much as we can, but if this keeps happening, it's only a matter of time before she finds out. 'What did it say?'

'I took it to the police on my way here, but it said, *Rest in peace.*'

My breath catches in my throat. 'So it could be the people who attacked him? Jesus, Tom, how are we supposed to keep him safe?'

'At least in here he'll be okay. And then we'll have to sort out what to do when he comes home.'

'Where's Ava?'

'I... had to ask Carrie to stay with her. Ava wouldn't let anyone else come. She didn't want me to leave and Carrie was the only person she wanted to be with.'

I stare at Tom, unable to comprehend what he's said. 'Carrie? And she agreed to come to our house?'

He nods. 'She likes Ava and wanted to help. She was horrified about what's happened to Jacob. She's been helping Ava make some missing posters for Cooper. It can't be easy for her, can it?'

'But she hates Jacob.'

'No, she doesn't. She just needs to know why he lied. And so do I, Lucy. It doesn't sit right with me. I can't pretend that it does.'

And we're right back here again. At loggerheads. Neither of us capable of shifting our perspective. 'He's your son, Tom. That's all that matters. We need to support him.'

'Even if he's—'

'Don't!' I hiss. 'Don't even say it!'

There is only acrimony in Tom's expression. Nothing else. This move to Surrey was supposed to put things right for us; instead, all it's done is widen the cracks that were already there. 'Anyway, I'm here now. You can go home and I'll stay with Jacob.'

'You'll sit with him all night?'

He nods. 'Yes, Lucy. That's why I'm here.'

I walk away and head towards the lift, but before reaching it I turn back, imagining I will go back to him, make an attempt to reclaim my marriage. But when I see him take a seat outside Jacob's room, and bury his head in his hands instead of going inside, I know it's far too late for that.

The house is eerily silent when I get back, devoid of signs of life. Perhaps I misunderstood Tom, and he'd actually taken Ava to Carrie's instead of her coming here. That would make more sense; Carrie hasn't wanted to set foot in our home since Rose went missing.

But there's a light on in the kitchen, and I know Tom always checks lights before he leaves the house, so I head towards it, preparing to face Carrie. She looks up when I enter, but doesn't say a word. She's sitting alone; there is no sign of my daughter.

'Where's Ava?' I ask, dread slowly snaking its way through my body.

'She's asleep of course. It's late, isn't it? She went to bed a couple of hours ago.'

My shoulders relax. Even though Carrie has a glass of water in front of her, I offer her tea or coffee, which she immediately declines. 'Thanks for coming tonight. I know this must be hard for you.'

She watches me while I boil the kettle and find a mug. 'I'm doing it for Ava,' she says. 'That's not hard.'

'Well, I appreciate it.'

'How is Jacob doing, then?'

'Not good.' Is this what she wants to hear? Perhaps it helps her to know that he's suffering. I can't bear this thought. 'Carrie, he didn't do anything to Rose—'

She holds up her hand. 'Please don't. I didn't come here to argue about our children. Like I said, I'm here for Ava. And Tom. He needed to be with Jacob, didn't he?' She begins to stand but I stop her.

'Please, can we talk for a minute?'

'I don't think that's a good idea, is it? Your son's being questioned in the death of my daughter so this can't be... appropriate.'

I leave the kettle to boil and sit at the table. 'It's just us, Carrie. Two mums who want answers for our children.'

Her expression seems to soften but she remains standing. 'You know that feeling, Lucy, that gut instinct when it comes to your kids? The one you feel right here?' She thumps her chest. 'Well, mine tells me that Jacob has something to do with Rose's death. I don't know exactly how he's tied up in it, but I know for sure that he is.' She pauses to take a sip of water. 'And I'm guessing yours tells you that it couldn't have been him?'

'That's right. I know my son would never—'

'Well, we can't both be right, can we?'

There's no reply I can offer to that, and I won't argue with a woman who's just lost her daughter. Instead, I silently watch as she leaves without a glance backwards.

And then a cold shiver passes through me at the thought that a woman who hates my son so much has been alone in my house with my daughter.

TWENTY-THREE

LUCY

The days pass slowly as I wait for Jacob to heal in hospital. At least he will be safe here; the nurses know to only let Tom, Ava or me in his room, and there are CCTV cameras all over the hospital. Still, I won't rest until he's home.

Tom and I take it in turns to stay by Jacob's side, passing each other as we swap shifts with little more than barely discernible smiles. This is the first time I can remember Tom taking time off work for any reason other than a holiday I've coaxed him into taking. I'm keeping too much from him, and our marriage teeters on the brink of an abyss. I see how much he's there for Carrie at the moment, and what kind of person would I be to object to the amount of time he spends talking to her? She needs him, and along with that, I need space from him. From us. I will deal with whatever fallout there is later; right now, keeping Jacob safe is all I can focus on.

At least Cooper has been found – he was wandering around for a whole night before someone spotted him and took him to the vet. It's a small flicker of light in the darkness that surrounds us all.

On Jacob's fourth day in hospital, the doctor tells me that he should be well enough to go home the next day. It's what I've been planning for, yet the thought of this moment fills me with dread. Everything is about to change, and there's no way to determine what will happen.

Tom has to go back to work on the morning Jacob is discharged, so I pick our son up alone. DC Keller from the murder squad is due at the house this afternoon, to once again question Jacob. At least we knew where we were with DC Gillary. And his manner was kind. But when the new DC took over, Jacob seemed to close up even more. Today there will be more questions about Rose. More veiled accusations. If this is going to work, then we need to move quickly.

I tell Jacob what I've planned when we get home, only to be greeted with a stunned silence. The bags I've packed for us are already in the car; all I have to do is finish writing the letters I will leave for Ava and Tom. It's tearing me up to leave her, even for this short time, but I know she will be safe here with Tom. Right now it's Jacob who needs saving.

'We can't just leave,' Jacob says. 'Where will we go? The police will find us.' Panic works its way into his voice. 'We'll be arrested.'

I take a deep breath. 'I won't lie to you, Jacob – I don't have all the answers. And doing this definitely won't be easy. I just need to get you out of here, somewhere safe, and then we can work out what to do. Whoever did this to you could have killed you. Think about those notes, Jacob. We have no idea who's sending them. Maybe they're just meant to scare you but it could be more than that. I can't sit by and let people do this to you.'

He studies my face, not speaking for a moment. 'What about Ava and Dad?'

'They can't be a part of this – I've got to protect them from what we're doing. Your dad could lose his job, and Ava needs to stay in school. Her life's already been disrupted enough. I just need to buy us some time until we can figure this all out, or until the police find out who killed Rose. Then everyone will know and you'll be free to come home. To live your life without fearing for it.'

Jacob shakes his head. 'Mum, this is crazy. Even I can see that.'

'I know, but we don't have a choice.'

He continues to stare at me with wide eyes. 'What about school? My exams?'

'I've thought of that. I'll get you a tutor for maths – that's the only subject you might need a bit of help with. And I'll help you revise for everything else. You just have to be focused. Getting away from here will help you.'

Seconds tick by and he doesn't speak. 'Okay,' he says, eventually, shaking his head. 'But won't we be in serious trouble?'

I've had days to think this through. 'You haven't been arrested yet – you're only a person of interest. DC Keller hasn't told you not to leave home, has she?'

'They'll assume I'm guilty if I run away.'

'I'll make it clear to your dad that we're going for your protection. No other reason. Okay?'

'Yeah,' he says. 'But where will we go?'

'Cornwall,' I say. 'I've found a cottage in St Ives we can stay in.'

'That's miles away!'

'That's the point, Jacob. We need some distance. Space to think straight.'

Eventually he agrees, but he's far from convinced.

I reach into my bag and pull out the two cheap mobile phones I've bought. 'These are for us,' I explain. 'We have to switch off our mobiles now and not use them again until we can come back home. It's really important, Jacob.' I hand him his new phone. 'And in a minute, I'm cutting my hair much shorter. It won't take long. And you can wear a cap until we can get some clippers. Your dad's have broken.' Jacob's thick, dark hair is too distinctive.

'But why do we have to do that?' Jacob protests. 'You said we're not doing anything wrong by leaving!'

'Because you were attacked, Jacob. I don't want anyone tracking you down. There are crazy people out there. We need to be completely off-grid.' *And I don't want to admit this to myself, but I'm terrified the police will uncover something else. Another lie. Evidence that can't be refuted.*

Jacob opens his mouth, probably to object, but then he sighs. 'I don't have a choice, do I?'

'No, neither of us does. And there's one other thing,' I warn. 'I need you to promise me that you'll always tell me the truth, no matter what it might be. I will be by your side no matter what. Okay? But I need to know you're being honest, Jacob. There have been too many lies.'

'I promise,' he says.' But he's not looking at me when he utters these words.

He falls asleep in the car, still exhausted by the brutal battering his body received. I'm grateful for this; it's respite for him and it means he doesn't see the state I'm in after having to leave Ava behind. I only pray that the words I've written for her will help her to understand why I'm doing this. And it won't be for long. Jacob is innocent and the truth will come out.

As we leave Surrey behind and head through Salisbury, some of the tension leaves my body. I know running like this will bring a whole set of new problems, but at least my son is safe.

While he stirs beside me, still softly sleeping, I turn on Heart radio and try to block everything out. Ava. Tom. The realisation that now there is no turning back.

· · ·

Even though the sky is interspersed with grey clouds when we arrive in St Ives, it's pleasantly warm, and Jacob is almost smiling as he steps out of the car, the fresh sea air surrounding us.

'It's nice, isn't it,' I say, breathing in deeply. 'Ava would love it here. We'll come back here – all of us – when this is over.'

He doesn't reply but gazes around, and when I take his arm and lead him towards the cottage, he's still silently taking everything in. At least his silence isn't an objection.

It's a pretty building with a thatched roof and pale yellow walls. The sky-blue door looks freshly painted, and it's just the kind of place I would have imagined Tom and I retiring to one day. Before all of this. Now our future is too fragile, too unstable to have any romantic notions in my head.

'Jayne Cassidy, the owner, said she'd meet us at five p.m.' I tell Jacob. It's almost half past, and I hope she's still here, and hasn't assumed we're not coming.

I press the doorbell and stand back to wait, smiling at Jacob to show him that everything will be okay now. His face is still badly bruised, but I've already planned how I'll explain it.

The door opens almost immediately. Jayne is older than she sounded on the phone, and must be at least in her sixties. 'Hello,' she says. 'You must be Kate?'

I hold out my hand to shake hers. 'Yes, and this is my son, Josh.'

She turns to Jacob, and her eyes widen when she takes in his appearance. 'Lovely to meet you,' she says, and I'm grateful she doesn't mention his bruises. 'Come in, then, and I'll show you around. I'm sorry but I'll have to be quick as I need to be somewhere at six thirty.'

'We got stuck in traffic,' I explain. 'I think I underestimated how long it would take to get here.'

She smiles. 'Oh, don't worry. London is a long way from

here. And you'll have had to make plenty of stops. That's a lot of driving for one person.'

Inside, she leads us through a narrow hallway, with a door on each side leading to the living room and kitchen. A winding staircase stands at the end of the cottage, and I'm struck by how clean and fresh the place looks. Exactly like the pictures I'd seen online.

Upstairs are two small bedrooms, both with double beds, one of which overlooks the sea. 'You have this one,' I say to Jacob, and Jayne smiles at us.

'I have to say,' Jayne says, 'I wasn't expecting to get any takers for the property this soon after the Easter holidays. I was planning on doing a bit of redecorating while it's quiet, actually.' She glances at Jacob. 'But that can wait. I'm happy that you want to stay here, of course. Are you not in school, then, Josh?'

Jacob glances at me. 'Yeah, I am. I just—'

'Josh is having a few issues at school,' I interject. 'With bullying. I wanted him to get away for a week or two, just until his exams start. So that he can focus on schoolwork without worrying about... people. The school agreed it was a good idea.'

'How awful,' she says, still eyeing Jacob carefully. 'Is that what happened to your face? My daughter was bullied at school, you know. And now she's a very successful doctor. Partner in her GP surgery.' She smiles. 'So, don't you let them get you down, okay? Those people will amount to nothing when they leave school, but you'll fly high.'

Jacob glances at me again before nodding. 'Thanks, Mrs Cassidy.'

'Oh, it's Jayne, dear. We're not very formal around here. You'll see.' She turns back to me. 'Won't he be missing out on important things at school, though?'

'We'll be studying here, won't we, Josh? Every day. Home schooling. And I'll be getting him a maths tutor. He's doing very well in all the other subjects. Actually, Jayne, I don't suppose you know anyone? Or know where I could find someone local to help?'

'Hmm, I can't think of anyone offhand, but I can get my daughter Hazel to post something on the local Facebook group. I don't bother with all that myself, but she's good at that stuff.'

'Thank you, I'd really appreciate that. The sooner we can find someone, the better.'

'Of course, dear, leave it with me.' She glances at her watch. 'I'd better get going. Now, I've left a few things in the kitchen for you. Bread, cheese, ham, milk, biscuits and some butter. I hope that keeps you going until you get to the shops.'

Thanking her, I rummage in my bag for my purse. 'You said on the phone cash would be okay?' I don't look at her as I say this. I already feel bad for misleading her.

'Yes, yes, that's fine. I know most places avoid it like the plague nowadays, but I prefer it. It's nice to know your money actually exists! I don't like everything being online.' She laughs, and I try my best to smile, to hide that my hands are shaking from all the lies I've fed this kind woman.

I hand her the envelope of cash I've already prepared. 'This will cover two weeks, but as I said on the phone, we may need to stay a bit longer.'

'No problem,' she says, taking the money. 'I don't have another booking until the May half-term so there's a bit of flexibility. I'll need to know your plans in advance, though, if you don't mind?'

'Of course.'

We say goodbye and Jacob and I stand by the living room window, watching as she heads to her red Volkswagen Polo.

'She was nice,' Jacob says. '*Josh*. Really, Mum?'

'I wanted a name with the same initial. I thought maybe it would make things a bit easier.'

'Why didn't you use my middle name? You're using yours.'

'Just trying to be careful. Besides, Sullivan's too rare a name.'

He doesn't say anything but stares through the window at the waves swallowing up the shore. I look at the bruises on his face, the reminder of why we're here, and push away the sadness I feel that I won't see Ava tonight. I won't be there to put away the book that will have slipped onto her duvet, wide open, when she falls asleep reading in bed.

Jacob reaches for my arm. 'We'll be all right, Mum. Now that we're here. Everything will be okay.'

I nod, and turn to watch the sea. Boats bob on the turquoise water, and there are still people scattered around the beach. 'How about we go and get fish and chips for dinner?' I suggest. 'It's getting a bit late to cook now and that drive's tired me out.'

'Yeah, I'd like that.'

'Just remember you can't use your old mobile or even turn it on, okay? Not even for a second.'

'We sound like fugitives,' Jacob says, and he chuckles. It's the first time I've seen him smile since Rose went missing, and I can't help but wonder how he's able to smile now.

Later, when Jacob's in bed, I head out for a walk along the beach. The air is chilly now, and I wrap my cardigan tighter around my body and fold my arms. It does little to fend off the breeze, and the sea crashes angrily against the rocks. It's twilight now, and the beach has emptied. I try to picture what Ava and Tom are doing at this moment, but my brain can't grasp any image. Their lives will be in even more turmoil because of my decision to run. *Please don't hate me.* I say this aloud to the sea, repeating it over and over. *I had no choice.*

When a mobile phone rings, it takes me a moment to register that it's mine, unfamiliar as I am with the ringtone of my new phone.

'Kate? It's Jayne Cassidy.'

My stomach somersaults. She's found out who we are and has probably called the police. I force out some words. 'Hi Jayne, is everything okay?'

'Yes, dear, sorry to call so late. I just wanted to let you know that I've found a tutor for you. He's a friend of my daughter's called Mitch. She says he's lovely and he has availability at the moment. I explained a bit of your situation and he really wants to help. Shall I send you his number?'

'Yes please, that's great. Thanks, Jayne.' I exhale with relief.

'Oh, it's no problem. I'm happy to help. Poor Josh, he really looks like he's been in the wars, and it's not fair that he has to miss school. Hopefully Mitch will keep him on track for his maths at least.'

'Yes, that's what he needs help with. He'll be okay with the other subjects.'

'I'm sure he will, dear. Lovely boy. Anyway, I'll let you get on with your night.'

We say goodbye and I sink to the sand and watch the ocean, trying to let it calm me. This is what it's going to be like living here – constantly looking over our shoulders, waiting to be exposed. The sooner this is over, the better, for all our sakes.

TWENTY-FOUR

CARRIE

Four days ago, she'd had it all figured out. Carrie had tucked Rose's mobile into Jacob's dressing gown pocket, right where Ava had found it. And all Carrie had to do was work out the best way of telling the police. She could have told Michelle, but surely that would raise questions about what Carrie was doing rooting through Jacob's bedroom. Carrie's no expert, but she couldn't risk throwing doubt on the validity of the evidence. It needed to come from Ava. But when Carrie had texted her after she'd got home that night, Ava had replied saying that she couldn't do it, and that she was freaking out. As much as Carrie had wanted to try and persuade her, she is mindful that Ava is only twelve.

And then she got the call from Tom, which is why she's now sitting in his kitchen, with Ava's questioning gaze on her.

'I can't believe she's done this,' Tom says. Understandably, he's distraught, and he paces the kitchen, while Ava sits at the table, rereading the letter Lucy has written her. Every few seconds she looks up at Carrie, who can tell that Ava is desperate for them to speak alone.

'Tell me again what exactly her note says,' Carrie says, taking Tom's arm to stop him pacing. It's making her uneasy, and she needs to get a grip on this situation. There is too much at stake.

Tom sighs. 'It just says she's sorry, but she needs to keep Jacob safe and this is the only way. They'll be back when this is all worked out, when the police have found out who did that to Rose, or at least when they stop considering that he might be involved.'

A swell of anger rises in Carrie's body. She needs to be calm for Tom and Ava, though. With Lucy gone, they will need her. And she needs them. 'Okay, let's talk this through. But I can't do that while you're pacing around.' She pulls out a chair. 'Please, Tom.'

When he nods, it feels strange that she is the one in control now.

Carrie takes a deep breath. She needs to keep Tom onside. 'I can understand why Lucy's gone. I'm not agreeing with it in any way, course I'm not – but as a mother, I think she's just done what's necessary to protect her son.'

With a glance at Ava, Tom shakes his head. 'She also has another child. She can't just think about Jacob. We're supposed to be a family. What happened to that?'

'I know.' Carrie turns to Ava and reaches across the table for her hand. 'How are you doing?'

'I don't like it,' Ava says. 'But... I sort of get it. Mum refuses to believe Jacob has anything to do with what happened. She's blind to it. So that's why she's done this.' She turns to Tom. 'Will Mum get into trouble? For taking Jacob away when the police wanted to speak to him? Isn't that like harbouring a fugitive?'

'I don't know,' Tom says. 'Possibly. But Jacob hasn't been arrested. I think DC Keller's wondering why they've gone. All I could do was show her the letters. Listen, why don't you get ready for bed while I sort out what we can do?'

Reluctantly, she stands, picking up the letter and folding it neatly. 'But will Carrie stay?'

Carrie smiles. 'Oh, I don't think—'

'Please stay with us,' Ava begs.

Carrie turns to Tom, who offers a nod. 'Okay, then. Just for one night, though.'

When Ava disappears upstairs, Tom begins pacing again. 'I can't believe Lucy's done this. She didn't say a word about what she was planning. Why? This isn't just about her wanting to protect my career, as she claims. This goes deeper than that. It must do.'

Carrie senses her opportunity. 'You're probably right. This is about the fact that the two of you don't agree on Jacob's innocence. It's so divisive, Tom. Can you see that?'

He stares at her for a moment before nodding. 'But Lucy leaving like this is even more so. How can I forgive her? Leaving me is one thing, but to leave Ava behind? That's unforgivable.'

There are so many things Carrie could say to defend Lucy, to chip away at Tom's anger. But she needs him to feel like this, because she is right where she needs to be: in this house. She likes being around Ava; it allows her to feel like a mum still. That urge to protect hasn't been eradicated because Rose is gone. It's as strong as ever, so she needs to channel that energy somewhere. And knowing how much Rose meant to Ava is a comfort to Carrie.

'Let's just try to focus on Ava,' she tells Tom. 'That's all we can do.'

A thin, sad smile stretches across his face. 'I like hearing you say *we*. It means a lot, Carrie.'

A wave of guilt rushes over her, but she won't let it deter her. 'I bet you're hungry,' she says. If she's using Tom in this way, then at least she'll do as much as she can for him. 'Let me check the cupboards. I can't promise it will be a gourmet meal, but anything's better than being hungry, isn't it?'

Later, while Tom's working, she goes upstairs to check on Ava. First, though, she pops her head into Jacob's room and reaches behind the door for the dressing gown.

It's gone.

Which means so, too, has the phone.

Don't jump to conclusions – maybe Ava has it.

Carrie doesn't expect the child to be awake when she slowly opens the door and peeps in, but then Ava calls her name.

'Yes, it's me. Are you okay?'

Ava pulls herself up in bed. 'No. I need to talk to you Carrie. I'm worried about Mum, and about the phone.' She rubs her eyes. 'You haven't told the police, have you?'

Carrie glances at the door before sitting on the floor by Ava's bed. 'I gave you my word, didn't I? But the thing is, Ava – the phone's gone. I just checked and Jacob's dressing gown is missing. Which means they must have packed it to take with them. Unless... you know where it is?'

Ava frowns. 'No, I don't. Then her mouth hangs open. 'What if Mum saw it and... and that's what made them go? She could be protecting Jacob from the police! What if it's not about his safety at all?'

'Ava, I know this is upsetting, but please try to be calm. We can't make assumptions. The truth will come out. If – and it's a big if – Lucy is doing that, then it will all catch up with her.' *And will what I'm doing catch up with me?*

'It's Dad I feel sorry for,' Ava says. Mum's just shut him out and he's done nothing wrong! Why couldn't she just tell him what she was doing?'

Carrie moves closer and puts her arm around Ava. 'Listen, people follow their hearts and do what they think is right in the heat of the moment. You and your dad just need to be

there for each other, and help each other through this awful
time.'

'I'm sorry, Carrie.'

'What for?'

'For not talking to the police. Then the phone would have
been found by now and Jacob would be arrested, wouldn't he?'

Carrie nods. 'Most likely. But what's done is done.'

She gets up to leave and Ava grabs her arm. 'Will you be
there for us, Carrie? I know you've lost Rose, but—'

'Of course I will. Don't you ever worry about that.'

But standing outside Ava's door, Carrie wonders if this is a
promise she'll be able to keep.

It feels strange to be in Lucy and Tom's guest bedroom, lying
under the freshly made sheets Tom's put on just for her. It's a
small room, but neat and clean, and there's a vase of dried
flowers on the chest of drawers. The unfamiliar smell of fabric
conditioner is too flowery, too sweet for her liking. But at least
she's here.

She thinks about Tom, lying in his own bed, the other side
of it conspicuously vacant, and she wonders how he's feeling.
Does he miss Lucy? Or is the chasm between them wide
enough for him to feel only anger? However awful he might be
feeling, it can't touch her pain. His child hasn't been murdered.
But still, his life has been ripped apart by this. Lucy leaving has
given Carrie an opportunity she has to take, no matter how
wrong it feels to mislead Tom.

It's past midnight now and she's thirsty. Making her way to
the stairs, she notices Tom's door is open so she peers in. He's
not in bed yet, so she assumes he must be working in his study
in the converted loft. Quietly she tiptoes downstairs, noticing
how soft the carpet that's so much thicker than hers is against
her bare feet.

'Couldn't sleep?'

Tom's voice startles her. He's in the living room, sitting on the sofa with his laptop balanced on his knees.

'Just needed some water,' Carrie says, peering into the darkened room. Only the glare from his computer lights his face. She turns to leave but changes her mind, stepping into the living room so she can see Tom more clearly. 'Can I ask you something?'

He raises his eyebrows. 'Yes, of course.'

She walks over to him and sits beside him on the sofa. 'What did you tell the police? They were meant to talk to Jacob after school yesterday, weren't they?'

Tom nods. 'DC Keller turned up and there was nobody here. That's when I got the call. I rushed back from work and found the letters. Even if the police hadn't been due to speak to Jacob, I would have told them. I can't let myself get tangled up in that. My career would be over. I was honest with them and said I have no idea where they'll have gone. That's the truth, Carrie. No idea. I've called her parents and they haven't heard from her. Because neither of them is in the best of health, she didn't even tell them what's been going on. She didn't want them to worry and insist on coming all the way down from Yorkshire.'

'I can see why she doesn't want them to know,' Carrie offers. 'My mum died a couple of years ago and if she hadn't, then Rose's death would have finished her off.' Telling Tom this, a pang of sadness hits her as she remembers she is now the only one left of her family.

'I'm sorry,' Tom says. 'You've been through so much.'

'What about your parents?' Carrie asks, to deflect from her pain.

'They live in London, but I haven't told them either. We're... not that close unfortunately. We talk on the phone every few weeks and it's all very polite, but that's about the extent of our relationship. And I have a brother in New Zealand. They're all very far removed from me.'

'That must be hard.'

He curls his lips. 'It's just the way it's always been. Since the kids have got older none of them have shown much interest in Ava or Jacob either.' He turns to Carrie. 'Can I ask you something? How have you found it in your heart to do all this for us? Be here for Ava. And for me. How do you do it when Jacob might—'

'Because you and Ava are nothing to do with it. We are not our children's actions; they make their own choices. And you... you've always seen my side of it. You didn't just rush to Jacob's defence, even though he's your son.'

'Because I'm a lawyer, Carrie. I deal with what's right and wrong every day. At least according to our law. Everything is black and white with my work, and that's how I understand the world. I don't do well with shades in between.' He sighs. 'I realise that probably makes me sound... narrow-minded?'

Somehow, even though she sees the world differently, she understands. 'No, it doesn't. I get it. And your support has meant everything to me, when I've felt so... so alone. Joe's just... Well, I don't need to tell you what he is, and as for Rose's dad – he couldn't give a damn. He didn't even make it over for her funeral.' The tears that fall aren't forced; Carrie is sinking and she needs to save herself.

Without a word, Tom pulls her close to him and holds her tightly, just like he did that time in her flat. This man, who is another woman's husband, is holding her as if she is everything in the world to him.

'Thank you,' she whispers close to his ear. Her lips brush against his skin, and she knows immediately what she needs to do. She cups his face in her hands and turns his head, her mouth finding his, tentatively. Carrie doesn't know if he'll respond, but what has she got to lose? He doesn't stop her, and within seconds he is kissing her back, pressing into her urgently, his hands exploring her body.

After a moment he pulls away. 'I'm sorry,' he says. 'I'm so sorry.'

'No, don't stop.' She pulls him back and loses herself in him.

And then there is no going back for either of them.

TWENTY-FIVE

ROSE

There was one thing you couldn't stop me doing, and that was seeing Ava. We'd grown close over those months, and I wasn't going to let what you did stop me being there for her. She needed me, you see, and I quickly learnt that I needed her too.

'Rose, can I ask you something?' she said to me, a few days after my fight with Nina. We'd bumped into each other leaving school and had headed home together. I noticed a lot of girls in her year walk past us, and not one of them acknowledged her.

'As long as it doesn't involve money,' I joked, 'then yeah, go for it!'

She smiled at my poor attempt at humour. 'You seem a bit... um... down lately?'

I offloaded an excuse about having a lot of revision to do, how it was all a bit intense. But I couldn't meet her eyes – Ava has an uncanny ability to read people. A group of year nine girls barged past us, knocking her onto the road. None of them seemed to notice what they'd done, lost as they were in their meaningless chatter.

'Are you okay?' I asked, glowering at their backs and helping Ava back to the pavement.

'Yeah, I'm fine. They didn't mean to do it.'

Although she brushed it off, it must have lingered with her because something changed in her after that. I didn't see it at the time, but the carelessness of those girls must have triggered a painful memory for Ava. Still, she turned her focus back to me. That's the thing about Ava – she always puts everyone else first.

'You haven't been at the house for ages,' she said. We turned onto the main road, where the heavy roar of traffic forced her to raise her voice. 'I asked Jacob if you were okay and he told me to mind my own business. He was really horrible about it, actually.'

Of course, this didn't surprise me. 'Sorry he said that. He's... Well, you know what Jacob's like.' I tried to make light of it, but the truth is that everything Ava said was like a knife slicing through my skin.

'Ava, listen, I...' Part of me wanted to tell her everything that day – to be honest about it all – but I knew it would destroy her. 'Um, don't worry about Jacob. He doesn't like people knowing his business, does he?' Ava believed that Rose and Jacob were in it for the long haul and I wasn't going to be the one to shatter her illusion. No, you would do that all by yourself. It was only a matter of time. It hurt to think that Ava would end up as collateral damage, but there was nothing I could do, other than be there to pick up the pieces. She would understand it all, I hoped. Ava always did.

'The best thing to do is just ask *me* if you want to know what's going on,' I advised her. 'Okay?'

She nodded and we continued walking. 'How about we stop at the coffee shop for a Coke and then I'll walk you home?' I suggested.

Her face lit up. 'Yeah. But, ugh, d'you know how much sugar is in that stuff? I'll have something else, though.'

I couldn't help but smile. 'Anything you like. My treat.'

Because I owed her, far more than I could ever repay, even though she didn't know it.

It was crowded when we got to Esquires, full of mothers hanging around until pick-up time at the primary school across the road. It was far too loud for me, but I'd promised Ava, and I knew this was important to her. She didn't have many friends at school yet, and I wasn't sure she ever would with the barriers she faced on a daily basis. Sitting with a friend after school would mean the world to her. Even if I was her brother's girlfriend.

Ava was silent when we finally got seats, and the silence meant that my focus was drawn to the hiss of the espresso machine, and the clatter of china. I didn't want to hear these sounds; I only wanted Ava to chatter away effusively like she always did to me. Nobody that young should be so sad. I blamed you for some of it. Everything always came back to you.

'Those girls who knocked into you,' I began. 'Is that what you're thinking about?'

She stared at her orange juice, twirled her paper straw around the glass. 'That was just an accident,' she insisted. 'They didn't do it on purpose. I don't even know them.'

'I'm not saying they meant to do it. But it... it got to you. Because of your old school.'

I only knew snippets of what life had been like for Ava in London, and the bullying she'd endured; I'd heard a lot of it through you. But I wasn't quite prepared to learn the full story.

'I don't make friends easily,' she began, looking around. She lowered her voice. 'I never have. I'm sure you've noticed.' She gave a small smile. 'Mum just thought it was something I'd grow out of. She assumed I'd learn to *socialise*. After all, I was completely normal, wasn't I?' She took a sip of juice.

'There's no such thing as normal, Ava,' I explained, as if I possessed deep wisdom.

'But there *is*,' she insisted. 'It just means what most people are like, or what most people do.' Now she was the wise one.

'Okay, but—'

'Can I just finish or I'll never get out all this stuff that's in my head?'

I apologised and told her to carry on.

'I was fine in primary school. Kids mostly knew to leave me to be by myself. They knew that was what made me happy and soon stopped trying to include me. It was just kind of peaceful. Then I started year seven and everything changed. It was bigger, faster, the kids were horrible. Like wild things who'd lost all their innocence over the summer holidays. They didn't just accept who I was and leave me alone. They flooded my social media with nasty comments and I had to delete all my accounts. I was okay with that, though.'

I took Ava's hand. 'Did you tell anyone?'

'No. I was ashamed. I felt like I... kind of like I deserved it because, well, I *was* weird, wasn't I? I just wanted to spend lunchtimes reading books – I wasn't interested in boys. I'm still not. But some girls already had boyfriends. Or girlfriends. Or both. I just had myself.'

'You sound like me when I started secondary school. Well, until I met Nina. She was my only real friend.'

She looked up. 'Was?'

'I mean is.'

Ava narrowed her eyes, but continued. 'I would have been fine, except things got worse. There was this boy called Finn. He didn't join in with the others and one day he was really kind to me. He defended me when some girls were saying nasty stuff right in front of me. They weren't even bothering to hide behind their screens. The trolls were making an appearance in person.' She fell silent. 'That's different, isn't it? When they're right there in front of you. They're not hiding, they're not scared.'

I nodded. 'What happened?'

'He... he told me he liked me and asked me to meet him after school, by the boating lake in the park near my old school. I remember feeling nervous when I was walking to meet him. Worrying about my hair. It was a bit frizzy that day.' She smiled. 'It was the happiest I'd felt for so long, and I remember thinking I wish I could bottle this feeling and keep it for whenever the kids at school were getting me down.' Ava sighed. 'And then when I got there, there was a whole bunch of them, jeering and laughing at me. Pointing at me. Did I actually believe Finn would like me, they screeched.' She averted her eyes. 'It was like something from a film. I didn't think people would do that stuff in real life.'

When she said this, I thought of the film *Carrie*. I'd begged my mum to let me watch it when I turned fifteen, just because it had her name in the title.

Ava was crying as she recalled what took place, and I squeezed her hand tighter.

'I've never done anything like this in my life before but I was so humiliated and upset, I think something in me just snapped. I grabbed one of the girl's hair and screamed in her face to shut up and leave me alone. The next second, hands were flying everywhere trying to help her and someone punched me in the stomach, so hard I went flying and smashed my head on the rocks. I can't be sure but I think it was Finn who did it. None of them ever admitted it. They all just said I fell. Every last one of them stuck together.'

My jaw dropped. 'Jesus, Ava! I had no idea.' You hadn't even told me that part. Perhaps you were protecting her privacy.

'We don't talk about it,' Ava said. 'Moving here was supposed to be a fresh start. It's as if Mum and Dad think I can just erase the person I was in London and be this shiny new... I don't know... social butterfly.'

As I listened to her, I pictured that boy Finn – even though

I had no idea what he looked like – and my fury with you inter-mingled with rage at him so that it became one and the same. Ava was powerless, just like I was with you.

'Boys need to stop thinking they can do what they like to us and diminish us,' I said. 'Take away our power.'

'It wasn't just him,' she said. 'It was all those girls too.'

But I wasn't listening, because I was too focused on destroying you.

TWENTY-SIX
LUCY

It's impossible to sleep in this unfamiliar place, especially when I know it might only be a matter of time before the police come looking for us. Perhaps I haven't covered our tracks carefully enough. Maybe they know where we are and have alerted local officers here, and as I lie in this strange bed, with its mattress that sags a little in the middle, they're on their way to arrest us. Changing our hair won't be enough. I've tried my best to make sure we can't be traced, but my knowledge of things like this is limited; nothing can be guaranteed. I wonder if Tom has shown them the letters, and my instinct tells me he has. There is no way he will have covered for us.

Tom. So many times during the night I've wanted to call him, just to tell him and Ava that we're okay. I know our love for each other seems unreachable, or obliterated, but if there's any fragment of friendship remaining, then perhaps he will understand the choice I've had to make. Life or death. That's what it's come down to.

At five a.m. I give up trying to force sleep, and climbing out of bed, I make my way to the kitchen, checking on Jacob on my way. He's sleeping soundly on his back, one arm dangling off the side of the bed. Downstairs, I make coffee and sit by the kitchen door, looking out at the small garden, where there's only space for a small table and two chairs. I miss my work, and I can't even check my email to see what jobs are coming in, but I assure myself this is temporary.

There's a small TV on the worktop in the corner of the room, and I switch it on, holding my breath as I wait to see our faces plastered across the screen. So far, Rose's death has only been covered on our local news, but this could change in an instant. After a few moments of watching, my shoulders begin to drop, and some of the tension releases as I exhale.

After a quick shower, I wake Jacob. Normally I'd let him sleep in, especially as he's still in pain after the attack, but he fell asleep at nine last night, so he's had a good rest. We have a lot to sort out, and who knows how little time?

'Mum, it's too early. Can't I just sleep a bit more?' he moans, rolling over.

'Jacob, you'll have to rest later, I'm afraid. I've made you some toast. There's no jam but we'll get some this morning, okay?'

Mumbling under his breath, he pulls the sheets aside and slowly heaves his legs over the side of the bed, burying his head in his hands.

I go over to him and sit beside him, leaning across to give him a hug. 'It will get easier for you. It just takes time.'

He looks at me. 'Yeah, everything just takes time, doesn't it? Getting over Rose, healing from my injuries, the police finding who killed her.'

'Jacob, I—'

'Don't, Mum, just don't.'

'I'll get breakfast ready,' I say, leaving him to get dressed. When Jacob shuts down there is no point trying to push him to talk.

When he finally makes it to the kitchen, the toast is already growing cold on a plate.

'Jacob, listen,' I say, pouring him some orange juice. 'I've got a lot to sort out today. I need to get some food for us and buy some clippers for your hair so you don't have to keep wearing a cap. Will you be okay here on your own for a while? I'll be as quick as I can.'

'Can't I come with you?' he asks. 'I'm feeling okay to walk.' He picks up a slice of toast, turning it over to inspect it.

'You need to rest,' I warn. 'The doctor said to take it easy until your body heals.'

'I'm fine,' he protests, as stubborn as ever.

'I saw the way you winced when you got out of bed, Jacob. Look, I think it's best if I go alone. And you need to revise. This will all be cleared up soon and you need to be ready to sit those exams.'

He stares at me as if I've spoken another language. 'Mum, do you really believe that? The police think I'm guilty so they won't be looking for anyone else, will they?'

This is my fear too, but I can't dwell on that. We have to keep moving forward. 'Just remember, they don't have evidence linking you to any crime. They haven't arrested you.' I hate referencing Rose in this way; she deserved so much more than that.

'I bet that's never stopped them before.' Jacob puts down his half-eaten toast and wipes his mouth, then he stands, leaving his glass untouched.

'Where are you going?'

'You told me to revise.'

'Can we talk first? I need to talk to you about Nina.'

'What about her?'

'Why do you think she lied? She said she didn't see you the night Rose died, but you swear that you were with her.'

'I don't know, Mum. She's... I don't know why she wouldn't tell anyone.'

I study his face, try to read it, search for something I can believe without a doubt. But there is nothing I can grasp hold of. 'So, there was nothing going on with you two? Rose was wrong about that?'

'I've told you all this before. Why won't you believe me?'

'I do, Jacob. It's just... There's always a reason people lie. I'm just trying to work out what Nina's is.' I walk over to him. 'This is important, Jacob. It could mean finding something that clears your name. And then we can go home. Isn't that what you want?'

He takes a long time to answer. 'I don't even care any more. I'll always be guilty to people online, even if the police clear me of any charges. Don't you see? Everything that's ever posted online stays there forever. What kind of life can I have now?'

'Eventually people will find something else to talk about. Move on to the next thing. It will be okay,' I say, trying to reassure myself as much as him. 'We'll get through this, Jacob, I promise. And you don't have to stay in Guildford forever. You'll go off to uni soon enough and then—'

'Mum, please stop! I can't think about any future. Not without Rose.'

As I watch him head upstairs, I have the overwhelming feeling that Nina is important in all of this.

I try to blend in as I traipse around shops, hunting for everything we need. It saddens me that I can't stop and take a moment to look through the windows of the boutique stores. This is a beautiful place, but even as I walk along the stone streets, I feel as though I'm not quite touching the ground, only half here.

My new phone rings as I'm leaving the supermarket, and it can only be one person. 'Hi Jayne. How are you?'

'I'm very well, thanks, dear. How are you and Josh settling in?'

I make my way to a low stone wall overlooking the harbour and sit down. 'The cottage is lovely, thank you. It's perfect.'

'Good. I'm just calling because I've spoken to Mitch Pierce, the maths tutor, and he said he's very happy to help Josh. He said he can meet you both this afternoon to go over everything. Is that okay with you? I don't know what plans you might have.'

'No plans. This afternoon is fine. Thanks, Jayne.'

'He's teaching all day so he asked me to arrange it. He said he can meet you after school? Mitch knows where the cottage is. Is four o'clock okay? I'll text you his number in a minute.'

I tell Jayne that's perfect and we end the call. It's not even midday yet, and the long day stretches before me, vast yet claustrophobic because the truth is that we don't have much time. We can't stay here forever, running from everyone and everything. And what if I can't fix this? All I know is that I need Jacob to talk to me. I need to know everything that happened leading up to Rose's disappearance. And then I can work out what to do.

Back at the cottage, Jacob is dressed and sitting at the kitchen table, his books spread across it like a tablecloth.

'See, I've been revising,' he says, holding up a book.

'That's great, Jacob.'

'Who's Jacob? I'm Josh, remember?' He smiles.

Hopefully I won't slip up when we have company. I begin unpacking the bags. 'Good news – the maths tutor can come and see us today at four. Just to go through what you need to revise.'

'Okay,' he says. He puts down his pen. 'What if he asks questions, Mum? Like what we're doing here when my exams are in a few weeks?'

I've given this plenty of thought during my sleep-void night. 'We tell him the same thing we told Jayne. You were being bullied, and after you were attacked, we decided to get you away from there for a while. Just don't go into too much detail. I'm sure it won't even come up. He'll just come here, teach you and then be on his way.' I fold the bag I've just unpacked, and place it in a drawer. 'I think we should ask if he can come every day, though.'

'But that's too—'

'I know it's a lot, but you'd be at school, wouldn't you? Every day you'd be having lessons.'

'I suppose.'

'And Jacob, if you want us to be able to go home quickly, please start talking to me. After we've done your hair. I need to write down everything you can remember about Rose in the weeks leading up to her disappearance. It's important.'

He stares at his hands and takes a moment to answer. 'Okay. But not now, please, Mum. I'm really tired and need a break before that tutor gets here.'

It looks like I don't have a choice; I can't force Jacob to talk.

Mitch is nothing like I expected. I sit in the living room with my notebook while he and Jacob sit at the kitchen table and go through everything they'll need to cover. And even though I'm busy writing notes about Rose, my ears are attuned to their conversation. He's a lot younger than I'd imagined, mid to late thirties I'm guessing, and he's dressed in jeans and a hooded top.

'Excuse my clothes,' he'd said when I'd answered the door. 'After wearing a suit all day, I just want to be comfortable when I get home.' As long as he helps Jacob, I don't care how he's dressed.

The two of them seem to be getting along, and I'm surprised by how attentive Jacob is being.

When they've finished talking, Jacob says he needs to have a shower before dinner. I've promised him we can eat out this evening, even though I need to be careful with money. I took out quite a bit, but eventually it will run out, and I can't use my bank cards.

'That went well,' Mitch says, putting his empty coffee cup in the sink. 'I've got a good idea of where he is, so I can put together a plan to lead him up to the exams.'

'Thanks. It will just be for a couple of weeks. He'll be back at school after that.'

His eyes narrow. 'Course.' He pauses. 'I heard what happened to Josh, and I'm sorry he experienced that. He's a good kid. I can tell.' He picks up his backpack. 'Well, I'll be off. See you same time tomorrow.'

Once he's gone, fear and regret overwhelm me. I'm torn between feeling guilty that I've lied to someone who seems like a decent person, and the anxiety that he didn't buy our story.

After dinner, Jacob and I sit at the table with mugs of green tea. I don't think he's ever had it before, but after seeing mine, he asked if he could try some. He's not touching it now, though, and instead of drinking stares at his hands, waiting.

'You need to talk to me, Jacob. For us to go back home now, we need something compelling to take to the police. Evidence that you couldn't have done anything to Rose, or something that points to someone else.'

He nods, staring at his mug, picking it up and placing the tea back down again untouched. 'Yeah, I know. But what?'

'Let's start at the beginning. Days before the barbeque. What can you remember about how Rose was acting?'

He cups his face in his hands and lets out a deep breath. 'I hardly saw her the week before the barbeque. We... just seemed to be busy doing our own thing. She was so focused on studying,

I think she saw me as a distraction. I didn't like it but I understood. She wanted to do well in the exams. Nothing was going to stop her.'

'So, you didn't see her at all?'

'No, I tried to get her to come over but she just couldn't fit it in.'

'And how did you end up looking for her at Nina's?'

'I'd been trying to call her all day and she wasn't answering.'

'Had you argued?'

'No, not then. That was later, after the barbeque. Just let me finish. She wasn't at home so I guessed she must be with Nina. But she wasn't there either. It was weird.'

'Why didn't you tell the police any of this? You told them nothing was wrong.'

'Because if I'd told them, they would think I was angry with Rose and that I hurt her.'

'You should never fear the truth, Jacob. Never. Whatever it might be.'

'I'm telling the truth now, Mum. All of it. When I went to Nina's she let me in and we just talked for a bit. Nothing happened. But... the next day Rose wouldn't talk to me when I went to her house. Joe was there. He said she was out, but I know she was there because I saw her through the window upstairs.'

'And did you talk to her after that? What happened?'

'I don't know, Mum. I didn't speak to her again until the barbeque.'

I try to make sense of what Jacob's telling me. 'I don't understand. Why did Rose end up coming if the two of you weren't even talking?'

He frowns. 'It's not like we weren't talking. We just hadn't had a chance to see each other. Nothing was wrong. At least not until the barbeque. And then Ava was just hogging all her time so I couldn't even talk to her then.'

'Do you think she could have been avoiding you because she thought you liked Nina?'

'Who knows, Mum? All I know is that she started acting crazy for no reason at all when I walked her home. I didn't even do anything.'

This doesn't sound like Rose. Is Jacob lying to me?

We let the silence wrap itself around us as we get sucked into our own thoughts.

'There was one thing,' Jacob says, after a while. 'I didn't think about it until now, but when I went to see if Rose was at home and Joe answered the door, there was something off about him.'

'What do you mean by *off*?'

'As if he was gloating. Happy that I couldn't find Rose. He seemed to be enjoying it.'

'Yes, I'd say that sounds exactly like Joe.'

'No, but you don't get it. Joe's always been all right with me. He's always been cool. Even though he and Rose couldn't stand each other, we actually got on all right.'

I try to work out what this could mean. 'Maybe he was happy that Rose was suffering?'

'No, don't you see? Joe must have been helping her. He knew she was upstairs, so Rose must have told him to tell me she wasn't in!'

'That doesn't mean—'

'It means he must know something. And we need to talk to him!'

TWENTY-SEVEN

CARRIE

People talk in their circles, and it's not long before word gets back to Joe that she's been staying at Tom's house.

He's waiting for her after work on Friday, walking up and down the pavement outside the hospital, a lit cigarette in his hand. 'What are you playing at?' he says, grabbing her arm.

Carrie glares at him. 'Get off me!'

Slowly, he releases her arm. 'Sorry, I... Everyone's talking down the pub. Saying something's going on with you and Tom Adams. What the hell, Carrie? What are you doing? His son killed your daughter!'

'People need to mind their own business,' she hisses, turning back to make sure no one she works with has spotted them. 'And you shouldn't be smoking here.'

He takes a short drag on his cigarette then throws it onto the road. Carrie doesn't have the energy to protest and insist he pick it up.

'It *is* their business!' Joe says. 'The whole community has been there for you, looking for Rose, supporting you. I got everyone down the pub to go and search. And now you've shacked up with her murderer's dad! It's disgusting, Carrie, that's what it is. What would Rose think?'

She'd be proud of me, that I'm doing everything I can to find answers. Carrie takes his arm and manoeuvres him away, towards the steps leading up to the car park. She's mortified that Joe's shown up like this, shouting at her in front of hospital visitors and people she works with.

'You're causing a scene, Joe. Lower your voice. There's nothing going on with me and Tom, I've just been helping him with Ava. She needed me there. Her mother's gone and... it's hard for her. She's just a kid.'

They reach the top of the steps, where a queue has formed by the ticket machine. 'Bleeding heart,' Joe mumbles. 'It's not for you to help them, is it? You should be staying away from that whole family, Carrie.'

'You wouldn't understand.' She turns away, heading towards her car. 'I'm not talking to you about this.'

Joe grabs her arm again. 'I need to talk to you,' he says. 'Not about this. Something else. It's important.'

'Get your hands off me, Joe.'

'Please, Carrie.'

She tells him she can't; she's promised to take Ava to her piano lesson, and she can't be late. The teacher doesn't like students showing up late, eating into their lesson time. Both Ava and Tom have warned her about that. And she's not about to let Ava down.

'When then? It has to be soon, Carrie. It won't wait.'

She softens at the sight of him begging like this. 'I'll call you. I can't deal with anything else right now, Joe.' She spots her car and pulls out her keys, turning away from Joe.

'You won't, though, will you?' he shouts after her. 'I need to talk to you, Carrie!'

Carrie keeps walking, letting his words ricochet off her

back. Joe is in the past now, buried along with the rest of her life.

Tom and Ava. They are her future.

Ava is quiet in the car after her piano lesson. They're heading to Carrie's house, so that she can pick up some things and stay another night with them both. Ava had begged, so how could Carrie refuse? She wonders if Ava would want her there if she knew what had happened between Carrie and her dad the other night.

Tom had felt a huge surge of guilt afterwards, and he'd clung to her, whispering that he was sorry, that he should have fought his urge for her because she's grieving. And so, too, is he. Grieving for his marriage, and for the family he feels is slipping away from him. Carrie had held him, and she didn't say a word when she felt a tear drip onto her shoulder. She doesn't know if it will happen again between them – maybe it won't – but Tom had asked her to stay another few nights. 'For Ava,' he'd said.

'You miss your mum, don't you?' Carrie asks Ava.

'Yeah,' Ava says, 'but it's not that. Everything's just a mess. This is worse than the bullying at my old school, and I didn't think *anything* could be worse than that.'

'Do you know what it all means, though?' Carrie says, briefly glancing at her. 'It means you're strong. That you can get through anything life throws your way.'

From the corner of her eye, Carrie sees a thin smile forming on Ava's lips. 'Yeah, I like that. And I'm going to write a book one day – you need life experiences to be able to write, don't you? Rose told me that, and I think she's right.'

'Yes, definitely.' Carrie supposes this could be true, although she wouldn't have the first idea how to write anything other than her reports and emails at work. Factual things she can do.

'I'm doing it for Rose,' Ava continues. 'I'll dedicate it to her.'

Carrie feels a twinge in her stomach. 'She'd love that.'

'Who's that over there?' Ava says, as they approach Carrie's house. 'There's a man on your doorstep.'

Carrie assumes it's Joe, remembering that he said he had something to tell her. She's not going to talk to him now; not in front of Ava. But as she pulls up, it's clear that the man standing at her door is not Joe.

She gets out and slams her door shut, striding up to him. 'What are you doing here?'

'I couldn't come any earlier. But I'm here now. Not for long, but I came.'

The car door slams and Ava joins her, staring at this stranger dressed in smart black trousers and a navy shirt.

The man smiles. 'Hello, and who might you be?'

Ava glances at Carrie. 'I'm... Ava Adams.'

'Hi, Ava, it's nice to meet you.' He holds out his hand. *As charming as ever*. 'I'm Hugh, Rose's dad.'

Carrie feels sick. She hasn't set eyes on Hugh since he walked out on them, not in person at least. She's seen fleeting images of him on FaceTime on the few occasions when he called Rose, but most of the time Carrie made sure she wasn't in the room. Avoided him at all costs. Seeing him now, and how much Rose resembled him as she got older, is bringing her a whole new level of pain.

'What are you doing here?' she asks, when Ava settles at the kitchen table with her homework. She and Hugh are in the living room and Carrie shuts the door.

'I explained about the funeral, Carrie. I tried my best but I just couldn't make it. I've said goodbye to Rose in my own way. Don't think I haven't grieved for our daughter.'

The daughter you walked out on. But now is not the time to bring this up. Ava doesn't need to hear it. Besides, it will be nothing Carrie hasn't already said to Hugh.

'Silvana's got breast cancer,' Hugh says. 'It's terminal. She'd been ill for a while and then her results came the day before I was supposed to fly. She got worse and was rushed into hospital. It was all so awful and I ended up leaving the hospital so late that I missed my flight. And then Silvana needed me. I'm sorry, Carrie.'

Carrie takes a moment for this revelation to sink in. 'I'm sorry,' she says. She's never met Silvana, and the woman had nothing to do with Hugh leaving her and Rose, but even if she had been the reason for her divorce, nobody deserves to be inflicted with such a devastating illness.

Hugh sits on the sofa. 'Now do you understand why I couldn't come? It's all just such terrible timing.'

'Right,' Carrie says. *But there were a million other chances to see your daughter. Out of sight, out of mind, is that it?*

'I've been an idiot, Carrie. Staying away from Rose all these years. I... I have no excuse. I was... I just put work before anything else. And now I realise how wrong that was. Now she's gone...' He turns away and stares out of the window.

'Well, we can't change the past.'

'No,' he says. 'But what the hell happened to her, Carrie? Who is this boy?'

Conscious that Ava's in the kitchen, and the walls in the house are paper thin, Carrie explains everything as quickly as she can, bringing him up to date.

'What a mess,' Hugh says when she's finished. 'And the police think it's him?'

'Well, they don't have evidence, but everything points that way. He's a person of interest. But as soon as they find any evidence, they'll arrest him straight away.'

'I see. Oh, Carrie, why are you mixed up with his family, then? What are you thinking?'

Carrie glances at the closed door, hoping Ava can't hear. 'It's what Rose would have wanted. She loved Ava. She's got nothing to do with this.' *Except that she wouldn't tell the police about Rose's phone.*

'It's asking for trouble,' Hugh warns.

'Let me worry about that.'

'Seems to me you might need a bit of help. And that's where I can actually do something for Rose.'

Carrie looks up, stunned. 'Like what?'

'I'm going to hire a private investigator. I've already done some research on the plane and they often get results before the police. They can even work with the police. Let me pay for it, Carrie. It's the least I can do.'

And right there, in that moment, Carrie is torn between wanting to throw him out of her house and wanting to hug him.

She sits with Ava in the Adams's living room, both of them reading. Carrie's reading material might only be a magazine, but it's still words on a page. And the important thing is that they're together, keeping each other company until Tom gets home. Comfortable in the silence.

It's after seven p.m. when Tom walks through the door, and Carrie's surprised that after he's hugged Ava, he comes to her and pulls her into a hug. As if they are a family.

'Are you both okay?' he asks.

'We've been reading,' Carrie says, rising from the sofa and picking up her magazine. 'Listen, Tom, maybe I should get going and give you two some time together?'

'No!' Ava protests. 'She doesn't have to go, does she, Dad?'

Tom looks at her. 'We'd both like it if you stayed,' he says. 'That is unless you need to get home?'

Carrie thinks of all that awaits her at home. Empty walls, suffocating loneliness, the ghost of her daughter. 'I'm happy to stay however long you need me here,' she says. 'I have an early shift tomorrow, though, so I'll get some sleep now if you don't mind?'

'Go ahead,' Tom says.

She leaves them both and makes her way upstairs, as if it is her own house.

Lying in the bed which has quickly become a comfort to her, Carrie thinks about what will happen next. She doesn't want to accept help from Hugh, but doesn't he owe them after being absent for such a large chunk of Rose's life? Now she might get some answers. A private investigator will find evidence. And then there will be no more running for Jacob.

TWENTY-EIGHT

LUCY

Days pass and Jacob and I begin to settle into life in Cornwall. Secluded. Out of touch with the rest of the world. We don't watch the news, or browse the web; it's best if we don't know what's going on out there. What we've left behind. But my heart aches for Ava, gut-wrenching pain that I have to fight against with every inch of my being. And still, I have no answers. I don't know how I'm going to find a way to keep Jacob safe and get back to Ava.

Every evening, after Mitch has gone, Jacob and I sit down together and go over everything that might help us, but despite our best efforts, we are getting nowhere.

'Mum,' Jacob says, rapping his knuckles on the table. 'Maybe we're looking at this all wrong. We're thinking someone who knew Rose did this, but what if it was a stranger. Someone who just saw her walking out alone? There's no way we can get proof for the police if that's what happened, is there?'

I've thought about this, of course I have, and I have no answer for Jacob. 'I need time,' I tell him. 'To work this all out. Just focus on your studies and let me worry about everything else.'

His shoulders unhunch when I say this and he lets out a deep breath. He's counting on me, my son believes I can put this right, so that's what I have to do.

Mitch takes me by surprise the following day when he suggests he and I take a walk along the beach to go over Jacob's progress so far. I've grown to like this man over the last few days – Jayne leaves us alone so he's the only person we have any contact with. He stops us feeling so isolated.

'Josh is a great kid,' he says as we walk across the sand, holding coffee cups from the café on the promenade.

'Thanks, I think so too.'

'If he stays this focused, then I can see him getting at least a five, possibly a six.'

'That's what he's aiming for,' I say. 'He's always found maths a little challenging, but he's doing well in all the other subjects.'

'You're not the first parent to say that. And so many adults find it hard too. I think it scares them. But if people could break down those walls, conquer that fear, then I think they'd find it enjoyable. Maybe even learn to love numbers.' He laughs. 'I sound like a right geek, don't I?'

I nod. 'Hmm. I'm not sure about loving numbers,' I counter. 'I'd rather write an essay.'

Mitch laughs again. 'Well, the world would be boring if we were all the same.' He slows down and turns to me. 'Can I ask you something? And I hope you don't mind. I-I know about the issues Josh has had at school, but I just wanted to make sure that you were both okay.'

'Yeah, we're fine. Just having a time-out.'

'It's just, you hear about women – men too – who've had to leave their homes because of... someone they live with. I just wanted to check in with you that you're okay. Not worried or anything. I know we don't know each other well, but I'm a good friend of Jayne's daughter. She can vouch for me that I'm actually an okay guy.'

I smile, touched by the concern of a virtual stranger. 'Thanks, Mitch, but honestly, I'm not in an abusive relationship. Thankfully.' I almost explain that my husband is at home with my daughter, and then I realise I can't be Lucy Adams while I'm here. I can't have the life she has. 'My husband died,' I say, and an image of Alistair flashes before me, as vivid and painful as if it had just happened yesterday. 'When Josh was nearly three. It's just the two of us now.'

Mitch stops walking and turns to me. 'I'm so sorry, Kate. I can't imagine... I haven't found anyone that special yet but... it must have been so hard.'

'You're still young – there's plenty of time,' I say, looking out at the shimmering turquoise sea.

Mitch chuckles. 'I'm not much younger than you.'

In a different time, in a different world, Mitch might have been someone I could enjoy getting to know, seeing what road a friendship would take us down. But I have Tom. I love him, and that can't just switch itself off.

'What's London like to live in?' Mitch asks, as we continue walking. It's getting cooler now and I fasten the buttons on my denim jacket. 'I've only ever been there for short visits.'

'It's... vibrant, full of life. Full of opportunities, I guess. But... it's not like here. It's not easy to make friends.' I picture the house we lived in before we moved. 'I don't even know the neighbours' names. I bet you know all of yours.'

'Yep. Which is good in some ways, but a bit stifling in others. I can't do anything without people knowing about it.'

I smile. 'And what exactly have you been doing that you don't want people to know about, then?'

He winks. 'All in good time, Kate. But for now, tell me what is it you do?'

By the time Mitch and I have walked along the beach and

back, I've almost forgotten the trouble Jacob and I are in. For the last hour, I've been a different person. Kate. Uncomplicated and unburdened, a fictional character I've had to create. I've tried to be as honest as I can with Mitch, feeding him details that, while not currently true, are part of who I've been before, not a complete fabrication.

'Thanks for this,' he says. 'I needed a break from teaching. Don't get me wrong – I love my job, but it's nice to have some company other than my students. Nice to do adult speak.'

I'm about to tell him that the only company I have other than my kids is my flowers, but I stop myself before I make the mistake of saying anything out loud. This is too difficult; if I keep talking to Mitch, or anyone else, then I'm bound to slip up.

'I have to go,' I say. 'I've just remembered some emails I need to send urgently. 'Sorry.'

I'm already turning and walking away when he calls out goodbye.

Jacob's watching a Marvel film when I get home. He doesn't normally watch television, but with no Xbox around, he's making do with whatever entertainment he can get in the evenings. He's so engrossed in the film that he doesn't hear me come in at first.

I stand in the doorway watching him for a moment, and I feel pride that he is handling this so well, mixed with sadness that this is happening to him. He's only sixteen and has not only lost his girlfriend, but is considered a suspect in her murder.

After a moment he looks away from the film and sees me there. 'I didn't hear you come in,' he says.

'Must be a good film.'

He shrugs. 'It's all right. Rather have my Xbox.'

'Soon,' I say, desperate for this to be true. 'I'm just going up to sort some washing out.'

'Okay,' Jacob says, turning back to his film.

Upstairs, I realise Jacob still hasn't unpacked a lot of his things. His navy blue suitcase lies open on the floor, clothes pouring out of it like soap suds from an overflowing sink. With a sigh, I begin to sort through his clothes, hanging them in the small oak wardrobe. I can understand why Jacob didn't want to unpack anything – it makes this arrangement feel more permanent.

I reach for the last item of clothing – Jacob's red fleece dressing gown – and when I lift it, something thuds to the floor. A phone. With a rose gold case.

My body freezes, and I stare at what I know is Rose's phone. I've seen her with it enough times to be sure. Slowly, I reach for it and pick it up, turning it over to find the initials I know will be there. RN. Struggling to breathe, I shove the phone in my pocket and walk out, shutting the door behind me.

In my bedroom, I sink to the floor and pull out the phone, examining it as if it will somehow change, and won't be Rose's phone after all. My mind can't comprehend what Jacob having it in his possession means – it's too heinous, too horrific.

Downstairs I can hear music signalling that the film is over. Jacob will be up here in a moment and I have no idea what to say to him. What words to begin with. I rush to the bathroom and lock the door, only just making it to the sink before I lose the contents of my stomach.

TWENTY-NINE

ROSE

Control. It's a horrible word. Especially when it creeps up on you so innocuously to start with. Disguised as something else. Passion. Love. Call it what you want, but at its core is a toxicity that destroys lives.

Despite the rage I felt towards you, things calmed down for me after I spoke to Ava. She had sent me a message to say that she'd read in a book once that it did no good to harbour resentment. That forgiveness was the only thing that could set us free. She said she even forgave Finn, the boy who had made her torment even greater.

I didn't see you for days and I think that helped. I began to catch a glimpse of who the old Rose had been, and maybe I began to heal. It was as if you'd slowly been flushed out of my system, the more time I spent away from you. I began to see that I could move on, and put what we'd done behind me. I had choices – I didn't have to let you destroy me.

I even began to laugh again, to feel like Rose Nyler, a girl who was gaining her power back. But then you came to my house that night, and everything changed again.

Mum was working that night. You must have known she

would be. Were you watching me from the house? I've had time to think about this and you must have been stalking me. Otherwise you couldn't have known she wouldn't be there. Joe too. You knew he often stayed even when Mum wasn't there.

We stood staring at each other for a moment before you spoke. 'Can I come in?' you asked, when I opened the door. I should have ignored the doorbell – but I didn't have the benefit of hindsight. Letting you in was the biggest mistake I could have made.

I didn't make it easy for you, though. 'Why are you here?' I demanded.

'Can we talk? Please, Rose. Can you just let me in?'

Silently cursing myself, I stepped aside to let you in.

As soon as I'd shut the door behind you, you grabbed my arm and pulled me towards you. 'I've missed you, Rose. So much. It's been unbearable.'

There was something about you using that word, as if you'd been tormented. I know you had been, but not for the reason you were explaining. I pulled away from you. 'I think you should go. Now. Just get out.'

'Rose, please. Will you just hear me out?' Your begging diminished you. I'd never seen you like this before and I almost felt sorry for you.

Ignoring you, I walked into the kitchen and poured myself a glass of water. I wasn't sure if the cup I'd grabbed from the worktop was mine or mum's, or even Joe's, but I didn't care. My hands were trembling and my whole body was flushing. I needed a distraction. I desperately hoped you hadn't noticed, that you couldn't sense my weakness.

You followed me and carried on talking, spouting stuff about how much you regret what happened the last time we were together. I did a good job of fending you off, because I'd vowed to myself that I would be okay, but you didn't give up.

Control. You see, it's not so overt. Yours was subtle, manipulative. And you'd been doing it for our whole relationship.

It was the tears that got me. The anguish on your face seemed genuine, and I wasn't wrong to believe that. Of course you were distraught; after all, I knew something about you that you'd never want anyone to find out, and the only thing that had stopped me exposing you was Ava. I couldn't do that to her, not when her mental health was already as fragile as a cobweb.

When you reached for me, I went with it this time, and I closed my eyes as your hands explored my body, tentatively at first, then ravenously. 'Let's go upstairs,' you whispered, leading me up there. 'I've missed you so much. I need you, Rose.'

Of course I had a choice – I know that. But your words were powerful; they won me over, and I became yours once more.

Afterwards, there were a few minutes when I believed everything would be okay. I started talking to you about my birthday – it was only a week away, and maybe now I could let myself enjoy it. You held me and stroked my hair, and I sensed none of the regret that you'd had after that first time. It was just the two of us.

Until it wasn't.

'Rose,' you whispered, pulling away. 'I need to know that you won't tell anyone about... you know. I've been expecting you to. Every day. It's been... awful for me. I have nightmares. I can't sleep. Please, Rose. Promise me.'

I stared at you, aware in that instant of the real reason you were there in my bed. I pulled the duvet over my naked body, inched away from you. You had made me feel vulnerable. Exposed. Violated. 'Get out,' I said.

'Rose, wait, what's wrong?'

I grabbed my mobile and waved it. 'See this? I'm about to call 999. Get the fuck out of my house.'

THIRTY

LUCY

Jacob looks up and gives me a nod when he notices I'm standing in the doorway.

'Can we talk?' I say, joining him on the sofa.

He moves his legs to give me more space. 'Mum, I'm really tired. Can it wait till tomorrow?'

I tell him it can't, and when he looks at me, I wonder if I'll be able to go through with this. For the past hour, as I sat on the bathroom floor, I've been debating what to do. There are options. It would be easy to ignore the phone, carry on with things as if I'd never found it. Get rid of the evidence. Or I could call the police. If it was anybody else, then that's what I'd do with no hesitation.

'I found something, Jacob, and I'm being honest with you and I need you to do the same.'

He frowns. 'I don't understand. Why are you being weird?'

I pull out the phone and hand it to him. This is it. No going back now.

Jacob takes it and examines it, the puzzled look on his face quickly transforming into horror. 'This is Rose's phone. What are you doing with it? What's going on, Mum?'

'I found it,' I say, reaching for the phone, snatching it back. 'It was in your dressing gown.'

Jacob's eyes narrow and he shakes his head. 'My dressing gown?' He frowns. 'No... that's impossible. Why would it be there?'

'That's what I need to know, Jacob. Can you tell me?'

'I have no idea! I didn't know it was there. I never even use that stupid dressing gown – it just hangs on the door.'

'Well, that's exactly where it was. It fell out when I was unpacking your things.'

He stands up, walks over to the window and back again. 'Why were you going through my things? You can't do that!' His forehead is flushed.

'I was just trying to... Wait, I don't have to explain myself, Jacob. I've just found Rose's phone in your things and I want to know what you're doing with it.' I reach for his hand. 'Listen, whatever's happened, I'll be here for you. I'm your mum, and whatever you've done—'

'But I haven't done anything!'

'You've got Rose's phone! And she was killed by someone, Jacob! You must realise how serious this is.'

He doesn't answer, but buries his head in his hands, howling. I move next to him and throw my arms around him, holding him as he lets out a waterfall of tears. 'It's okay,' I assure him. 'Everything will be okay.' Futile promises I won't be able to keep.

Eventually the tears subside and he straightens. 'Can I... can we talk in the morning? I'm so tired, Mum, and my ribs are aching.'

I don't want to have to wait until the morning, but I can tell he's finding this difficult. It's late now, and I won't do anything until tomorrow anyway, not until I find out from Jacob what happened, so I agree.

As soon as Jacob's closes his bedroom door, I can no longer

fight my nausea, so I rush to the bathroom again. My stomach is raw and empty now, hollow like the rest of my body. Eventually I retreat to bed, knowing without a doubt that I won't sleep. How can I when I am the mother of a murderer?

For hours I lie in bed, running through my options, until I realise there is only one thing I can do: hear Jacob's side of the story then go with him to the police. There is no other option – I have to do what's right, and Jacob must take responsibility for his actions. *If* he did anything to Rose. I don't want to believe it, and my mind desperately searches for another reason Jacob might have had her phone.

Sleep must overcome me in the early hours because suddenly I'm awake, reality hitting me like a truck. It's six fifteen. Jacob won't be awake yet, so I head downstairs and make coffee. My stomach aches, still feeling hollow, but a hot drink is all I can face.

I take my coffee upstairs and knock on Jacob's door. A few seconds pass and there's no answer. I call his name, and let him know I'm coming in, but he still doesn't respond. Usually I would leave him to wake up on his own when he doesn't have to rush to get ready for school, but this morning's talk can't wait any longer.

I know before I've even opened the door that something is wrong; I sense the emptiness in the room before I've fully opened the door. And observing the bedroom only confirms that I'm right.

Jacob is gone, his room is empty except for the furniture. It's tidy too, the bed neatly made, and everything back in the place it was when Jayne showed us around.

Even though I know he's not in the cottage – I've already been downstairs this morning – I still check every room, even my own bedroom.

I check my phone, and find a message from him.

I can't stay here in Cornwall. Please don't worry about me. It's
better if you don't know where I am, then you can't get in trou-
ble. I promise I'll pay you back the money I've borrowed from
your bag. I didn't do anything to Rose.

I try to call Jacob's new phone, but it's switched off. He doesn't want to be found, and there's not much I can do without the police becoming involved.

With my head feeling like it's being crushed, I start packing my things, and once I've filled my case, I spend over an hour cleaning every inch of the cottage. It's the least I can do for Jayne, when she's shown us such kindness. I call her when I've finished, and when it goes to her voicemail, I leave a message. A family emergency, I explain.

Then I lock up the house and post the key through the letterbox. I have no choice but to go home now and tell Tom what's happened. And then wait for the police to find Jacob. Before anyone else gets to him.

It's two in the afternoon when I pull up at the house. For the whole drive here, I tried to focus on only driving, attempting to shut out the thoughts intruding into my mind. What Jacob has done. Where he's gone. I can't process any of it, so I'm simply going through the motions, one step at a time. Get home first. Then together Tom and I can work out what to do.

Stepping inside, the house feels unfamiliar, even though everything looks the same. The smell is different, as if my scent disappeared when I left. I've got about an hour until Ava gets home from school, so I dump my suitcase in the bedroom and go to check on my cutting garden. I'd expected to find most of my flowers dying, but to my shock, they look vibrant and healthy, as if someone has been taking care of them. It wouldn't be Tom, so that only leaves Ava. She's never shown much interest in my flowers, so it lifts my spirits that she's done this for me.

I try Jacob's phone again, still using my new phone, but again there's no answer. I leave a message begging him to come home, that I will help him sort this out, but I know he won't listen. It's going to take more than me asking him to come back.

After that, I sit in the kitchen with my laptop and open my inbox. There are over thirty emails from prospective customers, so I send out a general message saying I will reply to them as soon as I can. There is no space in my head for work at the moment, not until Jacob comes home. Not until I know he's safe.

When my phone rings, no caller ID shows on the screen. I waste no time answering, desperate to hear my son's voice. 'Hello?'

There's a moment of silence before anyone speaks. 'Mum, it's me.'

I jump up. 'Jacob, where are you? Are you okay?'

'I'm fine. I'm... I can't tell you where I am. But I promise I'm okay.'

He doesn't sound like he's in distress, so I have no choice but to believe him. 'But you're not in Cornwall?'

'No. There was nothing for me there.'

'Please come home.'

'I can't. Nobody will believe I'm innocent. Not after the phone thing. And what will happen? I'll be in prison for something I didn't do, or I'll be dead. Those are my only two options if I come home.'

With sinking dread in my heart, I don't know how to convince him this isn't the case – not when I don't believe it myself. And I won't lie to convince Jacob to come home. 'Tell me again. I need to hear it from you.'

He knows exactly what I mean. 'I didn't kill Rose, Mum. I

watched her leave her house and that was the last time I saw her.'

This is all I need to hear. 'Then I believe you. And I'm going to make sure everyone else does to.'

'How?'

'I don't know yet. I need to think. But will you promise me something? I need you to text me on this phone, at the same time every night so that I know you're okay. Nine o'clock. Then I won't be worrying so much and I can focus on finding out the truth.'

He agrees, and I tell him I'll make sure I'm always alone when he messages.

'What about Rose's phone?' he asks. 'I've been thinking about it and I just don't know how it got in there. I think maybe... I don't know, maybe she put it there herself? I can't think why but what else could it be?'

In that moment I finally make the decision that I won't tell anyone about the phone. I believe in my son. I always have, and now I have to fight for him.

'Nobody has to know about it,' I say. 'And I won't tell anyone I've heard from you. We'll make sure they know you're innocent, Jacob – I promise.' I hear Ava's key turn in the door. 'I have to go. Text me later.'

Slipping the new phone in my jeans pocket, I rush to the door.

'Carrie, are you here?' Ava calls, and then she looks up and sees me.

'Mum!' she rushes towards me and throws her arms around me. After a moment she looks up. 'Are you back for good?' Then she looks past me. 'Is Jacob here?'

'No, he didn't come back with me. Ava, listen to me – there's a lot I need to talk to you and Dad about. But first I need to call him and get him home. Can you just hang on for a bit, until he's back? Then I'll answer all your questions, I promise.'

She nods.

'Has school been okay?'

Ava tells me the kids are still talking about Jacob, even more so since we left. Speculation is rife in the corridors, and online.

'I'm so sorry, Ava, I just did what I thought was best to protect him.'

'But where is he now?'

'I don't know. He... I think he thought it would be better for all of us if he just ran.'

When Ava looks at me there are tears in her eyes. 'He did it, didn't he, Mum?'

I didn't think it would feel so strange seeing Tom again. I've only been away from home for two weeks, yet it feels like a lifetime since I last saw him. I half expected to feel a rush of love, a sense of belonging, but it feels like I'm face to face with a stranger.

I talk, and he sits on the edge of the sofa, barely looking at me. He fiddles with his tie, flipping the end and examining it, and intermittently glancing at Ava. 'We need to go to the police, you know that, don't you?' he says, still avoiding eye contact. 'For his own safety, and because they still need to talk to him.'

'I know. I will. I just wanted to talk to you both first.'

He turns to me, tears in the corners of his eyes. 'What did you think you'd achieve by running away? You left us, and for what?'

'I'm sorry. I just wanted to keep Jacob safe.'

'But he's not safe, is he? And now he's run off and neither of us knows where he is!' Tom stands up. 'Ava, please could you let your mum and me talk? And then maybe we'll go out and get some food, okay?'

Ava folds her arms. 'That's not fair, Dad! This involves me too. I'm part of this family!'

'Yes, you are. But there are some things I need to talk to your mum about, so please just give us a few minutes.'

Without a word, Ava storms off, slamming her door when she reaches her bedroom.

Tom closes the living room door, even though with her door shut, there's no way Ava would be able to hear us.

'Have there been any more notes?' I ask.

'No. But that probably means whoever's sending them knew he'd gone. Someone's watching us. And you just decide to leave. We're supposed to be sticking together, Lucy, aren't we?'

'Tom, I'm sorry I—'

'I'm broken, Lucy. I always thought our marriage was solid, that nothing could destroy it.' He shakes his head. 'I actually thought we'd get through anything. But I never had this in mind. Our son being accused of murder.'

'But he hasn't—'

'And the worst thing – even worse than all of that – is that he did it, didn't he?' Tom looks directly at me, shaking his head. 'I think you know that, don't you? You must do. But you just won't let yourself do the right thing.'

'I came back to do what's right.' And this is true, even though it's not what Tom is talking about.

'It's too little, too late, Lucy. I can't do this any more. I'm not the only thing that's broken – our marriage is too, isn't it? We've been fooling ourselves.'

I could sit here and fight for our life together, clutch onto it with a vice grip, but the truth is Tom is right. And we were broken long before this. 'Okay, you're right,' I admit. 'And I can't be with someone who doesn't believe in his own son.'

Tom sighs. 'He's not really mine, though, is he? No matter how much we've both wanted him to be. He's Alistair's. He's never felt connected to me, has he? But that was fine – I still wanted to be there for him, to be the dad he deserved to have. I put everything else aside.'

'And are you, Tom? Are you the dad he deserved?'

The tears in his eyes are flooding out now, splattering onto his tie. 'I've tried. And maybe I haven't been good enough. That's been eating me up for years, Lucy.'

I think I've always known this, but Tom would never open up about it until now.

'Every time I look at Jacob, I see Alistair,' he says. 'The man you loved. The man you would have still been with if he hadn't died. And I know how dreadful that sounds, what kind of person it makes me, but I need to be honest, Lucy. For once, I need to get it all out. I've despised myself for years for feeling like this, but it never goes away. That's why... now it's time for me to walk away.'

Now he's said it, a minuscule part of me understands. It's always been there, looming over us while we tried to lose ourselves in our happy family. Something secret I didn't want to share with anyone, even myself.

'For now, though,' Tom continues, 'we need to stick together for Ava's sake. And to find Jacob of course. We'll live separate lives and I'll move into the spare room. Then when this is all over we can sort out what to do.'

I stand up and pull my bag over my head; I can't think about this now – I need to help Jacob.

'Where are you going?'

'To see DC Keller. I've got some explaining to do.'

THIRTY-ONE

CARRIE

Michelle has told her that Lucy has come home. But there's no sign of Jacob. He's run away, apparently, and even his mum doesn't know where he is. It's puzzling to Carrie. Why would Jacob run off when his mother was already hiding him from the police, and from everyone? And what about the phone? Jacob will have had plenty of chances to dispose of it by now, but she wonders if Lucy found it before he did. It's a waiting game for these answers to reveal themselves – Lucy is only just speaking to DC Keller now.

Carrie desperately needs to speak to Tom, to hear things from his perspective and find out what he knows. But she's giving him some space to get his head around what's happening. He will come to her when he's ready. Carrie hasn't yet told him that Hugh is in the country, not because she thinks it would bother him, but she doesn't want the separate parts of her life colliding. It's easy enough to keep Joe out of their conversations, but Hugh had a much bigger role in Carrie's life.

This morning, she's finished a night shift at the hospital and sits by the window in her living room, a bowl of cornflakes on her lap. She doesn't want to eat, but she needs her body to feel strong. Otherwise, how else will she fight for justice? Rose loved cornflakes as a toddler, and would eat them dry, with no milk. Carrie smiles as she remembers this, but it's quickly followed by a sharp jolt of pain in her chest.

Outside, one of the twins is running across the road, back and forth, flapping his arms as if he's trying to take off. It's as if he's waiting for a car to dodge. When his mum doesn't appear, Carrie jumps up; it may be a quiet road, but it only takes one car to tear around the corner and not notice him until it's too late.

'Hey,' she calls, running over to him and stopping him before he tries to run again. 'It's not safe playing out here on the road. Shall we get you home?'

He appraises her before nodding. 'You're that sad lady.'

Carrie takes his hand, checking the road before they cross. 'Yeah, I suppose I am.'

'I liked Rose Flower. She was nice to us.'

She's so shocked to hear her daughter's name coming from the mouth of this child that she can't find any words to reply. 'Shall we go and find your mummy?' Carrie says, that pain surging through her gut once more.

They reach the Nelson's closed front door, and in the absence of a doorbell, she raps her knuckles against the red wooden frame, still clutching the boy's hand. She feels terrible that she doesn't know which twin she's delivering back home, doesn't even know either of their names.

Lia Nelson answers the door, her eyes flicking between Carrie and her son. 'Kian – what are you doing?' she cries. 'I thought you were upstairs!' She reaches for him and pulls him towards her before turning to Carrie. 'Sorry about that. What was he doing?'

'I saw him in the road,' Carrie explains. 'Thought I'd better bring him home in case... you know.'

Lia nods. 'Yeah. Thanks. I dunno what he thinks he was

doing. I've told them not to be playing outside any more. Not when...'

A small face appears behind Lia. 'He got out, Mum. But *I* stayed in. I'm being good.'

'Just get inside please, Ryan.'

At least now Carrie knows their names. 'Well, okay, then, I'll—'

'Do you wanna come in? For a cuppa? Kettle's just boiled.'

Carrie glances back at her empty house. 'Um, okay. Thanks.'

Toy cars and Duplo pieces lie scattered all over the hallway, and Carrie can see straight through to the kitchen where bowls of cereal have been abandoned on the kitchen table.

'Excuse the mess,' Lia says. 'I'm having a nightmare morning here. These boys are running me ragged already, and they've only been awake for an hour!'

Carrie studies her, and notices the deep lines on her forehead, the grey circles under her eyes. Close up, she looks older than Carrie assumed she was. Lia can't be even thirty yet. 'You sit down,' Carrie says. 'I'll make us tea. And then I'll help tidy up this mess.'

Lia offers a vague smile. 'Thanks, but you don't have to do that.' She bites her lip. 'I'm sorry about Rose. I was out looking for her for days. I can't believe it. She was a lovely girl – used to always stop and say hello to the boys. Teenagers get a bad rap don't they, but Rose was proof that they're not all the same.'

'Thanks,' Carrie says. 'I didn't even realise Kian and Ryan knew her.' Now that Carrie knows their names, she will make sure she never forgets.

'Oh yeah. They called her Rose Flower.' Lia chuckles. 'I've always thought that's sweet. They're rough and tumble and all that, but they're good boys.'

I nod. 'I've just learnt about their nickname for her.'

Lia pulls two mugs from a cupboard, inspecting them

before she plunks a teabag in each. While she does this, Carrie gathers up the toys from the floor and places them all in an empty fabric toy basket in the corner of the room. By the time Lia's made their tea, the place looks a lot tidier, and Lia flashes a smile of gratitude.

'I can't imagine what you've been through,' Lia says, handing her a mug.

The tea is far too strong, but Carrie will make sure she drinks it. She doesn't know how to respond to Lia's statement. That's the trouble – people never seem to know how to talk to her. There isn't actually anything to say; Carrie just wants people to be normal around her. Distract her.

'I should have come and spoken to you before,' Lia continues. 'We've been neighbours for years, haven't we? What is it now – six or seven? I moved here a few years before the twins came along, didn't I?'

Carrie nods, even though she has no idea really. She, like Lia is now, was too caught up in trying to raise her daughter alone. She was oblivious to everything going on around her.

'Well, I should have come and spoken to you. We all liked Rose. She was a lovely girl. That's why I wanted to be out searching for her.'

'Thank you, I appreciate that.' Carrie takes a sip of tea. It's still too hot and burns the roof of her mouth. She needs to change the subject; she doesn't want to break down in front of Lia. 'It must be hard having twins. I found just Rose a handful enough at that age.'

'Yep. I'm just counting the months until they can start school so I can get back to work.' She clamps her hand over her mouth. 'Oh, I'm sorry, that's a terrible thing to say to you. I know I should be cherishing every second with them and all that, but... they're hard work.'

'Do you have anyone to help you?'

'Their dad lives close by but he's useless. He rarely sees

them. My mum's just round the corner. But she's a bit forgetful when it comes to keeping an eye on them.' Lia rolls her eyes. 'Actually, so am I obviously. I really had no idea Kian was out!'

'We all make mistakes,' Carrie offers. 'Nobody's perfect, are they?'

Lia nods. 'That boy – Jacob? He and Rose always seemed so happy. I used to see them walking along sometimes, holding hands. And I'd think, wow, if only I had that kind of love. Where you just want to hold hands all the time.' She sighs. 'Do the police really think he did it?'

'They definitely suspect him,' Carrie explains. 'Because he's lied so much. But they have no evidence to actually arrest him formally. Not yet, anyway.' And now Rose's phone has disappeared, Carrie will have to rethink her strategy.

'It's just baffling isn't it? Why would he do that to her?' Lia takes a sip of tea. 'Oh, look, sorry. You probably don't want to talk about this. Anyway, I haven't seen your man around for a while. Is he okay?'

As much as Carrie doesn't want to discuss her ex-partner, it's a preferable topic to the previous one. 'Joe and me... we're not together any more.'

Lia's eyes widen. 'Oh, sorry. I didn't know.'

'Don't apologise. It was my choice. I should have done it ages ago.' Carrie turns her attention back to her tea, and she can feel Lia eyes on her.

'I always thought Joe was okay to be honest,' Lia says. 'He was kind to me.'

Because you're an attractive female. 'Yeah. Shame he wasn't kind to Rose.'

Lia frowns. 'I didn't know that. What a jerk, then.'

'Well, how could you know what happens in our house when the doors are shut? They just argued a lot, that's all. Nothing worse than that.'

'A shame,' Lia says, wrapping her hands around her mug. 'I

just know that the night he nearly drove into Ryan when I was walking the boys home from Mum's, he was really good about it. And it *was* Ryan's fault. He just decided to run right out into the road just as Joe was coming along. Nearly gave me a heart attack! I tried to apologise to Joe and he kept saying not to worry, no harm done and all that. Really good of him.'

Carrie doesn't recall this incident, and it's the sort of thing Joe would grumble to her about. He was always moaning about the unruly twins across the road, despite playing Mr Nice Guy to Lia. 'When was this?' Carrie asks.

'Oh, I only remember cos it was the Saturday night that Rose went missing.'

Carrie stares at her. 'Are you sure? Joe wasn't here that evening. He was working then he went home.'

'I'm positive. I remember because the next day we were all out searching. I just kept thinking what a close call we'd had with Ryan, and I felt bad that now Joe and you were suffering because Rose hadn't come home.'

Carrie's whole body has become a furnace, her insides burning. 'Yeah,' she says. 'You must be right. I'm glad Ryan was okay.' She stands up and grabs her keys and phone. 'Listen, I need to get home, I've just remembered there's something I need to do before it gets too late. But thanks for the tea.'

'But you haven't even drunk it,' Lia says.

'Sorry,' Carrie says, rushing out of the house.

Outside, Carrie runs to her car, throwing her phone on the passenger seat and starting the ignition.

Joe has lied to her and she needs to find out why.

THIRTY-TWO

LUCY

I step out of the police station feeling like a criminal. I'm certain I will be watched now, as if I'm guilty of a heinous crime. I've lied to the police, omitted to tell them about Rose's phone, and that I've heard from Jacob. If I wasn't before, now I am as equally entrenched in this as Jacob.

Moments ago, DC Keller had grilled me about why I'd taken Jacob away, but I was steadfast in my reasoning: to keep him safe. 'And he wasn't under arrest,' I'd insisted. Still, all eyes will now be on me, which will make it harder to fight for my son.

In the car, I head towards Joe's flat. I have no idea what his shift pattern is, but I've got to try something. There's no sign of his car, the silver Volvo I've seen countless times outside Carrie's whenever I've picked up Jacob. But still, I park up and press his buzzer.

As I expected, there's no answer, but I'm not giving up. I'll find Joe before the day is over.

It's around lunchtime when I drive up to the large modern building he works in, so I'm not surprised to see him outside, strolling towards the row of shops further down the road, one hand buried in his pocket, and the other clutching a cigarette. It's seeing Carrie rush towards him and grab hold of him that shocks me. I pull up and cut the ignition, rolling my window down so I can hear what they're saying.

'You lied to me, Joe!' Carrie screams. 'You said you didn't see Rose that night, but you were at my house! You'd better tell me what the hell happened. Right now. Tell me!'

Joe pulls away from her. 'Just calm down, will you. I work here.'

'I don't give a shit! Just tell me!'

Scanning the area, he drops his cigarette on the ground and grinds it with his foot. 'All right. Bloody hell. I was there that night, okay? I came to see you but you weren't back from the barbeque, so I left. It's no big deal. I didn't even see Rose, so there was no need to tell you.'

'You're lying!' Carrie can no longer believe what anyone says.

'No, I swear I'm not. I'm not Jacob.'

Hearing my son's name, I feel a surge of anger as I watch the two of them.

Carrie is shaking her head, pointing her finger close to Joe's face. I've never seen her like this before. 'You're lying!' she repeats, screaming this time.

Taking a step backwards, Joe holds up his hands. 'It's the truth. I didn't stay long enough to see her.'

'Then why didn't you tell the police? You're as bad as Jacob!'

Again, I am riled by how they use Jacob's name when he isn't here to defend himself. I reach for the handle, but think better of it.

Now Joe steps forward, thrusting his face into Carrie's. 'Don't say that to me. I'm not a murderer!'

'You are a liar, though,' Carrie responds. Her voice is calmer now. She believes him. So easily.

'Was this what you wanted to talk to me about?' Carrie continues. 'The other day you said you needed to tell me something. Tell me now.'

Joe falls silent. 'Not here. I'll come over tonight. Nine o'clock. Now, please, Carrie – can you let me go? I need to grab lunch and get back to work.'

I watch in disbelief as Joe stalks off, leaving Carrie staring after him. She watches him for a moment, before turning away and heading back to where I assume her car must be parked. Thankfully she's too consumed with what's just happened to notice me. I don't have an excuse prepared for being here, and it's better for Jacob if Carrie doesn't know I've overheard her argument with Joe. That man is tied up in this – I know it.

Carrie disappears from view, but I stay in my car, silently replaying their conversation. Joe was there the night Rose disappeared. And the night before that he'd lied to Jacob, telling him Rose wasn't home, when Jacob had seen her at the window.

Reaching across to my bag on the passenger seat, I pull out my new phone and text Jacob.

Joe was at Carrie's that night after the barbeque. Did you see him? Did you see anything at all?

I press send. I know it's unlikely that Jacob saw Joe – he would have mentioned it long before now if he had, but it might trigger a memory. Jacob is grieving, as well as being under immense pressure; who knows what that's done to his mind?

After a few minutes, there's no reply. It's not yet time for our scheduled communication, so I try not to panic. It's feasible that Jacob is waiting until nine o'clock to reply. The familiar sense of panic begins to descend on me. I don't know where my son is or what he's doing. Somehow, I fight through the fear. *Nothing will happen to him. Jacob is fine.* I force this mantra to circulate through my mind. My focus needs to be only on helping Jacob. I've got just under an hour until school finishes, enough time to get home and take Cooper for a walk. And then there's someone I need to see.

I stand across the road from the school gates and see Ava walking out, her head down as she stares at the ground, avoiding looking at anyone. She used to be invisible, someone kids would barge past, not noticing, but now everyone turns to look at her. I can only imagine what it's doing to her already fragile self-esteem. I fight my urge to run to her and shield her from their intrusive stares; it's something she wouldn't thank me for, and I don't want to do any further damage to our relationship. And it's not Ava I've come to find today.

I've almost given up hope of finding Nina when the swarm of school children scurrying from the building dwindles. Then, just as it occurs to me that she could be off sick, I see her approaching the gates, walking side by side with a boy I don't recognise.

'Nina,' I call, rushing over to her.

She turns, her eyes widening as she realises who's called her name. 'Oh,' she says, turning to her friend. 'Um, you go on, this might be long.'

The boy shrugs then walks off. He turns back to watch us for a moment before carrying on.

'Nina, I'm sorry to catch you after school like this, but I really need to talk to you. Is that okay?'

'I don't think I should,' she says. 'I mean, didn't you run away from the police with Jacob?' She starts walking.

'Wait, it wasn't like that, Nina. I just had to get him away for a while to keep him safe. Please can you just stop and listen to me. Please? You must have heard what those men did to him?'

She stops walking and lowers her eyes. 'Yeah. And I'm sorry that happened. But... I don't want to get in trouble.'

'I promise you, you won't be in any trouble. Just five minutes – please. Can you do it for Rose? And Jacob? You cared about them both, didn't you?'

Nina looks up at me, her mouth twisting. 'Okay. Five minutes. No more.'

I explain that my car is parked around the corner and she agrees to let me drive her home. And now I have one chance to get through to her, and I don't have much time.

Once we're in the car, I try to reassure her that it's fine for us to be talking, but I can tell from the way she cowers against the passenger door that she's nervous. We get stuck at some temporary traffic lights, and I'm grateful that this pause will buy me a bit more time.

'Where's Jacob now?' she asks, clutching her bag to her chest. 'They're saying he didn't come back with you, and I haven't seen him at school. Is it true?'

I keep my eyes on the road. 'Yes. Jacob ran away and I don't know where he is. I don't think he'll come back until his name is cleared. This has been so hard for him.'

'But—'

'He didn't do it, Nina. I promise you. I know he didn't.'

She turns to me, and if I could look at her now, instead of having to focus on the road, I'm sure she would see in my eyes what I know in my heart. 'Nina, I'm just going to pull up when we get through these next lights. And then after our five minutes is up, if you want to walk the rest of the way home, then I won't try and stop you.'

'Okay,' she says, her eyes scanning the road ahead.

We finally make it through the lights and I pull into Colts-foot Drive and turn off the ignition. Silence falls upon us as I turn to Nina. 'Jacob didn't do it. And I have to get evidence so that he can come home.'

'You keep saying that, but you can't *know*,' she insists. 'Nobody can.'

'One day you might be a mother yourself and then you'll understand, I promise. I can't explain it. It's just something I know.'

Nina turns away from me and stares out of the window. 'How can we ever really know anyone?' she says. 'Rose used to say that all the time.' She smiles as she turns back to me. 'She always knew what she was talking about.' Then tears begin to fall from her eyes, and I don't know whether she'll want me to comfort her, or just leave her.

I reach for her arm. 'This has been so hard for everyone. We all miss her so much. What happened to Rose was just so terrible and unfair. She had such a bright future ahead of her. Such a gift. But even more than that – she was a kind person.' As I say this, Jacob's words about nobody knowing Rose thunder into my head, jumbling my thoughts. *Why did he say that?*

Nina looks up at me. 'Rose was completely right.'

'What do you mean?'

'About nobody really knowing anyone. I... I thought I knew her, but in the end she was like a stranger to me. I couldn't understand her.'

'Nina, what do you mean?' I hold my breath and wait.

She stares through the windscreen. 'We... we had an argument a few days before she went missing. We weren't even talking when she died.' Nina begins to take shallow breaths, struggling to control her breathing. But she brushes me off when I try to help her. 'I'm fine.'

Of all the things I expected Nina to say, her revelation isn't one of them. 'What did you argue about? Can you tell me? It's really important, Nina. Whatever you say could end up helping Jacob.'

Nina takes so long to speak that I wonder if she ever will. But I remain silent and wait. She doesn't look at me as she begins to talk. 'A few weeks before the barbeque, she called me one night and asked if she could come over. It was late and I could tell she was upset. She just wasn't herself. Rose was always so positive about everything, wasn't she? I'd never seen her like that before.'

Nina pauses and looks at me, but I urge her to continue.

'Things were over with her and Jacob, and she was really gutted about it.'

My whole body turns cold. 'What?'

She nods. 'Yeah. Their relationship was over.'

'But that doesn't make sense. Jacob never said anything. And Rose came to the barbeque.' *Although she was barely talking to Jacob.* 'They even walked home together.'

Nina stares at her hand, twisting a small silver ring around her finger. 'I don't know why she went. She wasn't talking to me by then. It's probably because of Ava, though. Yeah, that must be it. She was always talking about how close she and Ava had become.'

'But Jacob walked Rose home. If they were no longer together, then why would he do that? Why would she let him?'

'I don't know anything!' Nina protests. 'I can't answer any of these questions because I wasn't around. I told you – Rose wasn't even talking to me. No messages. Nothing. She blanked me whenever she saw me at school.'

'Why didn't you tell the police any of this?' So many lies that they will eventually unravel, including my own.

'I did it for Jacob.' Nina sniffs, reaching into her bag for a tissue.

'Why, though? I don't understand?'

Again, her reply is a long time coming. 'Because there *was* something going on with me and Jacob.'

Carrie has been doing everything she can to make time pass more quickly. She's desperate to find out what Joe has been hiding; despite his insistence that he didn't see Rose that night, how can she trust him? And now, thinking about it, she's not sure she ever did.

She hadn't expected Tom to turn up at six o'clock, not when they'd agreed to give each other some space while he and Lucy sort things out. She has no idea what the outcome of that will be, so she needs to make the most of every moment she can spend with Tom. She needs to be the first to find out when Jacob comes back. *If* he does.

'I appreciate you cooking for me,' Tom says. 'All I've been eating recently is takeaways at work. I've been practically living at the office.'

'It must be difficult at home,' she says, offering him some garlic bread. She'd found lasagne in the freezer that she'd made months ago and had shared with Rose. There had been far too much for the two of them, so she'd frozen it and forgotten all about it until Tom had rung her doorbell this evening.

'We've... Lucy and I have agreed to separate for the time

being,' he says. 'I don't know what will happen in the future, but it feels like what we need to do right now.'

'I'm so sorry, Tom,' Carrie says. And she is, even though this will make things a lot easier for her.

She looks at Tom now and part of her wants to tell him about finding the phone. She could explain that Lucy might know about it herself now, after the dressing gown disappeared when she and Jacob left. But Carrie won't. Tom's clearly suffering so she doesn't want to add to his misery. His wife has lied to him, and what will he do when he finds out Carrie hasn't been honest with him either?

'I'm sorry too,' he says. 'Although I should have known this would happen.'

'What do you mean?'

'We can't control who we fall in love with, can we? And I don't think Lucy's ever truly moved on from Alistair. It's easy when someone dies to almost put them on a pedestal, and forget that they were only human and had faults, just like the rest of us. She never said it outright, but I've always felt she was comparing me to him. And I never lived up to the father he would have been to Jacob.'

Carrie puts down her fork. 'If that's true, then I'm sorry.'

'It's not her fault. Like I said, we can't choose who we want in our hearts.' He takes her hand. 'Like this. I felt something for you even before the barbeque, but of course I'd never have acted on it. But then life threw us a curveball and everything changed. But even now, I feel bad because of what you've been through. I don't want to take advantage of you in any way.'

Carrie looks away from him. She loathes being so deceitful. 'You're not,' she assures him. 'I know exactly what I'm doing. And it's what I want.'

'Do you think... maybe we could just slow it down, take our time and give each other space while still being there for each other? If that makes sense?'

'It does make sense,' she assures him.

'But I'm here for you. Whenever you need me. And whenever you want some company. Like now. This is nice, isn't it? We don't have to pretend we're okay, we can just... *be.*'

Carrie nods. 'And I'm here for you and Ava too.' She picks up her fork and prods her lasagne. She doesn't want to eat it. 'Do you want to stay tonight? I have to go and see someone at nine, but it won't take long. Just make yourself at home.'

Tom chews his lip. 'Um, okay, yeah. I'd like that. It will give Lucy and me some proper space from each other.'

They both turn back to their food, sitting together in comfortable silence.

'Can I ask you something?' Carrie asks. 'Have you ever felt as though Jacob's not your son?'

His answer is immediate. 'No. Never. But if I'm honest with myself, then it's always there in the back of my mind. Especially as he looks so much like Alistair. 'But I love him. Just as much as I love Ava, even though Lucy would dispute that.' He sighs. 'I've spent years trying to convince her of that and then this happens. And it's just confirmed to Lucy what she already believes.'

'Do you still think he's guilty?' Carrie asks, lifting her fork. There's no way she can put it in her mouth. All she wants to do is get to Joe's.

'The honest truth is... I don't know. Why did he run if he's innocent? That doesn't make sense.'

'It will all come out in the end,' Carrie says. And this is what keeps her going.

'Yes, you're right. But I think that terrifies me even more than not knowing for sure.'

She watches Tom as he finishes his lasagne. As close as she feels to him, there are things she can never let him know. And one of them is that these moments they're sharing can't possibly last.

· · ·

She's ten minutes early when she gets to Joe's flat, but she couldn't wait any longer. She left Tom working on his laptop, poring over a contract for a client. It was a bizarre scenario, as if they were a married couple. Or rather some strange parody of marriage, on her part at least; everything on the surface hiding dark truths within.

Joe lets her inside, his face riddled with frown lines. He's still dressed in his work uniform, and Carrie notices a small ketchup stain on his top.

'I didn't think you'd come,' he says, closing the door.

'It stinks of smoke in here.' Carrie holds her breath as she walks through the hallway to the living room.

Joe follows her. 'Sorry. Been smoking like a chimney since I got home from work. Can't even eat. I'll open the window.'

In the living room, Carrie turns to him. 'Are you going to tell me why you lied, Joe?' On the way over here, she'd determined to stay calm with Joe. Losing it will just anger him and force him to close up. He has a short fuse, and she doesn't want to ignite it.

'Yeah, yeah, I'm about to tell you,' Joe says. 'I just need a sec.' He grabs his cigarette packet and pulls one out, shoving it in his mouth and fumbling in his pocket for a lighter.

'No,' Carrie says, yanking it from his mouth. 'You know I hate smoking. Just talk to me, Joe.' She throws the unlit cigarette on the table, ignoring it when it rolls to the floor.

'At least sit down, will you?' Joe says, eyeing the cigarette. 'You're making me nervous.'

She sinks onto the sofa and folds her arms. 'Go on, then. I want to know everything that happened. Every single thing.' *And then I'll make up my own mind whether or not to believe it.*

Joe sits down and folds his hands into a steeple, pressing his head against them. 'I was supposed to come to the barbeque with you, wasn't I? But I got called into work.'

'I remember,' Carrie says. She'd been relieved that Joe wouldn't be coming. It meant she could be free to enjoy herself without worrying about what he was getting up to, or how he might embarrass her and Rose.

'But I got off earlyish and wanted to see you. I thought I'd surprise you. That's why I didn't text or anything before. Listen, Carrie. Everything I told you yesterday is true. You weren't home so I sat and watched TV for a bit. Had a beer. I must have fallen asleep.'

'I'd met Lorna at the pub.' Carrie recalls how her work friend had called her, begging her to get down there because she needed a drink and a chat. Something and nothing in the end – Lorna was thinking of leaving her husband and wanted someone to lend an ear while she talked it all through. And now, weeks later, the two of them are still together. How Carrie wishes now she'd said no to Lorna. Would Rose still be alive if Carrie had been home when she'd got back after arguing with Jacob?

Joe nods. 'Yeah, but I didn't know you'd gone down the pub. Or I would have just gone there to meet you. I thought you'd be coming back from the barbeque any minute. I mean, I didn't think that thing would last that long.' He sighs. 'If Rose came back, then I didn't hear her. And actually, what proof is there that she even came back home like Jacob claims? He's already lied, and—'

'So have you,' Carrie points out. 'You didn't tell the police you were at my house that night, did you?'

'No, you're right. But it's not relevant cos I never saw Rose!'

He's getting riled now; Carrie needs to tread carefully. And Joe has a point – other than Jacob, nobody witnessed Rose coming home that night. Her head throbs.

'When did you leave my house, then? You weren't there when I got back.'

'I dunno. Who checks these things? Maybe nine or something like that.'

Around the time that Rose and Jacob left the barbeque. If Joe's telling the truth, then they would have only narrowly missed each other.

'Okay, Joe, whatever you say.' She stands, hoisting her bag onto her shoulder.

'Wait Carrie, none of this is what I needed to tell you. There's something else.'

THIRTY-FOUR

ROSE

I grew up in that moment I discovered the truth about you, the reason you'd come crawling back. If I'd thought I was mature before, I was wrong. Maturity was forced upon me, instantly, and it allowed me to finally see reality.

I've never considered myself an actor, but that's what I had to do. If I'd been able to talk to Nina, then I would have told her everything right then. And it would have felt good to unburden, finally. I wanted to feel light again, to lose myself in schoolwork and my songs, to free myself of the darkness I'd been tainted with. Free myself of *you*.

Nina wouldn't even look at me at school, though, so if I'd tried to apologise to her, she wouldn't have heard it. And to be fair to her, I was the same. I didn't allow myself to look her way, even when I saw in my peripheral vision that she was close by. It was important that we weren't talking. For everything to fall into place as I wanted it to, I had to put barriers up, to block people from my life in order to protect them.

Everyone at school knew that Nina and I weren't speaking, so it was easy to get close to Rowena Hill without anyone questioning why. Rowena and I are polar opposites. She's a plastic barbie, while I'm... what? I no longer know. What I'm trying to say is that she is the complete contrast of me: make-up as heavily applied as she could get away with at school, no interest in studying, and all her focus is on growing her YouTube channel. To her credit, she's doing well, and has thousands of subscribers. I can't understand it – she's a sixteen-year-old, just like I am. What do we have to say that's worth sharing with the world? Literally, the world.

I told her I was interested in setting up a channel for my music, and she thought about this for a moment before she smiled. 'Yeah, I s'pose there's an audience for that kind of thing. If you do it right. I'll show you.'

And that was exactly what I wanted.

I have no idea what you were up to during this time. I threw myself into studying, and everyone bought the excuses I showered on them to explain why I had become reclusive. And shut away in my room, it was easy to work away on my phone, to lose myself in this project and let Mum think I was studying the whole time.

Ava was the one who told me about the barbeque, not long after my birthday. 'Mum just checked the weather forecast and decided we needed to make the most of this freak heatwave at the weekend. You're coming aren't you?' she asked. As far as she knew, or anyone else knew, nothing had happened; Rose and Jacob were still going strong. Neither of us was going to say anything, were we? That was the way it would be until I was ready. But still, I was distancing myself – to make things easier for people I didn't want to hurt – so I'd avoided your house for days. Nobody questioned my excuse that I had to focus on studying until the exams.

'I don't think I can, Ava. I really need to—'

'Oh, Rose, you could sit the exams now and get all nines. Everyone knows it.'

I smiled at her, and it broke me to know that I was about to destroy her life. That's the reason I agreed to go to the barbeque. It would be the calm before the storm, a last moment of serenity before the avalanche crushed us all. A last supper.

Later, while Mum was at work, I sat with Joe in the kitchen. Mum had made us some dinner, which Joe had heated up in the oven. A minced beef cobbler. Things were different between Joe and me now – the animosity between us had disappeared and left in its place something peaceful.

'I'm not seeing her any more,' he said, peering across at me. He was talking with his mouth full, and normally I would have pointed this out, but his disgusting habits no longer seemed to matter.

'Really?' I barely looked up from my plate.

'Nope. I love your mum. She's a good woman, Rose. I don't deserve her.'

'I'm not arguing with you there.'

'Ha, listen to you – the voice of wisdom. But you're still only just sixteen.' He shovelled another mouthful of mince into his mouth. 'I haven't forgotten what it was like at that age. Thinking you know everything. And then one day you'll be pushing forty and realise you didn't know a damn thing.'

Joe was right. At fifteen I'd thought I was grown up, practically an adult. It's only now, too late, I know my thinking was way off. Destructively so.

'So you're going to stop cheating on Mum? Treat her how she deserves to be treated?'

'Yep, I am. You have my word. Scout's honour.' He did a salute.

He was making something serious so light-hearted and it made me uneasy. Angry even.

But what he said next was the final nail in the coffin. 'You won't say anything to your mum, will you? Can I count on you, Rose?'

That was it. His words echoed yours, brought it all back to me how cheap you'd made me feel. How worthless.

I snapped. Picked up my plate and tipped the contents of it over his head. Then, before he was out of his chair, I ran upstairs and locked myself in the bathroom.

'You little bitch,' he shouted, thundering up the stairs. He pounded on the door for ages before he gave up.

It wouldn't be long before Mum would get home, and I know Joe wouldn't say anything about what I'd done. If he wanted me to keep his secret, then he'd be downstairs clearing up the mess, making sure Mum didn't need to ask any questions.

Even if he wasn't, there was something far more important I had to deal with, and tonight I would be putting it into place.

THIRTY-FIVE

LUCY

I should be used to being shocked to my core by now. First Jacob, and now Nina. So many lies. And all of them concealing what really happened to Rose, and why her life was taken. I study Nina, and wonder briefly if I've misunderstood her.

'You and Jacob? You were together?'

For a moment Nina sits staring through the windscreen. A young girl walks along the street, who for the briefest second reminds me of Rose. As she gets closer, though, it's clear that she's vastly different from Rose. She's older for a start, at least twenty, and everything about the way she holds herself is different. More conscious. As though she's aware of what she looks like. Rose didn't care about any of that.

'Nina, please talk to me,' I urge. 'I need to understand what's going on so I can help Jacob.'

She blows her nose again before beginning. 'I was the one who noticed Jacob first at school. I... kind of liked him straight away.' She looks right at me. 'He didn't like me, though, not like that. The second he saw Rose he couldn't stop looking at her.' Nina sniffs. 'It was like once he'd seen her, he couldn't pull his eyes off her. Ever. I was the one who pushed Rose to talk to him. She didn't seem interested to start with, but I had to keep forcing it, didn't I?' She looks away. 'I wish I hadn't.'

So many questions race through my mind, but I need to just let her speak.

'Then they got together, and everyone thought they were perfect together. Even I did to start with. But I know Rose, and she didn't say anything but I could tell something was off. Not straight away. But definitely towards the end. As much as Jacob had been into her, it just felt like... I don't know, like he wasn't that interested really. Like he wanted to show the world that he had a girlfriend, but really he wasn't that invested in her. And Rose used to say that she and Jacob were just friends, and she'd go on about his girlfriend from London.'

'Isla. She moved away, but, yes, Jacob still insisted they were together until he met Rose.' And I don't want to think about this – how odd things were between my son and Isla. 'Did Rose ever talk about her?'

Nina shakes her head. 'I tried to once, but she shut me down. She just wouldn't talk about it. I gave up after that. I get the feeling something happened there that made Jacob... weird. Sorry.'

'So, if Rose and Jacob were just friends to start with, when did it change? What happened?'

'I don't know. I didn't actually notice anything changing, but then one day she was calling him her boyfriend. But by then everyone thought they were together anyway so nothing was a big shock.'

None of this makes sense. How did I not see that something was wrong? I ask Nina what happened to Jacob and Rose.

She shakes her head. 'No idea. All I know is that Rose became weird. Distant. We never met up after school or anything. She always had an excuse not to. I asked her about it once and d'you know what she said? She said maybe she was just growing up. Adult friends don't live in each other's pockets. That's what she told me. I was a bit annoyed with her about that but I forgave her. She was my best friend. I'd known her since primary school.' She pauses for breath.

'I know this is hard for you, Nina. But what happened with you and Jacob?'

'I hung out with them both quite a bit so I got to know him, and I... Well, I'd liked him from the moment I saw him that first day at school. But I would never have done anything. Never. Even when he started to tell me that things weren't good between them. He said Rose was becoming cold and distant, not wanting to see him, or... you know *be* with him.'

I bury this thought – I can't deal with thinking about Jacob's sex life. I know that he's old enough now, but that's a part of his life that is not my business, except for me reminding him to always be safe.

'The night of the barbeque, Jacob *did* come round. He'd called me and I'd sneaked him in, so none of my family saw him. Mum would never have let him in that late.' Nina rolls her eyes. 'You know, because he's a boy. Anyway, he was distraught, telling me that Rose had accused him of being into me. He said he couldn't understand why she was saying all this, and I didn't tell him that she'd already said the same thing to me. We just talked and he was upset about Rose the whole time. Then he hugged me, telling me how he'd lost Rose and he couldn't bear it.' Nina hangs her head. 'I'm so ashamed of this. I was the second it happened, but I kissed him and begged him to sleep with me.' She starts to cry – slow tears that trickle down her cheeks, but quickly turning into loud, heavy sobs that make her chest heave.

'So, you and Jacob—'

'No,' she says, through her tears. 'He pushed me away and

said he could never hurt Rose, even though she was really distant with him. And then he left. He said he had to fix things with Rose. He couldn't get away from me faster.'

Hearing this, although I'm sad for Nina, I feel an intense surge of pride towards Jacob. Plenty of teenage boys wouldn't have turned Nina down.

'Listen to me. You never, ever have to offer yourself up like that. Never. You're worth so much more than that. When you find someone who's right for you, even if it's just the first of several relationships, you will never have to beg anyone to be with you.'

She nods. 'I know you're right. I just really liked Jacob. And I stupidly thought he could like me too. It's clear that Rose didn't love him.'

'I don't know, Nina. I've been kept in the dark about all this. I didn't even realise they were having problems. I did notice that she wasn't coming to the house over the last few weeks before the barbeque, but Jacob just told us she was focusing on revising.'

Why wouldn't he tell me that he and Rose were having problems? How did I not notice? All this time I've watched the kids like a hawk, ready to step in to protect them whenever they need it, yet all this was happening and I remained oblivious.

'Nina, I know this must be frightening for you, but do you realise that you're Jacob's alibi?' I ask. 'If you'd told the police all of this at the start, then it would have cleared his name. Why did you lie to them? You could have just told them Jacob came to see you.'

Nina shakes her head. 'I couldn't tell them. I was humiliated. And then it would have also come out about what I did with Jacob, and about my argument with Rose. Then they might have thought that I—'

'No, they wouldn't think that, Nina. You were at your house at the time of Rose's death.'

She chews her lip. 'How do the police even know when she died?'

'DC Keller told us that they could estimate it from the last thing Rose ate at the barbeque. They wouldn't tell us what it was, and the truth is I'd rather not know. But they did estimate the time of death to be between nine thirty and twelve thirty. The exact time that you were with Jacob.'

Nina considers this. 'But I was scared. I didn't know if Jacob hated me. He might have said I left the house. And then what would they think?'

I'm about to convince her that Jacob doesn't lie, but how can I when he's told so many? *Not about killing Rose, though. I can't let myself believe he is capable of that.*

Nina hugs her bag to her chest again. 'I was convinced Jacob would tell them everything. I can't believe he didn't.' She looks at me. 'He did it for me, though, didn't he? That just shows what a good person he is, doesn't it?'

And this is the boy I know. Kind. Loyal. *But I still can't explain why he had Rose's phone.*

'Nina, do you know anything about Rose's phone? Did she lose it or anything?'

'I wasn't talking to her, remember? I have no idea. But her mum would have known, wouldn't she?'

Nina's right – if Rose had lost her phone, then surely she would have told Carrie. 'Okay, look, we need to get you to the police station so you can tell them that Jacob was with you. You don't have to tell them what happened with you two that night, just tell the truth and let them know you were there with him. When Jacob comes back, I'll make sure he doesn't tell them what happened between you.'

'Adults always say things they don't mean. Promise us this and that. Then it never happens.'

'You may be right, Nina. But I'm asking you to give me a chance to not be the adult who does that. Please.'

Seconds tick by and I imagine Nina flinging open the car door and running, my chance to free Jacob from this disappearing with her.

'Okay,' she says, turning away to stare out of the passenger window. 'I'll do it.'

THIRTY-SIX

CARRIE

She stands with Hugh at Rose's grave, watching as he places a fresh bouquet of lilies against her shiny black headstone. The letters on it are engraved in rose gold, their daughter's favourite colour. Hugh takes her hand and they stay for a moment, united in their grief. Over the last couple of days she's come to understand that Hugh does feel the loss too, just not as deeply as Carrie does.

The words Joe uttered last night ring in her head. His confession, delivered while staring at his shoes. 'I was sleeping with another woman, Carrie.'

She'd almost laughed, because this hadn't been what she'd expected. She'd thought Joe was about to tell her something about Rose – maybe even that he'd been the one who'd killed her – so when he'd admitted having an affair, all she felt was relief. How could she have lived with herself knowing that she had brought Rose's killer into their lives? It didn't bear thinking about.

She'd even laughed, doubled over clutching her stomach because once she'd started, she couldn't stop. Hysteria, really. It was nothing more than that. Another side effect of grief, she's sure.

'Are you okay?' Hugh asks, nudging her. 'I mean, I know you're not, but you see what I mean.'

Carrie kneels on the grass by Rose's grave. 'I always make bad choices with men, don't I?' she says, not caring that the person she's addressing is one of those choices.

Hugh kneels beside her, rearranging the flowers she's so carefully placed. Carrie doesn't have the energy to object. 'I don't think you can think of it like that,' he says. 'Some relationships just don't work out. They feel right to begin with, then it just doesn't work as time goes by.'

'Like us?' She turns to him. He's still handsome, even with the flecks of grey scattered around his hairline. 'Why do you suppose we didn't work out, Hugh?'

'It was nothing you did. It was because I was young and stupid and didn't focus on the right things. I had it drummed into me that I needed to forge a career for myself, that nothing else mattered. But my parents were wrong. And now I've lost Rose and I didn't even have a chance to know her properly.' He looks at her grave. 'My own daughter.'

Carrie wants to feel sympathy for him, but it won't come. She hates clichés but it's too little, too late. 'You could do something to make up for it,' Carrie says. 'We need to find proof that it was Jacob who killed Rose. He's lying to everyone. And I think his mother knows where he is. I think she knows a lot more than that. In fact, I'm convinced she does.'

'I told you, I've got someone working on it. He's a bit slow, yeah, but these things take time. I did warn you nothing would happen overnight.'

'No, a private investigator is not enough. And he hasn't even contacted me. How can he be looking for Jacob without talking to people? Tom knows nothing him about him either.'

'Just let him do his job, Carrie. Jarvis knows what he's doing.'

Carrie thinks his name sounds nothing like the name of someone who should be investigating anything, and she tells Hugh that's not what she wants. 'There's something else you can help me with instead.'

'Why don't I like the sound of this?' Hugh says, studying her face.

'I don't care. You owe it to Rose to do this.' She doesn't wait for a reply. 'I need you to get into Jacob's house and search for a mobile phone. It has a rose gold case, and I know it's in that house somewhere. Or maybe in Lucy's workshop.'

Carrie doesn't like the frown that appears on his forehead. 'What phone?' he asks. 'Whose is it? Wait a minute, is this Rose's phone? Carrie, tell me!'

She can't tell him the truth. There is no way she'd be able to convince him to keep it between them. 'Rose's phone wasn't found on her. Or anywhere in the surrounding area. It's just a hunch but I think Jacob might have it.'

'The police would have found it, Carrie. You're not thinking straight.'

But he's wrong, she's never before had such clarity. 'It's worth a try,' she says. 'Will you do this or not?'

Hugh shakes his head. 'I'm not a spy or a criminal, Carrie! I wouldn't even know where to start.'

A young man walks past with his dog, clutching a small bunch of flowers. Red and pink roses.

'Come on, let's walk,' Carrie says, taking Hugh's arm.

'You're here for three more days, aren't you?' she asks. 'That gives you plenty of time. Ava will be at school during the day, Tom will be at work, and I'll find out exactly when Lucy won't be home.'

'And no prizes for guessing you'll do that by asking Tom,'

Hugh says. 'I know something's been going on with you and the dad of that boy. What are you playing at?'

'Oh, give it a rest,' Carrie snaps. She doesn't need another one of her exes lecturing her about her relationship with Tom.

'The answer's no,' Hugh says, standing and straightening his jeans. 'I'm not breaking into anyone's house.'

'You don't have to,' Carrie says, rummaging in her bag. She finds what she's looking for and dangles a key in front of Hugh. 'Because you'll have this.'

He stares at it. 'How did you get that?'

'That's the best thing about this. Nothing criminal took place. I was given that key when I was staying there.' Tom has just never asked for it back. He's probably forgotten she even has it. That's the funny thing; Carrie would never forget if she'd given someone her door key – it was the first thing she demanded to have back when she left Joe. But Tom is so focused on work that he gives no thought to domestic issues.

'Like I said,' Carrie continues, 'I'll find out when the house will be empty, and then all you have to do is let yourself in and see if you can find anything.'

'As easy as that.' Hugh frowns. 'I really don't like this.'

'Neither do I. But do it for Rose.'

They walk for a few more minutes before Hugh gives her a reply. 'Okay, Carrie, I'll do it. I'll get Jarvis to come with me – he'll be more likely to know what to look for.'

Carrie smiles. For once, Hugh is doing the right thing.

Getting information from Tom without arousing suspicion is harder than she expected. She's made the trip to his office to meet him for lunch. The drive up the A3 to London, although not far, took her longer than she'd thought, so her cheeks are flushed, sweat dripping down her chest, when she finally meets him at the café he suggested in Putney.

'Well, this is strange,' Tom says, hugging her. 'Seeing you out of context. Strange in a good way, I mean.'

'I thought you could do with a change to your day,' Carrie says. 'My treat.'

Tom holds up his hand. 'Absolutely not. My firm has an account here anyway, so I'll put it on our tab.'

'No,' Carrie says. 'I insist on paying.' She doesn't add that it's the least she can do when she's using Tom in such an underhand way. How did she become this person, when she's always cherished every relationship she's had, committed herself fully and fought for it with every inch of her being? But losing a child changes people, Carrie now knows. *We no longer know who we are.*

'How are things at home?' she asks when their food arrives, and she's given Tom some time to tell her what's happening at work.

'The phrase "ships passing in the night" comes to mind,' Tom says. 'It's all pleasant and courteous, but we barely speak.'

'How's Ava handling it?'

'Surprisingly well, actually. Maybe because we're both still in the house.' He sighs. 'I suppose a time will come when we have to sell up and go our separate ways, but for now at least she's still got stability. I can't stop worrying about Jacob, though.' He grimaces. 'Sorry, I know it must be hard for you to hear about him. But he's still my son, Carrie. Even after—'

'And he's a child,' Carrie says. 'It's awful that you don't know where he is. I know how that feels, don't I?' It was how it all started with Rose.

Tom reaches for her hand and holds it for a moment. A small action that speaks more than a thousand words.

'The police are looking for him,' Carrie says. 'They'll find him.'

'And as much as it hurts to say this, that will be good for you too.' He looks away, and Carrie is sure there is a glimmering tear in his eye.

She almost tells him she has to leave; she can't bear being a witness to his pain. But she came here with a purpose. 'How is Lucy doing? This must all be so awful for her.'

He nods. 'Yeah, it is. She's taking Ava to her brother's place on Saturday. I think she's hoping Jacob will be there. He's always been close to his uncle. I told her there's no way he'll go somewhere he can easily be tracked to. It will be good for Ava, though.'

'I can come and keep you company if you'd like me to?'

Tom doesn't hesitate. 'I would. I'll just be in the office during the day, though. But you could come over in the evening? I'll be back by seven.'

Again, Carrie is flooded with guilt. She has the information she needs now, and she didn't even have to press him too much. Everything is falling into place.

THIRTY-SEVEN

LUCY

In the evening I sit in my workshop and wait. I don't know where Tom is, but he keeps his distance from me, and Ava went to bed early, so I know I won't be disturbed when Jacob calls. To ground me, I try to focus on the hydrangeas I'm preparing to dry. It's four minutes past nine and my phone hasn't rung.

I fight against all my instincts to call him instead – I have to show him that I trust him, and that I'm giving him space to live his life. It's torture, though, and I turn my attention back to removing the leaves and greenery from the hydrangeas. If I want them to be ready in time, I need to prepare them now for the dried bouquet a client has ordered for two weeks' time.

It's nearly half past nine when the phone finally rings, and I rush to answer. 'Jacob, hi. Are you okay?'

'I'm all right,' he says. 'Sorry, I didn't turn my phone on until just now so I've only just seen your message. What did you need to tell me? What's happened?'

I tell him about my conversation with Nina and he silently listens, only speaking when I urge him to respond.

'I didn't think she'd ever tell anyone,' he says. 'Not after I shoved her away like that. I was horrible and I know I upset her.

But I love Rose. I could never do that to her, and Nina was all over me – I just had to get her off me.'

'I know, Jacob. It's okay. You did the right thing for Rose.' I need to tell him that I know he and Rose were having problems, but I'm not going to do that over the phone – I need to give him a reason to come home, not one to stay away.

'I tried to apologise to Nina after,' Jacob explains. 'At school. But it was like she hated me. She wouldn't even look at me.'

'But she's doing the right thing now,' I assure him. 'I'm taking her to the police station tomorrow after school. She's going to tell them you were with her the night Rose was killed. She said she'll do it even though she'll get into trouble for lying before. This is great news, Jacob. It means you can come home. This is the proof we've been waiting for.'

I'm greeted with silence. 'Not yet,' he says eventually. 'Not until the police stop thinking I'm a suspect.'

'Jacob—'

'No, Mum. I'm not risking being attacked again. Everyone needs to know I'm innocent before I come home.'

'But your exams, you need—'

'I've been studying, Mum. I swear. And Mitch has been tutoring me online instead. I reached out to him and he said he was happy to help.'

This news takes me by surprise, and I can't work out whether I'm proud of him for taking the initiative like this, or furious for putting himself at risk of being found. 'You haven't told Mitch anything, have you? He still thinks you're called Josh?'

'Yeah, course. I couldn't just come out and say we lied to you the whole time in Cornwall, could I? He's cool.'

For a second, when I remember how relaxed Jacob seemed in St Ives, I long to be back there, away from all of this. With Jacob and Ava. A fresh start. 'Then will you at least let me come and see you? On Saturday. I've told your dad I'm taking Ava to your uncle's. You tell me where to meet you and I'll be there. Wherever you are.'

He takes his time to consider my request, but eventually gives the answer I'm hoping for. 'Yeah, okay. I'll text you where we can meet later.'

Time crawls by the next day, while I watch the clock, waiting to pick up Nina after school. This morning I told Ava all about Nina's revelation, but Tom wasn't at home, so I assume he didn't come back last night.

'Really?' Ava asked. 'So... this means that Jacob couldn't have done that to Rose?'

'No,' I say. 'He was with Nina for several hours and then came home. The timeline all adds up.' *But not the mobile phone.* I'm ignoring it because I still believe my son is innocent. And sooner or later I'll have to decide what to do with Rose's phone.

Ava had rushed over to me and thrown her arms around me, just as she used to when she was younger. I dared to believe that everything might be coming together – that we are going to get through it.

After school, I wait for Nina, expecting her to be one of the last out, as she was yesterday. This time, though, at least she's expecting me.

The crowd of school children dwindles, and there's no sign of Nina. When another ten minutes passes and no more students leave the building, I know that she's not coming. I start the ignition and make my way to her house, praying traffic will allow me to reach her quickly.

I'm not expecting Sacha Owens to be in at this time of day, but she answers the door, frowning. 'Lucy. What's going on? Is everything okay?'

'Um, is Nina home? I was supposed to meet her after school.'

She stares at me, her frown deepening. 'Yes, I know all about that. And Nina will not be going to the police station, I'm afraid.'

'Wait. Please. I promise you I haven't forced Nina to do this. Yesterday she said she wanted to put things right, for Jacob's sake. I didn't—'

Sacha leans forward and lowers her voice. 'I don't think you understand. Nina is the one who doesn't want to go. It's not me stopping her – I would never do that. She's nearly sixteen, she can make those kinds of decisions for herself.'

I knew I should have taken her straight there yesterday, but she'd told me she needed to get home for an online tutoring session. Was she lying? 'Did Nina have tutoring yesterday after school?'

Sacha's mouth twists. 'Yes, she did. Why do you ask?'

Because I need to know what could have happened in between then and now to make her change her mind. 'It doesn't matter,' I say. 'Please, Sacha, can I just talk to her?'

'She doesn't want to, Lucy. I'm sorry but I can't force her. I really think you should go now. This is harassment.'

I gently grab her arm. 'As a mother, can't you see how important this is? Nina is Jacob's alibi. He was with her for hours after walking Rose home, so he couldn't have done anything. She's lied to the police, Sacha. If she doesn't tell them, then I'll do it myself.'

She stares at me, her eyes boring into me. 'There's only your word against hers, isn't there? Maybe your son is forcing Nina to say that he was here. I was home that evening and I didn't see Jacob here. Neither did Nina's dad.'

I stand back and look up at the house. 'No, but I bet *that* did.' I point towards the CCTV camera fixed to the top corner of the house.

Sacha stares at it, her eyes widening as it dawns on her what this means. Then she gives a huge sigh. 'I'll talk to her,' she says, her voice barely louder than a whisper. And then she is step-ping back inside and closing the door in my face.

Ava is silent, her head buried in a book as we sit on the Tube, heading towards Leicester Square. I know why Jacob's picked central London to meet; he doesn't want us to know exactly where he's been staying, but it must be somewhere in London. I pray that he isn't sleeping rough, that he's reached out to someone he knows from our old life for help. Every time we've spoken, he's refused to answer my questions, and I have no choice but to trust that after years of me hovering over him, he will be okay without me at his side.

Ava and I step out of the station, our eyes assaulted by bright sunlight, and I pull my sunglasses down and scan the busy square. 'He said to sit on a bench in the middle of the square and he'd find us,' I tell Ava, pointing towards the grassy area. Even though we're in the middle of London, it's easy to blend in to the mass of people strolling around, so I don't feel worried that we could be noticed by anyone, or overheard.

My breath is stripped away from me when, after a few minutes, I catch sight of Jacob walking towards us. He's always been thin, but now his frame is skeletal, and his walk is slower, less assured. Everything that's happened has changed my son beyond recognition, and looking at him now, I'm sure he'll never again be the boy that he was.

Ava shocks me by running up to him and throwing her arms around him, almost knocking him off balance. He reciprocates her hug, and that gesture assures me that we will be okay.

'Mum,' he says, looking up from Ava. 'This is weird.'

I can't speak, but I reach out and hold him too, so that the three of us are frozen for a moment, unaware of the bustle around us.

'We're getting some lunch,' I say. 'I know you haven't been eating.'

He shrugs. 'Not much,' he admits. 'But I'm okay.'

Ava insists on Pizza Express, and planning our lunch like this is a tiny piece of normality in the midst of this horrific situation.

While we eat, I watch my son and try to fight against the guilt that's swelling inside me. 'Jacob, I need you to listen to me. I need you to come home with us. Today.'

He puts down the slice of pizza he's been ravenously tucking into. 'No, I told you on the phone – I'm not coming back yet.'

'Nina's going to the police. Then they'll know you have a solid alibi.' I don't mention her change of heart, or that I've forced her mother into convincing her to speak to them.

'Has she done it yet?'

'She's going to, Jacob. We just have to be patient.' I would text Sacha to check, but I can't do anything that might cast doubt on Jacob's alibi. Once a text is sent, it can't be taken back.

'I'm not coming home until Nina's been to the police,' Jacob says. 'That's final, Mum.'

I hadn't counted on it being this difficult to convince Jacob. I thought Sacha's promise that she'll tell Nina to go would be enough.

'Just hear me out. You need to sit your exams, Jacob. We can't let this affect any more of your future than it has to. I know you're grieving for Rose, but is your life. What about your dreams? You want to go to uni and study business.'

'My only dream is to not be a murder suspect,' he says, tearing some pizza crust off a slice and discarding both on the plate.

With every passing second, my chances of getting him home are vanishing. 'Please, Jacob. What do you think Rose would say?'

'Listen to Mum, Jacob,' Ava urges, finally breaking her silence.

He pushes his plate aside and stands. 'I don't give a damn what Rose would say. She never gave a shit about me. So why should I care about her? She was just like Isla.'

And before I can attempt to stop him, he's through the doors of the restaurant and out of my sight.

THIRTY-EIGHT

CARRIE

Everything is in place for Hugh to go to Jacob's house tomorrow, but Carrie can't just sit around and wait. The police investigation is getting nowhere. She doesn't listen when Michelle and DC Keller insist that just because she can't see what they're doing, it doesn't mean things aren't happening. But Carrie has lost faith in them, and with Jacob missing, she struggles to believe that anything is happening at all. She could never have imagined it would be down to her to get things moving, to find something that they haven't been able to. She almost laughs at how ludicrous it is that she's having to do this, until she realises instead how tragic it is.

It was quite straightforward to find Isla Harding; her Facebook profile was open for the whole world to see, and Carrie could even work out what school she attends. She also discovered that the girl appears to work in a hair salon after school and at weekends.

She's glad Rose would open up to her while they chatted over dinner. When she'd first met Jacob at school, Rose had told her that Jacob had a girlfriend in London, and that she'd moved away but he still wanted to be with her. And Carrie listened.

She was good at remembering names. *Isla Harding. You might just be able to help me.*

What was interesting, though, was that the girl wasn't in Manchester, as Jacob had claimed, but that she and her family were living in Chingford. Right there in London.

This puzzles Carrie, but it's just more proof of the trail of deceit Jacob has laid. But she's not complaining – travelling to east London is a lot easier to fit in around work.

Now she stands outside Luscious Hair and Beauty, and takes a deep breath before she pushes through the door. So far this has been too easy, but now, she suspects, will come the tough part.

The young woman behind the reception desk flashes a toothy smile at Carrie. 'Hi, can I help?'

Carrie asks if she can have a word with the manager. She's learnt from Facebook that Isla's mum owns this place. People really should be more careful what they expose about themselves on social media.

'Oh, sorry, Lottie's not in today. Can I help with anything?'

Carrie's about to answer when she spots the girl whose face she's become so familiar with since yesterday evening. Isla. Her dark olive skin seems to glow, and her voluminous black hair hangs in loose curls around her shoulders, bouncing as she sweeps away hair from under a chair. Carrie hadn't expected to feel such a jolt of pain seeing in person the girl whom Jacob loved before Rose.

'Never mind,' Carrie says to the receptionist. 'I'll just have a quick word with Isla over there. I'm a friend of the family.' She turns away before the woman can question her, and heads straight over to Isla.

The girl looks up as Carrie approaches and smiles. 'Hi, can I help?'

Carrie takes a deep breath. 'Isla, I know this might come as a bit of a shock, but my daughter was a friend of Jacob Adams, and I was just wondering if I could ask you something. It won't take long, I promise.'

Isla's eyes widen and her face seems to pale. She turns away from Carrie and resumes sweeping. 'No. I... I don't even know Jacob any more. We moved away. I need to get back to work. Whatever this is, it's got nothing to do with me. Sorry.' She tries to get past Carrie.

'Please, Isla. It won't take long, I promise. Can we maybe go outside and talk? It's really important.'

She looks at Carrie and shakes her head. 'What's he done now? What's happened?'

'I'll tell you everything, if you'll give me a chance.'

Isla glances at the receptionist, then back at Carrie, biting her lip. 'I don't know. I... I don't want to think about Jacob. I've put that all behind me.'

'My daughter was his girlfriend, and now she's dead!' Carrie hadn't planned to drop this bomb on this poor girl, but she needs Isla to talk to her.

Isla stares open-mouthed for a moment. 'I, um...' She points to a door at the back of the salon. 'There's a patio out the back, where we go for breaks – we can go out there.'

Carrie follows her outside, relieved to be able to take in a lungful of fresh chilly air. They're in a small concrete garden, with a few plant pots placed around the edges – none of them with flowers or plants – and a rickety wooden bench at the back. 'Can we sit?' she asks.

'Yeah... but I don't have long. I'll get in trouble if I'm not back to help with clients.' She pulls her phone from her pocket. 'I am supposed to have a break, though.' She turns to Carrie. 'What happened to your daughter?'

They sit on the bench and Carrie pulls out her phone, showing Isla the screen. 'This is Rose.'

Isla looks at the photo of Rose. Carrie has chosen the one where she's sitting with her guitar. She never looked more at peace than when she was playing, especially if it was her own music.

'She's pretty,' Isla says. 'What happened? Was she ill or something?'

Carrie's not sure she's ready to begin explaining, but she has no choice. 'Rose was in Jacob's school in Guildford. You know that's where he moved, don't you?'

Isla shakes her head. 'I heard from someone at my old school that he was moving. Didn't know where, though? Where's Guildford?'

'Quite a long way from here,' Carrie says. 'In Surrey. Someone... killed her.' Carrie fights back tears – until now, she's never had to say this out loud. 'My daughter was murdered.'

Isla's mouth hangs open and she stares at Carrie. 'What... I'm so... Oh my God, that's horrible.'

'She and Jacob were in a relationship, and he was the last person to see her. He was walking her home and they had an argument. She was missing for three days before... before they found her body lying in some woods.'

Isla frowns. 'Wait, did Jacob—'

'The police don't have enough evidence. But he lied about the argument and...' Carrie can't mention finding Rose's phone. She still needs to work out what she will do about that. 'I know it was him. That's why I'm here.'

'But I don't even know your daughter!' Isla protests. 'And I haven't seen Jacob for months. How can I—'

'I know,' Carrie assures her. 'I was just wondering... Well, Rose knew all about you and I'm sorry to say this but I think Jacob must have been seeing her while the two of you were still together. I just—'

'Wait, you've got it wrong.' Isla frowns. 'Jacob and I were never together.'

Now it's Carrie who is speechless, as she silently attempts to make sense of Isla's words. 'I don't understand. Jacob told

Rose that you were his girlfriend. His whole family knew. Everyone at school knew he had a long-term girlfriend in London who moved away.'

Isla shakes her head. 'No, I was never his girlfriend. Never. And his parents believed whatever he wanted them to think. He was... obsessed with me. He used to follow me around everywhere and turn up wherever I was. I'd be meeting my friends and there he'd be, watching me. Most of the time he didn't even say anything, he'd just stare at me. It was so creepy.'

'But you must have been to his house? Otherwise surely his parents would have known you weren't his girlfriend?'

Isla sighs. 'We sat together in science,' she says. 'We used to talk a lot. I thought Jacob was okay. A lot of girls liked him, but I never did. I just wasn't into him like that. I suppose we were kind of friends, though, so, yeah, I did go to his house a few times, but I was never his girlfriend. We never even kissed. Never. I knew he liked me, that was obvious. But I never led him on. I swear. He just got really clingy, and wanted to see me all the time. He'd bombard me with messages asking where I was or where I'd been.' She sighs. 'It was stalking. But it took me a long time to realise that. Because we were kind of friends, I just didn't see it.'

'So, nothing ever happened between the two of you?' Carrie asks, her mind scrambling to keep up with what she's hearing.

Isla shakes her head. 'No.'

'Didn't you tell him to leave you alone?'

'That's the thing – it wasn't that easy. Like I said, he was a friend. So I didn't want to hurt his feelings, or make anyone think badly of him. I just kind of put up with it. I've learnt a lot since then, and I'd never accept it now. But then... I just tried to ignore it. I was only fourteen when it started.'

'So, you didn't know he was telling everyone he was your boyfriend?'

She rolls her eyes. 'I mean, people at school used to gossip, but I wouldn't say anything. I didn't know his family thought it too.'

Carrie struggles to understand. 'It doesn't make sense.'

'Not to you, but things are different now. In school, it matters what people think of you. That's *all* that matters.'

Hearing this saddens Carrie. 'I don't want to sound patronising, but one day you'll know that isn't what's important at all. It's what you think about yourself that matters.'

But Isla has turned away, swiping at her eyes with her sleeves.

'What is it?' Carrie asks. 'There's more about Jacob, isn't there?'

She nods, clasping her hands together. 'I couldn't tell anyone. Jacob was... One time when he was at my house, he somehow took a photo of me undressing. I didn't even know he was there – my mum must have let him in. I didn't think anyone was home. But he had this photo of me. And I was completely naked.' Isla bursts into tears. 'He said if I told anyone I wasn't his girlfriend then he'd look bad and he'd have no choice but to post this picture of me all over the internet. He said he knew how he could do it without it being traced to him.'

Disgusted, Carrie puts her arm around Isla. 'That's awful. I'm so sorry.'

'But not as bad as what he did to your daughter,' she manages to say, in between sobs. Suddenly Isla stops crying. 'Wait a minute. Did he do the same thing to your daughter?'

'No. One thing I do know is that they were together properly. Rose was always with him, and she talked about him a lot. The plans they'd make about their future. They seemed really happy together.'

'But then why would he do that to her?'

'I don't know. Maybe she was leaving him? I can't work it out. Jacob is the only one who knows the truth. I just wanted to hear from you, to see if there was anything in Jacob's past that might show his character. And it looks like I've found it. Sorry you had to go through all that. It must have been hard living every day wondering whether he'd post that photo.'

Isla nods. 'I couldn't have a boyfriend because Jacob would have got jealous. Besides, everyone thought we were together so how would that have looked? I'd have been the bitch who cheated on her boyfriend. I actually cried with happiness when Mum said we were moving and I'd have to change schools. She thought I'd be upset but it was the best moment of my life, because I could finally get away from Jacob.'

'I'm glad you got away from him,' Carrie says. 'I just wish my Rose had been able to.'

'I hope the police get him.'

'That's where you can help,' Carrie explains. 'If you could just give them a statement telling them what Jacob did, it would help to show what he's capable of. I know it's not really evidence in this case, but maybe it might make them take a closer look at him?'

Isla moves further away from Carrie. 'No, I can't. He's still got that photo of me so I'm not risking it. No way.'

THIRTY-NINE

ROSE

Today, everything will change. It's time for the world to know. At midnight tonight, all of our worlds will implode. It's bittersweet to know that you'll be watching this, watching me speak our truth to everyone. I'm relieved that everyone will finally know, but it's broken me too, because despite everything, I loved you.

So, here I am, speaking to you in this YouTube video, something I would never have imagined I'd be doing. The irony. Rose Nyler: the girl who hates social media. The girl who doesn't even have an Instagram or TikTok account. The girl who dared to think she was different.

I will go to the barbeque at your house tonight, because I owe that to Ava; I want her to have a normal day before her life changes forever. Because this will be the moment when everything changes for all of us. Both our families will be devastated by what I have to share, and I wish there was a way for me to shield them from the blast, but we're too far past that now.

People will have an opinion of me after this, and that's fine. But surely there is one indisputable fact here – something that isn't subjective. It's black and white, as plain as a cloudless sky.

Oh, of course you'll deny all this. Put it down to the rantings of a crazy girl. A jealous girl? Maybe you'll even say that I've done this for payback, because you turned me down. But I've thought of all that. I've covered every eventuality. And that's why when I've finished talking, you'll see photos of us in bed together. Every time you fell asleep, I took one. They are proof, and no one will dispute that there needs to be consequences for your actions.

I was fifteen years old when you started having sex with me.

And you were forty-five.

PART THREE

I've heard it in the chillest land -
   And on the strangest Sea -
   Yet - never - in Extremity,
   It asked a crumb - of me.

Emily Dickinson, '"Hope" is the thing with feathers'

FORTY

ROSE

Rose has changed her mind several times about what to wear to the barbeque, and that isn't like her. Usually she'll throw on anything, but today feels like too significant a day for randomness. Everything needs to be considered carefully.

In the end she decides on her baggy light blue jeans and the green crop top she bought the other day. It's one of her favourite colours – green reminds her of nature, and the beauty in this world that too many people ignore. She's been guilty of that herself for the last few months, but all of that will end tonight.

It makes things easier that her mum is on a morning shift at the hospital; she would see that Rose is on edge, and not herself. Her mum's good at reading her, she always has been. Somehow Rose has hidden everything so well over the last few months, but it's been getting harder to do.

Jacob calls her, and she lets it ring out. For months now she's been forcing a distance between them, just so that it's easier on him when things fall apart after tonight. It's been hard watching his confusion grow at her weird behaviour, and she's appalled with herself that she used him this way.

It was just another thing she was coerced into doing.

Her phone stops ringing and she switches it off and shoves it in her back pocket. She won't need it today.

There are more people than she'd expected at the barbeque, and she doesn't recognise half of them. There are a few mums from the school, and Rose is surprised that Nina's mum hasn't been invited. She'd half expected to find her friend here; after all, Jacob has been confiding in her a lot since she's pushed him away. But then again, after she accused him of liking Nina, he was bound to keep away from her. Rose didn't want that, she just needed an excuse, something that would force him to question their relationship, to make him realise for himself that he should end things, because nothing else was working.

She recalls those words now, and they sicken her: 'You need to keep seeing Jacob. It's the only way we can stay together. If people think you're with him, then they won't question anything, will they? They won't be looking, and even if they do see something, their minds will dismiss it, because it just won't seem likely. Do it for us, Rose.'

Force it away. This will soon be over.

And then she feels a heavy hand on her shoulder and she turns to find she's face to face with him.

'Hello, Rose,' he says. His smile is halfway between a smirk and scowl. If only he knew that tonight his life will crumble into pieces. He looks around, checking nobody can hear them. 'I hope you're not here to cause any trouble.'

She looks him directly in the eye. 'Nope,' she says. 'I'm just here to enjoy myself.' She hopes he doesn't notice that her hands are trembling.

'Good, because I'd hate anything to upset Lucy today. She's put a lot of effort into this.'

'Rose!' Ava's voice calls from somewhere, and then she is running up to me, waving a book in my face. 'I've just finished this. It was brilliant, thanks for recommending it. Now I can get started on *Girl, Missing!*' She turns to her dad. 'Mum's looking for you,' she says. 'I think she needs help in the kitchen.'

Rose watches as Tom excuses himself and leaves, and crippling fear threatens to overcome her. Being in such proximity to him has made this more real. More difficult. His presence scares her now, because she knows how worried he is. But she won't change her mind.

'Where's Jacob?' Rose asks, turning back to Ava.

'Probably in his bedroom trying to make himself look nice for you.'

When Ava laughs, Rose feels a sharp jolt of guilt. 'Come on, then,' she says, 'Let's get something to drink and then you can tell me all about that book.'

Ava frowns. 'Don't you want to go and find Jacob?'

'No, he'll be out when he's ready. So, I'm all yours!' Rose hopes Ava doesn't notice that her eyes are watering.

'Okay, but just so you know, there's no Coke here. Only orange and apple juice for the kids.'

The word rings in Rose's ear. *Kids.* Because no matter how grown up she's felt, that's what she is after all. She glances into the kitchen and sees Tom with his arm around Lucy, kissing her cheek, smiling at his beautiful wife. His kind wife. Lucy is a good person, and Rose has done this to her. *It's not just on me, though.* Tom knew she was a child when he first kissed her, and he didn't care. Not in the end. Yes, she was the one who pushed it, but he could have put a stop to it. Ultimately, he was the one with the power, no matter how much Rose wanted him.

'D'you know what?' Rose says to Ava. 'You go and get some juice. I'll be back in a sec.' She rushes upstairs before Ava can protest, and throws up all over the bathroom floor. 'Jesus,' she whispers to the empty room afterwards. And when she's cleaned up, all she can do is sink to the floor, and wait for it to pass.

When she comes out, Jacob is standing there, smiling at her. 'I didn't know if you'd come,' he says, reaching for he hand. She wants to cry then, because he's being so kind to her, and she's about to destroy his life. She knows what he went through with Isla, how fixated he became with her, how sure they had a connection, and this will be the second time it's all been in his mind. She feels sick again, and pulls her hand away.

She walks past him but stops at the top of the stairs. 'Ava invited me, and I thought it would look weird if I wasn't here.'

'What have I done, Rose?' he says, pulling her down so they're both sitting. 'Why are you being like this?' He buries his head in his hands. 'I've been going over and over it, and I just can't think what I've done.

Rose can't bear to look at him. 'I can't do this any more, Jacob. It's impossible. I think we should just be friends.' But she knows that's not possible. 'We need to just let each other move on.'

He won't listen. She should know from what he told her about Isla that he has trouble accepting things. 'But why? It doesn't make sense. Tell me what I've done!'

Rose has to be firm. She has to end this now. 'I know it's hard to get it. I just... I don't love you, Jacob.'

There, she's said it now; cold, harsh words that she knows will haunt him. And they'll leave a scar on Rose too. Because despite everything, she does care about Jacob.

'But you've been sleeping with me. We've been together, haven't we?'

She wants to scream at him that it's his own father who made her do that, but that will all come out in a few hours. Now is not the time. 'That doesn't mean—'

'Is this because of Isla?' Jacob demands. 'It's freaked you

out, hasn't it? I told you the truth about what I did and you can't deal with it.'

Rose should agree, and tell him that's exactly why she can't be with him, but he's already suffering enough over what he did to Isla.

'No, Jacob. It's not about Isla. I hate what you did to her, but I know how much you regretted it.'

'Then what? Is there someone else?'

'No,' Rose protests. She pictures Tom's face, how it felt when he was on top of her, and all she feels is disgust. Shame. Terror. She won't be able to face Jacob after today; the pain in his eyes will be too much to handle. 'I'm sorry,' she says, jumping up and bolting down the stairs.

At the bottom, she almost careers straight into Lucy. She's holding a plate full of raw sausages and only just manages to hold it out of Rose's way. 'Oh, hi, Rose. Everything okay?'

'Yeah, I-I... sorry.' Rose notices the royal blue midi dress Lucy's wearing, how it flatters her figure. She is a woman, unlike Rose. 'Your dress is lovely,' she says.

'Oh, thanks. It's old but I haven't worn it for ages.'

Rose forces a smile. 'I'm just going to look for my mum. She should be here by now.' She walks off, relieved that when she looks back at Lucy, she has already turned her attention back to the sausages.

Ava appears beside her and taps her arm. 'Can we go to my room for a bit? Way too many people here and it's freaking me out a bit.'

Rose has to admit it is a bit loud; so many different conversations all clashing together, merging into a cacophonous boom. 'Yeah, good idea. Come on.'

In Ava's room, Rose shuts the door and sits at Ava's desk. 'Is that better?' she asks.

'Yeah. Sorry. I just... all those people. I don't know why Mum wanted to have a barbeque.'

'I suppose she misses all her old friends from London, and wanted to show them your new house.'

'Yeah, but I hate it. It makes me... I don't know. Kind of sick.'

This would be a perfect chance for Rose to explain to Ava what she researched the other day online. She's not completely sure, but from everything she read, it does seem that Ava could have some level of social anxiety disorder, perhaps triggered by the bullying, but more likely it's always been there at some level. But it's too late for it to come from Rose; she will have to think of another way, because tomorrow Ava won't want to hear anything she has to say. Tomorrow Ava will no longer believe in her.

They sit for a while, talking about books they've both loved, then Rose tells her she needs to go and look for her mum. 'She doesn't really know anyone here apart from your parents, so I just want to check she's okay.' And Rose also needs to make sure that she didn't bring Joe with her. There is enough tension here already, without adding him to the mix.

'Something's going on with you and Jacob, isn't it?' Ava asks, as Rose stands.

'No, we're fine.'

'I'm not stupid! I'm not a little kid. Why can't you just tell me? I tell you everything, don't I? And you never say anything about what's going on with you. You're like... a closed book.'

'I'm sorry, Ava, I'm just a private person. I share my thoughts through my music, not really by talking. That's just who I am.'

'But that's not how friendships work. You can't just take, take, take, and never give anything of yourself.'

Rose is shocked by Ava's condemnation, and she struggles to work out how to respond. 'I care about you, Ava. But what happens between your brother and me is our business. I hope you can understand that. It doesn't change our friendship.'

Ava ignores her. 'I know you've been fighting, otherwise you'd be with him now, not me. And I heard him calling after you when you rushed downstairs. I'm sick of being treated like a baby.'

Rose can't listen to this. She needs to start distancing herself now. 'I need to go and find my mum. Can we talk about this later?'

'Just get out, then,' Ava hisses. 'I hate you all.'

Outside Ava's bedroom, she stands for a moment, composing herself. Ava's outburst has come out of the blue, and it hurts Rose to know she feels this way. Then she realises that perhaps it is better this way, it might make tomorrow just that little bit easier for Ava.

Downstairs, Rose brushes past a huddle of people, scanning the garden for her mum. Music plays from a smart speaker now, and a few people are dancing, raucous laughter floating into the warm April air. Jacob appears in front of her and grabs hold of her arm; his mouth is moving but she doesn't hear his words.

'Leave me alone,' she says, despite not knowing what he said.

There's no sign of her mum, so she makes her way through the garden, checking everywhere. And then she sees her, around the side of Lucy's workshop, a large wine glass in her hand, most of its contents sloshing over the side because she's dancing with a man, her arms wrapped around his neck. Rose can only see his back, but she can tell it's not Joe.

Rose smiles, happy that perhaps now her mum will finally escape Joe's clutches. But then she sees who the man is.

It's Tom Adams.

FORTY-ONE

CARRIE

She's been trying to get hold of Hugh all afternoon, and had no luck. His phone is off, and all the WhatsApp messages she bombards him with remain unread.

On the sofa, Tom is tapping away on his laptop, and has been since he got here, even though he'd come straight from the office. Carrie watches his furrowed brow, and wonders what he'd do if he knew she'd instructed her ex-husband to break into his house today. Although, she reminds herself, it's not breaking in if you have a key.

She goes to the kitchen to make coffee, anything to distract herself from fretting. What if Hugh got caught? Maybe a neighbour saw him and called the police? These scenarios play out in her mind, accompanied by the tapping of Tom's fingers on the keyboard.

Her phone pings while she's waiting for the kettle to boil. It's Hugh. Carrie stares at the words, her body sagging as she reads.

Couldn't do it. Don't hate me.

So, he has let her down again, just like every man who's come into her life. She turns to Tom. He's the only one who hasn't, and yet she is betraying him.

She finishes making the coffee and hands a mug to Tom. He smiles as he takes it. 'Thanks, Carrie. Not just for this, but for everything. I'd be a mess without you.'

She squeezes his shoulder. 'You'd be fine. I think I'm the one who needed you.'

Tom smiles. 'You don't need anyone, Carrie. I wish you could see that.'

Oh, but I do see it. She knows now that she was wrong to cling to relationships that weren't working, and weren't healthy. *Rose was the only person I needed in my life. And it's too late to tell her I see that now.*

Her phone rings and she takes it to the kitchen. There's no caller ID, but it's got to be Hugh.

'I can't believe you,' she says, without waiting for a greeting.

'Carrie? It's DC Keller.'

'Oh, I thought you were someone else.'

'Hmm. I hope everything's okay?' the detective says.

'Well, my daughter's dead, but apart from that...'

'Sorry. I didn't mean—'

'No, I'm sorry,' Carrie says. 'I'm just... It's not been a good day.'

'I have some news,' DC Keller begins.

And Carrie listens while she tells her that Jacob now has an alibi for the night Rose was killed. Nina. Rose's best friend. Carrie doesn't hear much else of what DC Keller tells her, because she is already grabbing her car keys and telling the detective she has to go.

'Just need to pop to the shops,' she calls to Tom as she's leaving. She just about hears him tell her the coffee's running low before she shuts the door.

. . .

Sacha doesn't look surprised to see Carrie, and she ushers her inside. 'I know why you're here, and I'm sorry, but all Nina did is tell the truth. Finally.' She holds out her arms and hugs Carrie. 'I'm sorry she lied before. It was a terrible thing to do, but it's all out in the open now.'

Carrie doesn't speak, but slowly pulls away from Sacha.

'This is a good thing, isn't it? It was awful to think that Jacob could have done that to Rose, wasn't it? This must bring some relief at least. I mean, that's what would haunt me if it had been Nina. How someone so close to her could—'

'Can I see Nina?'

Sacha smiles. 'Of course. She'd be happy to see you. I'll just go and get her.'

When she comes back down, Nina is behind her, her arms folded.

'Are you okay?' Carrie asks. She's always cared about Nina; she and Rose were friends for most of their lives. She can still picture them now as five-year-old girls, running around Carrie's tiny garden. The pain is unbearable, and Carrie grabs hold of the banister.

Nina nods. 'Yeah. I'm so sorry, Carrie.' She doesn't even look at Carrie as she speaks. 'I should never have lied. I just... I was confused.

'You've done the right thing now,' Carrie assures her. 'I just need to ask you two things and then I'll go. But I need to hear this from you.'

Nina seems to shrink backwards. 'Okay.' At least now she is looking at Carrie.

'Did Jacob or his mum force you to say that he was with you that night? Please look me in the eyes and tell me the truth, Nina. If they did, I'll sort it out for you. You don't have to worry about anything.'

Silence falls around them all, everyone watching Nina closely. 'No. I haven't seen Jacob since he was at school last,' she says. She glances at Sacha. 'I've seen his mum, but she didn't tell me to say this. It's the truth.'

'So you were with Jacob after he walked Rose home until he got back at one in the morning?'

She nods. 'Yes, Carrie. I'm not lying any more. I want to come clean about everything. I can't stand all this. It's horrible. Rose would never have lied like this.

And that's when she breaks down and tells Carrie all about the falling-out she had with Rose, and all about what happened with Jacob.

FORTY-TWO

LUCY

Ava and I rushed after Jacob when he left the restaurant, but we lost sight of him in the crowds of Leicester Square. Ava stood crying a flood of tears, while we both hopelessly continued to look around, rushing towards the station in case that's where he'd gone. But there are four entrances to Leicester Square station, making our search futile.

Tom didn't come home last night – I can only assume he stayed with Carrie again. On the surface, I'm okay with that – for Ava's sake – but I don't want to examine how I really feel.

DC Keller calls at around nine in the morning and tells me that Nina has finally given her statement. Jacob is no longer the suspect he was. 'He still lied to us, though,' she explains. 'And he ran away when we needed to question him. None of that's good. And the other team still need to speak to him about his attack. I must stress how important it is that you let us know if you hear from him.'

The sad truth for Carrie is that they have no leads; I can only imagine how she's feeling. For all these weeks she's had hope – however wrong it was – of justice for her daughter, but now that's been snatched away. *I wish things could have been different, that Carrie and I could have been friends.*

I end the call and turn to Ava, who sits beside me, waiting for me to fill her in. 'Jacob can come home. Nina gave her statement and told them he was with her.'

I reach for my other mobile and call my son. As I expected, he doesn't answer, so I repeat everything DC Keller said, and urge him to come home. 'I told you it would be okay. It's over, Jacob,' I say, before ending the message.

Ava is frowning when I put my phone on the table. 'But it's not over, is it? Because they still don't know who killed Rose. It's not over for Carrie.'

I put my arm around her. 'No, but it's over for Jacob. And now he can sit his exams.'

Ava doesn't say anything, but taps her fingers on the table.

'I need to call your dad. He needs to know about this,' I say, reaching for my phone.

He doesn't answer so I leave a message telling him to call me. 'I need to go and find him,' I tell Ava. 'He should hear it from me that his son is innocent.'

'Are you going to Carrie's?' Ava asks, pulling her hair into a ponytail.

'Yes. I think your dad's there.'

Ava insists on coming with me but I tell her she needs to stay with Cooper. Since he got lost when Jacob was attacked, he's been distressed every time one of us leaves the house. She reluctantly agrees, and I head upstairs to have a quick shower.

There's a knot of anxiety in my stomach as I wait for Carrie to come to the door. Her car is outside, so there's a good chance she's at home. But I've already checked the road outside and there's no sign of Tom's.

When the door finally opens, Carrie stands there in her

dressing gown, pulling it tightly around her body. I'm shocked at how skinny she looks, and how drawn her face is. She looks older than I know her to be.

'Why are you here?' Carrie asks.

'Have the police told you? He couldn't have killed her, Carrie. You must see that now?'

She glances past me then holds the door open, moving back. 'You'd better come in.'

I step inside and shut the door. 'Is Tom here? It's where he usually is, isn't it?'

Carrie stares at me. 'He's at the office. I'll just get dressed and I'll be down in a minute. I... didn't sleep well last night. After the police told me about Nina. You'd think it would make me feel better but it doesn't.'

'But don't you see? This is a good thing. Jacob didn't kill Rose. He loved her.'

Without a word, Carrie heads upstairs, each one creaking under her feet, leaving me to wonder what she is thinking.

She comes back before long, dressed in a long cardigan and jeans. She walks straight past me to the living room, staring out of the window. 'I wish I could have as much faith as you,' she says. 'I wish it could be as simple as just believing Nina's statement.'

'It *is*, Carrie. I know you want answers, and it probably helps if someone is held responsible, but you have to accept that my son didn't do it. He loved your daughter.'

'And did he love Isla too?'

I'm taken aback at her mention of this name. 'Isla? What are you talking about?'

'Did Jacob love her?'

'I don't know. Maybe he thought he did. Carrie, what's that got to do with anything?'

She walks across to the window and peers out. 'Everything.'

She turns back to me. 'What do you know about their relationship?'

'They were together, and then we moved.'

'Wrong!' Carrie shouts. 'I saw Isla Harding. Lovely girl. She told me everything.'

Whatever Carrie's talking about, I don't think I want to hear it. I don't answer her. And even when she's telling me how Jacob was stalking Isla, how they were never together and he built their relationship up in his head, how he blackmailed her with a naked photo – I'm done with all of this.

But I need to say something. 'Jacob's done wrong,' I say. 'But he's not guilty of murder.'

Slowly Carrie turns to me, shaking her head. 'Then how do you explain Rose's phone being in Jacob's dressing gown pocket?'

Heat courses through my body and I can't speak. This is the last thing I expected Carrie to throw my way. After a moment, I regain my composure. 'How did you—'

'I spent a lot of time in your house when you and Jacob disappeared. Ava needed me, and to be honest, I needed her too. It felt good being able to look after someone again. Not that Rose needed looking after.' She pauses and studies my face. 'Sorry, I'm not answering your question. 'I found the phone.' Again, she stops and looks at me. 'You don't seem that shocked, Lucy. You found it, too, didn't you?'

I nod, still struggling to respond because I have never known what to think about Rose's phone.

'You look like you need to sit down. I think we both do.' She gestures to the sofa.

Finally, I find my voice. 'Why didn't you go to the police? All these weeks you've had and you didn't say anything.'

'I couldn't, could I, when it disappeared. And you could have told the police. Why didn't you?'

'Because I know Jacob isn't guilty. Rose could have easily

left the phone there. She was all over our house on the day of the barbeque. She could have lost it.'

'That's what I thought. But it still would have shown Jacob was lying about more than just their argument that night, wouldn't it? And strange how it couldn't have been there when the police searched, and then suddenly there it was. I was planning to tell the police, but then you and Jacob were gone, and so was the dressing gown. I couldn't do anything. Then you were back and it was too late.'

'Nina's statement is proof of his innocence,' I say.

Carrie stares at me for so long that I wonder if she'll ever speak again. 'Yes, I think that's probably true. You see, I've had so much time to think about it all, in the empty days and evenings when I'm not at work, and if it wasn't Jacob, then I think I've worked it all out.'

Now it's my turn to stare. 'What do you mean?'

'Ava,' she says. 'It all comes back to Ava.'

FORTY-THREE

ROSE

She stands and watches her mum and Tom for a while, her nausea intensifying every second her eyes are on them. Her mother is giggling, fawning all over him, touching his arm or his chest at every opportunity.

Tom sees Rose and grins, leaning in to whisper something to Carrie, who throws her head back and laughs. Her mother still hasn't seen her.

She's seen enough, and needs to get out of there, far from all of them.

'Rose, can we please talk?' Jacob appears in front of her. He's everywhere; she can't get away from him. 'Just for a minute. Then, if it's still what you want, I promise I'll leave you alone.'

Rose knows that he won't – he didn't leave Isla alone until she moved away, and they weren't even in a relationship. It had all been in Jacob's head. But on reflection, she's quite certain that after tonight, he will want to stay as far away from her as possible.

A chill runs down her spine; she hasn't stopped to consider fully that Jacob's reaction might not be what she's expecting.

She's assumed he'll be hurt, but it's plausible that he'll be full of rage. Hatred. He's unpredictable. His track record shows that he's capable of horrible acts, even if he claims he's changed. Still, she can't change anything now. This is the way it has to be, a risk she must take.

'I'm leaving now,' she says. After all, what is there for her to stay for? Ava? Her mum? Rose starts to walk off.

'Wait, I'll walk you home,' Jacob says. 'It's dark.'

She doesn't agree to his offer, but neither does she object. Glancing at her mum, who's now dancing on her own again, she heads to the side gate, feeling Jacob's heavy presence behind her. Before heading through it, she takes one last look around at the garden. She knows this will be the last time she sets foot in this place.

And there is no sign of Tom.

As they walk, Rose begins to feel relieved that Jacob is with her. It will be a chance for her to make this easier for him. She's got to help him realise that she's no good for him, that there is someone better out there for him. Someone far different from her, or even Isla. Someone who will love him.

'Will you do me a favour?' Rose asks. 'Promise me something?'

'Course. What is it?'

'No matter what happens, will you tell your mum that Ava might have social anxiety disorder?'

'I don't get it. What's that?'

She explains all that she's found online, and how a lot of it could relate to Ava. 'She needs help, Jacob.'

He agrees, and they continue walking, but it's not long before Jacob brings the conversation back to them. 'Why can't you give us a chance?' he asks. 'Everything's been good all this time, hasn't it? We've been happy. Just you and me.'

And now Rose tells him that things change. Nothing can stay the same. She hopes some small part of him will understand, but there's a blankness about his face. As if there's nothing there. He's not hearing her, and it's starting to scare her.

'That's bullshit,' he says.

'Nina likes you.' Rose hasn't planned to say this, but she wants to offer him some kind of comfort. 'She has from the minute she saw you in school. You must have noticed?'

'I don't give a damn,' he says. 'Nina's cool, but I'm not into her.' He looks at Rose, and then his eyes narrow. 'Just like you've never been into me, have you?

When she doesn't reply, Jacob grabs her arm. 'Tell me the truth!'

She yanks her arm out of his grip and walks off, her heart racing. 'Leave me alone, Jacob! It's over, why can't you get that through your head? You don't know me, I'm a terrible person... you know nothing about me. Just go.' She walks faster, convinced that this time he won't follow.

And then she hears him right behind her, wrenching her arm so hard that she screams.

FORTY-FOUR

LUCY

'What are you talking about?' I ask. 'Ava's got nothing to do with this.'

Carrie shakes her head. 'I didn't find Rose's phone myself. One night, when I was searching Jacob's room, Ava was just standing in the doorway, holding the phone. She told me she'd found it in his dressing gown pocket.'

'That's where *I* found it,' Lucy says. 'When we were in Cornwall, I was unpacking his suitcase and it fell out.'

Carrie nods. 'You found it because I told Ava we needed to put it back there. Like I said, I wanted to make sure the police found it, but then I guessed you must have found it. I actually thought that was the reason you and Jacob fled.'

'No. I didn't know about it until we'd already gone. I can't believe Ava didn't tell me.'

'She couldn't, could she? You were so convinced of Jacob's innocence that you would have dismissed anything that proved otherwise.'

'No,' I insist. 'If it had been anything that proved he was guilty, then of course I would have reported it. But the phone.

That doesn't prove anything. And now it doesn't matter because we know Jacob's innocent.'

'You took Jacob and ran, Lucy. How can you expect me to believe anything you say when it comes to defending your son? Why were you so convinced he was innocent? Before you knew for sure he was at Nina's?'

It feels strange to be talking about this to Carrie, but something has changed between us. For the better. 'I just *knew*.' I don't admit that in some of my darkest moments, those long nights I lay awake in Cornwall, desperate for sleep to grab hold of me, I wondered if I was deluding myself. Too blind to be rational. Subjective. I feared that the past had clouded my judgement. 'You still haven't explained what you meant about Ava.'

'After I spoke to Nina,' Carrie replies, 'I gave it a lot of thought and something occurred to me. How do I actually know where Ava found the phone? Or how she had it at all?'

I see exactly what Carrie is suggesting, and I'm not sure I can handle hearing it. But I listen while she tells me how she and Ava planned it all together.

'I'm not saying Ava did anything to Rose, I just think she might know more than she's telling us. Don't misunderstand me – I really care about Ava. She meant a lot to Rose and now she means a lot to me. But no other explanation makes sense. If it's not Jacob, then who? Maybe Ava is the one who can tell us.'

Ava's in the back garden playing with Cooper when I get home from Carrie's. There's no sign of Tom, and Jacob hasn't yet come home. Driving here, in between worrying about Ava and how she's mixed up in all this, I wondered if he ever will.

I watch her for a moment as she throws a ball for the dog to catch, and then I head to the kitchen doors and beckon her in.

She looks up and rushes over. 'Is Jacob back?'

'No, not yet. Can we have a quick chat?'

She nods, and tells me she needs to wash her hands first. 'That ball's filthy,' she explains, holding up hands that are caked in mud.

I follow her to the downstairs toilet. 'Ava, I know about Rose's phone.'

She stops scrubbing and turns to me, before quickly resuming washing her hands. 'What?'

'Carrie told me everything. How you found Rose's phone in Jacob's dressing gown pocket. And you gave it to her. How you both planned to put it somewhere and tell the police to search the house.'

Ava dries her hands, avoiding my gaze.

'Please talk to me. What happened?'

'I don't need to tell you,' she says, 'because Carrie already has.'

'But a lot of it doesn't make sense. We know now that Jacob didn't do it. So why would he have Rose's phone?'

'I don't know.'

'I asked him, Ava, and he swears he has no idea how it got there.'

'That's where I found it, Mum – I swear!'

'Ava, look at me. Do you promise? That's exactly where you found it? And you don't know anything else about how it got there or what happened to Rose?'

'No!' She storms out of the toilet and heads straight for the stairs. 'Why don't you believe me?' she shouts when she gets to the top. 'You were so quick to believe Jacob!' And then her door slams shut.

'I do believe you,' I say. But she doesn't hear me.

Something wakes me in the night. It takes a moment for my senses to come into focus, and then I realise that it's Ava. Screaming. Crying. Calling my name.

I throw the duvet off and bolt for her room, almost falling over Cooper, who's lying asleep in the hallway. He looks up before settling back down again.

I don't know what I expected to see when I reach her room – she often had nightmares when we were in London – but I'm taken aback to see her sitting on the floor in the darkness with her laptop on her knees. 'Mum,' she says. And then I can't make sense of anything else. Not only are Ava's words muffled by tears, but what she's telling me is abhorrent. Something nobody should ever have to hear.

Rushing over to her, I sink to the floor and stare at the video she's watching. Rose Nyler's face fills the screen, bright and alive, her dark eyes staring. Her voice floods into the room, calm and sweet, as if she's here with us. As if she's talking to us.

'There are two parts to my life,' she is saying, 'and each has been severed, leaving nothing but a jagged edge. A protective fence around two distinct Roses. You didn't know the Rose before, and I doubt you would have liked her. I might be barely sixteen, but I'm far more than that. Especially now.

Because of you.'

FORTY-FIVE

ROSE

She runs, feeling him right behind her, closing in on her. She needs to lose him, so she runs faster, even though she knows he'll soon catch up. Rose curses herself for spending too much time cooped up in her room writing music, when she could have been out jogging.

Her panting is so loud, she would normally be embarrassed, but now isn't the time to care about that.

Jacob is shouting. 'I won't let you leave me. Never. We're meant to be together, don't you see that?'

She knew it would come to this, even in those early days. As soon as he'd told her about Isla she knew. But Tom's insistence that she maintain a relationship with Jacob was mentally beaten into her, so even when Rose had reservations about what she was doing, she continued regardless. For Tom. Because he made her think that was the right thing to do.

'Rose, stop!'

But she doesn't, she keeps running, and then her road is in sight. She's nearly home. She can't hear Jacob any more, so she slows down and turns to check. He isn't there. Still running, she makes it to her house, her door key already in her hand. *Don't drop it. Just don't drop it.*

When she gets inside, she rushes to the window and peers out, but there's still no sign of Jacob. And then it hits her that she needs to warn her mum about Tom. Rose isn't sure what was going on with her and Tom at the barbeque, but at the very least it looked like she was flirting with him. It's not her mum's fault. She doesn't know what's been going on, and she was probably just looking for a distraction from her broken relationship with Joe.

She reaches into her back pocket for her phone, but the denim she feels is flat. There's nothing in there. She checks the other one, but that, too, is empty. 'Shit,' she says aloud. Rose can't even remember the last time she was aware of it being in there. It's either at Jacob's house, or she dropped it when she was running. Either way, she'll have to find it. When everything kicks off at midnight, she wants to witness what happens.

At the window, she checks outside again but there's no sign of Jacob. It's dark, but there are plenty of street lights lining their road. Rose leaves the house, heading in the direction she's just run, her eyes scanning the pavement.

A car passes by, and she's comforted by this; she was starting to feel like she's the only person inhabiting this world. Rose continues walking, and there's still no sign of her phone. And the further she gets from her house, the more she's convinced it must be at Jacob's. Or in his garden. Surely she would have heard it if it had fallen from her pocket? And it was tightly wedged inside; it never slips out easily.

She's so consumed with having to face Jacob again at his house, and Ava, that she doesn't notice the figure across the road until he calls her name. 'I really need to talk to you,' he says.

She should ignore him and continue walking. It's not like he can force her to talk to him. But then she remembers the video, and how he's living on borrowed time. What the hell, she thinks. It won't do any harm hearing what he's got to say. There's nothing he can do to change anything.

'What are you doing here, Tom? Shouldn't you be entertaining guests at your barbeque?'

'Everyone's leaving,' he says. 'And Lucy's taking care of all that.'

'Lucy will wonder where you are.'

'She's too drunk to notice anything. She's not a big drinker so the alcohol's gone straight to her head.'

'I don't care about any of this,' Rose says. 'Can't you just leave me alone? You and Jacob are as bad as each other.' She resumes walking.

'What's Jacob done?' Tom asks. He's talking as if the two of them being out here like this in the middle of the street is nothing out of the ordinary. It's funny – up until now Tom would never have been seen alone with her around here. The only time he broke his rule was when they went up to London on the train.

'He hasn't done anything.' Rose will never tell anyone about what Jacob did to Isla; she's given him her word and she won't break her promise. 'Nothing at all.'

'But you were arguing. I hope you weren't telling him about us?'

'Leave me alone, Tom.'

'Where are you going, Rose?' he asks. 'It's not safe for you to be out here wandering around. It's late. And dark.'

'I'm fine,' she insists. 'Just say what you've got to say and then go.'

'Can we just walk? There's a lot I need to tell you. To explain. And I want to say sorry.' His voice is softer now. Kinder.

Her instinct screams at her that she shouldn't listen. There is nothing he can say that she needs to hear. She's well on her way to washing her hands of him, so why do this to herself?

But it all comes back to this: kindness is too important to her. And shouldn't she at least show him some now, when he looks so pitiful?

'Okay. Go on then.'

'Walk with me, Rose. Please. Let's go that way.' He points to the right, towards the subway that leads to the school.

'I'm not a bad person,' he explains. 'At least, I never used to be. I wouldn't have done what we did with anyone else but you. I mean that, Rose. You got under my skin. Being with you over-shadowed everything. My sanity. I lost control. I owe you an apology for that.'

She doesn't say anything, his words rebound off her skin, unable to touch her. It's far too late for any of this.

They're heading towards the woods where they first slept together, and it's darker now, for there are far fewer street lights. And no cars driving past them.

'I don't believe you,' she says. 'I was *fifteen*. I was a kid. I still am. Look at me. It's a sickness, Tom. You're sick in the head. To look at me and think I'm a woman? No, that wasn't what you wanted. You liked that I wasn't like Lucy. And that makes you a paedo! I didn't see it at first – I was so sure you liked me because I was so mature, so much an adult. But that's all bullshit, isn't it?'

Tom stops walking. They're at the woods now. 'What did you call me?'

'You heard me.'

In the darkness, his face twists, panic flooding his eyes. 'No,' he says. 'That's not true! I would never—'

'But you did! You slept with me. Over and over. And I was fifteen!' She stares at him, and it's the first time she's ever seen him so diminished. 'You'll go to prison,' she says. She is enjoying having her power back. She never should have given it away.

'No, it wasn't like that,' Tom insists. 'And I don't know why I've been worrying you might tell someone – nobody would believe you. You... you were just obsessed with me, coming on to me all the time, and I never even touched you.' He glares at her. 'Yeah, who the hell would believe you?'

The swell of anger forces her hand. 'I have proof.' she says. So, you can say what you want.'

Tom stares at her. 'What? You're lying. There's no proof. We didn't text each other, or call or email. Ever. You have no proof, Rose.'

'Oh, but I do. And it's all about to come out. What time do you make it? I reckon you've got about three hours left.'

And now, seeing his cheeks erupt into fiery red, Rose knows she's made a big mistake.

She runs, heading straight towards the woods because Tom's blocking the way back. She stumbles over tree branches and then she's in darkness, barely able to see in front of her. But Tom's too fast, catching up to her within seconds.

'What have you done?' he says grabbing her and shoving her to the ground.

Her head smashes against the root of a tree, and she clutches it, wincing at the searing pain. 'Tom, stop. I—'

He's standing over her now, in a reversal of power, because ultimately, hasn't it always been his? 'I said what did you do? Have you told someone?' he says, his voice eerily calm now. 'Tell me, Rose.'

But she won't. He needs to be held accountable for what he's done. She doesn't speak. She's not sure she could, even if she wanted to – the crushing pain in her head is making her vision blur.

'On your phone?' Tom kneels down and pats down her pockets, quickly realising that she doesn't have it on her. 'Where is it?'

'I lost it,' she manages to say.

'Why are you lying, Rose? Surely Carrie taught you that it's not kind to lie?'

Something snaps inside her when he mentions her mum, and she pictures them dancing together at the barbeque. Maybe her mum didn't know what kind of man she was flirting with, but Tom knew exactly what he was doing.

Rose musters all her energy and smashes her foot into his stomach, knocking him backwards. It buys her a couple of seconds to act, and she pulls herself up and runs into the darkness.

FORTY-SIX

CARRIE

Carrie lies in bed, unable to sleep. It's nearly midnight, and Tom is either asleep downstairs on the sofa or he's on his laptop, throwing himself into work as usual. She really should tell him he needs more of a work–life balance. But then, from tomorrow it will no longer be any of her business. She's setting him free, ending whatever this is they're doing, because she needs to cut ties with every single member of that family. Even Ava. She's sad about that; Carrie has grown fond of her, and she's enjoyed being there for Ava in the absence of her Rose.

Besides, Tom has served his purpose now. She only needed him while she thought Jacob had murdered her daughter. Now it's looking likely it was a stranger attack, and whoever did it might never be caught. Carrie doesn't know how she'll live with that, without it eating away at her every day. No resolution. No closure. Just an unanswered question.

She hears the floor outside her door creak, followed by a soft tap. 'Carrie, are you awake?'

She sits up and turns on her bedside lamp, then smooths her hair. 'Yeah, come in.'

Tom opens the door slowly, peering in. He's wearing only a

T-shirt and boxers. 'I couldn't sleep. Wondered if you were having trouble too.'

Patting the empty side of the bed, she asks him if this is about Jacob.

'Yeah. I feel awful. Guilty. For not believing in him like Lucy did.' He sits on the bed, turning to her.

Carrie strokes his arm. 'It's not your fault. And you had me going on about how it must have been him. That couldn't have helped.'

He shuffles closer to her and takes her hand. 'You're what's got me through all this. And I know we talked about not rushing into anything, but maybe I was wrong. What if we both went away somewhere? To get away from all the painful memories for a while? What do you think?'

Carrie smiles. She can't think of anything worse. The last thing she wants to do is leave her home, where she feels the presence of Rose. Over the weeks it's become a comfort to her, not something she wants to run from. 'Maybe,' she says. That's all she needs to tell him – he'll know the truth of it tomorrow when she ends things.

Tom smiles. 'I'll start looking in the morning. See where we can go.'

'If you get time,' Carrie says. 'You're so busy with work, aren't you?'

Tom's eyes narrow. 'Yeah, but I'm sure I can squeeze in a browse on the web.'

'If you don't mind, I might try to get some sleep now,' Carrie says. 'I'm on an early shift tomorrow.'

Taking her by surprise, Tom leans over and kisses her, running his hands along her arms. She shouldn't let him – it's not fair on him – but it feels nice so she kisses him back, pulling him on top of her. They might not have tomorrow, but she can at least give him this last night.

. . .

Afterwards, Carrie still can't sleep. Beside her, Tom is already lost to slumber, but her mind won't let her rest. She jolts upright when her phone vibrates on the bedside table, and she snatches it up, expecting it to be the police. She hasn't heard from Michelle for a couple of days. Or DC Keller.

But it's Lucy's name on her phone. Glancing at Tom, who hasn't stirred, she climbs out of bed and tiptoes out, only answering once she's downstairs.

'What's happened?' Carrie asks, heading straight for the kitchen and shutting the door behind her. She turns on the light. 'Is Ava okay?' She can't think of any other reason why Lucy would call her at this hour. Perhaps she's trying to get hold of Tom.

'Carrie... Have you seen?'

Lucy's voice doesn't sound right. 'Seen what? What is it? What's going on?' Carrie asks. Fear instantly seeps into her bones, chilling her.

'I'm sending you a link right now. Check your texts. I'm so sorry. I'm so sorry, Carrie.' And then Carrie can hear Ava in the background, her wails sounding like an animal being slaughtered.

Without another word, Carrie puts Lucy on speakerphone and checks the message that pings through. It's a YouTube link. Her body freezes when she sees her daughter's name. And then she taps play, and listens while her daughter's words drift through the room, melodic and tuneful, harsh and devastating. They are all of these things. And now, finally, when she gets to the end of the video, tears splattering onto her pyjamas, she is a crumpled heap on the floor.

Lucy's voice brings Carrie back to life. 'Carrie? Is he there? Is Tom at your house?'

'He's upstairs asleep.' Carrie manages to say. *In her bed. Sleeping soundly, as if there's no weight on his shoulders.* 'We just... we... oh my God.' Carrie throws up on the floor.

'I'll call the police,' Lucy says. 'And you need to get out of the house. He could be the one who killed Rose. I'm so sorry, Carrie.'

'Okay,' Carrie says. She's still numb, but there's something else too – rage. Pulling herself up, she ends the call and walks towards the worktop, her eyes fixing on the wooden knife block in the corner. She'd always considered it a waste of money – she only ever uses two of the six knifes, and she can't even remember what most of them do, but now she picks up the largest one and stares at it.

She heads upstairs, hovering outside her bedroom for a moment, caught at a crucial junction. Whatever she does next will change the course of her life.

It takes less than a few seconds to decide. Holding the knife behind her back, she opens the door, taking a deep breath as she prepares herself to confront the man who slept with her daughter. Her *child*. And who is most likely the one who killed her.

Tom has gone.

The duvet is neatly made, and there's no sign that he was ever there.

FORTY-SEVEN

LUCY

Neither Ava nor I sleep. We sit up together all night, cuddled on the sofa, trying to make sense of everything. The tears we've both shed could fill an ocean, but at least we're not keeping our grief trapped inside. *Always better to release the pain, set it free.*

By now, Jacob must have seen the video. It's been plastered all over social media and the local news. Wherever he is in London, he must know what's happened. And it saddens me even more that he'll be dealing with it on his own. I've messaged him to come home, but now I have to leave it up to him.

No matter what I'm experiencing now, this pain is nothing compared to what Carrie will be feeling. And Tom had been sleeping upstairs in her room when she found out. It's not difficult to work out what the two of them had been doing. Which makes it all the more devastating for Carrie.

'Mum, what's going to happen to Dad?' Ava asks.

Night has merged into dawn, and I need to message the school to tell them Ava won't be in. 'The police will need to speak to him. When they find him, they'll need to question him about the video and the photos.'

'And about Rose's death?'

'Yes, probably that too.'

'But he was here, wasn't he? He was working and then he went to bed – so he couldn't have done it. Could he?'

I'd been so focused on working out what Jacob had been doing that night, that it never occurred to me to wonder about Tom. Why would I have? There had never been a reason to suspect anything had been going on between him and Rose. They both hid it well.

'Ava, I can't really answer that. I think he was here, but I didn't actually see him. He was working in his study. He wasn't even drinking that night. We know what he's done, but that doesn't mean he's a murderer.' As I say this, it hits me that I didn't know my husband at all. He could easily have left the house – I wouldn't have noticed.

The doorbell rings, and I heave myself from the sofa, preparing to speak to the police. I've got Rose's phone in my pocket, ready to hand over to them, and I'm prepared to tell them everything.

Jacob stands there, the gym bag he took to Cornwall on the doorstep next to him. 'I don't have my key,' he says.

I rush forward and hug him. He doesn't wince this time. His wounds are slowly healing.

Ava rushes to him too, grabbing hold of him and squeezing him tightly. 'I'm sorry for not believing you,' she says. 'And about the phone. It's all my fault.' She pulls back. 'You saw the video?'

'Yeah.'

'Oh, Jacob, I'm so sorry. This is devastating. Your dad is... He's done a terrible thing.'

'He's not my dad,' Jacob says calmly. 'Is he?'

I look at Ava, who is opening her mouth to say something. 'I know why you feel that way right now,' I say. 'Let's just try to get through this together.'

'Can I have some food?' He looks past me to the kitchen.

'Of course. What would you like?'

'It's okay, Mum. I can do it myself.'

I tell them both I need to have a shower before the police come, and I urge Ava to get dressed too. There is no telling what this day will bring.

Carrie turns up in the evening, asking to see Jacob. 'I just want to tell him how sorry I am,' she explains. 'I was wrong, and I owe him an apology.'

'It's okay, Mum,' Jacob says. 'I want to talk to Carrie.'

I leave them alone in the living room and go upstairs to check on Ava. An hour ago, she said she was going to her room to read, and I'm not surprised to find her asleep with the book lying open on her bed. I pull her blind down and shut the door. At least she's getting some respite from all of this emotional pain.

In the kitchen, Cooper scratches at the door and yelps when he sees me, reminding me that he hasn't had a walk today. 'Come on then,' I say. 'Let's get you out.'

It will soon be dusk, and the temperature has dropped. I have a cardigan on, but it's only thin, so I walk faster to warm myself up, heading towards the Downs. 'Just a short walk today,' I tell Cooper. 'We need to be back before it gets too dark.'

He gives a small bark, as if he understands me.

I've only been walking for ten minutes when I hear someone close behind me. I spin around, and freeze when I see Tom standing before me. I take in his dishevelled appearance – he is a shadow of the man I married – and then quickly step backwards, pulling Cooper closer towards me. My whole body turns cold. All day I've imagined what I will say to him when we're face to face, but now that we are, all I want to do is run. I don't want to hear a thing he has to say. I know all I need to.

'I didn't mean to scare you,' he says. 'I needed to see you, Lucy. It's all such a mess, and... I don't know what to do.'

I scan the area – we're alone here as far as I can tell. 'The police are looking for you, Tom. You need to talk to them. Hiding isn't the answer.'

'That's what you and Jacob did.' He edges towards me.

I recoil. 'And what good did it do?'

Tom lifts both hands and grips his hair, pulling tightly. 'I didn't kill her, Lucy. I promise. I didn't do it.' His face is anguished.

'You did enough.'

He hangs his head. 'It just got out of control – Rose and I. I tried to stop myself but—'

'No!' I shout. 'I don't want to hear it.' I reach for my phone, relieved to find it's there in my pocket.

'Okay,' he says, holding up his hand. 'I get it. But I need your help. Please.'

I need to keep him talking, to distract him so I can dial 999 and let everything he says be heard. But he's watching me carefully, and he'll notice if I make any movement. And then what? I no longer know what he's capable of.

'I didn't kill her,' he repeats. 'And I need you to tell the police that you know I was at home. I was working, wasn't I? In my study all night. And then I went to bed. You know that, Lucy, don't you?'

Cooper pulls on his lead, urging me to keep walking. 'Tom, I need to let him off, he's going crazy. He needs to run around.' I lean down to unclasp the lead, but Tom keeps his eyes fixed on me. Cooper runs off, but he knows the Downs well so he won't get lost.

'But I didn't see you, did I? I'd had too much to drink.' Shame floods my body, even though Tom has done something so much worse. 'How did you know about the video?' I ask. 'You were asleep at Carrie's, according to her. So how did you know?'

Even as I ask this, I don't expect him to tell me, so I'm surprised when he does.

'I woke up when Carrie got a phone call,' he begins. 'She thought I was asleep. I thought it might be the police so I went downstairs and I heard her talking to you. Then I heard the start of the video.' He frowns. 'Why did it only publish this long after the barbeque? It doesn't make sense. She said in the video that tonight would be the night everything came out.'

The police have a theory about this: that Rose entered the wrong date when she scheduled the video to upload to YouTube. That's the most likely explanation. I don't mention this to Tom, though; he doesn't deserve any answers. He can work it out for himself.

Tom shrugs, and continues explaining, as if by doing so he can cleanse himself. 'I didn't know what the video was all about at that point, but I knew I had to get out of there.'

'Even if you didn't do it, and I don't believe that for a second – you disgust me,' I say. 'You slept with Rose and she was a *child*. And then you start sleeping with her mother. What the hell is wrong with you?'

'I didn't plan for that to happen,' Tom mumbles. 'Carrie and I just... had a connection. We needed each other.'

'I can't listen to any more.' I walk off after Cooper, but Tom catches up with me. 'Wait. I'm sorry, Lucy. I'm so sorry for all of it.'

'For murdering Rose?' I'm shouting now, but there's nobody around to hear us, no witnesses if Tom were to do anything to me. I feel trapped. Vulnerable. Is this how Rose felt?

'So, what exactly were you planning to do?' I ask, even though the rational side of me insists I don't want answers to what he was doing in this sordid clandestine life he led. 'With Rose? Were you planning on leaving me? Running off together? What happened?'

Tom looks away and I slide my hand into my pocket. 'No,

he says. I ended it. She wasn't happy about it. I think that's why she made that video. It had been going on for months and she never said a word to anyone, then all of a sudden when I end things she wants... I don't know, some kind of revenge.' He kicks at the ground.

My stomach lurches; I want to smash my fists into his face for what he's done, and it takes all my willpower to remain in control. 'That wasn't what that video was, Tom.' I picture Rose's face as she spoke, the words that I can almost recite by heart now. 'She grew up in the time that you abused her. You used your power as an adult and controlled her, and by the end she realised it. Only it was too late because you'd already scarred her irrevocably.' I shake my head, disgusted with this despicable human being who stands before me. Who I married. 'Did you think about that? How what you considered to be a *relationship* would taint everything she did for the rest of her life? You moulded her and made her into something she was never supposed to be.'

Tears fall from my eyes. Anger and sadness intermingling to blind my vision. But I've never seen things more clearly. 'She was supposed to be Rose, the singer-songwriter, the academic high-achiever. The girl who would move mountains. And instead she became a teenage girl who slept with a middle-aged man. Who thought she loved him. Jesus, it's sickening.'

Something shifts in his expression then – the begging, sorrowful man before me morphs into the monster he is. I've never seen this in Tom and it scares me. I need to ground him, to bring back his humanity, if he has any left.

'The kids, Tom. What about them? Jacob loved Rose. And Ava did. Did you think about what this would do to them?' My hand is still in my pocket, but it's impossible to call any number without pulling it out.

'Ava,' he whispers. 'My Ava. How is she?'

'How do you think? She was suffering enough before all of

this, so take a guess what this might have done to her.' It's hard to keep my voice calm.

Tom sinks to the ground, burying his head in his hands. 'I never wanted to hurt her. Or any of you. I swear to you.'

But I'm no longer listening. While Tom isn't watching me, I pull out my phone and dial 999, only just managing to shove it back in my pocket before he looks up.

'You never loved me, did you, Lucy?'

I have never in my life been so sure of anything, so ready to admit the truth. 'No. I couldn't.' I want to believe this is because deep down I knew there was something toxic in Tom, but that's only partly true. 'I loved Alistair,' I say, for the first time allowing myself to acknowledge the truth. 'And you were never him. You never even came close.'

Tom is howling now, but instead of evoking sympathy, it makes me loathe him even more.

'Rose loved me,' he says, looking up. 'The way she looked at me – it was… intoxicating. You never looked at me like that. And I needed it, Lucy. I needed to feel wanted. But you, no, you never needed me. Never. At work I was climbing the ladder, proving myself, being successful, and then I'd come home and… you diminished me.'

Rage builds inside me, but I will let him have his say. The longer I keep him talking, the more time the police have to get here.

'And then there was Jacob. He never felt like I was his dad. He didn't even know Alistair, but I still wasn't good enough to be his father.'

Keep quiet. Don't say a word. I will only have to endure this for a few minutes more.

'Ava loved you,' I tell him.

'Yeah, she's the only one. But I felt like a failure there too, because I could never see what she was going through. It was down to you. You were the one who got us out of London, and she was much better here, wasn't she?'

I don't answer, because the truth is, I don't know what difference it made. And if we'd stayed in London, then Rose would still be alive. A stranger to us all, yes, but still alive.

'Lucy, I'm begging you,' Tom pleads. 'Tell them I was in bed. You saw me. I never left the house.'

'I'm not lying for you, Tom. Never.'

'I didn't do it,' he says. 'And it's time you knew the truth. 'It was Jacob. He found out about me and Rose and he confronted me at the barbeque. That must have been what they were arguing about when he walked her home.'

'No, you're lying.'

'I'm not, Lucy. And I think you know that. Didn't you wonder why I was so sure that Jacob was guilty? It's because I knew he had a motive. He was jealous. Full of rage that she'd done that.'

I think of Isla. There's no denying that Jacob is capable of possessive behaviour. 'No,' I repeat. 'Jacob didn't kill Rose.'

'You're blind to it, Lucy. What Jacob is really like. You've never been able to see.'

Tom's words fill me with rage. 'You've never given him a chance.'

And then it all becomes perfectly clear. Even if there was the smallest chance that Tom is telling the truth, he is still guilty of everything else.

'You're a despicable human being. You're not even human. Doing that to Rose is bad enough but then to try and blame your own son.' And then it hits me. 'You're the one who put Rose's phone in Jacob's room, aren't you? He was telling the truth when he said he didn't know how it got there.'

Tom doesn't say a word, but he doesn't need to.

There's a faint sound of sirens in the distance, and I watch him, ready to run after him when he realises they're coming, that this is it for him, but he stays still.

And he still doesn't move when two police officers run up to us and begin reading him his rights, throwing on handcuffs. He turns back to me as they lead him to their car. 'Please, Lucy. Tell them it wasn't me,' he says.

Turning away, I whistle for Cooper and clip his lead back on. 'Come on, boy, let's get you home.' I'm grateful that the dark night will hide my tears.

FORTY-EIGHT

CARRIE

It's been three weeks since she first watched Rose's YouTube video and Carrie's life exploded again. Now her house is empty once more – just as it should be – and each day she is focusing on healing herself.

On occasions, it's hard to remove the image of Rose and Tom together from her head, and the crushing pain it brings is compounded because Carrie shared her bed with this man too. 'You didn't know,' Lucy has told her several times. But ignorance doesn't mean you're not culpable.

Tom still protests his innocence regarding Rose's death, but the police search of his car turned up something interesting: Rose's mobile phone, hidden under the driver's seat of his car. Carrie thinks of this now and it brings a thin smile to her face.

'Carrie?' Lucy's voice brings her back to the present. 'Are you okay? You've drifted again. She hands Carrie a mug of coffee. There's a chip on the inside, just under the rim. Carrie really should get a new set.

'Thanks. I'm doing okay.' How funny, Carrie thinks, that she and Lucy seem to have fallen into an odd friendship, bound together by their grief. United because both of their worlds have been turned inside out.

But piece by piece, she will rebuild everything. Her life will be different, of course, but she will carry on. Rose would be proud of her.

Lucy doesn't say much about how she's feeling. In some ways she is an enigma to Carrie, but it's got to be hard for her – she was married to Tom when he started his affair with Rose. And then there is Jacob. That poor boy must have been broken to learn that the girl he loved was sleeping with his father. But, no, Lucy doesn't discuss this much, she just busies herself with her floristry business and checking in on Carrie, making her cups of tea or coffee she doesn't want.

'So, how did Jacob's first exam go?' Carrie asks.

Lucy shakes her head. 'He thinks he's failed. It was maths.'

Carrie nods. 'I remember him saying it's his least favourite subject.'

'Well, he's had lots of help from Mitch, so—'

'Ah, yes – Mitch.' Carrie nods and smiles.

'And what does that mean?'

'Nothing at all,' Carrie says, noticing Lucy's cheeks redden.

'Hmm. Well, life has to go on, doesn't it? We just learn to live with the pain, put it away in a little box and let it visit us once in a while.'

'Do you know what I was thinking about the other day? The irony of it all. The whole time I was getting closer to Tom to try and find out things about Jacob, he was doing exactly the same to me. That's my theory anyway. He wanted to make sure if anything ever came out about him, that he'd find out about it first.'

'Perhaps,' Lucy says. 'Who knows how his twisted mind works. We're well rid of him.'

Carrie's phone rings, and Joe's name appears on the screen. She ignores it.

'Joe?' Lucy asks, taking a sip of coffee.

'Yeah. Some people have trouble accepting when something's over.' She looks at Lucy. 'Oh, sorry, I wasn't talking about Jacob.'

Lucy sighs. 'Thank you for telling me about Isla. I'm not sure Jacob ever would have. He feels so awful about what he did. I just don't get it. There were plenty of girls who liked him – I'm not sure why he chose to fixate on someone who clearly didn't.'

'The heart wants what it wants,' Carrie says.

They fall silent, and Carrie is sure they're both thinking the same thing: that his relationship with Rose wasn't real either.

'I'd better get ready for work in a minute,' Carrie says, finishing her coffee.

'I'll come over after you finish,' Lucy says. 'Maybe cook dinner? Ava would love to see you.'

Carrie stands. 'Thanks, but I'll be okay, Lucy. You don't have to do that. Anyway, I'm driving up to Derbyshire tonight, to visit an old school friend. I'll be there all weekend.'

Lucy looks surprised. 'Oh, okay. Well, I'll see you next week then.' She stands too, and pulls on her coat.

From the window, Carrie watches her drive away. The street is silent, and there's no sign of the twins, or Lia. She must check in on them, give Lia that break she desperately needs.

As she turns away, her eyes are drawn to her car, parked outside the house in its usual spot. She must remember to move it somewhere else this weekend, just in case Lucy happens to pass by.

Carrie picks up the two empty cups and lets out a heavy sigh. 'It's just you and me now, Rose,' she says to the empty house. 'Just the way it should be.'

FORTY-NINE

ROSE

Darkness envelopes her, folding in on her, smothering her. Rose has lost her bearings now, and has no sense of where she is. *Just keep running, it doesn't matter.* Twigs and stones crunch under her feet, and surely it's only a matter of time before she falls, or smashes into something. She needs to get as far away from him as she can. *Don't look back.*

She's making so much noise as she runs that she can't hear whether or not he's catching her up, and she daren't stop to check. He runs fast for his age.

Then she feels a presence behind her, right before arms clasp her, squeezing so tightly she feels as though her ribs will crack. 'I need to know what you've done, Rose,' Tom pants into her ear. 'Tell me.' His voice is too calm, despite the heaviness of his breath.

'Nothing,' she manages to say. 'I was lying. Trying to scare you. I haven't done anything.'

'I don't believe you.' He spits his words at her, grabbing her hair and pulling her head back so hard she feels as though her neck will snap.

'It's too late, Tom,' she laughs. 'There's nothing you can do.'

She kicks backwards into his groin, sending him to the floor, and then she runs.

But he recovers too quickly and within seconds he's behind her, his arms crushing her in a chokehold. She can't turn around to face him, and force him to look her in the eye as he squeezes her last desperate breaths from her. She wants to fight back but she's powerless. Her eyes close, and everything begins to fade.

Rose's last thought is that at least she has the video, scheduled to publish at midnight.

FIFTY

LUCY

Ava was the one who suggested we move back to London after the school year was out. The bullying she experienced was nothing compared to what happened in Surrey. I have to agree that it had been hard to continue living in our house after knowing how much time Rose spent there with Tom, under the false pretence that she was waiting for Jacob. The ghost of her was in every corner of that place, and day by day it was tearing Jacob apart.

I don't blame Rose; it's Tom who needs to take full responsibility for everything that happened. He was the one who should have known better. The blame lies on his shoulders; Tom set in motion the avalanche that crashed down on all of us.

I stand in the garden of our rented house in Palmers Green – it's small with flowerbeds framing a neat lawn. I just need to plant some seeds. Roses, Ava suggested, but I'm not sure I could deal with a constant reminder. I will remember Rose in some different way. There's no space for a cutting garden here, but this is only a stopgap until our house is sold. Then I will find the perfect home for the three of us. My breath catches in my throat. This is our family now.

Ava joins me outside, holding one of the warm fresh croissants I've bought us for breakfast. 'Jacob's still asleep,' she says. 'Why does he sleep so much?'

I turn to her, and there are so many things I long to tell her, but they must all stay hidden. I still have that desperate urge to protect my children, even though now I am able to keep it balanced. To know when I'm overstepping, when it's time to let them be who they are, to make their own mistakes, to learn everything they need to know about life.

'He's exhausted after working so hard for his exams. That's probably why he needs so much sleep.' I smile at Ava. 'And you've been working hard in your counselling sessions, haven't you? I know it's not easy opening up to someone, spilling out all your thoughts and feelings.'

'I like Wendy, though,' Ava says. 'I think she's really helping me.'

'Good,' I say, looking around the garden again. Even Jacob has warmed to Wendy, and I'm hoping to see progress with him too. That might take more time, though.

'Will Mitch be coming over today?' Ava asks. 'He spends a lot of time in London, doesn't he?'

I smile. 'He does seem to like it here.'

Ava bites into her croissant and chews thoughtfully. 'Hmm,' she says when she's finished her mouthful. 'I don't think it's just London he likes!'

My cheeks flush and Ava and I both smile. It feels good. It wasn't easy explaining our situation to Mitch, and that I wasn't called Kate. And even now he still sometimes calls Jacob Josh by mistake. Like everything else, it will just take time.

Upstairs, I open Jacob's door and peer in. He's sleeping soundly, his body and most of his head hidden under the duvet. Ava's taking Cooper for a walk so I stand in his doorway and listen for a moment, wondering if I'll hear it again. But nothing fills the silence other than the sound of soft, steady breathing.

This shouldn't surprise me – it's only ever been at night that he's subconsciously spoken out loud the anguished thoughts bottled up in his mind. *I'm sorry, Rose. I'm sorry.*

A LETTER FROM KATHRYN

Thank you so much for choosing to read *The Lie*. If this is the first book of mine you've read, then thank you so much for taking a chance on me. And if you've read any of my others, thank you for your continued support. I really do hope you enjoyed this book, and that the characters and plot took you on a suspenseful journey. Hopefully the plot twist took you by surprise!

If you would like to keep up to date with all my latest releases, please feel free to sign up at the following link. Your email address will never be shared and you can unsubscribe at any time.

www.bookouture.com/kathryn-croft

If you liked the book, it would be fantastic if you could spare a couple of minutes to leave a review on Amazon or wherever you bought the book. Reviews have such great importance to authors as your valuable feedback helps us to reach other readers who may not have discovered our books.

Please also feel free to connect with me via my website, Facebook, Instagram, or Twitter. I'd love to hear from you!

Thank you again for all your support – it is very much appreciated!

Kathryn x

KEEP IN TOUCH WITH KATHRYN

www.kathryncroft.com

facebook.com/authorkathryncroft

twitter.com/katcroft

instagram.com/authorkathryncroft

ACKNOWLEDGEMENTS

This book really was a huge team effort and I have many people to thank for helping me bring it to life.

Thank you to Hannah Todd, my agent, for always being so approachable, kind and full of fantastic advice and guidance.

Once again, this book wouldn't be what it is without the talented and insightful editorial eye of Lydia Vassar-Smith, a wonderful editor to work with and a lovely person. Thank you to the whole Bookouture team for everything you do for me and all your authors.

I owe a debt of gratitude to Holly Tree, from Flowers by Holly Tree, for taking the time to talk me through everything to do with running a floristry business. I learnt so much from you and hope I've been able to convey your passion through my main character.

This book deals with the most complex police procedure that I've written so far, and I am eternally grateful to Stuart Gibbon, Joanna Sidaway and Michelle Langford for all the time you gave up to check through every detail of the police investigation for accuracy. Your advice was invaluable and is much appreciated. I thoroughly enjoyed learning from you all. Any errors in police procedure are my own.

Thank you to Olivia Roche and Shane Wheeler-Kingshott for taking the time to talk to me about what life is like for teenagers today. It's been a long time since I was that young, and the world has changed a lot!

I'm always grateful to everyone who has picked up any of my books to read or review – thank you so much!

And to my husband, parents and my whole family – always supportive and always there.

To my amazing children – I'm starting to see a little hint of pride when you tell people that 'Mummy writes books' and that means the world to me!

Printed in Great Britain
by Amazon

28809504R00189